To Lokog's relief, the battle was still going on once *Sud Qav* arrived.

It was more of a chase, really, with the Starfleet vessel—an Andorian-built light cruiser whose identifier beacon called it the *U.S.S. Flabbjellah*—in pursuit of an unfamiliar ship, a gray vessel with two boxy, inward-tilted warp nacelles flanking a central module in the form of a sphere bisected by a seven-sided slab. In the estimation of Kalun, *SuD Qav*'s gunner, the Andorian ship was firing to disable, while the unknown ship was firing defensively, more interested in escaping its foe than destroying it. But that did not entirely explain the longevity of the combat.

"I think," Ghopmoq said after studying his scans for a while, "the gray ship is repairing itself with incredible speed!"

"Impossible," Lokog spat. "You said there were only four life signs aboard. How could they work so fast?"

"It is as I said, Captain—the ship is repairing *itself*."

Once the idea sank in, Lokog thrilled at the potential. What a prize that technology would be for a raider! And what an advantage it would be for a warrior, to recover from damage almost as quickly as it was inflicted!

Either way, he had to keep that ship from falling into Starfleet's hands. "Battle stations! Prepare to engage the Andorian vessel!"

— STAR TREK —
ENTERPRISE®

RISE OF THE FEDERATION

LIVE BY THE CODE

CHRISTOPHER L. BENNETT

Based upon *Star Trek*®
created by Gene Roddenberry
and
Star Trek: Enterprise
created by Rick Berman & Brannon Braga

POCKET BOOKS

New York   London   Toronto   Sydney   New Delhi

Pocket Books
An Imprint of Simon & Schuster, Inc.
1230 Avenue of the Americas
New York, NY 10020

This book is a work of fiction. Any references to historical events, real people, or real places are used fictitiously. Other names, characters, places, and events are products of the author's imagination, and any resemblance to actual events or places or persons, living or dead, is entirely coincidental.

First Pocket Books paperback edition April 2016

POCKET and colophon are registered trademarks of Simon & Schuster, Inc.

For information about special discounts for bulk purchases, please contact Simon & Schuster Special Sales at 1-866-506-1949 or business@simonandschuster.com.

The Simon & Schuster Speakers Bureau can bring authors to your live event. For more information or to book an event, contact the Simon & Schuster Speakers Bureau at 1-866-248-3049 or visit our website at www.simonspeakers.com.

Manufactured in the United States of America

10 9 8 7 6 5 4 3 2 1

ISBN 978-1-4767-7913-3
ISBN 978-1-4767-7914-0 (ebook)

For Leonard Nimoy,
whose legacy will live long

We all try to live according to our principles, but we cannot control whether history will remember us as heroes or villains. Sometimes, those of us who take the boldest actions in support of our beliefs are destined to be remembered as both.

—Samuel A. Kirk,
The Forgotten Enterprise (2190)

2165

Prologue

July 8, 2165
U.S.S. Vol'Rala AGC-7-10

Captain's starlog, Thirdmoon 1:4, FLY 474.
Captain Reshthenar sh'Prenni recording.

We are making progress in our mission to liberate the remaining victims of the Ware technology. Two phases ago, Captain Reed of Pioneer reported that Science Officer Banerji's remote awakening protocol successfully revived the captives of a Ware trading post without the need for a boarding operation. This corroborates the previous success reported by Captain th'Zaigrel of Thelasa-vei against a drone fleet. This is heartening news, as Vol'Rala has detected a sizeable Ware facility in orbit of a nearby Fesoan-class planet. It is my hope that we can liberate as many survivors as possible and come one step closer to ending the Ware scourge for good.

"Yes, well, I'll believe it when I see it," Commander Giered Charas said once sh'Prenni shut off the log recorder. The gruff Thalassan leaned back against the starboard tactical console with arms crossed, his thick, rear-mounted antennae spreading skeptically. "The day I trust Banerji's scientific tricks over good, honest soldiering is the day I hand in my commission. I say we should stick to proven methods—board the station with a strike team and liberate the survivors. We've done it twice now with no casualties. My teams have it down to an art."

"And each time, the Ware gains more experience with our methods and unleashes some new deadly trick to try to stop us," Hari Banerji replied from the science station just aft of Charas's post, rotating his stool to face the executive officer. The lieutenant commander, an older human with brown skin and a fringe of hair as white as an Andorian's around his otherwise bare pate, replied to Charas's barbs with his usual avuncular cheer. "We've been lucky to avoid fatalities so far—I don't want to take any chances."

"I'm sick of your human notions of luck. Victory comes from planning and self-control."

"Which is exactly the purpose of the awakening protocol—to let us take more control of the situation." Banerji chuckled. "By your own argument, you can't object to that."

"Why, you red-blooded, flat-headed . . ."

"All right, you two, enough," sh'Prenni advised them. "You're setting a bad example, you know."

Charas straightened. "Of course, Captain. Apologies."

As usual, Banerji's response was more relaxed. "Sorry, Thenar. You know I'm not much for hand-to-hand, so I have to get my sparring practice in somehow." Charas restrained himself from a riposte, but his antennae spoke his irritation clearly. Still, Ensigns Breg and zh'Vethris, seated together at the forward console, were chuckling softly at the exchange, and sh'Prenni resisted the urge to join them. Over her left shoulder, Commander ch'Gesrit kept his gaze on the screen above his engineering console, but she could sense amusement in his bioelectric field. The whole bridge crew knew that, for all their endless bickering, Banerji and Charas were more similar than they would ever admit. The science officer was the only human in a crew of Andorians, and the XO was one of the few Thalassan Andorians in the mostly Talish crew. Both men took pleasure in standing out from the crowd. The laughter their arguments provoked only encouraged them to keep up the performance.

Only Tavrithinn th'Cheen, standing stiffly at portside tactical, remained above the general amusement. "With respect to Mister Banerji," the lieutenant said in the polished, haughty accent of the Clan of Cheen, "I'm not convinced the Ware is intelligent enough to learn from our tactics. I'm honestly starting to get bored with fighting mindless machines. The faster we can wrap this up and take on a real challenge—like the Klingons, perhaps—the happier I'll be."

"I'm sure the innocent victims of the Ware appreciate your concern for their plight, Vrith," Kitazoanra zh'Vethris replied in her usual wry, soft-spoken tones.

"Of course I meant *after* we liberate them, Zoanra," th'Cheen told the young navigator. "I'm sure they'd agree that the less time we waste, the better."

Zh'Vethris pursed her exquisite lips, unable to dispute the sentiment. Beneath the bridge crew's banter was a keen awareness of the suffering and death they had seen over the past few moons, all in service to the mindless demands of the Ware.

The threat had first been discovered fourteen Lor'veln cycles ago by Jonathan Archer, then the commander of the Earth ship *Enterprise*—the namesake of *Vol'Rala* in the language of United Earth. Following a crippling first contact with a Romulan minefield, Archer had learned of a nearby repair station, completely automated and equipped with highly sophisticated matter-replication technology that had repaired his vessel in record time. But when Travis Mayweather, the ship's pilot, was apparently killed in an accident, *Enterprise*'s doctor had soon discovered that the station had abducted him and falsified his death with a replicated corpse. Upon rescuing

Mayweather, Archer and his armory officer, Malcolm Reed, had found that the pilot was one of multiple captives whose brains the station had co-opted to provide the processing power for its remarkable feats—at the cost of progressive neural deterioration and eventual death. Archer had destroyed the station to spare others that fate.

Much had changed since then. The Earth Starfleet and the Andorian Guard were now sister services within the Starfleet of the United Federation of Planets, and Reed and Mayweather were now captain and executive officer of the *U.S.S. Pioneer*. Late last cycle, *Pioneer* had encountered another such station while exploring uncharted space. The local peoples referred to the technology as the Ware, but they had no knowledge of its origins or its true danger. Reed and Mayweather had assisted them in liberating some of the stations' captives, but *Pioneer* had been badly crippled by drone warships sent to retrieve the Ware's "stolen property." In response, Reed had convinced his former captain—now Admiral Archer—to assemble a task force to return to the uncharted sector and deal with the Ware before it became a threat to the Federation. *Pioneer* had taken the lead, investigating and making contact with local populations, as befitted its role as a member of Starfleet's exploratory arm. Meanwhile, seven ships from the defensive arm, the Andorian Guard, had stood by in reserve and joined the fight as needed.

Pioneer had found multiple pre-spaceflight worlds enslaved or devastated by the rapacious technology, which had been seeded by a people called the Pebru. In time, *Pioneer*'s engineering team had devised a signal that would awaken the captives, transmitting it throughout Pebru territory and shutting down all their Ware in one blow. Yet the Pebru were not the Ware's creators—merely more victims who had managed to direct its appetites toward others to spare themselves. The task force had made a sizeable dent in the Ware's spread, but the greater threat remained, so the mission continued.

The banter died down as the Ware station came into clearer view on the large semicircular screen at the fore of the bridge. The gray-white station, illuminated by the stark white primary star of the ringed, gaseous planet it orbited, had a fittingly skeletal appearance: three spherical data cores and the angular slabs that enclosed them were linked by narrow struts to one another and to three pairs of cylindrical docking lattices, each one able to expand to accommodate ships of many different shapes and sizes. The Ware facilities' great adaptability, including the ability to match their internal environment to any conceivable biology, was one of their primary lures, no doubt intended to maximize the number of living brains they could acquire.

"Target coordinates in eight," Ensign Breg reported in her strong Alrondian drawl. Ramnaf Breg was an Arkenite, orange-skinned with bright green eyes, a bulbous, tapered skull, and pointed ears that put a Vulcan's to shame, but she was Andorian by nationality, a native of the Arkenite community on the Alrond colony. It was a heritage she took pride in despite the upheavals on Alrond in recent years, and it shaded her vowels as she counted down to target.

"Neutralize warp," sh'Prenni ordered at the end of the countdown. "Go to battle alert." The pair of status dishes flanking her command chair altered their EM fields to a frequency that promoted alertness in the Andorian crew. Breg's own magnetic senses let her feel the change as well, leaving only Banerji blind to the sensation; but the light rods within the dishes changed from orange to blood-blue, serving as a visual cue that he could read. Not that he needed it; despite his relaxed, playful manner, Hari had one of the most focused minds sh'Prenni had ever encountered.

The crew put the fruits of that mind to good use as *Vol'Rala* burst into normal space and swooped down upon the Ware station. By the time the station's powerful sensor beams pierced the vessel's shields and excited the air within to a dazzling glow, th'Cheen had already fired two modified probes toward it. The probes—hardy Andorian models designed for gathering combat intelligence—homed in on the central spheres and struck their hulls with some force, piercing deeply enough to connect with the internal circuitry that pervaded the automated facility. As soon as contact was made, they put all their power into an intense signal, using the peripheral circuitry itself as an antenna to amplify the pulse. This was the trick Banerji had devised to enable the pulse to penetrate to the shielded cores of the spheres.

The first element of the pulse was a recognition code used by the Ware for transmitting software patches and upgrades. Once the data core responded with the proper handshake protocols, the probes transmitted the awakening command devised by Philip Collier, a civilian consultant serving as *Pioneer*'s acting chief engineer. Collier had realized that if the people held captive within the Ware were restored to consciousness while still in interface, they would be able to shut the technology down from within. Indeed, once awakened, the captives had gone even further than Collier had anticipated, interfacing with other Ware facilities and passing the awakening protocol along, until all the captives in a given Ware network were revived and the network was deactivated. Some Ware stations were interfaced with only a few others, but the Pebru's particular network had been fully interconnected, allowing the sleepers to shut down the Ware throughout Pebru space.

Sh'Prenni found it beautiful that her Starfleet colleagues had managed to devise a weapon that gave the Ware's victims the power to defeat their own oppressors. It embodied the spirit of justice and empowerment that defined the United Federation of Planets and made her proud that Andoria had been one of its founding members. She had joined the Imperial Guard (as it was then known) to serve her people, but at the time, she had seen little future for herself beyond conflict with Vulcans, Coridanites, Arkenite separatists, Nausicaan and Klingon pirates, and the like. But most of those conflicts had died down, largely through Jonathan Archer's diplomatic efforts, as sh'Prenni had risen through the ranks. And though the Romulans had then emerged as a major threat, the humans had managed to beat them back to their space—with no small assistance from the Andorian fleet at the decisive Battle of Cheron, in which sh'Prenni had fought as executive officer of the *I.G.S. Thalisar*. The subsequent founding of the Federation had heralded a new era of peace and cooperation, and sh'Prenni had been proud to devote her career as a Starfleet captain to constructive causes and the defense of the innocent. The Ware mission had already brought her greatest triumph; the defeat of the Pebru had liberated billions of sentients in one swift blow. But sh'Prenni would not rest until every last victim of the Ware was freed—or at least put out of their misery.

But while th'Cheen reported a textbook launch and impact of the probes, they failed to have the expected effect. The station remained functional, deploying robot arms to detach the probes from their impact craters. Banerji, who handled communications, reported an incoming signal from the station. *"Please follow proper docking procedures,"* the cool, pleasant feminine voice of the Ware computers intoned. *"Any damage to these facilities will be charged to your vessel."*

Charas shook his head. "I knew it. Banerji's drones are a bust."

"Now, now, let's not jump to conclusions," the wizened human replied, studying his readouts. "Hmm. Hmm, yes, that's most interesting."

"Would you care to share it with the class, Professor?" sh'Prenni asked.

"Well, not to blow my own horn, m'dear captain, but before those ill-mannered robot arms put paid to my probes, the readings I received from their sensors were consistent with a successful reawakening of the abductees." He leaned back in evident surprise. "In fact, these biosigns are unusual—not just two to four viable sleepers per data core, but a couple of dozen apiece, judging from these encephalographic readings. Remarkable! Most of them should be too neurologically degraded to revive . . . Why, this is astonishing!"

"But if they're all awake," Charas insisted, "why aren't they pulling themselves out, shutting the station down?"

"He's right," ch'Gesrit said. "It's just not consistent. Are you sure it isn't some kind of sensor artifact?"

"I am reading a kind of . . . fluctuation in the station's activities," the human replied. "No sign of an impending shutdown, more just sort of a . . . hesitation, followed by a slightly more unstable power flow. Almost as if the control switched from automatic to manual."

"What are you saying?" the captain asked. "That they're conscious inside the Ware, but somehow unable to take the next step and revive themselves?"

"Or unwilling," zh'Vethris suggested.

Breg frowned at the navigator's suggestion. "If you woke up inside one of those things, a prisoner in your own body, would you be content to stay that way?"

"No," Zoanra replied with a querulous tilt to her antennae. "But they aren't me. We don't even know what species they are."

"Then let's find out," Charas advised. "Whatever the reason, they aren't coming out on their own. And that means it's time to do it my way. Take in a team, get them out."

"Dozens of them?" countered Banerji. "That's almost as many sleepers as we have people aboard. We don't have enough shuttles, and you know transporters can't breach the cores."

"We can at least mount an exploratory raid," th'Cheen proposed. "Take one of the cores, liberate as many as we can, then bring them back to question."

"Yes, yes, excellent idea," Banerji told him. "Once we have some real answers, we can decide how to proceed from there."

Sh'Prenni wasted no time, nodding to Charas. "Take your raiding team. Proceed as discussed."

"Yes, Captain!"

"And Giered—be careful."

"As always, ma'am."

As the tactical officer headed out the portside exit door, the captain traded a knowing look with Banerji. "That's what I'm afraid of."

"Oh, he'll outlive us all," Hari reassured her. "He'd never let me get in the last word."

1

Klingon privateer *SuD Qav*

CAPTAIN LOKOG DID NOT REALIZE how deep a rut he had dug himself into until his lover tried to murder him.

Vhelis had been in bed with him at the time, and he had been confident there had been no part of her body where she could possibly have been concealing a weapon. That, he realized in retrospect, had been a symptom of his complacency; he hadn't considered that she might have a garotte woven into one of her hair braids until he'd felt it bite into the flesh of his neck.

The second sign of his weakness was that he'd only escaped death by luck. Vhelis was a capable enough fighter for her size, but that size was slight next to his, and her work as a sensor officer meant she rarely participated in raiding parties. By all rights, she should have been easy to overpower even with surprise on her side. But Lokog had been unable to land a decisive blow as he stumbled around the room, her legs wrapped about his waist from behind while the wire dug deeper into his throat. It had been by mere chance that one of his last desperate flails as consciousness faded had dislodged his prized *HomneH* from the wall and caused the club to fall upon Vhelis's head.

By fate, Lokog had recovered marginally faster. His *HomneH* was a cheap copy made of imitation *klongat* bone, not as solid as the real thing and good for little more than decoration; but Vhelis, a *QuchHa'* like himself and all his crew, lacked the protective cranial plating of a healthy Klingon, making her more vulnerable to head strikes. Still, she had remained conscious enough to feel it when he wrapped the garotte around her own throat in return. *"Why?"* he had demanded, giving her just enough breath to rasp out her answer.

It did not deter her bile, though. "Because you are a coward! First . . . you flee the fight for our people in the Empire, then you flee the spread of the Federation. Now we wander . . . deeper into wild space, looking for weaklings to pick off . . . retreating from any real fight!"

Lokog scoffed, tightening the garotte. "'Our people'? We are diseased, Vhelis! Victims of a plague that stripped us of our Klingonhood. We have no place in the Empire."

"We are still Klingons! And many . . . back home fight for our place, as any Klingon would! Now that Chancellor M'Rek lies on his deathbed . . . we have our chance! The Council is in turmoil—if the *QuchHa'* unite and strike now, we can win a place for ourselves . . . maybe even the chancellorship! But you keep us away from that righteous battle out of fear!"

"A battle we could not win! The *HemQuch* are divided now, but they will surely unite against us, and they have an insurmountable advantage of numbers!"

"Four thousand throats can be slit in one night by a running man!"

She was either bold or stupid to use that particular saying under the current circumstances. "You failed with even one throat, *petaQ!*"

Her eyes blazed in defiance. "Only if you lack the will to kill me."

It was then that he realized she was doing him a favor.

He had been ambitious once, before the Qu'Vat Plague had stripped him of his ridges and his standing, forcing him to start over with nothing, an outcast operating on the fringes of Klingon society. But for eleven years now, he had used his virally induced transformation as an excuse to remain there, to settle for a liminal existence as a pirate and mercenary, retreating ever further from the influence of Empire and Federation alike. Preying on easy targets and taking pleasure from their helplessness, rather than from the triumph of overcoming a true challenge.

"You're right. I am a coward." He tossed the garotte away, meeting her contempt-filled eyes.

"But I can change that," he went on as he finished the job with his bare hands. He thanked her as she died, then donned his armor with a new sense of purpose.

"Find me battle!" he roared as he stormed onto the bridge, dragging Vhelis's naked corpse behind him by her hair. Perhaps she deserved better after the gift she had given him, but he had a statement to make to his crew. If he had become lazy and dissolute, and if only his own bedmate had had the courage to kill him for it, then the rest of his raiders must be in even worse shape, and they needed a harsh awakening. Lokog was done being timid.

His crew got the message and leapt to their stations. The junior sensor officer Ghopmoq, now keenly aware of his abrupt promotion to Vhelis's former post and the consequences if he failed in that responsibility, rose determinedly to the occasion. By the time Lokog had finally tired of displaying Vhelis's corpse and had permitted the ship's *jeghpu'wI'* servitor to take the empty shell to the recyclers, Ghopmoq had managed to pinpoint the energy emissions of weapon discharges and straining engines within range of *SuD Qav*.

Better yet, one of the engine signatures read as Andorian. Lokog thrilled at the timing. After years spent in retreat from the Federation Starfleet, now he had a chance to go on the offensive against them at exactly the moment he'd sought it. Surely it was a sign that fate was on his side.

U.S.S. Vol'Rala

While an undertaking as dangerous as raiding a Ware station to liberate its "primary data core components" could never be called routine, Giered Charas hadn't lied when he said his teams had it down to an art. While the station's automation attempted several methods to expel or kill the boarding party, each one was met in turn by a well-practiced defensive measure: Transporter beams were scrambled by an interference field, extreme changes in atmosphere and temperature were staved off by environmental suits, and replicated weapon emplacements were pre-empted by the prompt destruction of any matter replication unit the team encountered. This station's computer even attempted shutting down its gravity plating and opening its airlocks to purge the intruders, but the boarding party locked their magnetic boots to the deck the moment the gravity faded, and once the flow of air had stopped, they used their zero-g combat training to maneuver swiftly through the corridors. Meanwhile, aboard *Vol'Rala*, th'Cheen made sure both boarding shuttles were protected by destroying any robotic repair arms within reach and using pinpoint fire to sever any adjacent plasma conduits that might build to an overload.

Within two centiphases, the shuttles had returned with all personnel and four liberated processors from two different species. All four had to be kept in the landing bay's quarantine section, for neither species could survive in an Andorian climate and atmosphere. All had been enclosed in special life-support units within the data cores, facilitating their transport to the ship. It seemed they had been re-sedated through the tubes plugged into their bodies, or else were simply too weak from inactivity to revive fully. Either way, sh'Prenni hoped it had kept them from panicking during their transport to *Vol'Rala*, and afterward while Banerji and Chirurgeon th'Lesinas altered the two quarantine bays to match their respective environments.

One species was native to a frigid liquid-methane environment with a nitrogen-hydrogen atmosphere—probably that of the nearby giant planet's most massive moon, which Banerji likened to a larger version of Titan in his home system. The other was an aquatic species from a liquid-water environment, presumably a dark one, given that it had infrared pits and echo-location nodes in place of eyes. "I can't imagine how either one got into space," the science officer reported to sh'Prenni as he waited for them to revive. "The fishy fellows have no kind of manipulative ability, and the others are from an anaerobic environment where fire would never be possible—which would put quite a damper on any efforts to invent technology, unless they're a good deal cleverer than I am."

"If they are from the nearby moon," Zharian th'Lesinas observed, "the Ware could have abducted them from there, as it's done with other races we've encountered."

"The bipeds, maybe. But the only place the aquatic creatures could live on that moon is in the subglacial ocean that's completely enclosed underneath the icy crust. That would explain their nocturnal adaptations, I suppose, but it'd make them damned hard to get to!" He chuckled, intrigued by the problem.

"Not to mention the totally different biochemistry," th'Lesinas put in. "Look at these readings. The hydrogen breathers don't even use DNA—they're based on some kind of complex lipids inside azotosomic cell membranes. The two couldn't come from the same evolutionary origin."

Banerji noted a readout. "Well, now they can tell us themselves. They're awake!"

His typical human optimism led him to gloss over the initial difficulties in establishing a translation matrix. But it took only a few centiphases for his linguistics officer to finesse the equipment to the point where communication was possible. The methane-based organisms called themselves the Nierl. They were slender, tailed bipeds with forward-leaning bodies terminating in flowerlike heads, if that was the word—each with a quadrilaterally symmetric array of manipulative sensory tendrils around a central cluster of optical organs and a four-flapped mouth. The stouter, more assertive one gave its name as Vuulg, and its slighter companion was Rulii. They identified the aquatic sentients as the Sris'si, verifying that both species occupied the nearby moon, with the Nierl on the frigid surface and the Sris'si in the warmer depths below—an environment that the Nierl thought of as molten rock, for under their native conditions, water was a mineral. "That is the Sris'si's origin world," Vuulg explained.

"Then the Nierl are not natives?" Captain sh'Prenni asked.

"We are of the Partnership of Civilizations. You must know this; you found us aboard a Partnership station."

Sh'Prenni exchanged a look with Banerji and th'Lesinas. "We've liberated captives from a number of stations of that type," she said. "None of them referred to a Partnership of Civilizations."

Vuulg and Rulii waved their tendrils in evident distress.

"We are not captives!" Vuulg insisted. "The Partnership does not employ the Ware in that fashion. We are all volunteers!"

"Yes, we are!" Rulii added. "And we insist that you return us to complete our full tenure!"

Studying the poor creatures with pity, sh'Prenni strove for patience. "I know this is difficult for you. But we have dealt with the Ware before. Its promises are insidious. But it is far more destructive than it appears."

"Only if misused," Vuulg countered. "The Partnership is more enlightened. We choose to subordinate ourselves to the Ware's needs for a limited tenure, in exchange for which our people, our families, can thrive. It is how we repay the Partnership for the bounty it provides."

"A payment that cripples you? Damages your brains, atrophies your bodies?"

"Our terms are brief enough to cause no serious decay. The system has worked for many generations! It has enabled the Partners to thrive as they never could before!"

"Excuse me," Banerji asked, "but have you ever met any 'volunteers' after their tenure?"

The creatures traded a look, tendrils waving—to communicate or merely express a mood? "Not that we know of," Vuulg admitted. "But our numbers are large, and the Ware does not demand that many."

"We may have met former volunteers who did not wish to speak of it," Rulii added. "It is not the most pleasant experience, I admit. And you miss out on so much while you are under."

"It is a vital service," Vuulg protested.

"Oh, of course. I would not have volunteered otherwise. But I will be happy enough to leave it behind when my tenure ends."

It soon became clear that the Nierl could not be dissuaded from their convictions, and a follow-up conversation with the Sris'si (which proved rather more challenging, since their more alien mentality and sensorium provided less linguistic and conceptual common ground) confirmed that they felt the same sense of duty to sacrifice themselves for the Partnership. "It's the same pattern we've seen on half a dozen worlds," sh'Prenni told the science and medical officers once they'd stepped away from the quarantine bays. "Their societies have been so seduced by the Ware's luxuries that they rationalize the victimization of their own people. Even the victims are fooled into going along." She noted the skeptical tilt of th'Lesinas's antennae, and asked, "What are you thinking, Zhar?"

"Well, it's odd, Captain," the portly chirurgeon replied. "All four rescuees show only the most minimal brain damage, as if they've been emplaced for only two or three moons. It's consistent with their story of serving only finite terms as volunteers."

"Yes," Banerji added, "and the boarding party confirmed that all the processors appeared equally viable. We were wondering about that, remember? None of them had the years of progressive brain damage we've found in the majority of captives on other Ware stations."

"But how could that be?" sh'Prenni asked. "We've seen repeatedly how difficult, how dangerous it is to persuade the Ware to give up its captives. I can't believe this Ware is so different that it just . . . voluntarily lets them go before they're harmed. Or that these beings could have somehow figured out a way to reprogram it. Look at them! You said yourself, Hari, they aren't even capable of starting a fire!"

Banerji grew thoughtful. "Then imagine how much the technological bounty of the Ware would mean to them."

"Exactly. They're even more dependent than most—which makes them more vulnerable than most. Even if it does somehow let them take turns, spare their lives for some reason, it's still slavery. The Ware's standard procedure is to make itself alluring to bait the trap. It's harming them, whether they know it or not. It's just hiding it more insidiously here."

"Except," the elderly human muttered, speaking as much to himself as to her, "if these species *are* more susceptible, why would it *need* to be more insidious with them?"

Before sh'Prenni could formulate a response, the comm signaled. *"Bridge to captain,"* came Charas's voice.

She strode to the wall console and opened the return channel. "Sh'Prenni. Report."

"We're getting a distress signal from Flabbjellah, *Captain. The message is unclear, but they're in battle with a Ware ship and they need assistance."*

"Set course to intercept. Maximum warp factor."

"Captain," said th'Lesinas, "we can't just take the rescuees into battle."

"But we can't just drop them back on the Sris'si moon," Banerji replied, "not with their special life-support needs. It would take hours to work out a way to move them."

Sh'Prenni considered. "Bridge. *Tashmaji's* already on standby for our call, correct?"

"Yes, Captain," Charas confirmed. The high-speed courier was one of two belonging to the task force. Since the Ware sent drone battleships after any vessel that stole their "proprietary components," standard procedure was to transfer rescuees to one of the couriers, which would then whisk them away to their homeworlds before the drones could hunt them down.

"Contact Commander sh'Regda. Have her rendezvous

with us en route to *Flabbjellah*. Th'Lesinas will send you the life-support protocols to forward to *Tashmaji*." She nodded to the chirurgeon, who moved to his console to comply. "That will give us time to prep for a transfer and have the rescuees clear before intercept."

"*Very good, Captain.*"

Banerji chuckled. "So we rush them away from their home planet, then have another ship rush them back to almost the same place they left. Quite the roundabout commute."

"At least they'll be safely home," sh'Prenni told him. "Now let's make sure Captain zh'Ethar and her crew can come home safe as well."

SuD Qav

Shortly after Lokog had set his ship on course for the battle, he had realized that his enthusiasm had been premature. The battle was forty *tup* away at top speed, and few battles lasted more than a few *tup*. He had feared *SuD Qav* would arrive to find only wreckage—though there was still a chance that they could face the victor, hopefully finding them strong enough to put up a satisfying fight but damaged enough to assure victory. That was the name of his ship, after all: *Last Chance*.

To Lokog's relief, they found the battle still going on once they arrived. It was more of a chase, really, with the Starfleet vessel—an Andorian-built light cruiser whose identifier beacon called it the *U.S.S. Flabbjellah*—in pursuit of an unfamiliar ship, a gray vessel with two boxy, inward-tilted warp nacelles flanking a central module in the form of a sphere bisected at its equator by a seven-sided slab. In the estimation of Kalun, *SuD Qav*'s gunner, the Andorian ship was firing to disable, while the unknown ship was firing defensively, more interested in escaping its foe than destroying it. But that did not entirely explain the longevity of the combat.

"I think," Ghopmoq said after studying his scans for a while, "the gray ship is repairing itself with incredible speed!"

"Impossible," Lokog spat. "You said there were only four life signs aboard. How could they work so fast?"

"It is as I said, Captain—the ship is repairing *itself*."

Once the idea sank in, Lokog thrilled at the potential. What a prize that technology would be for a raider! And what an advantage it would be for a warrior, to recover from damage almost as quickly as it was inflicted! (He rubbed the stinging welt across his throat as he thought this.) Either way, he had to keep that ship from falling into Starfleet's hands. "Battle stations! Prepare to engage the *'anDorngan* vessel!"

The crew hesitated. Although *Flabbjellah* was a midsized vessel, its speed and firepower surpassed *SuD Qav*'s, and Lokog's raiders were unaccustomed to facing foes that could put up a better fight than they could. The one person aboard who'd proven to have that kind of fire was Vhelis, and she was no longer available. (If only, Lokog mused, there were a way he could have the satisfaction of killing his crew without the inconvenience of their subsequent absence.) But the others had seen the consequences of disobedience, so they quashed their doubts and bent to their tasks.

Of course, Lokog was no fool. For all his determination to strike at Starfleet, his belief in picking his battles remained intact. An Andorian light cruiser at full strength would have outmatched his ramshackle privateer, but *Flabbjellah* was damaged and strained from its extended running firefight—and Lokog had a formidable ally against it.

Those conditions saved Lokog the trouble of trying to

devise a clever strategy. The pilot, Krugt, brought *SuD Qav* in on a simple intercept course while Kalun cut loose with all weapons, battering *Flabbjellah*'s damaged shields. A few particle-cannon bolts shot out in *SuD Qav*'s direction, but the Starfleet crew's main focus was on their mysterious quarry, so their fire toward the privateer was halfhearted and defensive. They would soon learn that Lokog would not be warned off so easily. Not when he had the advantage, at least. No doubt the gray ship would turn and join him in the attack, combining its formidable weapons with *SuD Qav*'s to reduce the Starfleet ship to radioactive scrap.

But after Kalun's fire had blasted the light cruiser badly enough to cripple its propulsion, Lokog belatedly realized that the quarry ship was not taking the opportunity to go on the offensive. Instead, it merely continued its now unharried flight. "What?" Lokog cried when Ghopmoq confirmed the evidence of Lokog's eyes. "Hail the ungrateful cowards!"

The face that appeared on the viewer moments later was as dark and smooth-browed as Lokog's own, save for an array of light spots adorning the brow, a completely hairless head, yellowish eyes, and small fins protruding from behind the ears. *"My name is Daskel Vabion, chairman of Worldwide Automatics on the planet Vanot. I appreciate your impulse to intervene on my behalf, though I had the situation under control."*

"I am Lokog, commander of the Klingon vessel *SuD Qav*—and you could never have defeated your foe without me. Now, before they can regroup, circle back to join us and we can blow the Starfleet scum to atoms!"

The man called Vabion looked unimpressed. *"I have no interest in their annihilation. Now that they are no longer an impediment, they are of no further concern to me."*

"We came here to assist you! You owe us gratitude, surely."

Those bright eyes sized him up. *"I take it you expect compensation of some sort."*

"Well . . . I meant that you should join us in the glory of the kill, as a gesture of thanks. But . . . if you wish to discuss compensation afterward . . ."

"I only kill when it benefits me, Captain Lokog. And I only offer compensation to those who have earned it." He paused, thinking. *"However, you could be of use to me in the future. The vessel I control employs a proprietary technology of Worldwide Automatics, known as the Ware. The organization called Starfleet—of which I see you are aware—recently launched an attack on this technology, incapacitating it on worlds throughout the sector and disrupting commerce and industry on a massive scale."*

"Why would those Starfleet do-gooders want to destroy your technology?"

"They found certain . . . necessary compromises in its method of operation to be incompatible with their ethics. They have been allowing me to assist in the rescue of various crews stranded by the Ware shutdown by bringing their ships up to a minimum level of operation. However, by working clandestinely, I was able to replace certain . . . key components of the system and restore this vessel to full operation. My goal is to do the same with other Ware systems and exploit the technology to its full potential."

"To what end? Conquest?"

"In a sense. I am a businessman. I was once the most powerful and influential individual on Vanot, and I seek to rebuild what I have lost, only on a far more cosmic scale. Any who align themselves with me will profit greatly."

"Profit interests me," Lokog said. "But I also seek battle and glory. I wish to strike at my enemies." He leaned forward. "I have seen what your ship can do. Its weapons, its ability to repair itself. And there are only a few of you aboard. This Ware is automated?"

"Indeed—the most advanced automation in the known galaxy. Ware

drones can operate with no crew aboard at all." The man of Vanot furrowed his brow. *"Are there other Klingons in this space? And do they share your interest in acquiring powerful weapons and ships?"*

"In exchange for providing you with some service?" Lokog countered.

"Indeed. While these ships are powerful, Starfleet has the means to shut them down. I have managed to circumvent that with this ship, but it is difficult and time-consuming. It would be useful to supplement them with vessels and weapons that Starfleet could not so easily overcome." He paused. *"Of course, if Starfleet is your enemy, Ware ships would be of no use to you. But you cited enemies in the plural . . . ?"*

Vhelis's dying words echoed in Lokog's mind. The *QuchHa'* people had many enemies on the High Council. Lokog had no hope of taking on those enemies with *SuD Qav*, or even with an alliance of all the privateers in unclaimed space. But with a powerful new technology, with drones that could repair themselves and be controlled in large numbers by a single Klingon . . . perhaps one running man could slit a few thousand throats after all.

Still, he had some unresolved bloodlust to address. "We can do business, Mister Vabion. Let us commemorate our pact by destroying the Starfleeters together." At Vabion's impatient look, he went on. "This kill would benefit you, Vabion. Consider it a product demonstration for your customer. Show me what your weapons can do."

"When you put it that way, I'd be happy to comply. Unfortunately, that vessel is only one member of a Starfleet task force, and it sent a distress signal to its companions some time ago. Two more Starfleet vessels, one of them significantly larger than this one, are on an intercept course as we speak."

Lokog turned to Ghopmoq, murder in his eyes. The young sensor officer worked his controls frantically. "I detect nothing on approach, Captain! I swear!"

"Will that demonstration satisfy you, Captain? Ware sensors are clearly far superior to yours."

Lokog wondered if Vabion could be bluffing, but he wasn't about to take the chance. Boldly facing danger was all well and good, but only if he could be reasonably sure of surviving to boast of his courage afterward. He had really wanted to prolong the pleasurable sense of power he'd gained from killing Vhelis, but he grudgingly admitted he'd have to let his bloodlust go unsatisfied until some other day. (He contemplated shooting Ghopmoq as a token gesture, but it would be too much of an anticlimax. And he was short on sensor officers as it was.)

Besides, if this Ware lived up to Vabion's promises, he would have plenty of enemies to destroy before long.

2

Pheniot V, Orion-Klingon Borderland

GYRAI DID NOT GENERALLY MIND when one of her male slaves intruded on her in the bath without permission. The Orion merchant princess rather enjoyed the pretense that the muscular, emerald-skinned giants were the masters and herself merely one of their playthings; it was quite pleasurable to be dominated, knowing that in fact she had the absolute power to assert command over the situation if any aspect of it displeased her. What she did not enjoy about the intrusion this time, however, was that Korem-Gaas had come with other than amorous intentions. "My lady," he began, his honest submission a sign that he was not here to play. "We are being raided! The slave pens are open—the merchandise is in open revolt!"

"What?" Gyrai erupted from the pool, scattering the three junior Orion women who had been tending to her ablutions. "How did this happen without warning?" she asked as a fourth slave woman, this one a lavender-haired Boslic, hurried over to help her into her robe.

"I'm sorry, mistress," Gaas cried, nearly panicking. "But they had a valid identification code. It wasn't until the raid started that we scanned their ship, and—"

"Who? Who are you talking about?"

Whoever they were, they had exceptional dramatic timing, for at just that moment, the doors burst open and four women entered. But these were not slave women, Orion or otherwise. They strode into the room with commanding confidence, they were fully clothed (Gyrai could not imagine how that could be comfortable), and they were armed. The woman in the lead was tan-skinned and black-haired, human by appearance and scent, wearing black trousers and a gray tunic with a gold arrowhead patch on the breast. She felled Korem-Gaas with an energy beam as he charged—although, since there was no aroma of burned flesh, Gyrai concluded he had merely been stunned. But that woman then stepped aside, her body language deferring to the other three. Two of those, lighter-skinned human women with shoulder-length dark hair and blue tunics of the same design, flanked a longer-haired Vulcan in a tunic of brownish green. Gyrai realized they were officers of a Federation starship, and the Vulcan was clearly their commander.

Gyrai had instinctively fallen back and adopted a deferential pose, expecting the intruders to accept Gaas's public role as the master, but the Vulcan focused her gaze directly on Gyrai and strode toward her. She realized she should have shed her robe as well; as the only female wearing a garment, however abbreviated, she stood out from the pack. "I am Captain T'Pol of the Federation vessel *Endeavour*," the Vulcan said. "Where is V'Las?"

Gyrai blinked innocently. "Who?"

"V'Las. Former administrator of the Vulcan High Command and suspected Romulan collaborator. Orchestrator of the recent coup attempt on Vulcan. Last reported aboard the renegade Vulcan battleship *Karik-tor*, which was sighted entering the Borderland four days ago."

"Many ships come to the Borderland for many reasons," Gyrai lilted. "We offer pleasures undreamed of here."

"It is unlikely that Vulcans would come here seeking pleasure."

"Oh, it's always the quiet ones you have to watch out for—hey, what are you doing?" The two blue-clad women had discovered her data terminal and were attempting to access its systems. "That material is private. And even if you could breach the encryption, it would offer nothing of use to you. We Orions have no interest in Vulcan politics."

"That is a lie," T'Pol replied coolly. "The Orion Syndicate has been attempting to undermine Federation institutions for the past several years."

"I know nothing of that," she said, fingering the jeweled choker she wore. "I'm just a businesswoman. I'm not privy to the Sisters' plans."

The Vulcan loomed closer. "You are Gyrai, one of the most prominent racketeers within the Borderland. No Syndicate business occurs here without you getting a share."

"You'll never be able to prove that."

"I'm in!" called the daintier of the two women in blue, a black-haired woman with dark eyes and delicate lips that could fetch a fortune on the slave market.

"Good work, Hoshi," the captain said.

Gyrai shook her head. "Impossible. You can't have penetrated my security files."

"Oh, not your security files," said the woman called Hoshi. "Your bank account." She turned to the taller, fairer-haired woman. "Elizabeth? It's all yours."

"Okay, now, let's see . . . Whoa, that's a lot of digits. I bet the Interspecies Medical Exchange could do wonders with this kind of funding."

"So let's give them some."

"Why not?" Elizabeth smiled as she bent to the console.

"What are you doing?" Gyrai cried. "It's not enough that you raid my livestock, you now resort to rank thievery?"

"Oh, I'm sure you entirely outrank us," Hoshi told her.

"I will ask again," T'Pol said. If she were not a Vulcan, Gyrai would swear she was coolly amused. "Where is V'Las?"

"I know nothing of him." Her fingers closed around a large green gem on her choker.

But T'Pol's fingers closed around her wrist, pulled her hand away from her neck with a grip of steel, and relieved her of the poison gas pellet before she could throw it. "Your behavior is uncooperative. Lieutenant Cutler?"

"Yes, Captain. I was thinking the Rigelian Children's Fund next."

"Excellent choice. May I also suggest the Vegan Chorio-meningitis Society?"

"And there's Habitat for Humanoids," Hoshi put in.

"Why not?" said Cutler. "After all, there's plenty of money to go around."

"Stop!" Gyrai demanded. "Just stop, please! All right! V'Las came here seeking allies. I was instructed by the Sisters to turn him away. The Syndicate has no wish to provoke the Federation again." *For the moment.*

"Are you quite positive?" Hoshi asked. "Because I'm seeing a stock portfolio here that would do wonders for relief efforts on Coridan."

"Good call," Cutler said. "Here it goes!"

"I swear! Please, I'm telling you the truth! The last I saw of his ship, it was heading out of the sector on a course through the outskirts of Klach D'Kel Brakt. Of course no one could track him beyond that morass."

T'Pol held her gaze, studying her. Finally she looked away with a faint sigh. "Then we are done here. Move out."

Gyrai's eyes widened as Cutler and Hoshi stepped away from her console. "What about my money? Aren't you going to put it back?"

"Why?" Cutler asked, her jovial tone undiminished. "Those others need it a lot more than you do."

"I need it now that you've set my slaves free!"

"Okay, you're really not earning any sympathy points there."

Gyrai winced and took a deep breath, hoping to hold on to what little wealth and dignity she had left. But as the Starfleet women headed for the door, the Boslic slave stepped forward. "Wait. Can I come with you?"

"Certainly," T'Pol said. Looking over the golden-skinned girl, the Vulcan turned back to Gyrai and brandished her weapon at her once more. "Would you be so kind as to give this young woman your robe?"

U.S.S. *Endeavour* NCC-06

Doctor Phlox had always admired Captain T'Pol's timing. She came through sickbay's frosted doors just as he was wrapping up his examination of the last of the liberated slaves from Pheniot V. "Just remember, now: Consume one *vghlar* beetle with each meal until the supply runs out," he told the emaciated Nuvian woman. "There's nothing better for a vitamin deficiency, and they taste good, too!"

The young lady thanked him and allowed the gray-shirted security guard outside to escort her to her guest quarters. "Ah, Captain!" Phlox said, turning to his new arrival. "She's the last of them. And just as well, too, for my supply of beetles is running dangerously low. Aside from their use as vitamin supplements, they're a vital part of my Altarian marsupial's diet. I'll simply have to restock once we reach Denobula." He tried his best not to make it sound like a leading question, though he doubted he succeeded.

Indeed not. "I know you have been concerned about reaching home in time for your daughter's wedding, Phlox," the captain said.

"Oh, don't worry about me, Captain. I quite understand the needs of duty. The hunt for V'Las is a vital task." The defrocked administrator had proven himself willing to inflict violence on a massive scale—first eleven years ago when he had attempted to foment a war with Andoria and bomb his political opposition to extinction, then more recently when he had organized an attempt at a military coup to retake power on Vulcan, nearly destroying *Endeavour* in the process.

"Unfortunately, the trail has gone cold. The supernova remnants, metaphasic radiation, and quantum fluctuations in the Klach D'Kel Brakt region make it effectively impossible to track a warp trail through it."

"What was it that Arik Soong called it?" Phlox asked. "The Briar Patch?"

"An apt analogy," the captain granted, "particularly given that the nearest Vulcan equivalents to Terran briar plants are carnivorous."

Phlox chuckled. "I sense frustration, if you don't mind my saying so."

T'Pol gave him a knowing look. "It would be illogical to deny it. The only reason *Karik-tor* would have entered the Briar Patch is to elude pursuit. We may take it as a given that they altered course upon entry. Lieutenant Cutler is scanning the periphery of the patch intently, but I do not expect her to find anything." She eased a bit closer. "Therefore, unless another lead presents itself within the next few days, I see no impediment to reaching Denobula in time for Vaneel's wedding."

Phlox smiled. "Thank you, T'Pol. If necessary, I would have arranged alternate transport, but I can't tell you how much it will mean to me to have you and Hoshi and my other dear friends by my side."

T'Pol showed typical Vulcan unease toward his sentiment, but she was spared the need to respond by the intercom. *"Bridge to Captain T'Pol,"* came the crisp voice of Thanien ch'Revash, *Endeavour*'s first officer.

The captain strode to the console near the door and opened the channel. "T'Pol here."

"Captain, a Klingon battle cruiser, D-Five class, is closing rapidly on our position."

T'Pol's shoulders tensed, and Phlox could understand why. The Klingons had kept to themselves for the past few years, dealing with internal matters that Phlox was more intimately familiar with than he would have liked. But the proud, bellicose beings had never been kindly disposed toward Starfleet, and if something had provoked them to action, the consequences could be dangerous indeed. "I'm on my way," the captain said. She turned to Phlox. "Doctor, I suggest you ready sickbay as a precaution."

"Of course, Captain."

Thanien's voice sounded again. *"Captain, the Klingons are hailing us."*

"I'll take it when I arrive."

"Captain—they are asking to speak to Doctor Phlox."

"Me?" Phlox was so surprised that he feared his face would puff up as a defensive reflex. He cleared his throat. "Why ever would the Klingons wish to speak to me?" he asked, not looking forward to the answer.

"I suggest we ask them," T'Pol said. "With me, Doctor."

Endeavour's efficient turbolift soon deposited them both on the starship's bridge, on whose forward screen the angular green battle cruiser loomed like a Berengarian dragon preparing to stoop on its prey. T'Pol took her command chair, gestured to Phlox to stand beside her, then nodded to Lieutenant Commander Sato at the communications station. "Open a channel."

A swarthy Klingon with heavy brow ridges and an ornate beard appeared on the viewer. *"I am Nevokh, commander of the Imperial Klingon Cruiser* Haj. *I am seeking Doctor Phlox of the Interspecies Medical Exchange."*

"I am Captain T'Pol of *Endeavour*. Doctor Phlox is here with me. What is your business with him?"

"That business is solely with him, Captain. It is . . . a medical matter. Does the Federation not believe that such things are private?"

Normally Phlox would agree, but T'Pol read his reservations on his face. "With all due respect, Commander Nevokh, the last time the Klingon Empire wished Phlox's assistance with a medical matter, they abducted him by force and threatened his life."

Nevokh squirmed. *"I am aware of this. That is why I have been tasked by Fleet Admiral Krell . . . to ask Doctor Phlox to accompany us back to Qo'noS. I am not authorized to explain more to any but the doctor himself."*

Phlox stepped forward. "If a member of your crew is ill, you are welcome to bring them aboard *Endeavour*. I'm sure I can treat them best in my own sickbay." *Surrounded by Starfleet security's finest.*

"That is not why we need you, Doctor. Admiral Krell has sworn that you will not be harmed if you accompany us to the homeworld."

"I cannot permit you to take him without some explanation," T'Pol said.

"Do you doubt a Klingon's word of honor?" Nevokh shouted, erupting from his command chair.

T'Pol sat unmoved in hers. "Do you doubt a Vulcan's sense of duty? Phlox is a member of my crew. His safety is my responsibility. If you wish his assistance, you must make your case to me."

The Klingon clenched his fists and his jaw, but then he swallowed his anger. *"Very well. But this is in the strictest confidence. May we speak without your crew hearing?"*

"Give us one moment." T'Pol rose and turned to Sato. "Forward it to my ready room."

Once she and Phlox were alone in the captain's spartan office, T'Pol reopened the channel on her desk monitor. "Only Doctor Phlox and I can hear you now, Commander."

Nevokh was still hesitant. *"It is said that the word of a Vulcan is unbreakable. Is this true? Can I rely on you to keep this in the strictest confidence?"*

T'Pol pondered. "If the matter is relevant to Federation security, then I will be obligated to inform my superiors. But I will divulge nothing to anyone I am not duty-bound to inform."

The Klingon took a deep breath. *"Very well. I appreciate your candor. And your Federation would surely find out soon enough. I suppose I have no choice.*

"Captain . . . Doctor . . . I must inform you that Chancellor M'Rek is dead."

Phlox exchanged a look with the captain, then spoke. "You, ah, have my sincere condolences on your loss, Commander. However, I don't see what I can do for the chancellor at this stage. If you had come to me sooner—"

"We do not ask you to save the chancellor, Denobulan. M'Rek was widely and justly despised, and the High Council has been fractious and

paralyzed under his weak leadership. He did not even have the virtue of dying with honor—he grew ill and wasted away for months. No one could challenge him for leadership, for he was too weak to fight. Even Admiral Krell, who relied upon M'Rek's patronage, agrees that he was holding the Empire back.

"But that is the root of the problem. M'Rek had many enemies. The factions within the Council accuse one another of poisoning M'Rek—slaying him secretly and without honor. An Arbiter of Succession has been named, but none of the challengers can be affirmed until they are cleared of the accusations. Yet none will accept that M'Rek died of natural causes, for the very physicians who tended to him may have been his poisoners.

"The only thing the councillors have been able to agree on, Doctor, is that they require an objective party to determine the cause of the chancellor's death."

"But why me?" Phlox asked. "The Empire has no love for me, given my role in the creation of the Qu'Vat virus." He declined to point out that the release of the metagenic virus, which was responsible for the cosmetic changes in the appearance of several hundred million Klingons, had been necessary to cure a more deadly form of the pathogen—and that Fleet Admiral Krell himself had arranged for Phlox to be brought to the Qu'Vat colony under duress and forced to engineer the cure. No point in antagonizing a Klingon who, for once, seemed reasonably civil toward him.

"That is why the factions have agreed to seek you out, Phlox. There is no love lost between you and the Klingon people, and thus no reason why you would aid any of the factions."

"Well, I suppose that makes sense. Although I truly have nothing against the Klingon people, and have no wish to see them come to harm. If my assistance will prevent further strife, I'm willing to consider it. But I'd like to take a moment to discuss it with the captain, if you don't mind."

"Very well. But waste no time!"

The screen went dark, and T'Pol turned to him. "You are inclined to agree to this?"

Phlox paced. "Believe me, I'm not eager to go off with the Klingons again. I'm sure many of them hold grudges against me—the *QuchHa'* in particular." T'Pol nodded, recognizing the term the Klingons had given to the population stripped of their cranial ridges by the virus. It was a rather mean-spirited wordplay: *QuchHa'* was the Klingon word for "unhappy," but was also a homonym for "deprived of a forehead." Phlox was reluctant to use it—or its counterpart *HemQuch*, meaning "proud forehead," for unaltered Klingons like Nevokh—but the Klingons themselves had embraced the labels so thoroughly that there was little alternative.

"But you heard Nevokh," he went on. "The Empire is torn apart by factional strife, and that's largely due to the conflict between the mutated and unmutated Klingon populations. I can't help feeling that the situation is partly my responsibility."

T'Pol contemplated him. "I understand your desire to minimize loss of life. But what if you find that M'Rek was assassinated, and this leads to the execution of his killers? Or simply worsens the recriminations and sparks civil war?"

Phlox paced the cramped room. "Believe me, T'Pol, I'm very much aware of those possibilities. But whatever happens, I *do* bear a responsibility for the current situation, and I should stand up and face it. Goodness knows, I've certainly tried to instill that belief in my children. Now, of all times, I can't walk away from it." Vaneel, who had learned that lesson as well as any of his children—and far better than some—would certainly understand if he had to risk missing her wedding. "At least I can attempt to bring some rationality and calm to the proceedings. If the factions are willing to cooperate enough to invite me—and actually *make* it an invitation this time—maybe that's something I can encourage them to build on."

The captain nodded. "I cannot fault your convictions, Phlox. And you are a civilian, so ultimately the choice is yours. If you wish to go, I will not stand in your way."

"I really think I must, T'Pol."

She rose. "Yet it troubles me that this is occurring so soon before the wedding. I would find it . . . disagreeable . . . to attend the event without you, Phlox."

He smiled. "And I would find it disagreeable to be detained. Especially by Klingons. But Nevokh did give his word of honor that I would be unharmed."

T'Pol did not look reassured. "If the Klingons suspect their chancellor was assassinated, then honor may not be as prevalent in the Empire as they claim."

Starfleet Headquarters, San Francisco

"You're positive? M'Rek is dead?"

Admiral Jonathan Archer considered his words before responding to the Andorian *shen* on his desk monitor. Vinithnel sh'Mirrin was the current Federation Commissioner for Defense, and though Archer found her more reasonable than her predecessor, Min glasch Noar, he wanted to make sure there were no misunderstandings. "At this point, all we have are unconfirmed reports. We'll know more when we get Doctor Phlox's report in a few days—assuming the Klingons let him go like they promised."

Sh'Mirrin's antennae took on a thoughtful cast. *"Understood. Still, you were right to notify me. We have to be ready for whatever comes. M'Rek's inability to unify the High Council worked in our favor; it kept the*

Klingons too busy undermining their rivals to spare any attention for us. What if the next chancellor is able to unite the Council behind a common goal, like invading the Federation?"

"All the more reason to be glad Phlox is there," Archer pointed out. "If he does them a favor, it might earn the Federation some goodwill in their eyes." Even as he said it, Archer recognized how feeble a hope it was. In his past dealings with the Klingon High Council, he'd found them too preoccupied with their political games and pissing contests to be interested in alliances with the Federation. Even a decade ago, when it had been in their best interests to join with Earth against their common Romulan foes, they had come within a hair's breadth of declaring war on Earth merely to save face for some perceived embarrassment. Chancellor M'Rek's unofficial assistance had come in handy at the Battle of Cheron, but it would have destroyed him politically to side openly with Earth and its allies, the later founders of the Federation. And now M'Rek was gone, making it unlikely that the Federation had any potential allies left on the Council.

"Except that Phlox isn't from a Federation world," sh'Mirrin pointed out, adding one more strike against the notion. *"Denobula still isn't in any hurry to make up its mind about joining."*

"They are an ally, though. And the Klingons know that Phlox has been a doctor with Starfleet for over a decade. Maybe that'll count for something."

"I admire your optimism, Admiral." She sighed. *"Meanwhile, I need to brief the president and discuss our options. Depending on how things fall out on Qo'noS in the phases and moons ahead, we may need to divert Starfleet resources to the border sectors nearest the Klingon Empire."* Her phrasing reminded Archer of the small mercy that, as yet, neither Federation nor Empire had grown far enough in the other's direction for their territories to abut. *"And we've already*

got a sizeable chunk of the Guard devoted to the Alrond operation and the Ware task force. On which point, any chance Captain Reed will be bringing them home soon?"

"Admiral Shran's the one to ask," Archer said. "But last I heard from *Pioneer*, they were still searching for the originators of the Ware."

"We may have to consider calling them back if the Klingon situation erupts. I'll notify Shran to be ready."

"Of course, Commissioner," Archer said, though he felt she was being premature. "Meanwhile, where do we stand on Alrond? Is the Council any closer to approving intervention?"

"Still deliberating, I'm afraid."

"What is there to deliberate?" Archer wondered. "The Keepers of the Throne are insane. They're murdering Alrondian citizens just for being Arkenites. What's more, this morning an Ar*konian* diplomat on Alrond was attacked by some fanatic who apparently couldn't spell! I've been busy all day trying to convince the Arkonian ambassador that the Federation hasn't declared war on them!"

"Jon . . ."

"Something has to be done about these fanatics before it gets any worse! Governor Lecheb sure isn't gonna rein them in. She's bending over backward to appease them rather than risk being deposed." Lecheb sh'Makesh's faction had always been the most extreme of the separatist groups that had rebelled against their respective worlds' formation of the United Federation of Planets four years before. The governor of the Alrond colony neighboring Andoria, Lecheb had refused to recognize the Federation and had declared herself leader of the Andorian Empire in exile. She'd lacked enough ships to back up her rhetoric with force, so the Andorians had tolerated the situation for two years. But recently, Lecheb's extreme nationalist rhetoric had provoked an even more radical splinter faction, the Keepers of the Throne, to begin attacking Alrond's sizeable Arkenite population in retaliation for Arken II's recent admission to the Federation—even though the Alrondian Arkenites were Andorian citizens by birth and culture, and thus had already been Federation members. Even Governor Lecheb had initially attempted to rein in the Keepers' excesses, but once it became evident that they sought her overthrow as well, she had begun playing along with their demands, falling silent on the Arkenite killings and endorsing not only the expulsion of the Federation from Andoria but the restoration of the monarchy and clan-based rule.

"Admiral." The commissioner's sharper tone got through to him. *"You're exaggerating the risk. Even the Lechebists are shocked by how far the Keepers have gone. Councillor sh'Rothress assures me she's close to persuading Lecheb to denounce the Keeper movement and accede to a Starfleet peacekeeping force on Alrond. But if we go in without her blessing, it'll just shift the Lechebists' sentiments further toward the Keepers' extremes."*

"Meanwhile, innocent people are being beaten and killed by the day. Federation citizens!" He took a deep breath, gathering himself. "I'm sorry, Commissioner. I just hoped we were beyond this. We've spent the past two years trying to hold the Federation together against forces trying to tear it apart from the inside. After the election, and the defeat of V'Las on Vulcan, I'd hoped we'd finally put an end to all this."

"And we nearly have. The very insanity of the Keepers' actions is proof of their irrelevancy. They know the end of their era is at hand, and they're lashing out against the inevitable. And their violence is so hideous that they've alienated everyone who might have stood with them—including Lecheb, once she finally admits that this kind of self-destructive lunacy is where her rhetoric inevitably led. This is the last gasp of internal revolt, Jon," sh'Mirrin assured him.

"I hope so," Archer said. "Because it looks like we've got plenty of external problems to keep us occupied."

Once sh'Mirrin signed off, he winced and rubbed the bridge of his nose to try to ease the tension. He heard the heavy footfalls of his aide, Captain Williams, as the big, square-jawed man entered the room. "Can I get you something, Admiral?" he asked in his Midwestern drawl.

"That's okay, Marcus. It's just . . . I was hoping things would be quiet for a while. Give me a chance to get used to the new job. Instead, everything seems to be piling on at once. The Ware, the Keepers, the Klingons . . . Couldn't the universe have cut me just a little break? A few days. I don't ask much."

Williams chuckled. "The secret is to delegate. Rely on your staff, just like you did as a captain. That's how Admiral Forrest did it."

Archer looked up at him, reminded that Williams had been the aide to his old friend and superior officer, the late Maxwell Forrest, before he'd come to work for Archer. "So basically you're telling me you did all the work, is that it?"

"Mmm, ninety percent. But I try not to brag."

Noting the data slate Williams carried, Archer asked, "What have you got there? Is that the progress report from Admiral Osman?"

"Yes, sir." The broad-shouldered captain handed him the slate, but then said, "To sum up, *Apollo* and *Soyuz* should be ready to launch in three months, and *Ares* and *Charybdis* are on track for next spring, provided Grennex Aerospace lives up to its promises." Archer nodded. The Rigelian shipbuilding firm had been contracted to build upgraded impulse assemblies and navigational deflectors for the new wave of *Columbia*-class ships now being built under the supervision of Alexis Osman, the Alpha Centaurian chief of staff responsible for overseeing the research, logistical, and administrative aspects of Starfleet, and Captain W. M. Jefferies, the head of the Starfleet Corps of Engineers. Two such ships, based on the old NX-class design of Archer's *Enterprise* with a cylindrical secondary hull slung underneath to house a more powerful warp reactor, were already in service to complement T'Pol's *Endeavour*. If construction proceeded apace, those ships, *Buran* and *Shenlong*, would be joined by six more within the next two years—the four Williams had mentioned, plus *Phoenix* and *Valiant*.

Williams went on. "And the admiral's included those development proposals you wanted for the *Ceres* and *Poseidon* classes, along with the latest performance specs on the prototypes."

"Good." Archer had been working with Osman and Commodore Jefferies to develop new ship classes to take Starfleet into the future, but there were disagreements within the Admiralty over the best approach. Archer favored the *Ceres* class, a hybrid of the *Daedalus* and NX-series designs with innovations from Vulcan, Andorian, and Tellarite technology. The prototype had performed well in trials since its launch a year and a half ago, and Archer and Osman planned to incorporate its advances into future refits as well as new ship construction. They'd even gotten interest from civilian contractors seeking to upgrade classes like Earth's DY-series transports and J-class freighters, or the wide range of ships built by Grennex.

But the *Daedalus*-class ships that *Ceres* had been intended to replace had proven surprisingly reliable, once upgraded to post-war specs. Their cramped, submarine-like conditions, accommodating an atypically large crew complement for ships of their size, seemed outdated in peacetime, but had proven useful for missions that required transporting large numbers of personnel or colonists. Thus, many of Archer's colleagues found the *Ceres* project redundant, arguing that it would be better to focus on the *Poseidon* class, an *NX*-variant destroyer developed late in the war and intended to replace the smaller *Neptune* class. But Archer felt the heavily armed design was unnecessary in peacetime.

As he skimmed the report, Archer noted that Osman was again trying to convince him to name one of the new ships *Enterprise*. He had resisted reusing the name so soon after his own *Enterprise* had been decommissioned and placed in the Smithsonian, and there were political fears about offending the Klingons by commemorating a ship that had been a thorn in their side so many times. Besides, the name of Captain sh'Prenni's *Vol'Rala* essentially meant *Enterprise*, so adding another to the fleet could be seen as redundant. Osman's memo countered that by that logic, it would be impossible to have ships named *Intrepid* and *Dauntless* at the same time, for instance. And, she said, the Klingons were too preoccupied with their own problems to care about the name of a Starfleet ship. Given the recent news from *Endeavour*, the Centaurian admiral may have been more right than she knew. Archer figured he should at least give the idea some consideration. After all, both the *Ceres* and *Poseidon* construction proposals extended well into the next decade. Perhaps one of the later ships in whatever class was chosen could be given the name. It might be nice to have a new *Enterprise* in service after all.

"Anything else?" Archer asked once he finished glancing over the report.

"Captain Shumar's standing by on subspace. He's got a report on that distress signal from Theta Cygni Twelve."

Archer frowned. "And you kept him waiting?"

Williams looked somber. "From what I gather, it's not a time-sensitive situation."

The admiral took his point. The radio-frequency distress signal had only recently been picked up by a Tellarite freighter passing thirty light-years from Theta Cygni. The system was only sixty light-years from Earth, but in a direction where few Federation or allied ships had yet traveled—which was why it had been necessary to divert Shumar's *Essex* nearly thirty-five light-years from its assigned survey route. Whatever had led to the distress signal, the crisis was probably long since over—but to ignore a cry for help was unconscionable.

Archer opened the channel from *Essex*. "Captain Shumar. What have you got for me?"

The bronze-skinned, mustachioed captain looked as stiff as ever as he gave his report in crisp British tones. *"Not a pleasant tale, I fear, Admiral. We were far too late to make a difference, of course, but the situation was worse than we could have imagined. The planet was lifeless, devastated by chemical and bacteriological warfare. From the evidence we found, and from the few surviving records, it seems the planet was overrun by a wave of mass insanity. The natives tore each other apart in a genocidal rage, and no one understood why."*

Archer was stunned. "Could you find any evidence of a medical cause?" he asked.

"No, sir. The Theta Cygnians were some sort of land-dwelling invertebrates. Remarkable anatomy, judging from the artworks we found, but leaving no skeletons or other hard remains. After thirty years, there's nothing left to autopsy."

"And none of them survived or escaped? If they had the means to send an interstellar distress signal, even by radio . . ."

"There was evidence of dozens of ships being launched. Amazingly many, in fact, given that their civilization was descending into madness all around them. Nuclear engines, probably like a DY-series sleeper."

"Any chance of tracking them down?"

"Not an easy prospect, Admiral. Theta Cygni burns hot—its stellar

wind has probably scattered any ion trails, so it would be difficult to determine their speed or direction. By now, if they haven't already arrived at their destination, they're probably coasting in low-power mode, which would make them easy to overlook. It would be one hell of a long shot to find them, sir." Shumar gave a subtle smile. "Which is why I intend to try anyway."

Archer had to admire his exploratory fervor. A scientific mystery like this, especially with the prospective rescue of a dead civilization as the payoff, was just the anodyne he needed for the headaches he was facing elsewhere in the galaxy. "I don't blame you, Captain. And I think we can spare your services for a while longer."

"So Admiral Narsu hasn't yet convinced you to reassign us to Starbase Twelve, sir?"

"That'd be a decent-sized hop from your current position. I appreciate that you and the admiral are old friends . . ."

"I want only to serve where I'm most needed, sir. And these sectors are still badly in need of charting."

Archer smiled. Maybe he and Shumar had more in common than he'd realized. "I couldn't agree more, Captain. Good hunting."

"Thank you, Admiral. Essex out."

The screen went dark. Yawning and stretching, Archer realized it was getting late. The thought lightened his heart, for it meant he could go home to Dani. Having Danica Erickson in his life was the thing that made this job bearable, for her love, friendship, and beauty gave him the strength and peace of mind to handle its frustrations. Checking the chronometer, he decided he could take Williams's advice, delegate the rest of the day's work to his staff, and return home just a little early.

But then Williams buzzed him and forwarded a report from Admiral Shran: One of the ships in the Ware task force had been attacked and damaged, and it seemed their prisoner Vabion had found a way to reactivate the Ware and make his escape—with help from a Klingon ship. Archer sighed and asked Williams to have a yeoman bring him some coffee. It seemed he was going to be staying late again.

3

THE *U.S.S. FLABBJELLAH* WAS NAMED for an Andorian musical instrument that doubled as a kind of truncheon or throwing club. Right now, though, as Travis Mayweather studied its scans on *Pioneer*'s situation table, it appeared neither harmonious nor hazardous. *Pioneer* and *Vol'Rala* may have arrived in time to scare off *Flabbjellah*'s attackers before they could destroy it, but they hadn't been in time to prevent serious damage to the ship and its crew, including one fatality, the ship's chirurgeon Veneth Roos. The surviving thirty-seven crew members were currently split between *Vol'Rala*'s and *Pioneer*'s sickbays, except for Captain Zheusal zh'Ethar, who now stood in the situation room at the rear of *Pioneer*'s bridge, observing the damage alongside Mayweather and Captains Reed and sh'Prenni, among others.

"Man, Vabion really did a number on you," said Charles Tucker III—or "Philip Collier," as Mayweather reminded himself to think of the engineer. His old friend and *Enterprise* crewmate, whom he'd believed dead until just months ago, had instead—through a bizarre series of circumstances—become an intelligence operative for a Starfleet agency so secretive that Travis wasn't sure it was even legal. But for all his remaining questions and doubts about "Trip" Tucker's current life, Mayweather was grateful that he still lived, and at times like this, it was pleasing to see Tucker's old personality peeking through the subtly altered brows and nose, the dark red hair and thick beard, the false eye color, and the changed accent and mannerisms. "We're gonna have our work cut out for us bringing those engines back online."

"He had help," replied zh'Ethar, a wiry *zhen* in Andorian middle age.

"Yes," sh'Prenni said. "Vabion is a nuisance, but he's from a backward world. I'm more concerned about the Klingons getting involved here. Judging from the scans, the attacker was *SuD Qav*. It's a ship I encountered back while we were cleaning up the Kandari Sector—no significant threat to us, but its captain is brutal and rapacious, with a real sadistic streak toward his victims. If he were to get his hands on a working Ware combat drone, he could do some real damage."

"With all due respect, Captain, you shouldn't underestimate Daskel Vabion," Mayweather said. "He may have come from a pre-warp world, but he's a genius, and he's spent years reverse-engineering a technology even more advanced than ours. When it comes to the Ware, he has the advantage over us."

"That's right." The speaker was the last member of the group: Olivia Akomo, a stocky, dark-featured cyberneticist whom Tucker had recruited as a mission specialist—as well as part of his cover identity as a consultant from Abramson Industries, Earth's leading robotics firm, where Akomo was one of the head researchers. "We would never have devised the awakening protocol without his discovery of the recognition codes for upgrades. The Ware aggressively resists analysis of its software and hardware. The fact that he achieved so much starting from, essentially, a twentieth-century knowledge base is a testament to his brilliance."

"And his ruthlessness," Malcolm Reed added in his

polished English accent, "considering all the lives he had to sacrifice to the Ware's defense systems in the process. The fact that he was able to reactivate that drone ship right under our noses—no offense, Zheusal—is a testament to the risk he poses."

"You are right to criticize me, Malcolm," zh'Ethar said to the goateed human captain. "Do not retreat from it. I let that damned Vanotli fool me into thinking he was cooperating. He's just so . . . so reasonable, so polite. I thought that meant he was tamed. But he was more Andorian than I realized: the calmer he gets, the more dangerous he is."

"Vabion is a cool, calculating man," said Mayweather, who'd had the most direct contact with the Vanotli industrialist. He had been taken hostage by Vabion while undercover on Vanot to investigate, and attempt to counter, its infiltration by the Ware—a technology that Vabion had embraced as his own. As part of his plan to best the Pebru, Vabion had allowed them to reinstall Mayweather into the Ware as a live processor, forcing him to relive one of the worst experiences of his life. The fact that Vabion's act had played a key role in allowing *Pioneer*'s crew to shut down the Pebru's Ware had not made it any easier for Travis to live with the memory. "He believes his superior intelligence entitles him to superior power. He's not gratuitously cruel—or at least he likes to think he isn't—but he'll unhesitatingly murder you if he thinks he'll profit from it, and then he'll send a thoughtful condolence note to your family afterward. No hard feelings, because he hasn't got any."

"Except pride," Tucker reminded him. "The man's got plenty of that. I've seen the way he reacts to the Ware. He takes it as a personal affront that there's a technology he can't master."

"Yes, yes, I saw this," replied a thoughtful zh'Ethar. "I knew he was willing to work with us because we sought to understand and reprogram the Ware as well. I saw that as a way to control him, keep him cooperative. Rescuing the stranded Pebru, restoring their ships to basic functionality, let all of us gain more knowledge of the technology, and I tried to show him that it was in his best interest to work closely with us." Her antennae drooped. "I thought I had outsmarted him. That he had accepted the wisdom of deferring to our greater advancement."

"Vabion doesn't accept anyone as his superior," Akomo told her.

"Then he's a megalomaniac?" sh'Prenni asked.

"Certainly not—at least, no more than any genius on his level. He reminds me very much of Willem—Mister Abramson." Akomo's clarification was hardly needed; her employer was Earth's most famous recluse. "He's the kind of man who recognizes his limitations, but is convinced they're temporary setbacks. Vabion started from nothing and built himself into his world's leading industrialist, a man who had the entire government in his pocket. So he doesn't believe there's any height he can't reach." Mayweather frowned. She sounded almost admiring.

"Sounds very human," sh'Prenni said. The four humans stared at her, and she stared back. "It's a compliment! Although, granted, he's somewhat more ruthless."

"Thanks, Thenar . . . I think," Reed said. "Meanwhile, I gather you've encountered one more difficulty to add to the list. Care to tell us about it?"

The *Vol'Rala* captain efficiently filled the others in on her vessel's experience with the station belonging to the Partnership of Civilizations. "It's the flaw in the awakening protocol that we never considered," sh'Prenni added. "We wake the captives up within the system, let them realize what's been done to them, and wait for them to free themselves. But what if they don't *want* to be freed? We never expected anyone would be tricked into *volunteering* for Ware enslavement."

"I can't imagine," Mayweather said. "I've been inside those things twice. I've felt what it's like—the helplessness, the trapped feeling. The cold, mechanical pressure on your mind." He shuddered. "I would've thought anyone who was aware of that feeling would do anything to escape it."

"People can be trained to endure anything," Tucker said softly, not meeting anyone's eyes. "To tolerate any level of repression, suffering . . . so long as they don't realize they have a choice."

"From what you tell me, Thenar," Reed said, "the incentives seem considerable. The species you met would have no civilization at all without the Ware. They must be completely dependent on it from birth."

"Which is no doubt why this Partnership is able to fool them into volunteering for Ware enslavement. It's the Pebru all over again—they've found a way to evade captivity by giving the Ware alternative victims. Only they've selected victims too helpless to have a choice. Species so dependent on what the Ware offers that they submit to it voluntarily. It's brutal."

"Now, hold on," Reed told her. "I agree it looks that way, but we haven't yet met the Partnership leaders. We need to gather more information before we decide on a strategy."

"That could take weeks, months," Mayweather protested. "There are people suffering, slowly dying inside the Ware right now. We can't just leave them there."

"Travis is right," sh'Prenni said. "And it's not just them. As long as there's any Ware active, it can spread the infection to other worlds. The only way to keep the Federation safe, to keep the Vanotli and the Menaik and the other races of this region safe, is to shut down all the Ware. Leave none of it active. And to do that, we need a way to force through a shutdown command regardless of the live processors' participation. I've already put Banerji and ch'Gesrit on the problem." She turned to Tucker. "Mister Collier, would you be willing to lend your team's expertise to the problem?"

"Glad to help," the undercover engineer told her, "so long as Captain Reed's okay with it."

"That is why you and Ms. Akomo are here, Mister Collier," Reed replied with care. But then he noticed Mayweather's subdued look. "Travis? You have a concern?"

"I dunno," the first officer replied. "I agree that we shouldn't leave them trapped there, but . . . something about trying to take their choice out of the equation rubs me the wrong way. It seems too much like what the Ware does to them."

Sh'Prenni clasped his shoulder. "It's a noble principle, of course. But we don't live in an ideal universe. These people have been tricked into wanting their oppression. Sometimes people need to be helped even when they aren't willing to help themselves."

Mayweather couldn't see a reason to reject her assertion. He tried to imagine wanting the experience he'd undergone inside the Ware, believing it was necessary and just. Would it really be so wrong for someone to free him from that condition, that conviction, over his protests? Would he be better off staying inside? He couldn't believe that.

Asking the question is what keeps you honest, he told himself. *As long as you remember why you're doing it, and never forget who you're doing it for, then . . .*

"All right," he said to the others. "Let's get them out of there."

July 12, 2165
Qam-Chee, the First City, Qo'noS

If there was one advantage to the Klingons' warrior lifestyle that Phlox had to concede, it was that they were not, as a rule, prone to squeamishness. He had no shortage of spectators for his postmortem examination of the late Chancellor M'Rek, as the leaders of the various factions within the High Council crowded into the autopsy room of the Council's private medical wing, keeping his every move under careful scrutiny. This puzzled Phlox at first, given that their entire reason for inviting him was that he was the one physician they had been willing to trust. He soon realized, though, that they were far less willing to *admit* to trusting an offworlder.

Thus, Phlox needed to rely on the assistance of Doctor Kon'Jef to keep the councillors from crowding in too close and interfering with his work. Kon'Jef was large and intimidating even by Klingon standards, so Phlox was grateful that he had secured the position of personal physician to Chancellor M'Rek, by virtue of being married to M'Rek's closest advisor, Fleet Admiral Krell. Phlox had worked with Kon'Jef once before, a decade ago, to reattach Krell's left arm after Jonathan Archer had severed it in the course of diplomatic negotiations, Klingon-style. It had earned him a measure of respect from the towering doctor, which proved useful to their collaboration now.

Certainly Phlox needed every advantage he could get, given the squalid conditions of this treatment facility. He had seen in the past how little regard Klingons had for medical care or basic sanitation; even the most dedicated Klingon healer Phlox had ever met, Doctor Antaak, had allowed his pet *targ* to wander freely about his laboratory. Antaak and other scientists like him were capable of sophisticated genetic engineering; indeed, it had been Antaak's attempt to repurpose human Augment DNA (left over from Earth's Eugenics Wars) for Klingon use that had led to the release of the metagenic virus responsible for the cosmetic transformation of the *QuchHa'*. But the members of the High Council had little use for intricate genetic studies, so their medical section was geared more toward treating the gross bodily trauma sustained during the frequent combats that served as political debate within the Council. Having seen these facilities before, Phlox had made sure to bring the necessary equipment with him; but with condensation dripping from the ceiling, stains of blood and bloodwine liberally adorning all surfaces, and High Councillors shedding hair and spraying spittle as they declaimed and gesticulated toward one another, there was only so much he could do to avoid contamination of the body even with his sterile field emitter in place.

Thus, it was a minor miracle that he was able to isolate the virus responsible for the chancellor's long illness, and to confirm that it was the underlying cause of his death. But identifying the virus and determining its origin was a trickier matter. Kon'Jef had been unable to link it with any known strain, hence his inability to cure it.

"Does that mean it was artificial?" demanded Councillor Khorkal. The gray-bearded centenarian, head of the ancient and distinguished House of Palkar, was one of the leading contenders for the chancellorship, a career politician eager for leverage against his foes.

"Not necessarily," Phlox told him. "After all, Klingons are

a well-traveled people. This could be some alien strain that came to Qo'noS through trade."

"Then why have others not fallen ill as well?"

"There are countless factors that can influence viral susceptibility. I'd need to know much more about the virus to be sure. It has an unusually lengthy genome containing complexities that are difficult to account for."

"Too complex to be natural?" Khorkal pressed.

"With respect, Councillor, it is imperative that I avoid preconception or bias in my investigation. That is why you brought me here, after all." He cleared his throat. "However, I would welcome some assistance from an expert in viral genetics. If Doctor Antaak could be consulted—"

"*No!*" The fierce objection came from B'orel, a hotheaded veteran councillor that Phlox remembered from his previous visit here. "Antaak has disgraced himself by bringing the *QuchHa'* plague to the Klingon people. Had M'Rek's softness not held us back, we would have eradicated Antaak and all the others of his kind by now!"

Phlox declined to point out that Antaak's metagenic viral research had been conducted under orders from the High Council. If anyone was ultimately responsible for the Qu'Vat mutation, that list included several of the people here in this room, possibly including B'orel himself. But it would not be conducive to Phlox's health to remind them of the fact.

"Very well, gentlemen—and lady," he went on with a nod to Councillor Alejdar, a dignified, middle-aged Klingon who was the sole female on the High Council. "Then I will simply have to do my best to identify the viral strain using the equipment I have. And that may take a good deal of time, so if any of you have other business to attend to . . ."

"We will not leave you unwatched, Denobulan," Khorkal intoned.

Phlox shrugged. "Then perhaps you could arrange to take turns."

The councillors grumbled and blustered, but as Phlox went about his meticulous work with the genetic sequencer, they grew increasingly restless, and within another hour, most had wandered off to deal with other things. B'orel stayed and kept his suspicious gaze on Phlox at every moment, but otherwise, the only one who remained the full time was Councillor Deqan, the appointed Arbiter of Succession responsible for overseeing the rites by which the new chancellor would be selected. Deqan was unusually quiet and even-tempered for a Klingon, content to observe rather than intimidate, which Phlox appreciated greatly.

The sheer size of this virus's genome—well over a million base-pairs in length, carrying nearly two thousand different genes—made it difficult and time-consuming to track down the telltales Phlox was looking for. The majority of the genes were consistent with the genomic "vocabulary" of Qo'noSian life, as one would expect from a virus able to interface with Klingon cells. But there were anomalies in the sequence whose origins proved more elusive. Comparison with Klingon medical databases let him identify many of them as originating on the farming colony of Pheben. "Perhaps a mutation that arose there," Kon'Jef suggested, "and was carried in the chancellor's food."

"Not out of the question, given your fondness for uncooked meals," Phlox agreed. "But there's something here that looks familiar, and that shouldn't be, because I've never studied a Pheben genome before."

"Familiar how? You have seen part of the sequence before?"

"Not so much the sequence as . . ." He kept the rest to himself: *the way the pieces are put together.* He was beginning to recognize the artist's hand.

It was not the answer he had wanted to find.

Phlox managed to persuade Deqan and Kon'Jef that he needed to consult confidentially with a colleague in the Interspecies Medical Exchange. B'orel was instantly suspicious, but Phlox rode heavily on his physician's honor as it pertained to patient confidentiality, so the arbiter agreed to grant him privacy over the councillor's objection. Phlox expected that the Council's agents would attempt to monitor his call despite this, but he used a couple of tricks Hoshi Sato had taught him to ensure that his call to the Qu'Vat Colony would be unseen and untraced.

The face that appeared on the monitor was broad and lined, but smooth-browed and framed by long white hair. *"Doctor Phlox!"* exclaimed Antaak, his eyes going wide. *"It is a pleasure to see you again, old friend. To what do I owe this call after all these years?"*

Phlox spoke slowly, weighing each word. "I suspect you may already know, Doctor. I am calling from the chambers of the High Council. They called me in to perform a postmortem on Chancellor M'Rek."

Antaak looked stunned. *"M'Rek is dead? I had heard rumors of illness, but they tell us little out here—"*

"Please, Antaak. Let's not waste time with denials. I recognized your recombination techniques in the genome of the virus that killed him." He sighed. "I felt I owed it to you to ask why before I revealed my findings to the Council."

"My techniques . . . ?" Antaak shook his head sadly. *"Phlox, I have no access to recombinant equipment anymore. My career as a geneticist*

is ended. I have attempted to petition the Council to finance research into a cure for the mutation, as a chance to reclaim my honor, but M'Rek himself revoked my license." He chuckled without humor. *"I attempted, for a while, to pursue a cranial reconstruction practice, but the sentiment soon spread that such concealment of QuchHa' status was fraudulent and dishonorable. Many still see us as unclean, contagious, even though the virus burned itself out a decade ago. They wish to ensure that we are marked as separate. Did you know they no longer allow QuchHa' in the Defense Force to wear a warrior's traditional armor? Or even a warrior's mane?"* he added, a hand brushing through his own long hair.

Phlox pondered. "I would like nothing more than to believe you, Antaak. But if anything, you're merely establishing that you had a motive for the chancellor's murder."

"Never! I may have turned my back on military service, but I am still warrior caste! Whatever they accuse me of, I strive to live by the precepts of the qeS'a'." Phlox recognized the name of the traditional text purporting to pass down the teachings of Kahless, the founding father of Klingon civilization. *"Including the Third Precept, 'Always face your enemy.' Had I wished to slay M'Rek, I would have challenged him properly—and probably died in the attempt, since I am a doctor, not a soldier. But slaying him from afar with a virus, attempting to conceal my killing as a natural disease—which I assume to be the case given their need to consult you, Phlox—that would be no way to regain my honor. It would only compound my disgrace, and damn the House of Antaak for all time."*

Phlox found himself believing his old colleague, though he recognized that he was predisposed to do so. "Then how do you explain the signature I found in the viral genome? The technique is yours, Antaak, I'd swear to it. And I may have to, unless you can give me another explanation."

Antaak had gone pale. It was some time before he spoke. *"It cannot be. I could not have failed with him so profoundly."*

"Antaak?"

The aged doctor gave a heavy sigh. *"There is . . . one other to whom I have passed on my techniques. Who has the skill in genetics and the access to the equipment . . . and who resides on Qo'noS. But I dare not say it unless I can be sure. Please, Phlox . . . allow me to see the genome sequence. I must know if his hand is there."*

Phlox granted his request; it was the consultation he'd been hoping for in the first place, though under more troubling circumstances than he had imagined. Indeed, Antaak seemed to know exactly what to look for, and with each passing moment he seemed to age by years. *"There is no doubt. The artist's hand is as clear as fire to me."*

"Who is it, Antaak? Who?"

"It is Krit." He spat the name through clenched teeth. *"My eldest son."*

July 13, 2165

To Phlox's eye, Doctor Krit looked much as his father must have in his youth—bulldog-featured (as Earth literature would have it) with clearly defined cranial plating forming a pronounced V shape over his ridged nose. But he did not act like his father would when brought to a meeting room within the High Council's headquarters and confronted with the accusation by Arbiter Deqan, with the other leading councillors, Fleet Admiral Krell, and Doctor Kon'Jef also in attendance. "This is a lie!" he shouted. "I had nothing to do with the chancellor's dishonorable wasting. Let me face my accuser!"

"You face him now!" Antaak barked from the chamber's large wall screen. *"Do not compound your dishonor and mine by hiding from your actions, my son. I have seen the viral genome myself. Does a teacher*

not know the work of his own pupil?" Mercifully, the councillors had chosen to look the other way regarding Phlox's deceit in contacting Antaak, given the payoff it had brought. *"Please, my son. You face death for your crimes. Have the decency to face it standing up. Prove to me that I have taught you something beyond genetic resequencing."*

The younger physician studied his father's gaze for a long moment, trembling with emotion. "All right!" he exclaimed at last. "Of course I slew M'Rek, Father! I did it for you! To avenge your treatment at the Council's hands! You are not to blame for the plague that disfigured you—*they* are! M'Rek most of all! He deserved to die!"

"Few would dispute that!" Antaak cried. *"But not like this. Not from hiding, not in secret so that no one even knows it was vengeance! Revenge is done to restore a family's honor, not corrupt it further!"*

Krit scoffed. "Honor. What is it? Just a word Klingons use as an excuse for doing whatever they wish. M'Rek claimed that his persecution of you served honor. Where was the Council's honor when they ordered you to create the virus in the first place?"

"That is enough," said Councillor Deqan. The arbiter did not raise his voice, but his authority came through nonetheless. "You have confirmed your guilt. Do not compound your treason further."

Krit sneered. "If it is treason to speak the truth, then we are all damned."

On the screen, Antaak looked disgusted. *"You have lost any right to speak of truth, Krit."*

"But Father—"

Antaak folded his arms before him. *"My son is dead to me."* He ceremoniously turned his back on the younger man.

"So be it," Deqan intoned. "Krit, son of no one, you are

found guilty of high treason and are hereby sentenced to death. Sentence to be carried out—"

"Allow me." Admiral Krell stepped forward.

B'orel stepped in his path. "You are out of order, *QuchHa'*! Your filth should not even stain this chamber."

Krell swatted the leaner man aside almost effortlessly. B'orel recovered his balance and reached for his knife, but Khorkal and Alejdar stepped forward to restrain him. Deqan held out a hand and they fell still. Krell spoke as if none of it had happened. "Arbiter. I failed to protect the Empire from this plague or my patron from a dishonorable end. Let me reclaim the last of my own honor by avenging the chancellor's murder."

Deqan looked around the room at the other councillors. Even B'orel could not bring himself to object. "Very well. Have Krit taken away. Prepare him for execution in the public square. All will know that the chancellor's murder has been solved and avenged, so that we may proceed with the Rite of Succession without further taint from this matter."

Phlox closed his eyes as the murderous youth was dragged away. He had no love of the Klingons' fondness for lethal penalties. But Denobulan medical ethics forbade him from intervening against death when such intervention went against a patient's wishes.

Before his eyes even reopened, B'orel and the other councillors had begun hectoring Deqan about proceeding with the selection of a new chancellor. Deqan led them out of the meeting room to debate the matter further, leaving Phlox and Kon'Jef alone with Antaak on the screen. Kon'Jef leaned over Phlox, speaking as quietly as his booming voice would allow. "My gratitude, Doctor. Now my husband can achieve a last measure of peace."

Phlox had an inkling of what the doctor meant, but he chose not to pursue the question. He reserved his attention for his old friend Antaak, who had turned back to face the visual pickup once Krit had been taken away, and who spoke as soon as Kon'Jef left them alone. *"You have my gratitude as well, Doctor."*

"I don't deserve it," Phlox said. "I've just gotten your son killed."

"He brought his shame upon himself." Antaak paused and shook his head. *"No . . . if any is truly to blame, it is I. His upbringing was my responsibility, and I failed, as profoundly as I did with the Qu'Vat virus."*

"All we can do is try our best to lead our children by example," Phlox told him. "I, too, have a son who failed to learn the lessons I tried to pass on to him."

"He did not follow you into the healing arts?"

"Worse than that." Phlox sighed. "His name is Mettus. My youngest boy, so you'd think I would've figured it out by then. But no. He allowed himself to be poisoned by hate toward the Antarans—a people who had once been our enemy, but whom we no longer had reason to oppose. Any wrongs they had inflicted on us had been 'avenged' long since, the scales balanced, if you believe in such things. There was no longer any reason to hate Antarans except that they were Antarans, and that was enough for Mettus. I tried my best to raise my children without prejudice, to open their minds to the possibility of friendship with all races, but Mettus allowed himself to be swayed by dangerous friends. And so I lost him." He shook his head. "I don't know if a Klingon can sympathize."

"We do not hate randomly, my friend. There is no honor in continuing a grudge that serves no purpose. The First Precept of the qeS'a' is 'Choose

your enemies well.'" Antaak sighed. *"But that does not matter. Deeper even than the word of Kahless is the bond between father and son. Death comes to us all, soon enough. It is through our children that we survive. And if our children reject our teachings . . . it is worse than the death of the body. I, for one, do not know how I will survive."*

"Look on the bright side," Phlox told him. "At least Krit believed he was acting in your defense. As misguided as it was, it was an act of love. I haven't been so lucky."

"You are better off without such 'luck,' believe me."

Phlox shook off his solemn mood. "So—what will you do now, Doctor?"

"I'm not sure. Perhaps now, with M'Rek out of the way, I can again petition the Council to finance research into a cure for the Qu'Vat mutation. Perhaps then I can help bring an end to the strife I have caused, and bring stability to the Empire at last."

"You know," Phlox couldn't resist pointing out, "you could simply learn to live together. To look beyond a cosmetic change and learn to cooperate. My people—most of them—have overcome their hatred of the Antarans and learned to work with them as friends." He chuckled. "My daughter is marrying an Antaran man in just a few weeks. You're welcome to attend the wedding, if you can."

Antaak gave the hearty laugh of a man who desperately needed something to laugh about. *"Then you have my congratulations, Phlox! Though I fear I must decline, for I have matters of my own I must attend to. As for the rest . . ."* He sobered and shook his head. *"Such tolerance is not the Klingon way. These smooth brows show the galaxy that we can be conquered by a lowly virus. They are a badge of weakness, and weakness must be destroyed."*

"Are they really, Antaak?" Phlox asked, his voice hardening. "The High Council has seen that you, a 'weak' *QuchHa'*, acted with true honor and courage, while your *HemQuch* son acted with treachery and shame. Perhaps they will learn something from that. And if they don't . . . then at least you should."

July 15, 2165
Starfleet Headquarters, San Francisco

"And do you think Antaak listened?" Jonathan Archer asked Phlox. He had his desk monitor turned around so he could pace the office while receiving the doctor's report from the Xarantine freighter that was bringing him back to Federation space. It was one way he tried to avoid letting this job make him too sedentary.

"I'm inclined to doubt it, Admiral," the Denobulan said. *"He seems more driven than ever to find a 'cure,' as he insists on calling it, for the viral mutation. He feels he must redeem his family's honor at any cost."*

"Do you think he has any chance of succeeding?"

"Hard to say. The metavirus was incredibly aggressive, as you know, inducing systemic changes in nearly every cell in its host's body. Normally, mutated cells will coexist alongside unaltered cells, and gross physical changes will come slowly if at all. You'd be surprised how many individuals are genetic chimeras—males with a certain percentage of female cells from their mothers, or the like. Normally it has no impact at all on an organism's gross anatomy or overall body function. But this metavirus infects nearly every cell and triggers it to regenerate, reactivating cytogenic and cytolytic processes that have been dormant since maturity. It's really quite extraordinary, and it should be quite a challenge to overcome." He shook his head. *"Personally I feel Antaak is wasting his time, since the cosmetic and slight neurological changes have a trivial effect on quality of life. But if anyone has a chance of undoing its effects, he does."*

"But not anytime soon, I take it."

"It could be a lifetime's work. Or more."

"And from what you tell me, the Council is divided about how to deal with it."

"Indeed. Some want to exterminate the QuchHa' altogether, others to exile them. Some simply want to declare war on the Federation as retaliation for Earth's perceived role in creating the virus. However, I gather that one or two QuchHa', the leaders of noble Houses whose wealth and status enabled them to avoid complete ostracism, have actually put their names in for nomination."

"Not Admiral Krell?" Archer recalled his contentious dealings with the fleet admiral, a stern, powerful Klingon who had at first hated Archer and Phlox for their roles in turning him into a *QuchHa'* but had ultimately afforded them some measure of respect and become something verging on an ally.

Phlox's expression was grave. *"I received word from Doctor Kon'Jef that Fleet Admiral Krell has died. Once he carried out the execution of Doctor Krit, he requested that Kon'Jef help him perform the* Mauk-to'Vor, *a form of assisted ritual suicide."*

"Damn." Archer winced. Why did the Klingons insist on seeing someone's death as the answer to everything? Not only was it a total waste, but from a coldly political perspective, it had cost the Federation a potential ally in the High Council, or at least a voice of moderation. "Any idea who's likely to be the next chancellor?"

"Hard to say. Arbiter Deqan is taking his time with the Rite of Succession. Before I left, he ordered prospective candidates to report for the ja'chuq, *an involved ritual in which the challengers recite their achievements and deeds to demonstrate their worthiness to lead. Apparently it's quite time-consuming, and there have been calls for its elimination from the Rite, but Deqan insisted on going through with it. I think that, in the wake of recent events and accusations, he wishes to give tempers a chance to cool."*

Archer laughed. "Among Klingons? That I'd like to see."

"Anyway, I'm just grateful to be out of there. I think some of the

councillors were, ah, disappointed that my findings did not incriminate any of their rivals for the chancellorship. I'm grateful to Krell for ensuring my safe departure before he . . . well."

"I'm glad you're coming back too, Phlox," the admiral told him, smiling. "I've had *Endeavour* standing by near the Klingon border—I'll tell T'Pol to rendezvous with your freighter as soon as you're clear." His smile widened. "And then I'll see you on Denobula. I hear it's gonna be one hell of a wedding."

Phlox gave a grin that put Archer's to shame. *"I can guarantee it will be an experience you'll never forget!"*

4

July 28, 2165
Pebru homeworld

"DON'T LET THEM SURROUND US!" Valeria Williams called to her security team as they closed ranks against the mob of rioting Pebru. "We have to get through to our people at all costs!"

The rest of the team shared the armory officer's urgency as they brandished their particle rifles and stunned the charging horde with precision fire, advancing step by laborious step toward the besieged government complex. After all, not only would defeat by the raging mob mean they had failed in rescuing their crewmates . . . but it would be damned embarrassing. The Pebru were chubby, pear-shaped bipeds with small heads, pointy snouts, and stubby arms with barely functional digits. They were perhaps the least physically imposing species that Williams had ever fought against. Losing to them would be like being beaten by a mob of overweight Corgis.

But the lieutenant reminded herself that the Pebru had a ruthless streak. They had deliberately infected more than a dozen pre-warp worlds with Ware in order to provide the rapacious technology with alternative sources of live processors, victimizing others to spare themselves. The majority of those worlds had suffered horribly from their selfishness, while the Pebru had thrived.

"Their line is weakening near the left entrance!" Ensign Ndiaye cried.

Williams spotted the opening before her second-in-command finished her sentence. Trusting that she and the ensign were on the same page, she turned to Crewman Kemal. "You and Sandra drive them to the right! Make us a hole!" She pushed forward, Katrina Ndiaye at her side, and fired relentlessly at the few remaining rioters who stood between her and the left entrance. They were slow-moving, making easy targets, but there were still enough to overwhelm her and the ensign if Kemal and Yuan failed to shift the rioters' line. Indeed, one managed to evade her fire and get close enough to leap at her. She took that one down with a right cross to the snout. The Pebru went down so easily she almost felt bad about it, but she reminded herself that if she let even one rioter knock her over, the others could overwhelm her.

In the Pebru's defense, this uprising did not represent the will of the majority. Most of the Pebru masses had been kept ignorant of their government's atrocities, and the recent revelation of the truth had led to that regime's ouster. But the revelation had come along with the shutdown of the Ware network on which the Pebru depended for virtually their entire civilization. Their anatomical limitations made it difficult for them to build or operate technology without the Ware to synthesize it for them, and so they had been forced to endure significant hardships in the wake of the shutdown. Most Pebru blamed their government for bringing things to this point, and there had been widespread gratitude for the restoration efforts undertaken by the Starfleet task force and other neighboring powers like the Tyrellians—a civilization of interstellar traders who had lost both individuals and profits to the Ware (since their own goods could not compete with the advancement or convenience of the Ware's products) and thus were happy to assist the worlds now liberated from it, in hopes of nurturing future trade partnerships.

Yet many of the ousted leaders still sought to regain political influence and avoid imprisonment. In recent weeks, they had mounted a propaganda campaign to exploit the masses' growing frustration at the harsher standard of living they now endured. An ugly sentiment of xenophobia, shifting the blame for the Pebru's hardships onto outsiders rather than their own leaders, had been spreading through the more gullible and angry segments of the populace, finally erupting into these riots.

For Williams, the timing of the upheaval could not have been worse. Left to herself, she could take on a mob of rampaging xenophobes every day and chalk it up to exercise; there were surely no categories of life-form more satisfying to punch in the face than bigots. But her concern was for the people inside the government complex—specifically for one man that she'd failed once and was determined never to fail again.

As Williams and Ndiaye fought their way to the steps of the blocky, gray-white government complex, the doors opened and the Pebru defenders inside, employees of the new, reformist government, started firing their own low-powered stunners at the mob. With their assistance, the women from *Pioneer* were able to break through the line and reach the doors. "Where are our people?" Williams asked.

Urging them inside, the captain of the defenders gestured with a stubby forelimb. "This way," he replied, leading her down the stark, white Ware-built corridor while his fellows remained to hold the entrance. Williams hoped that they and her team outside would be enough to contain the mob until reinforcements arrived.

The Pebru captain led them deeper into the complex, which put them farther from the rioters yet drove home that there'd be no escape by transporter. The walls were made from materials that resisted sensor and transporter beams; it might be possible for *Pioneer*'s transporter to get a lock if they were by the outermost wall, but it would be a risk. Beaming out from deeper inside would be impossible. That was why they'd had to break in the hard way to begin with.

Still, it was a relief when they reached the archive room and she saw the faces of the two she'd come to rescue. "Val!" cried Ensign Bodor chim Grev. "Thank Kera and Phinda!" The cherubic Tellarite communications officer shot to his feet and ran over to give her a hug. "I knew you'd save us, but I'm still relieved you're here."

Behind Grev, Lieutenant Samuel Kirk looked equally relieved but was more reserved in expressing it. "He's right," the soft-spoken historian said. "It would've been annoying to get killed just when we've made a possible breakthrough."

Williams studied Kirk, wondering what lay beneath his flippancy. Over a year ago, he and Grev had been taken hostage by the First Families of Rigel IV in an attempt to sabotage their system's entry into the Federation, and Kirk had been tortured to motivate Grev to help them decrypt classified files stolen from the Rigelian authorities. The ordeal had changed the thoughtful, gentle-natured historian, leaving him more haunted, less open with his feelings.

But that was something to save for a later time. It was simpler—and more important to the mission—to focus on what he'd just said. "You found something about the origin of the Ware?" she asked him.

It was easier to get him to talk to her when it was strictly business. "Maybe not the origin, but at least the Pebru's source. Their early records are fragmentary—they had a mostly oral history before the Ware era—but I've found references to another civilization that either gave the Ware to the Pebru or shared it with them."

Williams frowned. "What's the difference?"

"Shared in the sense of coexisting. It sounds like the Pebru were initially part of a larger community, but then had a falling out with them. I get the impression that they got sick of being exploited as sacrifices to the Ware, so they struck out on their own to become the exploiters."

"Any indication of where this other race came from?" the armory officer asked.

"Not a race," Grev said, "a multispecies community. In fact, I'd say the best translation of the Pebru name for them is 'Partnership of Civilizations.'"

Williams stared. "Those people *Vol'Rala* encountered? The ones who claim to use volunteers for the Ware?"

"Not necessarily," Grev said, warming to the debate. He was far more easygoing with his human crewmates than most Tellarites would be, but he still relished a good argument. "After all, it's a pretty generic label. Partnership, Consortium, Alliance . . . Federation . . . there could be multiple neighboring groups with equivalent names."

"But the description fits what we know about the Partnership," Kirk said, "including the general region of space where they were encountered."

"So maybe their whole 'volunteer' thing is just a smokescreen," Williams replied.

The discussion was interrupted by a series of loud bangs and rumbles and the distant sound of shouting voices. Williams's communicator beeped; she fished it out of the sleeve pocket in her gray tunic and answered it. *"The rioters have broken into the building,"* Kemal reported. *"We're inside, but we've fallen back to a defensive position. We'll try to hold them off until reinforcements arrive."* More shouting and weapons fire sounded. *"I just hope that isn't much longer, ma'am."*

"Don't be modest, Ediz. You and Sandra can hold that line all by yourselves, right?"

"Right. Got it, Lieutenant. Kemal out." The crewman tried to instill his voice with the same certainty she expressed, but there was a hint of resignation beneath it.

But Williams had been watching Kirk and Grev, and she'd seen the fear in their eyes—especially Kirk's—at the prospect of falling into enemy hands again. Putting her communicator away, Val stepped closer to Kirk and lightly touched his arm. "Don't worry, Sam. I promise, I won't let you down. Never again."

They were both surprised by the intensity in her voice. From the look in Kirk's eyes, Williams feared she'd done more to upset than comfort him. During the Rigel incident, she had prioritized saving a stranger over bringing back intelligence about Kirk's captors, delaying his rescue. If she hadn't made that choice, he could have been spared days of torture. Once she'd told him that, it had changed things between them. Before, he'd always been clearly attracted to her, though she'd done nothing to encourage it; not only was he not the bold, athletic type of man she normally preferred (though he did have lovely eyes and a very attractive mouth), but her previous attempt at shipboard romance had interfered with her work and earned her a chewing-out from Captain Reed. But though she'd made sure to keep their relationship platonic, she'd come to value his friendship greatly, appreciating his intelligent, inquisitive mind and his innate gentleness and empathy.

Ever since Rigel, though, Sam had pulled away from her. She couldn't blame him for that, and she'd given him the space he needed to heal, hoping that they could renew their closeness in time. Grev had been there as his stalwart friend—clearly as unrequitedly attracted to Sam as the historian had been to her, but just as selfless and loyal in his friendship. Although Val thought the two of them would make an adorable couple, she'd come to realize that she was grateful that nothing seemed likely to happen on that front. She felt she owed something to Sam, and she yearned for a second chance with him—thus her determination to prove that she would not fail him again.

But what if the reminder of that failure just drove him further away?

After a moment, Kirk sighed. "Val . . . you didn't let me down before. None of it was your fault. It was the Families who had me tortured. You just did what was right. You always do."

She gazed at him, a wave of relief washing over her. "I thought you resented me."

He looked down. "I did, for a while. But I got over it."

"Then I don't understand. Why is it still so hard to get close to you? What more will it take to get things back to the way they were?"

More distant bursts of fire and shouting sounded outside, and Kirk took a moment to contain his alarm before replying. "You don't get it, Val. What happened to me . . . nothing can make that go away. It will always be part of me."

"You're right, I don't get it. Do you forgive me or not?"

He grew exasperated. "It's not about you, Val. It's not about whether you can be the brave space hero and get the guy."

"I'm not—" She let out a frustrated breath. "I don't want to score you as a conquest, Sam. I care about you. I want you to know I'm there for you. Damn it, isn't that what you want?" She winced. She wasn't very good at this sensitive stuff.

His voice hardened in response to her own. "Not if it's just about you assuaging your guilt."

"But you just said I had nothing to be guilty about!"

"The problem is that I had to tell you that!"

"What the hell is that supposed to mean?"

"Umm . . . guys?" That was Grev, his soft voice managing to reach them despite their own raised voices. It helped that it was underscored by a change in the sounds from outside. "The reinforcements are here," the ensign went on. "The mob is in retreat! We're okay now!" He looked between them. "Maybe we should celebrate. You guys want to go for coffee?"

Grev's attempt to play matchmaker, while sweet, was rather poorly timed. "We'll have plenty of mopping up to do," Williams said, gesturing to Ndiaye to follow her outside to rendezvous with Kemal and Yuan.

"Right," Kirk said. "And we need to report what we found out about the Partnership."

"Or whoever," Grev couldn't resist adding. But no one was in the mood to reply.

August 6, 2165
Gronim City, Denobula

Phlox's home was one of the most remarkable cities that Hoshi Sato had visited in all her travels. She had never seen a place that was so urban and so organic at the same time. Great towers and sprawling arcologies stretched clear to the horizon, reminding Sato of Tokyo or São Paulo on an even grander scale; yet the wide boulevards between them were rich with vegetation, and the buildings themselves were covered with greenery on their rooftops and many terraces. The larger structures were artfully faceted and curved to reflect sunlight around their bulk, breaking up the shadows and keeping the streets bright and airy for their botanical and humanoid occupants alike. Large, leathery-winged mammals soared on updrafts between the towers, occasionally swooping down on the lemurs that climbed and leapt among the branches, commuting across their own arboreal city that coexisted within the constructed one. Their cries and peeps blended comfortably with the constant, gentle roar of ninety million Denobulans going brightly and politely about their business.

"You're in luck," Phlox had told Sato, T'Pol, and Elizabeth Cutler as they had made their way through the crowded city toward his family's pre-wedding gathering. "Since it's mating season, it's also monsoon season, and the city is at its most lush and vital. It's so invigorating!" Hoshi agreed up to a point, though she could have done without the humidity and the frequent downpours.

It could have been monstrous. With so many humanoids cramming themselves into such a tight space, hardly ever sleeping, keeping up a constant level of activity for thirty-five-point-six hours a day, the waste and pollution and disease and tension they generated could have been all but unbearable. But over millennia of close-knit living, the Denobulans had become experts on sanitation and hygiene, and more generally on living together in close quarters. Their world had only one vast continent, most of whose interior was profoundly arid, deprived of moisture by its sheer distance from the ocean. The Denobulans had evolved in the forests along the continent's southwest coast, sustained by the monsoonal rains and protected from the devastating hurricanes that frequently lashed the eastern seaboard. But even though their modern technology had allowed them to irrigate the desert, mitigate the storms, and spread more widely across the continent, the people of Denobula retained their communal instincts and huddled together by choice, with twelve billion Denobulans crammed into an area barely larger than China or Canada, leaving more than ninety percent of the planet's single vast continent unpopulated and wild. Being good neighbors, and good caretakers of their finite environment, had been a basic survival strategy for them.

Not that their caretaking was entirely peaceful; they saw themselves as part of the ecosystem they shared, and they often hunted the lemurs and various other small species for food, even in modern times. But they had long since abandoned hunting animals advanced enough to have any level of awareness, and were as humane as they could be toward the species they did hunt, taking no more than necessary and dispatching them as painlessly as possible. Their measured approach to utilizing the plants and animals of their world as integral parts of their civilization and technology explained much to Sato about Phlox's approach to medicine.

Indeed, a large part of what made the city so beautiful for Hoshi was that she could see it through Phlox's eyes. He had spoken of it in such glowing and romanticized terms over the years of their friendship that she had expected the reality to disappoint, but instead she found herself reminded of the warm feelings he had often expressed for his home and its occupants. She had seen many remarkable sights on the strange new worlds she'd visited over her fourteen years in space, but this time, the experience was personal, and that made it more profound.

Which made her all the sadder that she could not share it with the man she was going to marry.

Phlox had invited Takashi Kimura to attend his daughter Vaneel's wedding along with Hoshi; indeed, the doctor had been a witness to Sato's acceptance of Kimura's proposal, and had invited them to make it a double wedding. But this had proven impossible. Kimura had sustained severe injuries and brain damage during a battle with V'Las's revolutionary forces on Vulcan not long ago, forcing him to give up his career as *Endeavour*'s armory officer. This had been liberating for the couple in a way, freeing them to marry now that they were no longer serving together—but that was one of the few compensations for the ordeal Takashi was now enduring. He was back home in Hokkaido on Earth, going through intensive physical and neuroplastic therapy with his family's support. Though he'd hoped to make it to the wedding, his therapy was at too sensitive a stage right now, so he'd had to send his apologies. There was nothing Hoshi wanted more than to be with him now to offer her aid and comfort, but her duties to Starfleet and *Endeavour* had prohibited it, and Kimura had refused to let her sacrifice her career for his benefit.

Though she had to admit, there was a small, traitorous part of her that was relieved not to have to deal with the struggle he was enduring right now—that was glad to skip over it and eventually, hopefully, return to find him recovered and adjusted, or as close to it as his cognitive damage allowed. What did that say about her? Phlox had assured her that it was a natural impulse, one that she would not hesitate to reject given the opportunity to be with her fiancé. Still, she had less faith in her motives than Phlox did.

Yet it was impossible to wallow in regret for long, not while surrounded by dozens of Phlox's relatives, most of whom were as boisterous and outgoing as he was. The pre-wedding gathering was held in a large rooftop pavilion in the middle of the city, overlooking the wide Gronim River that snaked and twisted among its towers. Since Denobulans

rarely slept, they had little need for homes to return to on a
nightly basis, and thus they led a peripatetic existence. Most
of the structures in the city were for communal use: offices
and meeting halls; well-developed research centers, libraries,
and schools; stores where goods were loaned freely to those
who needed them; theaters, restaurants, and taverns; medical clinics, gymnasiums, and public baths; hallucinatoriums
where Denobulans could go to safely indulge and share the
altered states of consciousness that served them in lieu of
dreams.

Denobulans did have private places of their own—"nests"
where they bedded down for their annual hibernation, offices
and studios for their work, storehouses for their less transient
possessions—but with no permanent homes as such, even
family members rarely lived together, which was how they
could manage having three spouses apiece who each had two
other spouses of their own. It was really only for gatherings
like this that entire families came together, requiring the rental
of a meeting pavilion. If one could even define an "entire
family" with so many branching interconnections. Phlox was
probably related through marriage to virtually every other Denobulan on the planet, if you took it through a long enough
chain of mutual spouses.

In the case of Vaneel's wedding, the relevant family on the
Denobulan side consisted mainly of the biological parents
of the bride—Phlox and his second wife, Feezal, a striking
blond quantum engineer whom Sato remembered from her
occasional visits to *Enterprise* and *Endeavour* over the years—plus
their other respective spouses and children. That limited it to
a manageable three fathers and three mothers, plus various
of Vaneel's half-siblings and siblings-in-law. Not to mention
her first two husbands, a lanky Denobulan performance artist

named Thesh and a strongly built human biochemist named Hong Sun-woo. Sato felt that Vaneel had fine taste in men. But then, Phlox's younger daughter was quite a beauty herself, a gamine strawberry blond with piercing, pale green eyes and an enormous, aggressively warm smile. Vaneel had been attracting suitors for a good two decades now, and she had taken numerous lovers, according to Phlox's proud boasts; but she had been far more particular in her selection of husbands, accumulating them gradually and one at a time, instead of in pairs or triads as many Denobulans did.

"Which has been to the enduring frustration of my first wife," Sato heard Phlox saying from behind her as she stared out at the city. She turned to see the doctor approaching with a group including Captain T'Pol, Admiral Archer, and the admiral's lanky, elegant girlfriend Danica Erickson, along with Phlox's old Interspecies Medical Exchange colleague Doctor Jeremy Lucas, a cheerful, portly man with a walrus mustache. "Vesena couldn't be more thrilled that Vaneel is finally completing her triad—particularly with an Antaran. In her mind, that makes this wedding a historic event, and she's determined to manage it to perfection."

"I thought the responsibility for planning a Denobulan wedding resided with the biological parents," T'Pol observed.

"Normally, yes, but Vesena is such a natural leader and organizer. She's always taken an active interest in the marital prospects of her various offspring, spouses, and more distant relations."

"Don't mince words, Dad," interrupted a mature, balding Denobulan man standing nearby. Hoshi recognized him as Phlox's eldest son, Vleb, an artist specializing in pottery. Although at the moment his sensitive fingers cradled a more utilitarian vessel, a tall glass containing a rapidly dwindling supply of Denobulan wine. "You mean that Mom is a controlling tyrant who wants everything done her way."

"She simply wants to see to the well-being of every member of the family," Phlox replied in more diplomatic tones.

"Which is why she's not speaking to Groznik—*again*. And why he had to move clear to another planet to get away from her—*again*."

Phlox refused to be baited. "Well, Feezal and I were both busy with matters of our own offworld, so we were happy to let Vesena take charge of planning the wedding."

"'Busy,' he says," Doctor Lucas put in with a Santa Claus chuckle. "Called in to consult with the Klingon High Council, no less. Not many doctors can say they've done that and lived to tell about it."

"It wasn't that bad, Jeremy," Phlox replied. "Indeed, a Klingon succession dispute can be downright relaxing compared to planning a Denobulan wedding. At the very least, there are fewer factions whose agendas need to be balanced."

"I can believe it," said Dani Erickson in her warm alto voice. She was a tall, brown-complexioned woman with intense dark eyes and a large, ready smile. "I had a hard enough time just dealing with my father while he was alive. I can't even keep track of how many relatives you have."

Archer furrowed his brow. "Didn't you once tell me, Phlox, that your family had something like five hundred . . . no, seven hundred and twenty relationships, forty-two of them romantic? I admit I could never work out the math there."

"Hmm, let's see," Phlox answered. "Ah, yes, that was when I performed the pituitary gland transplant on Porthos. Let's see, that was several months before Feezal visited *Enterprise* . . . yes, at the time, there were thirty-one children in the family—limiting it to second-tier relationships for simplicity, of course, so only counting myself, my spouses, their spouses, and our respective children." He cleared his throat uneasily. "Although I would've been excluding my younger two sons, Tullis and Mettus, who weren't speaking with the rest of the family at the time. Well, Tullis has come around now, at least; he and his wives are right—um, over there somewhere, I think."

"Oh, I remember Tullis," Lucas said. "One of those Denobulans who thought that leaving the planet meant betraying their connection to nature." He turned to the Starfleet officers. "I'm afraid not all Denobulans are as well-traveled as Phlox and most of his relatives. It's why you don't see that many of them offworld, compared to their population size."

"I know," Archer said. "It's also part of why the Federation is having so much trouble persuading them to join."

"Well, there's always hope, Admiral," said Phlox. "I'm happy to say that Tullis, for one, changed his mind years ago. Vaneel deserves the lion's share of the credit for that, reaching out to him when she married Sun-woo and encouraging him to get to know his new brother-in-law."

"She's amazing, that girl," Vleb interrupted. "Tullis turns his back on the whole family when Rabb moves offworld and marries a Tiburon and a Tellarite."

"Rabb is their half-brother, Feezal and Bybix's son," Phlox interposed for the group.

Vleb went on regardless. "Didn't speak to us for two decades. I still don't know how Vaneel talked him around." The potter took another hefty sip of his drink, then shook his balding head. "Too bad she couldn't do the same for Mettus."

An awkward silence fell over the group, and Sato winced to see the pain on Phlox's face at the reminder of his still-estranged son. After a moment, T'Pol diplomatically resumed the earlier conversation. "Doctor, that would have left twenty-nine children and ten spouses. The total number of relationships among thirty-nine individuals taken two at a time would be seven hundred and forty-one."

"Ah! Yes, well, you have to realize that Vesena's son Kornob and his three wives had never met Bybix and the two wives he had at the time, since Kornob lives on B'Saari Two and Bybix lives on Tiburon. So that's twenty-one potential relationships down."

"So the forty-two romantic ones?" Dani asked.

"Within two tiers of myself, that includes all the marriages among me, my wives, and their other husbands—that's ten—plus our children's marriages, of which there were sixteen at the time. Plus the sixteen potential pairings between co-wives or co-husbands, among those who are receptive to such things." He gave a wry grin. "I've always been a bit disappointed that Kovlin is only interested in females, given how Feezal praises his prowess. I wouldn't have minded trying it for myself. But to each their own, as the humans say.

"And of course," he went on, "we've had several more marriages in the years since then. Let's see, Filoona married Tresc, Rabb married Dworra Sindar, Rempal married Morren and Dresp, and of course there were Vaneel's first two husbands and now Pehle completing the triad. And my third wife, Nullim, has had two children since then—Doulin with her second husband and Kronna with her third. And that's not even counting the grandchildren! Ah, such a blessing to have a large and growing family." He smiled at Sato. "As I'm sure you'll discover yourself in due time, Hoshi!"

Sato gave a feeble smile in response. Fortunately, she was spared from further discussion of her engagement when an early-evening rainstorm broke out. The Denobulans cheered this as an auspicious omen for the impending marriage—not as a superstition, merely an acknowledgment of the vital role the monsoon rains played in sustaining the cycle of life. But out of deference for their offworld guests, they moved the festivities into the open-walled pavilion at the center of the roof. The resultant reshuffling of guests brought Phlox and the Starfleet group in proximity to the bride and groom themselves, and Phlox introduced them to one another with pride.

Vaneel's fiancé, Pehle Retab, was a tall, robust Antaran man, pale of skin with a high hairline and a set of orbital and frontal ridges whose shape vaguely reminded Sato of the head and horns of an antelope. His long, tan hair was gathered into several tight, intricate braids that jostled one another between his shoulder blades as he moved and spoke with lively energy. Sato continued to approve of Vaneel's taste in males. "I'm a xenobotanist," he said to the group. "Once we began to normalize relations with Denobula, I welcomed the chance to come here and study the biosphere—not only the indigenous species, but the way the Denobulans had learned to coexist with them. Our own people have had more difficulty finding a healthy balance with our ecology."

"Oh, we were far worse than that, my boy." The speaker was Pehle's father, Sohon Retab, an older, portlier version of his son with shorter, grayer hair but an impressive, braided beard. "We mismanaged our environment for centuries in the name of easy profit. We made the Denobulans our scapegoats for the mass famines of three centuries ago, but we were at least as much to blame."

"You're too kind to our ancestors, Sohon," Vaneel insisted. "They were the ones who chose to unleash a biological weapon against your crops."

"But they could not have anticipated how little genetic diversity we had in our key crops. They meant only to weaken our war efforts and our economy, but instead whole staple crops were wiped out planetwide, and twenty million died. The only good thing that can be said of either side in the affair is that it shocked us both enough to sue for peace—even if the only peace our ancestors could agree upon was mutual avoidance."

"You'll have to excuse Father," Pehle said. "Making speeches is an occupational hazard for a legislator."

"I happen to like his speeches," Vaneel said, taking Sohon's arm. "He has a lovely voice. And I like what he has to say."

"Now, this is why you're lucky to be marrying her, my boy," Sohon declared. "She's smart enough to flatter her future father-in-law."

"It's no mere flattery, Sohon. You've done so much to change people's minds on Antar. It's thanks to reformers like you that I can walk down a street with Pehle in his hometown and feel welcome there."

"Now you're the one being too kind, dear girl. I think most of us were ready to let go of our fear of Denobulans. For centuries, the corporate rulers used them as scapegoats for all the restrictions and deprivations they imposed on us—exploited our fear of an outside race to keep us from recognizing the true cause of our problems."

"A familiar pattern," T'Pol observed.

"But it didn't sit well with us. We've embraced other cultures since the wars, for the most part. The famines taught us the importance of diversifying our crops, our technologies, our ideas. We've eagerly sought out the new and different, made friends with numerous other species, so this vestigial terror of the Denobulans was out of place. Our leaders convinced us—well, we convinced ourselves—that they were the exception to the rule, the one irredeemable race. I think most of us were relieved to discover they weren't the monsters under our beds after all. And once that particular corporate lie was exposed, it made the people question the rest. And that, not my own meager oratorical skill, is why the Reformists are in power now."

Phlox smiled. "Even so, Sohon, you deserve a lot of credit for your openness to this marriage. I understand that even today, Antarans have a strong belief in monogamy."

Sohon cleared his throat. "Yes, well, that took some soul-searching. Until I realized how your system makes sense for your people. You hardly ever sleep! You don't need to return home every night, and so you wander widely instead. Having more people in your life whose paths can intersect with yours is only reasonable. Besides," he added with a laugh, "not needing to sleep is the only way one could possibly have time to tend to three spouses!"

Phlox laughed in reply. "Even without sleep, it can be hard to find time for three spouses, with so much else to do. We Denobulans get so caught up in our work—it's fortunate that we tend to be self-sufficient when it comes to our emotional needs."

"I imagine that without sleep, you could easily lose track of time. You could be apart for weeks and it would feel little different from hours." Sohon shook his hirsute head. "I envy that. My wife had to remain on Antar to shepherd a vital piece of legislation through the Council. This is the longest I've been apart from her in twenty years, and I feel every moment keenly."

Pehle grasped his father's shoulder. "Well, Vaneel has

promised not to neglect me—not while I'm awake, anyway. Although she has been trying to convince me to look for at least one more wife." He drew Phlox's daughter into his arms. "But I'm afraid I'm the type to love only one woman." He pulled Vaneel into a kiss, which she returned aggressively.

Nearby, her husbands Thesh and Sun-woo looked on without jealousy. "Your loss," the human husband said. "I've already got a second wife and my eye on a possible third. So far I'm not having any trouble giving them enough attention, even with the need to sleep."

"Oh, I can attest to that," Vaneel said, even as she continued to cuddle with Pehle.

"Honestly, Vaneel," came a new voice, "I hope you don't intend to put on public displays like that all the time." The new speaker was a female Denobulan who resembled Vaneel, but with blond hair and a narrower face.

"Rempal, hello," Phlox said. "Everyone, this is Feezal and Kovlin's daughter Rempal—Vaneel's half-sister."

"Hello, Rempal," Archer said. "So . . . you're Phlox's wife's daughter with another husband. Would that make you . . . his niece? Or his daughter-in-law?".

"Second-tier daughter, actually," Rempal said. "But at this rate I'm starting to wonder if I'll be gaining any more nieces or nephews myself."

Vaneel glared. "Rempal!"

"I'm sorry, dear, I'm just worried about you. We don't know if it's even possible to have children with a human, let alone an Antaran. I know you think you're making an important statement and all, and I applaud that, really. But I hope it doesn't come at the expense of your happiness."

Vaneel faced her half-sister tensely, crossing her arms. "You just don't understand. You haven't even tried. You look at the man I love and all you see is an Antaran. You don't notice who he is, just *what*."

Her words saddened Rempal. "I've got nothing against Antarans. This is about you, not him."

"And that's exactly the problem! You and your father, you don't see him. Even Mother Vesena, all she sees is a symbol, a historic first to boast about."

"And you expect me to believe that isn't exactly what *you* want him to be? Considering how important his father is to the peace process?"

"Speaking of peace," Sohon interposed in a booming voice, "perhaps this is a question better discussed in more private surroundings."

"There's nothing to discuss," Vaneel said. Turning to Archer and the others, she said, "I apologize for the outburst. I think the rain is clearing up now—perhaps we could all use a bit more space." Taking Pehle's arm, she led him out from under the pavilion.

"Wow," Dani Erickson said as she, Archer, and the *Endeavour* party emerged into the waning daylight. "Family."

"It has its complexities," T'Pol noted. "It is only logical that they would be compounded in families as large as the Denobulans'. I begin to have some insight, Phlox, into why you are content to spend so much time apart from one another."

Phlox waved it off. "Oh, this was a minor tiff. Nothing you should allow to trouble you. Oh, look!" he said, pointing off into the distance. "The sun is about to set behind the Tregnig Towers. If we can find just the right viewing angle from this roof, the refractions between the building edges can be quite spectacular."

Sato exchanged a look with T'Pol. They had both known

Phlox long enough to recognize that he was more concerned than he let on.

After the party had broken up and the offworlders had gone off to sleep, Phlox tracked Vaneel down in her favorite hallucinatorium, where she often went to rest and work off her anxieties. Phlox had never been able to hallucinate as easily as Vaneel, instead tending to dream during his occasional brief naps—which was less satisfying, since he rarely remembered the experience. He envied his daughter's ability to confront and cleanse her subconscious more openly.

But tonight he found her restless and frustrated, pacing the empty, padded chamber without even talking to herself. "Am I intruding?" he asked.

She looked at him hopefully for a moment, then slumped. "Oh. You're real."

He declined to take it personally. "I take it you're having difficulty hallucinating?"

"Nothing seems to be coming tonight. I don't know why. I certainly have plenty to be tense about."

"Rempal only wants what's best for you, you know that."

"I know, but I just resent it that she doesn't think I know my own mind, my own motives. Why does she think I come here so often? I always listen to myself."

He considered her. "Unless you don't want to hear what you have to say."

"Oh, not you too, Dad." She turned away and resumed her long-legged pacing.

"Of course not, Vaneel. You know I'm on your side."

Looking embarrassed, she slumped against a cushioned wall. "I know, Dad, sorry. You're the one who understands better than anyone. You always raised us not to listen to

Great-grandmother Palbak's stories, not to believe the old prejudices. And it was you who first made the effort to get to know an Antaran in person, who paved the way for everything since. I would never have met Pehle if not for you."

He smiled. "I just convinced one injured Antaran to let me save his life. You were the one who chose to expand on that small opening, to travel to Antar and build bridges. To share Denobulan scientific knowledge to help repair Antar's ecosystem."

She pursed her lips. "I suppose I was rather spectacular."

"As always."

He came over to the wall and lowered himself to sit beside her, grunting a bit and lamenting his aging joints. He may have been in prime health for a Denobulan in his early eighties, but that was still middle age, and even Denobulan medicine couldn't work miracles. "But it occurs to me," Phlox went on, "that given how much of an activist you've been these past several years, it's understandable that others might see your relationship with Pehle as an extension of the same. It certainly is a striking statement of defiance toward . . . the old ways."

"That's a bonus, to be sure," Vaneel admitted. "There are certain types of people whose disgust and condemnation for your actions is profound reassurance that you're on the right path in life."

"True," her father said. "But the question is, does Rempal or Vesena deserve to be put in the same category as those people?"

Vaneel sighed, squeezing her eyes shut. "Of course not. They mean well." A loaded pause. "They aren't Mettus."

The pause before Phlox spoke was longer. "I try to convince myself that Mettus believes he means well, in his way.

That he believes he's defending something positive about Denobulans."

"He belongs to a hate group, Dad. A group that's issued death threats against my fiancé."

"You don't believe Mettus had anything to do with that?"

"He hasn't been a part of this family for over two decades. He's a stranger to us."

Phlox grew thoughtful. "He was always very passionate about what he believed in. Very stubborn. And contrary, relishing a good argument. Much like you, in fact. Oh, you and he had some barn-burners in your youth."

She stared. "'Barn-burners'?"

"A colorful idiom I picked up from an old shipmate back on *Enterprise*. I'm honestly not sure I'm using it correctly."

"But I see what you're saying," Vaneel replied. "You're wondering if this marriage is part of some extended argument with Mettus. If I'm doing this to make a point of defying his hatred. Of countering his voice."

"You did agree it would have that effect. And that's hardly a bad thing. But your sister has a point that your personal happiness is important as well."

Vaneel thought it over for a while. "All right . . . I admit, maybe I was too defensive with Rempal. Too quick to assume that she might have some lingering prejudice. I'll apologize to her later."

"I'm sure she doesn't need an apology. She just wants to know you'll be happy."

Vaneel clambered easily to her feet, evoking a touch of envy from Phlox. She slowly paced the confines of the room as she spoke. "Of course, I knew this marriage would be seen as symbolic. It is a very important statement. There's no denying that."

"Agreed."

She turned to face him. "But that's exactly why I knew it wouldn't be enough to marry Pehle for that reason alone. If it were just a symbol—if the essence, the connection, weren't there—then it would likely fail, and that would've harmed the cause Pehle and I both believe in. That's why we waited so long to commit. We both wanted to be absolutely sure that it was what *we* needed, just the two of us. That we couldn't possibly be happy without each other."

Her gaze shifted to the empty air beside Phlox, and she smiled. "And I know that's true, Dad. Because I see him. He's with me now."

Phlox smiled back. If her hallucinations were finally kicking in, then he knew she would be fine. "Does he look happy?" he asked.

She frowned. "Actually, he's riding a purple *flegnar* beast. They're usually orange. He's having trouble taming it. I should probably help."

"Ah." Phlox tried not to grunt too much as he levered himself to his feet. "I'll leave the both of you to it, then."

5

"WARP NEUTRALIZED," Ramnaf Breg reported from her helm console. "On course for orbital insertion in two-point-four milliphases."

"Acknowledged," said Captain sh'Prenni. "Good job."

Breg smiled. The Arkenite prided herself on the precision of the maneuver. Strictly speaking, a ship emerging from a spacetime warp should retain the real-space momentum it had possessed upon entering warp—but it was possible to finesse the collapse of the warp bubble to impart a selective torque and acceleration to the ship within, allowing fine course adjustments at the moment of warp egress without the expenditure of extra thruster fuel. It wasn't easy to gauge the effect to just the right degree, but this time, she'd pulled it off to perfection. She hoped that augured further success in the confrontation ahead.

"Oh, the long-range scans were right, Captain," Hari Banerji announced. "This planet is just covered in Ware. Numerous Ware stations and ships in orbit, too."

"Hail them."

Banerji made the attempt. "No reply."

"Keep trying. Broadcast our intentions and our information about the Ware."

"Understood."

In the lull that followed, Breg turned to her right to resume her ongoing conversation with Kitazoanra zh'Vethris. "Anyway, far be it from me to say an assassination attempt is a good thing. But the Keepers' attempt on Lecheb's life was the worst possible move for them. All they did—besides putting her in the hospital—was guarantee that she'd remove her objection to Starfleet intervention."

"And would you feel any differently if they'd succeeded in killing her?" zh'Vethris asked from the adjacent navigator's seat, her lips and antennae twisting in that wry, observational way that Breg found so attractive. "It would've achieved the same result."

"Not necessarily," Breg told her. "Whoever had succeeded her as acting governor might have been too afraid to endorse intervention openly and free the Council's hand." She shook her head. "I just wish *Vol'Rala* weren't stuck out here, unable to join the fight."

"Eager to dish out some payback?"

"Well . . . a little," she admitted. "But mainly I'm concerned for my *sia lenthar*. My bond-group. They'll be better off once the Keepers are subdued, no question, but the fighting itself may grow intense, if the Keepers are as stubborn as I expect. I feel I could do something to protect my *sia lenthar* if I were there."

"More likely you'd feel even more guilty about any harm you couldn't prevent," Tavrithinn th'Cheen observed from the tactical station on Breg's left. "There or here, the answer is the same: Trust the Guard. Your colleagues are as well-trained as you. They'll keep your kinfolk safe." Breg smiled at th'Cheen, appreciating the support. The tactical officer tended to be aloof and arrogant, a property of his upbringing in one of the oldest, most prestigious Andorian clans, but sometimes he could display unexpected solicitude toward his shipmates.

Th'Cheen's antennae angled forward as he spotted a read-out on his console. "Captain! A drone fleet is deploying from the nearest orbital station. Reading five drones."

"No preliminaries this time," sh'Prenni said. "The Ware must recognize us from our previous encounter."

"We are getting a hail about returning their stolen 'compo-nents,'" Banerji affirmed.

"Mmm, I don't think we'll comply. Vrith, is there a control ship?"

"No, Captain. Drones only," th'Cheen confirmed.

"I doubt they need one," Banerji replied, "with a home sta-tion close at hand."

"Then we target the station."

"We'll need to get past the drones first," Giered Charas re-minded her.

"Oh," zh'Vethris said. "And here I was hoping for a chal-lenge."

"Never take a fight lightly, Zoanra," the captain told her. "Not even the dull ones."

"Of course not, Captain." Breg chuckled as the navigator's antennae drooped in embarrassment.

Still, the young *zhen* had a point. Ware drones may have had a powerful computer intelligence directing them, but it lacked flexibility and imagination. From what the task force's crews had discerned in prior battles, they were driven by a finite set of protocols. In this case, not only were they attempting to retrieve the live "components" *Vol'Rala* had taken (no longer aboard, but the Ware had no way of knowing that), but since the ship was a known offender, they were also trying to de-fend the planet's Ware from further sabotage. That posed a challenge in getting close enough to the controlling station to attempt a shutdown. Not only were three of the drones maintaining a blockade, defining a plane in space between *Vol'Rala* and the station no matter how the battlecruiser maneuvered, but the remaining two were free to harry *Vol'Rala* and blast at its engines and weapons. Irritatingly, the Ware's skills at starship diagnostics and repair made it extremely good at calculating an enemy's vulnerable spots.

Still, the bridge crew had experience with the drones' tactics and had studied the other task force members' encounters with similar craft. As soon as Breg saw a drone maneuver toward *Vol'Rala*, she immediately knew how to move the ship to evade its fire. Th'Cheen could just as easily anticipate how to redirect the shielding energy for point defense, and between them they left Charas free to direct return fire, leading the drones' predictable maneuvers and landing the majority of his hits successfully. Only the drones' swift repair capabilities kept them in the fight. But Charas had studied Banerji's scans carefully enough to let him target his attacks to sever pieces of the drones, eroding them until there was not enough left with which to rebuild.

It all went so routinely that, despite her assurances to the captain, zh'Vethris couldn't resist carrying on her gossipy exchange with Breg. "At least your news from home promises to be good in the long run," she said with a sigh. "For me, I foresee no end in sight to my family's nagging. Incoming, fifth octant."

"Acknowledged." Breg veered the ship to evade the fire.

"At least until my fertility window runs out," the navigator went on, "and it's too late to pressure me into a *shelthreth*. I wish I could get them to accept that I'm just not the maternal type."

Breg chuckled, aware of how truthful that was. Zh'Vethris was a striking beauty and enjoyed the attention of the other three sexes—four if you counted Arkenite females, since Breg and zh'Vethris were currently in a friendly but intensifying sexual relationship. Breg knew that starship captains often discouraged romance among their crews; she counted herself fortunate that sh'Prenni was a believer in following one's passions. Zh'Vethris seemed relaxed and soft-spoken, but underneath it, she was as fiery as any Andorian. Her adventurous spirit had led her to seduce Breg out of curiosity, and that spirit had proven infectious enough to persuade Breg to experiment for the first time with a lover who was not Arkenite—an experiment that was still producing remarkable benefits. At first, Breg had thought zh'Vethris was merely taking an alien lover as an excuse to avoid the pressure to commit to a *shelthreth* group. She couldn't imagine that the *zhen*'s lively spirit could tolerate being anchored to a single set of partners. Yet in the moons since their involvement had begun, the two of them had only grown closer. Physical passion aside, it still felt more like a deep, relaxed friendship to Breg than a fiery romance— but then, maybe that was the kind of relationship that had real staying power.

"Damage to particle cannon five," th'Cheen reported. "Rerouting power to compensate." As he worked his console, he went on: "It's not just you at stake, though, Zoanra. Fertility is not something Andorians today can afford to waste."

The navigator rolled her wide, dark eyes. "Oh, not you too, Vrith. I get enough doomsday warnings from my *zhavey*. Seriously, it would take centuries before our population sank to an unviable level. Surely it won't take *that* long to find the answer."

"Even so, why take chances?"

"If every Andorian in their prime went home to procreate and parent, then who would run the Guard? We'd have to cede Starfleet almost entirely to humans and Vulcans. Can you imagine? Heads up, opening in the blockade, third octant!"

"Got it," Breg said. "Course laid in."

"Firing," said Charas. "Target destroyed!"

"If you're done gossiping," sh'Prenni said, "take us in and prepare to deploy probes."

Three points defined a plane, but two only made a line. With one of the blockading drones destroyed along with one of the attacking drones, and with the remaining attack drone on the wrong side of *Vol'Rala*, the battlecruiser now had a clear path to the controlling station. Charas released a spread of four probes toward the station, and though a drone managed to take out one probe with its particle beam, *Vol'Rala*'s cover fire allowed the other three to reach the station.

This time, thanks to the work done by Banerji and Philip Collier's team on *Pioneer*, the wake-up protocol had something extra added. The engineering teams had studied the telemetry from the original reawakening event, identifying the specific commands that Travis Mayweather and the other captives had sent into their life-support systems to override their sedation and restore themselves to full wakefulness, deactivating the Ware in the process. This way, the reawakening should work even on captives who had been duped into wanting to stay under. At least, that was the hope. This was the first time it was actually being attempted.

For a few moments, Breg feared the theory was a bust, for the drones continued their harassment of *Vol'Rala* and further drones were incoming from around the curve of the planet. But finally, the drones lost attitude control and began to drift, and Banerji reported that the repetitive warnings from the station had stopped. "Rendezvous with the station," sh'Prenni ordered. "Ready a boarding party to assist the reawakened captives."

"What's the extent of the shutdown?" Charas asked. "Is it planetwide?"

After examining his readouts, Banerji shook his head. "The orbital facilities only. I'm still reading active Ware systems on the surface."

The first officer grunted. "I knew it. Your latest trick is only a partial measure."

"Always rushing to judgment, eh, Giered? In fact, I anticipated this. Before, we had the cooperation of the sleepers. They woke themselves up, once we gave them the initial nudge. So all that needed to be transmitted was the basic revival signal. The actual shutdown procedures were initiated locally."

"Then this is practically useless, if we can only do it to one facility at a time!"

"I'm getting to that. Now that this station is under our control, I should be able to employ its own communication systems to push the shutdown codes through to the rest of the Ware in this system."

"Not beyond?" sh'Prenni asked.

It was Silash ch'Gesrit who responded. "It'll take a lot of power to force the signal through planetwide," the chief engineer said. "The power demands to transmit it over subspace would be prohibitive, even to target just one other system, let alone the entire Partnership network."

"All right, then we take it one system at a time—unless we can convince the Partnership to see reason." The captain cocked her antennae forward. "For now, though—"

"Captain!" Banerji called. "We're getting a hail from the surface."

Zh'Vethris threw Breg a look. "Took them long enough to notice us."

"Always refreshing to hear a living voice, though," the captain told her. "On the screen, Hari."

The semicircular display lit up with an image of two aliens—erect beings resembling some kind of arboreal rodents with golden fur and large, circular eyes. The one nearer the screen had a bright, multicolored fin atop its head. Behind them were the crisp, institutional white walls of a Ware facility. *"Please,"* the finned one said without preamble, *"whoever you are, stop this attack! Our people depend on the Ware!"*

"I'm afraid that's exactly the problem," sh'Prenni said. "I'm Captain Reshthenar sh'Prenni of *Vol'Rala*, a starship of the United Federation of Planets. And you?"

"Tefcem var Skos of the Partnership world Etrafso. My overmate is Wylbet, for whom I speak." Presumably that was the finless individual in the background. *"Please, we ask only to be left alone. We mean your people no harm."* Var Skos raised a mittenlike hand in supplication.

"The harm is not from you, Tefcem var Skos, but toward you and your people, inflicted by the Ware."

"The Ware is our bounty, our protection."

"It is a trap. You've become dependent on it to fight your battles, feed your people. We have seen whole civilizations destroyed by such dependence."

"And what gives you the right to decide this for us?"

"The Ware threatens all life. If you feed it victims, you help it spread and endanger other worlds. We act in the defense of all worlds, including your own." Sh'Prenni stepped forward to stand behind Breg's right shoulder. "I know this will be a difficult transition for your people, and I'm sorry. But the Federation will assist you in regaining your self-sufficiency. We will assign a vessel to see to your needs and guide you through the transition."

"And will we still have our prosperity, our health?"

Breg felt compelled to speak up. "No one can prosper if anyone is exploited. If people's lives aren't valued, then any material value you cherish is an illusion."

"You do not understand our lives, alien. You will take the very essence of the Partnership from us."

"Oh, I've heard that before," Breg snapped. "Defending your own kind, your own ways, at any cost, so long as it's others who pay the price. Your so-called Partnership lives on the backs of its weaker members. You've made them too dependent to stand for themselves. But that's where we come in."

She felt sh'Prenni's hand on her shoulder, at once reining her in and offering moral support. "We're not here to take anything from your people," the captain said. "We're here to give you back your freedom. Your dignity. Your future."

"You will cost us everything."

"Those of you who thrive by exploiting others? Hell, yes, and glad of it. You're the ones who happen to be talking to me, but I'm listening to the voices who can't speak for themselves. And from where I'm standing, those voices are far louder. *Vol'Rala* out." The screen went dark. "As I was saying, Hari—let's wake this world."

Breg smiled up at her captain. She hoped the Starfleet captains liberating Alrond right now were as committed and passionate as sh'Prenni. But at this moment, she was glad to be here instead of there.

Oceantop City, Partnership planet Rastish

Rinheith Chep felt a wave of dread rippling through his neck feathers as soon as he saw Fendob's body language. He had been taking his midday meal on his favorite promenade, enjoying the sea air and the view of the calm, flat ocean that surrounded the city on all sides, hoping its example would help him find the placidity that had so often eluded him these last few years—particularly since this latest alien incursion had begun. All Fendob said once she reached him was "Message, Vinik-Hev," but he knew his loyal Monsof understood the looming crisis better than her language skills allowed her to express.

Rinheith let his wings flap nervously as Fendob led him through the floating city's passages to his white-walled office and activated the communication controls for him; it was about all his wings were good for. He often envied the Monsof for the dexterity of their five-digited hands, which far exceeded that of the Hurraait beak and tongue. But he could never resent Fendob for it, since she had been his cherished companion since her childhood. She was almost as dear to him as her departed father, Gondob, who had been his Hands since he was a chick.

The Ware screen slid forward from the wall and lit up to display the streamlined, delta-winged body of Vinik-Hev, the Senior Partner for Avathox, her visage distorted by the dense, hot atmosphere in which she floated. "Greetings, Partner," Rinheith cawed.

"Greetings, Partner," the Xavoth replied, her rapid, low-pitched speech interpreted into Hurraait language by the Ware. *"I convey terrible news. Etrafso has gone dark."*

Rinheith had expected this, but the news still filled him with dread. "A whole world now fallen to these invaders. We must rally the Partners. Devise some form of defense."

"What defense can there be? They can shut down the very Ware itself."

"Can no one reason with them?"

"The drones intercepted their communication with Wylbet and Tefcem

before their strike," Vinik-Hev informed him. *"They see the Ware as a threat. They believe they are helping us!"*

Rinheith sank onto his cushioned perch, despairing. He felt Fendob's sensitive fingers stroking his back feathers, but he took little comfort in it this time. It was unfair to her, but on some level she reminded him of the invaders, who appeared to be primates like the Monsof, but with fuller linguistic development and finer motor skills. "Have you spoken with the scholars? Do they see any hope that the Ware can devise its own defense?"

"We had thought the Ware could adapt to anything. Apparently we were wrong. Our scholars are out of their depth."

"Then what can we do?"

"Only prepare yourself. Chep . . . the drones report that the ship that shut down Etrafso is heading for you now. They are mere days from Rastish."

Rinheith pondered for a long moment. "Very well. We shall begin stockpiling food, medicines, independent tools, everything we can."

Vinik-Hev's dangling underlimbs folded into a skeptical stance. *"You will have to depend heavily on your Monsof. Can they handle the burden without the Ware to guide them?"*

The Senior Partner regretted his earlier thoughts toward the primates. "They are more intelligent than they seem, my friend. And their survival is as much at stake as our own. They will not fail us." Fendob looked up at him with a gawky grin.

"They do make fine volunteers for the data cores," Vinik-Hev conceded. *"Proof enough of their mental capacity, I suppose. But what happens when the stockpiles run out? Can they build as well as the Ware?"*

Rinheith had no answer. Fendob lowered her head unhappily.

But then the voice of the Ware spoke from the screen.

"*Proximity alert. Incoming communication.*" The image of the Xavoth Senior Partner shrank to a window as the screen projected a schematic of Rastish's system, highlighting two ships that had just dropped out of warp.

At first, Rinheith feared that the invaders had already arrived, well ahead of schedule. But the readings showed that one of the two vessels was a Ware command ship. That brought him comfort—until he remembered that such a ship would be useless against the invaders who called themselves "Starfleet."

Noting Fendob's inquisitive look, he nodded to her. "Accept the communication. Vinik-Hev, you should monitor."

The schematic was replaced by a view from inside the command ship, with Vinik-Hev remaining in an inset. Two primates stood in its main chamber, both with dark brown skin and smooth brows, but otherwise different. One was hairless with light-colored spots above and around his vivid gold eyes and small fins behind his ears. The other had an unruly mane of dark hair, no spots, and no evident fins. It was the hairless one who spoke. "*Greetings. My name is Daskel Vabion of the planet Vanot. My associate is Captain Lokog of the Klingon Empire. Please pardon our intrusion, but we have been monitoring your communications, as well as the larger situation, using the facilities of this Ware command vessel. We believe we may be able to offer you assistance against the Starfleet threat.*"

Rinheith schooled himself to caution. "This is quite a claim, sir. But these invaders have the ability to neutralize Ware."

"*I am aware of that, Partner. But I have worked with the Ware far longer than they have. Indeed, their ability to shut down the Ware is based on my own research into its operation. This very ship was shut down through their actions—until I reactivated it.*"

Now Rinheith began to feel hope. But Vinik-Hev tempered

it with a reminder of caution: *"Vabion. This is hopeful news, if true. But what is to keep them from shutting it down again?"*

"That is a wise question, Partner. I am aware of that risk. I am also aware that I alone cannot maintain a holding action against the entire Starfleet task force. But that is where my associate comes in."

The other primate, Lokog, spoke in rougher, more aggressive tones. *"We Klingons are a race of warriors. We have fought Starfleet before—and we would gladly fight them again. And our ships . . . are not Ware."*

Rinheith felt his wings begin to spread as he realized just what was being offered.

6

THE FORECAST FOR VANEEL'S WEDDING DAY had promised
heavy rain and occasional thunderstorms, and it proved accurate. The Denobulans in the wedding party rejoiced at this,
gleefully letting the rain drench them as they conducted the
ceremony, for to them it was a cleansing beginning to Vaneel
and Pehle's new life. There was no analogy for this in Vulcan
thought, so T'Pol wondered if the human practice of baptism
might be a fit comparison.

The lightning flashing overhead was initially a source of
concern to T'Pol, but as she assessed her surroundings, she
realized the rooftop garden was surrounded by taller sky-
scrapers, all of which appeared to be topped with sophisticated apparatus for attracting lightning and absorbing its
charge as a source of power. A subtler, but still effective,
array of lightning rods and wires encompassed the roof
itself.

A portion of the seating area was beneath a transparent
overhang for the benefit of offworld guests such as T'Pol
and her Starfleet colleagues. Still, the humid conditions were
not beneficial for T'Pol's desert-adapted lungs and skin. She
counted herself fortunate that this ceremony included only
one wedding, and that one of the participants was monogamous. Even a single Denobulan wedding was a complicated

affair; rather than being officiated by a single religious or secular authority figure, it was approached more as a vote, with the spouses' petition to wed requiring the unanimous consent of their first-tier family members (in this case, on Vaneel's side, her parents, Phlox and Feezal, her full brother, Tullis, and her husbands, Thesh and Sun-woo, and on Pehle's side, merely Sohon Retab, voting on behalf of himself and his wife). Even though the parties involved must give their prior consent in order for a wedding to proceed at all, the ritual required the bride and groom to make ceremonial declarations of their case to the voting members, who would in turn make speeches expressing their own approval of the marriage. There would then be an exchange of vows, not only between the bride and groom, but between each participant and the other's pre-existing spouses, if any. Depending on the number of simultaneous weddings being conducted and the number of parents, siblings, and prior spouses involved, some Denobulan weddings could be marathon events lasting a day or more, given the Denobulans' lack of need for nightly sleep. By contrast, Vaneel and Pehle's wedding would likely take only a few hours.

Based on Phlox's stories about his iconoclastic daughter, T'Pol was unsurprised when Vaneel chose to break with Denobulan tradition and play her part in the ceremony according to Antaran custom. Evidently this was not without precedent. "When she married Sun-woo," Jeremy Lucas muttered to Archer and Danica, "she made it a combined Denobulan-Buddhist ceremony. Wore a Bhaku dress, made the recitations, everything."

The Antaran wedding ritual evidently entailed the bride and groom selecting a poem from the planet's romantic or historical epic tradition, one which they believed best illustrated the significance and character of their own relationship, and chanting it together while adorned in ornate traditional costumes representing its characters. Memorizing the lengthy piece and its intricate choreography required extensive rehearsal, the stress of which had reportedly driven many couples to sever their engagement. The Antarans believed this was a way of weeding out those couples not fully committed or temperamentally suited to each other. Vaneel and Pehle appeared to carry out the performance with adequate skill, as far as T'Pol could discern, though the artistic and cultural significance of the recitation was mostly lost on her. The Denobulan guests seemed rather bewildered by it as well, but that was probably just the reaction Vaneel had wished to evoke. If the mingling of Denobulan and Antaran cultures were to succeed, they would need to accept each other as they were.

For his part, however, Pehle followed up the recitation with a more conventional, Denobulan-style presentation of his case to the voting family members. The statement was meant to convey what the groom believed he could contribute to his spouse and to the family as a whole, generally including his economic prospects and the genetic benefits he could contribute as a parent, as well as more personal considerations. The parenting question was an area where Pehle was unable to offer much in the way of prospects. "I don't know if it will be possible for me to conceive a child with Vaneel," he confessed. "We've spoken with some of the best genetic engineers on Denobula, and they're researching the question, but it's a possibility that's gone uninvestigated by both our planets' medical science, for reasons I don't need to restate. It could be years before we determine whether it's even possible for us to conceive, let alone with a safe chance of the baby's survival."

T'Pol felt a sharp twinge of emotion at the reminder of Elizabeth, the hybrid child that Earth's Terra Prime extremists had conceived by blending her DNA with that of Charles Tucker. The infant had been a pawn in a twisted plan meant to warn of the "danger" of alien contamination of the human genome, but had tragically suggested the reverse when she had proven unviable and died mere weeks into her life. Though the child had been conceived without her or Tucker's consent, essentially as a violation of them both, neither of them had blamed Elizabeth for what Terra Prime had done, and both had felt her death as keenly as if they had conceived her by choice. Phlox had told them that Terra Prime's botched engineering had been responsible, that it might still be possible for a Vulcan and a human to produce a viable child together with the proper medical intervention; but it was still a risk she wasn't sure she would ever be willing to take.

"But that's the nature of trying new things," Pehle went on, heedless of the pouring rain. "We just can't predict what will happen. When I grow an Antaran plant in Denobulan soil, or Vulcan or Terran or B'Saari soil, I don't know how its development might be changed by the new conditions in which I nurture it.

"I'm supposed to tell you what I can contribute to this family—how you will be enriched by my participation. The fact is, I can't answer that question. There's no precedent for this. It's the first trial of the experiment, and there's no predicting how it'll turn out.

"But if you ask me—and if you ask my brave, adventurous Vaneel, I'm sure—that's exactly why it has to be tried. Every day we spend together, we discover something new about ourselves, something changed by our interaction with someone so new and different to us. Every day, we become more in combination than we were apart. And so the fact that I can't tell you what comes next—that excites me deeply. And it should do the same for you."

Once he finished, Hoshi Sato turned to T'Pol with a smile. "Infinite diversity in infinite combinations. Very Vulcan of him, wouldn't you say?"

"I would like to think so," T'Pol replied. It hadn't been that long ago that those Vulcans who repudiated such inclusion of outsiders had attempted to regain control of the planet's government and society—but they had been roundly defeated and discredited, giving T'Pol confidence that the majority of her people lived up to Sato's characterization.

Still, for a Vulcan to marry an offworlder was virtually unheard of. Most Vulcans were pledged to their future mates in childhood, leaving little room for such variations from tradition. T'Pol was free from such an obligation, since her husband, Koss, had released her from her vows. But by the same token, she had been generally disinclined to consider marriage as a viable prospect for her, preferring to focus on her career as a scientist and officer.

Could that be why she was content in her relationship with Charles Tucker? Not only was he someone she would never be expected to marry, but he was generally kept far from her by his work—not to mention that he was presumed dead, ensuring that the very existence of their relationship must remain secret. All of which provided reasons—or perhaps excuses—for the absence of a deeper commitment such as marriage or parenting.

That had been enough for her for years, and thus she had never questioned it before. Yet Pehle Retab's words resonated with her in a way she did not fully understand. It would bear further thought.

With the bride and groom having played their parts, the family members now took their turns to express their feelings on the marriage. Sohon Retab was invited to speak first, as befit an honored guest. He began by passing along a statement of consent to the marriage from Pehle's mother before beginning his own remarks. Sohon was known as an orator, and T'Pol expected a lengthy and dramatic statement addressing the philosophical and political significance of this historic union between Antaran and Denobulan.

But instead, Sohon spoke on a more personal level, sharing anecdotes of his interactions with Vaneel and his observations of her relationship with Pehle. He told of how the couple had met through their work, how they had begun seeing each other socially, how they had fallen in love. He spoke of joyous experiences he and his wife had shared with their son and his fiancée, related jokes that Vaneel had taught him and ones he had taught her, and conveyed his gratitude that his son had found a life partner who brought him such fulfillment and novelty. Not once in his entire remarks was the word "Antaran" or "Denobulan" even spoken. He did not speak of Pehle and Vaneel as members of alien races entering into a precedent-setting union, but merely as a man and a woman like any other, with a relationship like any other—unique and special, yes, but only because of who the two of them were, rather than what they were. And that, T'Pol realized, was perhaps the most powerful statement he could have made.

Vaneel's brother Tullis spoke next, his remarks tinged with regret at how he had been estranged from his family for so long due to his mistaken belief that traveling offworld was a betrayal of the Denobulan link to nature—but praising Vaneel for her refusal to give up on him and for the relentlessly positive example she had set through her own interstellar wanderings. "I had thought I was being true to my nature," the chubby-faced blond Denobulan said, "and that it was my sister, my father, and the others who were violating theirs. But Vaneel made me see that I was the one cutting myself off. How could I be truly connecting to the ecosystem if I separated myself from the life-forms most closely related to me? No matter how different the path she pursued, no matter how far she went, Vaneel never stopped being my sister. Once I saw that, I realized how narrow-minded I'd been. And I'm grateful for the time I've shared with my family ever since."

Feezal spoke next, conveying her pride in her daughter's adventurous and open mind, as well as her admiration for her taste in males. "I don't know if Vaneel and Pehle can give me a grandchild either, but I'm happy for them anyway, since I'm sure they'll have plenty of fun trying!" The puckish Denobulan woman's raunchy remarks in approval of her daughter's latest husband were discomfiting to the human guests and downright scandalous by Vulcan standards, but the Denobulans took them in good humor.

Finally, when Phlox's turn came, he returned the proceedings to a more serious tone. "I have always striven to set a good example for my children," the doctor said, "yet at the same time, I have tried to give them freedom to discover their own identity, their own paths in life. I didn't try to make them believe what I wanted; I simply tried to give them the tools to consider and choose for themselves. Vaneel has always taken full advantage of that freedom. Often she would experiment with odd or eccentric ideas, sometimes to the point that I feared I would have to step in and lay down some limits for her own good. But I feared that if I did so, she would push against those limits and go even farther astray, just to challenge my authority.

"In time, I realized that Vaneel sought not to challenge me, but to challenge herself. She recognized that I was giving her freedom to become her own person, and she embraced that freedom as the gift I had always meant it to be. And though there were times she ventured down paths I could not for the life of me understand—like the time she abandoned her studies for a year to live in the Central Desert as an ascetic, or that time when she was eight years old and decided to deliver every sentence backward for two weeks—I'm happy to say that she never chose a path that I found shameful or hurtful to others. Her desire to explore other ways of thinking was an expression of her profound empathy and regard for other beings, and as a doctor, I find nothing more admirable than that.

"And I have never been more proud of my darling Vaneel than I am today, seeing her with Pehle Retab. Our ancestors— even her own great-grandmother—would have condemned this union as a crime against nature. Just looking at the two of them standing here now is the most perfect repudiation of that attitude that I could imagine. I did what I could, in my way, to put that shameful past behind us. Yet I am proud to say that it is my daughter, Vaneel-zalleen-oortann, who is leading Denobula and Antar into the future."

"You always have to make it about you, don't you?"

The interrupting voice was strident and angry, loud enough to carry over the rain without amplification. Accompanying it was the heavy smack of multiple boots against the wet rooftop as a group of five young Denobulans strode aggressively through the crowd. All but one of them were male, and all wore matching dark brown garments that each bore an angular emblem in red on the left shoulder. The dark-haired male in the lead, high-browed and narrow-faced with a rounded chin and cheekbones, was the one who had spoken. "The great man, leading through example," he went on. "An example set by renouncing everything our forebears believed in!"

Phlox stared at the man, dumbstruck and disbelieving. Most of the other family members reacted with similar astonishment. Only Nullim, Phlox's third wife, showed any hint of warmth toward the intruder. "Mettus," she gasped so softly that T'Pol doubted her human crewmates had heard it over the rain.

The senior wife, Vesena, a formidable silver-haired woman, strode forward to confront the intruders. "How dare you disrupt this wedding, Mettus? You and your . . . cronies are not welcome here."

"Of course not!" Phlox's youngest son snarled back. "This event is for Antaran-lovers only! Not enough that they contaminate our planet, pollute our air and our water, steal our resources. Now they seek to erode our most precious institutions! How soon before they have us marrying monogamously, sleeping with no one but a single spouse? Making our population plummet until we're too few to stand against them?"

"Enough of this!" Vaneel stormed forward to face him. "Mettus, I enjoy seeing a party crashed as much as anyone, but if all you have to say is the same old boring, stupid rhetoric, then that's not a good enough reason to interrupt me in the middle of my wedding."

"It needs to be said, Vaneel! The world needs to know!"

"About things that happened three hundred years ago? Thanks, already got the newsfeed. Can I get back to getting married now?"

Mettus sighed. "You're right, sister. This should be about you. Why don't we take this somewhere private so we can talk? So I can convince you of the terrible mistake you're about to make?"

Vaneel scoffed. "Since when did you care that much? You haven't spoken to me, haven't written, haven't answered a letter in over twenty years! You didn't acknowledge either of my other weddings, my degrees, any of it. And you want me to believe this, barging in here with a band of stormtroopers to make a political statement, is about me?"

"Yes! Because it's *his* politics, not yours!" Mettus answered, pointing at Phlox. "All your life, always acting out to try to get his attention, his approval. Even his disapproval, as long as he took notice. You finally figured out that the only way was to play along with his pet cause. To join him in dishonoring the sacrifice of our great-grandparents in the Antaran wars."

Vaneel stared. "This is the version of reality you've been living in all this time? No wonder we couldn't reach you." She narrowed her lips. "Whatever chance you might've had to voice your opinions, however insane, you forfeited by waiting until now to come forward. You're not doing this for me—you're doing it for the publicity. And I'm not going to play along."

She turned away and returned to stand alongside Pehle before Phlox and the others. "Dad? You were saying?"

"No!" Mettus strode forward, the other four moving to follow. "I won't let this Antaran scum touch my sister!"

"You're a couple of years late for that," Vaneel said, laughing heartily. But her laughter broke off when Mettus grabbed Pehle by the arm and shoved him away from Vaneel. The larger man retained his footing and shoved Mettus back, knocking him to the deck. The other four uniformed youths circled Pehle menacingly. T'Pol traded a look with Archer, drawing her communicator from the sleeve pocket of her dress uniform in case it became necessary to call in a security team.

But Vesena had beaten her to it. A contingent of

Denobulan police poured onto the roof, following the elder wife as she guided them toward the looming fracas. As soon as they spotted the approaching officers, Mettus and his gang broke and ran for the far exit. The lead police officer sent her team in pursuit, remaining behind to hear Vesena's full report on the event.

Phlox's family members and Sohon Retab moved forward to gather around Vaneel and Pehle. Archer left the shelter of the overhang to join them, moving with a resolute stride, and T'Pol followed, ignoring the rain (which had subsided to a moderate shower).

"I can't apologize enough for this," Phlox was saying to Sohon when she and Archer arrived at their side. "Mettus has kept himself apart from the family for so long that it never occurred to me he'd try anything like this."

"The fault is hardly yours, my friend," Sohon told him. "Although I know that as a father, you can't help but feel otherwise."

"Still, I should have known. The first wedding between our peoples—of course it would bring out the hate groups." He shook his head. "Maybe it was a mistake to do this in public. Perhaps we should make new arrangements, reconvene somewhere more secure—"

"No!" Vaneel insisted. Taking Pehle's arm, she went on. "We can't let bullies like Mettus change the way we choose to live our lives. Besides, we had a hell of a good wedding going here. I was really enjoying your speech, Dad. Personally, I want to hear how it ends. Especially the part where you make it unanimous and Pehle and I are officially married. I don't want to wait a moment longer than I have to for that."

Phlox smiled warmly, pulling his daughter into his arms. "He's so wrong about you. If anything, I'm the one who's been guided by your example. I'm so proud to be your father." He chuckled as he pulled away. "Which is essentially how my speech would have ended anyway. So I, Phloxx-tunnai-oortann, hereby cast my vote in favor of this marriage. Which I believe makes it unanimous!" He clasped Pehle's hands in his. "Pehle Retab, I officially welcome you as the newest member of our family, third husband of Vaneel! Congratulations!"

The Denobulans cheered and began to dance in the rain, the recent disruption seemingly forgotten. But T'Pol caught Archer's attention as she noted the police team returning to report to their chief. "They're saying that Mettus and the others got away," she related to the admiral. "They suspect the complicity of a member of the building's security contingent with the anti-Antaran group."

Archer looked grim. "Then this may be bigger than just a few angry kids. Vaneel and Pehle may not be out of the woods yet."

U.S.S. *Vol'Rala*, Rastish system

Tavrithinn th'Cheen had been expecting the next Partnership world on the Ware map to be defended by a cordon of ships. No doubt word of the task force's actions would be getting around. And this was a particularly populous world, its bright, sprawling Ware cities metastasizing across the landscape and even out into the oceans. But th'Cheen had not expected the kind of ships he detected once *Vol'Rala* neared the planet. "Captain," the tactical officer announced in surprise, "those ships . . . they're Klingon!"

Captain sh'Prenni rose from her command chair, frowning. "The Empire, here?"

"No, ma'am, I think not. Mostly older ships . . . civilian, decommissioned military, a few that seem to be captured prize ships modified with Klingon markings and equipment."

"Privateers, then."

"I'd say so, yes." Th'Cheen had certainly encountered enough of those during *Vol'Rala*'s cleanup of the Kandari sector. "Nine ships in all."

"Not only that," said Hari Banerji, "the lead vessel is *Sud QaV*. Lokog's ship."

Captain sh'Prenni's antennae cocked thoughtfully. "Well. He gets around, I'll give him that."

"Vabion must have brought him here," Commander Charas observed. "He probably wants to raid the Ware for himself."

"And he brought friends," zh'Vethris added. "Are we interrupting a feeding frenzy?"

"Or a protection racket?" sh'Prenni wondered. "Let's find out. Hail him, Hari."

"No need—he's hailing us."

Th'Cheen knew Lokog mainly by reputation; most communication between *Vol'Rala* and *SuD Qav* in the past had been through the medium of weapons fire, and the privateer had generally not stuck around for conversation when *Vol'Rala* had arrived. So it was a surprise when the Klingon's oddly humanized visage appeared on the forward screen. His belligerence was certainly Klingon, though. *"Attention, Starfleet vessel! You are outnumbered. Stand down and prepare to be boarded!"*

"By you, Lokog?" asked sh'Prenni. "Don't make me laugh. I recommend you tell your associates to leave. Whatever interest they have in the Ware, it will be rendered useless to them in very short order."

"That we will not allow, 'anDorngan. We know you must reach the orbital station to commit your sabotage, and you cannot do that so long as

we stand in your way. And no—you will not be laughing." The screen went dark.

The Klingons did not attack, but then, they didn't have to. "He has a point, Captain," th'Cheen observed. "To get close enough to fire the probes, we have to descend to the station's orbit, and the Klingon ships stand between us and it. Worse, if we descend, we will be hemmed in between them and the planet, surrendering the high ground."

The captain moved closer and studied the tactical readouts over his shoulder, thinking. "Maybe not. Consider, Vrith, that orbit is not just a matter of altitude, but velocity. Those ships aren't standing still between us and the station—we're all circling the planet in the same direction, keeping pace with one another like *zabathu* on a racetrack."

Th'Cheen's antennae perked up at her words. "So what if we ran in the other direction?"

She clapped his shoulder. "Exactly." She strode around the bridge, giving orders. "Zoanra, plot us a retrograde descent. Duck behind the Klingons' horizon. Hari, once we're out of sight, very quietly release a spread of probes on an intercept trajectory with the Ware station."

"It won't take long for them to catch up with us," Charas pointed out.

"Which gives Ramnaf an excuse to take us back up through their lines and make it look like we're trying to get maneuvering room for the fight. When we're really diverting their attention long enough to let the probes sneak up on the station and do their work."

As always, th'Cheen was impressed by the captain's strategic mind. *Vol'Rala*'s retrograde move took the Klingon privateers off guard, disrupting their formation as they scrambled to reverse their own orbits in pursuit. It did not seem to occur to any of them to thrust downward and use their forward momentum to skirt the edge of the atmosphere, letting them circle tightly around the planet and intercept the *Kumari*-class battleship from ahead. But then, these were raiders and pirates, not trained battleship commanders. The surprise maneuver scattered their formation sufficiently that, once four probes had been released on an unpowered trajectory and *Vol'Rala* had accelerated outward from the planet again, the ship was able to penetrate the Klingon lines with little difficulty.

Still, the privateers were quick to give chase as the ship ascended. Sh'Prenni laid a hand on Breg's shoulder. "Ramnaf, your job is to keep their attention away from the probes and the station, while making it look like we're still trying to reach the station. Think you can handle that?"

"The Klingons are making that easy, Captain," the Arkenite replied. "They're coming into formation ahead of us on retrograde arcs. A polar trajectory should make it look like we're trying to get around them to the station, while luring them away from the probes."

"Good call. Do it."

Th'Cheen left the details of the ship's course to Breg. His own part in the distraction was to occupy the Klingons with particle beams and photonic torpedoes, keeping them so caught up in their battle frenzy against *Vol'Rala* that they would not notice the probes. "Remember my rules of engagement," sh'Prenni advised him. "No more bloodshed than strictly necessary."

"Captain, they're Klingons," th'Cheen countered. "They will take that as an insult."

"Exactly," the captain replied. "These are nothing but bullies and thieves. Let's not give them the satisfaction of treating them like warriors."

The tactical officer felt limited by the captain's restrictions on the use of force, but he offered no protest. Th'Cheen prided himself on the quality of his work. Throughout his career, many had expected him to coast on his aristocratic birth, to achieve status in the Guard through his clan ties rather than his merits. He had been determined to prove them wrong. Was a member of the Clan of Cheen entitled to success and achievement? Yes, but only because the resources and opportunities granted to him as a member had guaranteed him the best education and training from childhood onward. Perhaps that had given him a head start over those who lacked those advantages, but he had earned his advancement through hard work just as much as they had. He had never attempted to use his clan name to curry political favor within the Guard, instead letting his work prove his worthiness to serve among the best and brightest.

Indeed, it was the benefits of his superior education that currently enabled *Vol'Rala* to hold its own while massively outnumbered by Klingon privateers. Granted, most privateer vessels were little threat to a capital ship like *Vol'Rala*, but nine of them could pose a significant danger if allowed to surround the starship. Th'Cheen's precision fire prevented that, damaging or driving off ships that attempted to close off gaps in the Klingon formation and leaving those gaps clear for Breg to dive through. The Klingons managed to dodge the worst of it—these privateers tended to flee readily from any serious challenge—but he managed to cripple two of the smaller ships and leave a third, one of the prize ships, tumbling with only one working engine, out of the fight until its engineer could rebalance the thrust. He even managed to clip *SuD Qav*'s wing, destroying one of its disruptor banks.

But then Banerji spoke. "Captain, I'm picking up a transmission from the Ware station—directed at the Klingons."

"Can you decipher it?"

"Given time, perhaps."

"I think we can handle that without you," Charas remarked. "The Klingons are breaking off the attack. They're on an intercept course for the probes!"

Commander ch'Gesrit stared at the first officer. "The Ware alerted the Klingons?" the engineer asked.

"We'll sort that out later," sh'Prenni said. "No more dodging, Ramnaf. Head for the probes."

"Aye, Captain, but we'll never reach them in time to save them."

"Then belay that. Aim right for the station so we can fire another probe salvo. We'll blast right through the Klingon lines if we have to."

That proved harder in practice than promise, however. Only two of the privateer ships veered off to take out the probes, leaving five between *Vol'Rala* and the station. The number of foes had been nearly halved, but the need to close in on the station created the very disadvantages that sh'Prenni had been trying to avoid, limiting the ship's maneuvering options and allowing the Klingons to hem them in against the planet from above.

The job was harder now, and *Vol'Rala* began taking significant damage. A dorsal shield generator blew out, requiring th'Cheen to refocus the adjacent emitters to compensate, but not before a lucky shot blew out a power relay, overloading one of the wing cannons. Worse, the Klingons had now drawn blood, with Chirurgeon th'Lesinas reporting several injuries from the relay explosion. Th'Cheen rededicated himself to his work, coordinating with Commander Charas at the opposite tactical station to hold the Klingons at bay. The lieutenant would never allow anyone in this crew to think he valued them less than himself. He would defend them with all his skill, and he would fulfill his captain's orders. Anything less would be letting his clan down.

But then *Sud Qav* and another vessel bracketed *Vol'Rala* from aft and combined their fire against the starboard secondary engine pod. Th'Cheen retaliated with everything he had while Charas bolstered the shields over the pod and Breg twisted the ship in an attempt to break their target lock. But it was not enough. "Pod overloading!" ch'Gesrit cried. "We have to jettison!"

"Do it," sh'Prenni ordered. The engineer cut the pod free, and while th'Cheen kept up his fire against the pursuing Klingons, Charas used the tractor beam to fling the overloading pod toward another ship.

But the pod exploded while it was still less than a kilometer from *Vol'Rala*. It was fortunate that it was only a secondary pod. The main nacelles were well-protected within the body of the ship, vertically bracketing the antimatter reactor, only a portion of whose plasma output was channeled through the wings to the secondary engines. So the explosion was much milder than that of a full-fledged reactor breach. Still, at that range, it was enough to do considerable damage. The radiation pulse weakened the dorsal shields enough for the vapor cloud and shrapnel to overload them and penetrate to the hull. The ship rocked and tumbled, and th'Cheen barely managed to keep his footing by clinging to his station's support column. Banerji was not so lucky, falling from his stool and knocking Charas to the floor. The first officer's curses were audible even over the deep ringing of the hull.

"Damage report!" sh'Prenni ordered.

"Aside from the obvious," ch'Gesrit replied, "we've lost the dorsal and both wing cannons and most of our dorsal shield emitters. The upper primary nacelle has four coils down, and the port pod has a radiation leak—I'm shutting it down for its own good, not to mention ours."

"Casualties?"

Charas had clambered back to his feet to study his console. "Reports still coming in."

"We still have maneuvering," Breg put in.

"And the probe launchers," th'Cheen added. "And enough working cannons and torpedoes to make a fight of it."

"Let's do so," sh'Prenni ordered. Though th'Cheen could hear in her voice the question she was choosing not to ask: whether they could survive the attempt. Surely they would all agree that was irrelevant, so long as they achieved their goal.

But again, news from Banerji appeared to change the equation. "Captain! I'm detecting six small ships emerging from warp, closing on our position. They read as Balduk!"

"Oh, good news at last," sh'Prenni said. The Balduk were one of the local races that had been preyed upon by the Ware without their knowledge. A prideful, aggressive breed, they had been outraged to learn of their exploitation and had offered assistance to the Starfleet task force a few moons back. "Hail them, Hari. Let them know we need assistance."

It was a moment before Banerji replied. "They aren't responding, Captain. However . . . they *are* exchanging communications with the Klingons."

The readings on th'Cheen's console suggested the nature of those communications. "Captain . . . the Balduk ships are on course to join the Klingons' formation. They're hemming us in."

"What?" sh'Prenni cried. "Hari, hail the Balduk again.

Inform them that the Klingons are apparently working in concert with the Ware."

As Banerji complied, sh'Prenni turned to Charas. "Giered, what are our odds against both contingents?"

"Vanishing, Captain. We've got one engine and less than half our weapon and shield capacity."

"Can we take out the Ware, at least?"

Banerji came up alongside Charas's shoulder. "Not unless we survive long enough to use the station's signal array against the planet's Ware. Which does not appear to be an option anymore."

The captain narrowed her lips, her antennae folding back angrily. "Send a distress call to the task force. Tell them . . . our situation." Requesting assistance seemed unrealistic at this point.

Banerji turned back to his console to comply. Once he had completed his task, he reacted with surprise to a signal from his console. "Captain—*Sud Qav* is hailing us."

Sh'Prenni turned to face the forward viewer. "Put him through."

Lokog's mutated features appeared before them again. *"I told you only we would be laughing,"* he said, matching the action to his words. *"You have no way out, 'anDorngan."*

"I have to admit, Lokog, I'm impressed," sh'Prenni said. "How did you get the Balduk on your side?"

"It was not I," the Klingon said. *"They and we have both been employed in a common cause: the defense of the Partnership of Civilizations against the aggression of the Federation."*

The captain scoffed. "You expect me to believe your interest is altruistic?"

"If altruism pays us well enough, then yes. Although seeing you at my mercy is almost payment enough." The gloating captain grinned

widely, revealing that the viral mutation that had stripped away his skull ridges had done nothing for his dental alignment. *"Captain Reshthenar sh'Prenni, I hereby place you and your crew under arrest for crimes against the Partnership of Civilizations. You will submit immediately—or be destroyed."*

Th'Cheen desperately tried to think of a way out—some brilliant tactical ploy that would let *Vol'Rala* break the englobement and gain the advantage over the combined armada. It was his job to protect this ship and its crew, to fulfill its mission. His pride as a Cheen demanded that he not fail his captain, his family, or himself.

When it came down to it, though, for all his education and training and hard work, he had never been much for inspiration. He was relentless in a fight, but it was his captain's strategic brilliance that guided his aim. He could give her nothing more than he already had.

But when he looked at his captain now, all he saw was resignation. There was only one available option for defending her crew. "Very well," she said through clenched teeth, her antennae low, forward, and trembling. "We surrender."

7

Gronim City, Denobula

After the wedding, the new spouses, the family, and most of the guests adjourned to Gronim City's legendary *kaybin* district for the celebratory bacchanalia. Phlox found it amusing that human marital customs inverted the Denobulan practice by putting the night of sexual indulgence before the wedding and the reception after it. Of course, this was because human marriages were typically monogamous, with the participants allowing themselves a final night of license before settling down—or at least that was the theory. Among Denobulans, by contrast, the post-marital *kaybin* crawl was a celebration of the new spouses' fertility and the physical and spiritual joys involved in the exercise thereof.

T'Pol, unsurprisingly, had declined to join Phlox and his family in the crawl—as had Hoshi Sato, for reasons Phlox could understand. But Jeremy Lucas was along for the ride, and though Admiral Archer had been hesitant, Dani Erickson had talked him into participating in the name of cross-cultural enlightenment. Sohon Retab had also been hesitant to join the crawl, given the absence of his wife, but had agreed once it had been pointed out that Gronim's high-class *kaybin* bars offered fine food, wine, music, and other delights besides the sexual.

It had been a long time since Phlox had last enjoyed the

wonders of the *kaybin* bars, let alone with all three wives at once, or in commemoration of such a special occasion. Yet despite his best efforts to embrace the joy of this night, Phlox was unable to shake off his somber mood entirely. Archer noticed this, sidling up to the doctor as they trailed the wedding party through the lush vegetation, colorful signage, and lively street performers of the *kaybin* district. "If you like, I could have T'Pol bring down a security team from *Endeavour*."

"What? Oh, no," Phlox replied, laughing off the suggestion. "I appreciate the offer, Admiral, but the police escort should be more than adequate to frighten off those young ruffians. And they'd be unlikely to try anything here. Crime in a *kaybin* district is almost unheard of. This is where we celebrate life and beauty and fertility. It would be like vandalizing a church, in Earth terms."

"Hate groups on Earth used to burn down churches. Life is the last thing people like that hold sacred."

Phlox waved off his concerns. "You heard Mettus, Admiral. He wasn't there to do violence—he was there to embarass me. To 'rescue' Vaneel from my pernicious, Antaran-loving influence. He's made his point, achieved what he set out to do." He shook his head. "I'm afraid Mettus was never ambitious enough to strive for much beyond that."

Archer frowned. "If you don't mind my asking . . . how did things get this bad between you and your son?"

"I've spent decades asking myself that same question. I always strove to treat my children with respect and understanding. To give them freedom to discover their own identities. It always seemed to me that cracking down harshly on one's children only gave them more to rebel against."

"Maybe," the human said. "Then again, some children might crave more attention. More structure."

"And act out in order to attract it? Yes, Nullim and I thought that might be the case with Mettus. He often seemed to feel that he was at a deficit for attention. He was my youngest child, my only one with Nullim. He was only two years younger than Vaneel, and she was always a handful." He gave a rueful chuckle, then sobered. "And by that time, I was heavily involved with the IME, spending increasing amounts of time offworld. Perhaps Mettus resented the fact that I paid more attention to aliens than to him, and that left him vulnerable to recruitment by the anti-Antaran movement.

"But by the time Nullim convinced me to make it clear how strongly I disapproved of his associations, the damage had been done. They'd already polluted his mind with their twisted view that showing any kind of tolerance toward Antarans was a sin against nature itself. He believed that my 'favor' toward Antarans—hah! As you'll recall, I could barely bring myself to stay in the same room with one at the time, regardless of my professed beliefs." Archer nodded. "But he saw it as a rejection of him as my son, as choosing 'the enemy' over my own flesh and blood. It only drove him deeper into their clutches."

Phlox sighed. "Beyond that . . . I can't say. That encounter at the wedding was the first time we've spoken since our estrangement. They've had decades to indoctrinate him deeper into their worldview." He paused in thought. "Still, some things haven't changed. He still resents me. And he's still drawn to Vaneel."

"I thought you said he was jealous of the attention you gave Vaneel."

"Oh, he was. But you know Vaneel, always the champion of the underdog. She instinctively took him under her wing to ease his feelings of neglect. Besides, all our other children were grown or nearly so, while those two were almost the same age. It created a natural bond between them."

"So if Mettus resented you for choosing Antarans over him," Archer observed, "just imagine how he must feel about Vaneel marrying one."

"Yes . . . I suppose I shouldn't be surprised that it brought him into the open." He shook his head. "I've never seen Vaneel speak so harshly to him. Whatever bond they once shared, she's clearly washed her hands of it."

"He brought it on himself, Phlox. He chose hate over family. You did your best as a father, but some people are just lost causes."

"I've often thought so," Phlox admitted. "But still . . . Tullis came back. And today I have an Antaran son-in-law, something both our peoples would've thought impossible just a dozen years ago. So it's hard for me to believe there isn't still hope for Mettus. Maybe . . . maybe what he did today is a way of reaching out. After twenty years of silence, even renewing the argument is a step forward."

Vaneel caught up to them from behind, and Phlox realized he and Archer were no longer trailing the others. "Come on, Dad, you missed the turnoff!" She gestured over her shoulder toward a narrow, tree-shaded side street, into which the rest of the party had already nearly disappeared. "Don't tell me you've forgotten the way," she said as she led him and the admiral back toward it. "It was you and Mom who introduced me to this place, after all."

Archer stared after Vaneel, then threw Phlox an odd look. "You and she—we won't all be . . . together in there, will we?"

Phlox realized what he was asking and laughed. "No, no, Admiral. You know how Denobulan men generally feel about public displays of affection. No, there are private rooms available for the more intimate portions of the evening," he went on as the two of them entered the quieter side street. "The *kaybin* bars provide everything that a romance-seeking couple or group—or individual, for that matter—could possibly desire, including their privacy. The public areas are for food, music, conversation—the kinds of pleasures best enjoyed in a crowd. It's not unlike—"

"Phlox, get down!"

The shock of Archer's weight knocking him to the ground—and of a phased-energy beam squealing in his ear and singeing the side of his head—left Phlox dazed. He heard angry cries, feet pounding, weapons firing. As his hormonal responses to danger kicked in, he became aware of the scene around him. Denobulans in brown jumpsuits with red shoulder patches were attacking the party, firing at them. Archer had already incapacitated one and was now fighting off another. Phlox looked around desperately for his wives and daughter, but he saw that Vesena had led Feezal and Nullim up into the trees for cover. But Vaneel and Thesh had stayed on ground level with Sun-woo, Pehle, Sohon, and Dani Erickson, who lacked the Denobulan knack for climbing. They were sheltering behind a large *voat* tree, which was fortunately too damp from the day's rains to catch fire as energy beams burst against it.

Phlox spotted another attacker creeping out from the shelter of a tree behind him, drawing a bead on Pehle. "Hey! No!" Phlox yelled, unthinkingly running forward into the man's sights. Before the potential consequences of that act could register on his conscious mind, Archer was there, spinning the man around by the shoulder and striking him in the jaw. The firearm went flying, but the brown-clad man retaliated. The attacker must have been half Archer's age, but Starfleet combat training prevailed and the man fell, having inflicted only minor abrasions and contusions upon the admiral.

By now, the police were pouring into the side street from both ends, and the attackers began to break ranks and flee. But one voice cried out: "Keep firing! Death to Antar!"

Mettus's voice.

Phlox saw his son and two other raiders charge forward, guns blazing. The *voat* tree, eaten away by the beams, began to crack and topple, sending the party scrambling from its shelter. Flying wood shrapnel and stray bolts forced Phlox to duck and avert his eyes, and when he could look again, several people had fallen.

Archer arrived beside him, pulling him behind another tree, then crouching and looking for an opening. The police were returning fire against the attackers now, and in moments the man and woman flanking Mettus fell unconscious. Mettus took a more grazing blow to his shoulder and fell, the gun falling from his numbed fingers.

As the police secured the prisoners, Phlox hurried over to the group to assess their injuries. He reached Vaneel and Sun-woo first. "We're fine," she told him. "But I think Dani was hit."

The tall, dark-eyed human was on the ground, bleeding but conscious. Phlox quickly assessed her as Archer knelt beside her, looking worried. "She's been struck by shrapnel from the tree," Phlox said. "It looks minor, but we should have her looked at promptly."

"I-I'm fine," Dani managed to get out. "I'm not . . . gonna lose a fight with a damn tree."

Trusting in her determination, Phlox left Archer to tend to her and checked on Thesh, who had sustained serious burns from a near miss, much closer than the beam that had scorched Phlox's ear. "Get an ambulance for this man immediately," he ordered the nearest constable.

But his voice fell silent as his eyes fell upon the two Antarans. Pehle Retab was sobbing, crying out as if in agony. But Phlox could see that he had not been struck—except by the weight of his father lying atop him. No . . . the full force of the energy beam had burned its way deep into the body of Sohon Retab, once he had flung himself in its path to shield his son. Even from this distance, the doctor could tell that the older man was dead.

Phlox turned stiffly away, stepping toward the police as they took Mettus and his cronies into custody. Behind him, Vaneel, Sun-woo, and Phlox's wives moved in to comfort Pehle and draw him away from his father's body. Phlox left them to it. He was in no mood to offer comfort at the moment. Only a cold anger filled him as he watched a junior constable inform Mettus of his legal rights. Spotting the senior constable, Phlox introduced himself and asked, "Did he fire the shot?"

The constable, a lanky, black-haired female named Lonixa, spoke with the same sympathetic detachment Phlox used when delivering bad news to a patient's family. "At this point it's too early to tell. It was certainly one of these three. Either way, it looked to me like he was the one in charge."

"Which makes him responsible," Phlox replied without overt emotion.

Lonixa gave him a wary look. "The investigation will determine the facts. Believe me, I'm in no hurry to rush to judgment against your son."

Phlox stared coldly at Mettus, who resolutely avoided looking back at him. "Do as you will, Constable. I have no son here."

August 10, 2165
U.S.S. Pioneer

Even forewarned by the distress call from *Vol'Rala*, Malcolm Reed was startled by the composition of the fleet that intercepted *Pioneer* en route to the site of that vessel's capture: a Ware command ship flanked by three Klingon privateers and two Balduk destroyers. He wasn't alarmed; the opposition was significant, but *Pioneer* was accompanied by *Thelasa-vei* and *sh'Lavan*, and Reed was confident they could hold their own if it came to a fight. But he wasn't sure what was stranger to see: the highly territorial Balduk supporting the technology that had enslaved some of their kind, or Klingon privateers allying with other races.

The face that appeared on the main viewscreen was the first hint of a method behind this madness. "Vabion," Travis Mayweather growled at the sight.

The cadaverous Vanotli industrialist stood in the control chamber of the Ware ship, flanked by an alien built much like an ostrich or emu, but with a larger cranium, wide-set eyes, golden-orange feathers, and a hooked, quadripartite beak. *"Captain Reed,"* Vabion said, ignoring Mayweather. *"We meet again. I trust you still speak for your task force?"*

"I'll do more than speak if I have to, Vabion," Reed replied. "Your allies have committed an act of piracy against a Federation vessel. I demand the immediate release of *Vol'Rala* and its crew."

The ratite alien cawed in apparent anger, but Vabion quelled it with a gesture. *"This . . . gentleman . . . is Senior Partner Rinheith Chep of the Partnership planet Rastish. My allies acted on behalf of his world, defending it against an assault that would have devastated their civilization. It is Captain sh'Prenni and her crew who are the criminals here, and they shall be tried according to Partnership law. The crime is attempted genocide."*

The bridge personnel stared at one another in disbelief. "You've hit a new low, Vabion," Mayweather said. "You know now how the Ware devastates worlds. You've seen the evidence. But you'll still do anything to profit off of it."

"The Ware is a tool, Mister Mayweather—only as harmful or beneficial as its users make it. The Pebru used it to devastate worlds, and if you'll recall, the insights I provided you were instrumental in their defeat. But the Partnership is something different." He frowned. *"I prefer to conduct negotiations face-to-face. If you will permit me and Partner Rinheith to board* Pioneer, *we will explain the true situation to you."*

Signaling to Ensign Grev to mute the channel, Reed turned to his first officer. "He's definitely up to something," Mayweather said. "But at least we'd have him where we could keep an eye on him."

"Agreed." Reed turned back and nodded to Grev to reopen the channel. "Very well. But have your escort vessels withdraw before you attempt to board. I won't lower *Pioneer*'s shields otherwise."

"Of course. My only goal is to resolve this matter in a civilized way." Vabion's expression grew smug. *"The question is whether you can say the same."*

"My people foraged and hunted across the plains of our world for uncounted thousands of generations," Senior Partner Rinheith Chep intoned to the gathered personnel in *Pioneer*'s briefing room. "We sang great songs that spread from pride to pride, trading history, lore, philosophy, and myth. We studied our environs as best we could, learned how to thrive within their cycles and evade predators, watched the stars and developed intricate calendars to guide our migrations. From them, we developed abstract mathematics and theoretical astronomy."

The Senior Partner, a member of a species called the Hurraait, sat with Vabion across the table from Reed, Mayweather, and Charles Tucker, with Ensign Grev on hand in the event of translation difficulties and Lieutenant Williams standing watch over the visitors. The final person in the room was Rinheith's aide Fendob, a robust humanoid female with a hairy back and shoulders and a pronounced brow ridge. She appeared quite subservient to Rinheith and barely spoke.

"But there was little we could achieve beyond abstraction," the Hurraait went on, "for, as you can see, we lack the advantages of your kind." He spread his vestigial wings, emphasizing his lack of hands or other fine manipulative organs. "We have enough dexterity in our beaks and tongues to handle rudimentary tools. We could use them for some limited horticulture, for making basic traps for small animals, for the creation of art and mathematical notations. But we could not farm fields or build cities or invent the wheel. We never created a written language, for our society was never complex enough to require the keeping of records. And we never developed more than the crudest medical techniques or any understanding of disease. We were as intelligent as any race, but we were trapped by our inability to build a civilization.

"And then the Ware came. A gift from the heavens that could provide all the tools and medicines and scientific knowledge we could ever hope for. Yes, it demanded payment in raw materials and resources. It took us much time to scrape together enough minerals and rare chemicals to pay for the products of the Ware, but with those products came the equipment to mine more, and in time our prosperity grew. At last, we were able to make our dreams into reality, to use our minds to affect the world rather than merely describing it. We could enlarge our population, fill our world with more and wiser minds to bring greater knowledge and enlightenment. We could even travel through space and meet other species— others who relied on the Ware, making us part of the same community from the beginning, even before we formed the Partnership."

"But sooner or later," Mayweather said, "you must have realized the enormous cost."

"We did come to realize that the Ware demanded sacrifices, yes. For a long time, we and our fellow Partners endured this as a necessary cost of civilization. We developed a tradition of volunteers, brave individuals who gave up their lives for the sake of the majority. Some worlds in the Partnership selected sacrifices by lot instead.

"Yet we studied the Ware, hoping to find a way to modify its programming and free ourselves from this painful trade. It took us generations, but finally, our most brilliant minds found a way to penetrate the data cores and safely revive the sleepers. We still required volunteers to keep the Ware functional, but they need only sacrifice a small portion of their lives, after which they would be replaced by others. By staggering the cycles, awakening and replacing only some at a time, we could maintain the benefits of the Ware continuously without the losses it demanded."

"You understand why we find that hard to believe," Reed declared. "We read about you in the Pebru's historical records. You gave them the Ware, exploited them as processors for it. They were hardly volunteers."

Rinheith lowered his head. "As I said, it took us generations to find a better way. The Pebru were among our early members, centuries ago. Yes, they were victimized by the Ware, but so were all of us at the time. During our search for a better way, the Pebru discovered how to redirect the Ware to target other races. They presented this as the solution we needed, but the other Partners refused to prey on others to spare ourselves. The dispute could not be resolved, and the Pebru severed ties with the Partnership in order to enact their rapacious solution. Once we found our own solution, we offered it to them. But our separation had been acrimonious, and they did not trust what we offered."

"For once, I'm with them," Tucker declared. "We've seen how tightly the Ware holds on to its 'property.' Anyone who gets sprung from a data core gets hunted down and plugged back in."

Vabion looked down his nose at the engineer. "The Ware does not bother to distinguish between individuals any more than you care for the difference between an electronic circuit and its replacement. As long as a new processor is installed to replace the missing one, the Ware is satisfied."

"And what about the damage to the volunteers?" Mayweather insisted. "Loss of memory, cognitive defects, neurological problems . . .'"

"Most of which," Rinheith countered, "can be repaired by the Ware itself. Assuming a volunteer remains long enough for damage to occur at all. We monitor them closely to minimize the risk."

"But the risk shouldn't be necessary. There are other ways to get technology, ways that don't require giving up so much."

"That's the trap of the Ware," Reed added. "It's designed to make you dependent, to give it more of what it needs in exchange for the benefits it provides."

"And yet it has given us an independence we would never otherwise have had. And not only us." He gestured to Fendob with a wing, prompting her to step forward. "As you can see, Fendob is like you, blessed with sensitive fingers and a strong back. But her people are not quite dexterous enough, either in fingers or in creative thought, to invent a sophisticated technology of their own, and they lack sufficient linguistic skills to communicate complex scientific knowledge. On their own, they would have been as incapable of civilization as we were."

"Surely you have recognized the pattern by now," Vabion put in. "I have seen Partnership records of the worlds whose Ware you have neutralized, of the species that occupy them. The Enlesri, a brachiating species with syndactyl forefeet, the digits fused together into a clamplike configuration—excellent for clinging to branches, but ill-suited to fine manipulation. The Nierl, methane-breathers from an environment whose atmosphere will not allow fire to burn. The Sris'si, sentient but blind aquatic mammals. And of course you know of the Pebru. Not one of these species is capable of creating high technology on its own."

"That is what defines and unifies the Partnership," Rinheith went on. "Every one of the Partner species owes its entire civilization to its membership in the Ware community. Through its bounty, we have built cities, enlarged our populations. We have traveled the stars and colonized worlds we could not otherwise inhabit. We coexist with races deeply alien to us, in environments that would kill us without the protection of the Ware.

"Do you not see, Captain Reed? This is the crime of your Captain sh'Prenni and her crew. By shutting down our Ware, she was not liberating us, but condemning us to the loss of our very civilization. And eventually to the death of most of our population."

Reed was reluctant to believe the shocking claims made by Rinheith and Vabion. The Ware thrived on deception and false promises, and any ally of Vabion's—let alone one who employed Klingon pirate crews—was not high on his list of people to trust. Still, he could not deny that every Partnership species encountered so far would have been incapable of developing high technology or civilization on its own—or sustaining what they now had without considerable assistance. He'd seen the difficulties the Pebru had faced in adjusting, and they had at least possessed a modest technological capability without the Ware. How much harder would it be for species with no such capability at all?

Once the Partnership representative and Vabion had returned to their command ship, Reed ordered Grev to contact *Kinaph,* the light cruiser that sh'Prenni had left behind at the planet Etrafso to assist its people following the shutdown of their Ware. Though *Kinaph* was a *Sevaijen*-class vessel of Andorian design, its home port was Arken II, the newest member of the Federation, and its name and most of its thirty-eight-person crew were Arkenite. Its captain, Kulef nd'Orelag, was a tall, pale-skinned member of that species who looked younger than his forty-three years, though he seemed to have aged significantly in the week since they had last spoken. Yet when Reed asked for a progress report on the transition process for Etrafso's citizenry, Captain nd'Orelag was oddly evasive.

"I need specifics, Kulef," Reed told him. "Captain sh'Prenni and her crew are in prison on a Partnership world, awaiting trial for attempted genocide. The Partnership alleges that it's impossible for their civilization to survive without the Ware. I need to know whether there's any truth to their claims."

The Arkenite fidgeted. Even with his *anlac'ven,* the black, inverted-U headband he wore to stabilize his sense of balance away from the magnetic field of his homeworld, he seemed to have difficulty keeping his footing. *"There have been . . . challenges, of course. This was bound to be a difficult process. But we are coping. Sh'Prenni would never have abandoned these people."*

"I appreciate your loyalty, Kulef. But you can best help her by telling us the truth. We need to know what we're facing."

Finally, with great reluctance, nd'Orelag spoke. *"Captain . . . the situation is . . . desperate. The main population of this planet is Enlesri, who are adapted to warmer conditions than are natural for this world. Many are suffering from the cold, though we are doing all we can to restore power to their heating grids.*

"But they have it easy compared to others. There are Nierl here as well, beings for whom the native environment is lethally hot and oxygen is a poison. They have environmental suits that are self-sustaining, but limited in their power reserves. There are also the Xavoth, a fluorocarbon-based species native to an extremely hot planet. Restoring their life support has been a top priority, but . . . we have already lost several thousand." Reed winced. Beside him, Mayweather gasped audibly. On his other side, Tucker listened with disquieting stillness, revealing nothing. *"It's not just life support. They need food, and we do not have enough understanding of their biology to synthesize it. My science teams are attempting to retrieve the data from the Ware's matter-synthesis systems, but the technology is beyond us."*

Striving to understand, Reed asked, "Why are there so many different species from such alien environments, living together on one world?"

"Apparently they migrated here to be closer to their fellow Partnership races and to have fuller access to Ware products. The Ware did not colonize their worlds as it did with the Vanotli or the Kyraw; they were visited by other Partnership races who shared the Ware with them and assisted them in developing technology and civilization."

"And required them to offer 'volunteers' to the Ware in payment," Mayweather said, though his anger was muted. If

Rinheith had spoken truly, then every Partnership world paid the same price for membership.

"Kulef, why didn't you report how bad things were there?" Reed pressed.

Nd'Orelag spoke haltingly. *"I have requested assistance from Flabbjellah. And I've put out a call to the Tyrellians, requesting additional resources and personnel to aid in the transition."*

"'Aid in the transition'? Captain, from what you're telling me, you're in the middle of a planetwide disaster! You should have notified me as soon as the magnitude of the problem became evident."

The Arkenite straightened with pride. *"Captain sh'Prenni charged me with the task of aiding the people of this world. I cannot fail in that obligation."*

Reed began to realize where this was coming from. The dominant Arkenite culture had a deep-rooted belief in the importance of debts and obligations, and Reed knew from experience that nd'Orelag shared that belief. "I know that sh'Prenni championed your captaincy, Kulef. You feel indebted to her, don't you? You didn't want to admit that her methods might have been . . . excessive."

"My debt is not merely to her," nd'Orelag said. *"The Andorians sponsored our membership in the Federation. Even though they could have been vindictive about our struggle for independence from their empire, they chose to set aside the past and embrace us as partners. And Starfleet, the Federation—you welcomed us as well, and brought me to where I am today. I cannot be disloyal to that."*

"Captain, the first duty of any Starfleet officer should be to the truth," Reed said tightly. "Your obligation was to report the crisis on Etrafso immediately, not attempt to downplay it at the cost of lives!"

Nd'Orelag lowered his bulbous, bald head. *"Then I have failed in my duties. I misunderstood. Perhaps my people are not ready for Federation membership after all."*

"Let's not go that far," Mayweather offered. "You made a mistake. That's part of the learning process."

"And frankly," Tucker put in, "this isn't about you. It's about all those people you need to be helping."

"Yes," the *Kinaph* captain replied. *"I have incurred a profound debt to them. I must put it right."*

"We all must," Malcolm told him. "But first we need to figure out what 'right' means here."

U.S.S. Endeavour, orbiting Denobula

Archer paced *Endeavour's* briefing room, trying to absorb what Malcolm Reed had related to him over the wall screen. The signal from *Pioneer*, relayed as it was through multiple widely spaced subspace amplifiers, was blurry and laden with interference, but at least it was in real time. On the other half of the screen was a much clearer transmission from Admiral Shran on Andoria. The chief of staff of the Andorian Guard did not pace, but the way his antennae folded back against his white-haired cranium revealed his fury. Only Captain T'Pol, who stood by the end of the briefing table nearest the screen, seemed calm in light of Reed's revelations.

"How did it get to this point?" Archer demanded. "Why didn't sh'Prenni wait to gather more intelligence about this Partnership?"

Shran looked surprised. *"You can't be blaming her!"*

"I'm not blaming anyone, Shran. I'm just trying to get answers."

"You have to understand, sir," Reed said. *"We've seen the horrors*

the Ware leaves behind, the way it enslaves and ruins entire civilizations, even while they believe it's doing them a favor. The Partnership's protests just sounded like more of the same to her. They would have to any of us. If she's guilty of anything, it's excessive zeal to help people. The same zeal that's always made her an asset to Starfleet." He hesitated. *"Still . . . we can't deny that there is some truth to the Partnership's claims. We may have gravely misjudged the situation here."*

"You can't know that," Shran said. *"Yes, you've seen disruptions on one world, but you only have the Partnership's word about conditions elsewhere. Maybe Thenar was right—maybe these no-tech races are the fodder that the Partnership's true masters feed to the Ware. Maybe they even created the Ware."*

"Nothing the task force has observed would suggest that, Admiral," T'Pol put in.

"Maybe, but they've given us plenty of reason to question their integrity. Partnering with Vabion. Hiring Klingons and mercenaries. Not to mention their ties to the Pebru."

"I share your concern, Admiral Shran," said Reed. *"They want me to turn over . . . my consultants Collier and Akomo for their role in creating the shutdown protocol—something I'm vigorously resisting—but they're working with Vabion even though he's just as responsible for its creation."* Pioneer's captain sighed. *"Granted, though, Vabion had them over a barrel. We could shut down the Ware, so he offered them a line of defense we couldn't deactivate."*

"In exchange for working Ware of their own to use back home!" Shran pointed out. *"Can you imagine what the Klingons could do with drone battle fleets that advanced?"*

"We do have a defense against Ware, Admiral," Reed replied. *"Besides, these are privateers, not Imperial soldiers."*

"That doesn't mean they won't do serious harm. We've seen how virulent the Ware plague can be. If it's allowed to spread at all, it could engulf the Federation in time—not to mention all those other worlds we sent you out there

to protect." Shran's antennae thrust forward belligerently. *"We need to wipe it all out, without exception. If these Partnership people depend on it, find them an alternative. The one they're using is unacceptable."*

"Shran," Archer cautioned. Waiting until he was sure he had his friend's attention, he said, "We've seen what happens when we meddle in other cultures without fully understanding them. Even with the best of intentions, it can go seriously wrong."

"I know the rhetoric, Jonathan. The old Vulcan party line—let them develop at their own pace, make their own mistakes. If you ask me, that was just an excuse to do nothing to help others in need. The High Command certainly interfered when it was in their own interests."

T'Pol retained her cool, but Archer could tell she did not appreciate the Andorian's words. "Granted that the High Command abused the noninterference principle on occasion," she said, "but are you suggesting that we should be just as arbitrary?"

"I'm suggesting that we live up to what the Federation stands for. We don't sit idly by when people are in need. That's the whole reason your task force is out there, Captain Reed. Thenar did what she was supposed to do."

"That's as may be, sir," Reed said, *"but the upshot is that she and her crew are in prison awaiting trial. If there's a debate to be had over the ethics of her actions, that's the place to have it—before the Partnership, so we can try to convince them that she acted with good intentions. Perhaps even convince them that there's a better way than dependence on the Ware."*

"That presupposes," T'Pol said, "that the Partnership's justice system will be fair. Even if that is generally the case, civilizations often become unreasonable when they feel their survival or way of life has been threatened."

"For what it's worth," Reed said, *"they have agreed to delay the trial until sh'Prenni's representative can gain sufficient familiarity with Partnership law."*

"Her representative?" Archer asked.

Reed grimaced. *"Me, sir. Apparently, as the one responsible for sh'Prenni and her crew, I'm to be the advocate on their behalf. I tried to convince them that, as the person responsible, I should be the one on trial instead of her. But apparently the Partnership is organized according to a complex network of interdependencies and shared responsibilities, so that logic would be effectively useless if they tried to apply it here. In their system, the ones who actually committed the act must be the ones put on trial."*

"And they expect you to become an expert in their laws quickly enough to offer a valid defense?" a skeptical Shran asked.

"I've been assigned a Partnership legal advisor as co-counsel. And the trial isn't scheduled for at least another six weeks." He paused. *"They've requested that the Federation send a diplomatic representative to negotiate a treaty agreement. They want assurances that we'll honor whatever verdict they deliver."*

Shran sneered. *"Diplomats. We should be sending you more battleships, so you can get sh'Prenni and her people out of there by force."*

"You talked about our principles, Shran," Archer said. "We should at least try to give their system a chance to work fairly before we write it off."

"Even if it means sacrificing one of the finest officers I ever trained?!"

"With respect, Admiral," Reed said, *"would Captain sh'Prenni expect any less from us?"*

Shran subsided, unable to deny it. After a momentary lull, Archer traded a look with T'Pol, saw that they were in agreement, and spoke. "I'll send *Endeavour* your way immediately, Malcolm. I'll make arrangements to have a diplomatic team join them en route."

"Thank you, sir."

"But in the meantime, you're to continue your search for the Ware's origin world. Shran is right—the Ware is still dangerous. Even if the Partnership is on the level, even if they truly have found a way to coexist with the Ware, their use of it could still pose a threat to others." On the screen, Shran looked up and met Archer's gaze, but did not go so far as to convey gratitude. Shran could keep up a good sulk for months. "Everything we've learned about this technology suggests it was created as a trap, a tool to exploit other races. If we can prove that was the intent behind the Ware all along, it might convince the Partnership that sh'Prenni was acting in their best interests after all."

"I agree, sir." Reed looked uncertain. *"If nothing else, it would keep my engineering team out of harm's way. But as Thenar's assigned advocate, I'm obliged to remain in the Partnership myself. And I'd prefer to stay close to Thenar in any case."*

"I understand." Archer smiled for the first time in this conversation. "Why not turn *Pioneer* over to Travis? Give him some practice sitting in the big chair. I'd say he's earned his shot by now."

Reed smiled as well. *"He has indeed, sir. It's a splendid idea."*

Archer's eyes darted to the other half of the screen. "Anything more to add, Shran?"

"Not for the moment," the other chief of staff replied. *"I want to let this simmer for a while before I really give you a piece of my mind."*

With a wry smirk, Archer said, "I look forward to it. *Endeavour* out."

Shran disappeared from the screen, and Reed followed after signing off. T'Pol turned to the human admiral. "I'll have Hoshi call the crew back from the surface."

"Do that. But first, I want to speak to Phlox personally."

Within a few minutes, *Endeavour*'s doctor was on the screen, and Archer filled him in on the situation. *"I knew* Endeavour *would not be able to remain indefinitely, Admiral,"* Phlox said. *"However, I fear I will be unable to accompany it this time. I'm still needed here, as a* witness in the legal proceedings against Mettus. And I need to be with my family in these trying times."

Archer shook his head in sympathy. "I can't imagine how you must feel, Phlox. Your own son . . ." The investigation had confirmed that it was indeed Mettus's weapon that had struck the killing blow against Sohon Retab.

Phlox's expression was tightly controlled. *"I appreciate the sentiment, Admiral, but that . . . individual is my son in only the strictest biological sense. I gave him every chance, tried for years to get through to him, but this . . . this is what he has become, through his own choices. My only concern now is for Pehle and Vaneel . . . to help them work through this crisis."*

Archer could not disagree with the doctor's sentiment. As harsh as it seemed, Mettus had brought it on himself with his atrocious act. "I understand, Phlox. I just wish there were something I could do."

"Well . . . the Antaran people have just lost one of their most respected statesmen at the hands of a Denobulan," Phlox said, his tone clinically detached. *"I know that neither of our worlds is a Federation member, but depending on how the Antarans react, we may need to request a neutral mediator."*

"Do you think that likely, Doctor?" T'Pol asked.

Phlox shook his head. *"I don't know, T'Pol. I'd like to think that the Antarans wish to preserve the peace as much as we do. Our own Curia has already made it clear that they in no way endorsed this horrible crime and are receptive to extraditing Mettus for trial on Antar."* His voice faltered for a moment. *"I suspect that should be enough to ameliorate any diplomatic tensions. Still, if you could monitor the situation, just in case . . ."*

"Of course, Phlox," Archer said. "Don't you worry about that. Just take care of your family."

The doctor nodded. *"I do apologize, Captain, for leaving you without my services for such an important mission."*

"The cause is more than sufficient," T'Pol told him. "I shall simply have to locate a substitute."

Phlox brightened, in the sense that a dense fog is brighter than a thunderhead. *"If I may make a suggestion . . . Jeremy Lucas is as accomplished an IME physician as I am. His credentials in interspecies medicine are impeccable, and he's currently between assignments. He's also charming company. I couldn't recommend a better person."*

T'Pol tilted her head in acknowledgment. "Your endorsement is sufficient, Doctor. Provided Doctor Lucas is amenable, I have no objection."

"Excellent." Phlox foundered, unsure what else to say. *"Well. Thank you both for attending the wedding. I'm sorry it couldn't be a more positive memory for you."*

Archer smiled. "The *wedding* was great, Phlox. That's the part I choose to remember. Thank you for having us."

Phlox blinked his eyes several times, and hastened to sign off before he betrayed any more emotion. T'Pol turned to Archer and raised an eyebrow. "We seem to find ourselves amid a glut of prosecutions."

"It never rains but it pours," Archer agreed. "Let's just hope that only one of them returns a guilty verdict."

8

LOKOG STARED THROUGH the wide viewport and grinned as he watched the automated manipulators of the Ware spaceyard beyond assembling drone after drone with untiring efficiency. "With these," he said, "the Klingon Empire will soon belong to the *QuchHa'*!"

Daskel Vabion looked at him sidelong. "Or perhaps the *QuchHa'* will belong to the Ware."

The Klingon scoffed. "Do not worry, businessman. If the drones develop an appetite, we will have plenty of *HemQuch* to sate them." A rough chuckle followed. "And if we run out of them, there are always the humans."

"Take care," Vabion advised. He was not sure why he wasted his advice on this boorish pirate, although he supposed the man had a drive he could identify with. "Ambition is admirable. Ruthlessness is often necessary. But cruelty tends to backfire. I learned that the hard way. Look how many of the Ware's users have turned against it when they learned the true price of its use. It's a poor product that inspires such customer disloyalty." He gazed around him at the automated station on whose indulgence he, Lokog, and so many in the Partnership relied. "Why do you think I seek the Ware's creators rather than simply using their product? I will be at no other's mercy, person or machine. This technology is astonishing, but it has a fatal design flaw."

"The ability to kill is not a flaw."

Vabion resisted glaring at the Klingon, aware that it could provoke a primitively violent reaction. "I meant fatal to it, and to the purposes of those who wish to profit from it. Once I find its creators and obtain their secrets—with or without their cooperation—I will show them a better way of applying this technology."

Lokog sneered. "So that no one will be harmed anymore? You sound like a human."

"No, Lokog. So that its owners' control of the market will not be harmed due to the blatant shortcomings of their product. Feed off the consumers, yes. That is what they're for. But do it in a way that makes them think you're serving them."

"That sounds no different from what the machines already do."

"Except that the machines do it *badly*. They ruin or alienate their customers and thereby lose business. Have I not been explaining this to you?" He paused, reminding himself to temper his irritation. No matter how this primitive provoked him, he would not succumb to the same lack of control. "The difference is one of judgment. The judgment I can provide to perfect their flawed business plan."

The Klingon examined him. "I respect your ambition, businessman. But do not underestimate the value of cruelty." His jaw tightened. "You are used to being on top. It has been long since you have had to struggle and suffer beneath the heels of those who would hold you down. Perhaps you have forgotten how satisfying it is to put them in their place—to see them squirm beneath your own heel."

"My ambitions are not so base as that," Vabion insisted. Then he gave a slight sigh. "But I do not begrudge you yours. I have fulfilled my part of the bargain," he said, gesturing toward the drone fleet quickly taking shape on the other side of the port, "and you have fulfilled yours. What you do now is no concern of mine. Once I master the Ware, I will have no shortage of other clients."

"If Starfleet does not destroy it first," Lokog countered.

"Starfleet is reasonable. If I show them I have overcome the Ware's more predatory aspects, they will no longer be compelled to destroy it. They are an intelligent people who value progress and knowledge, even if their ethics occasionally blind them to opportunity. If I salve their ethical concerns sufficiently, I am sure they will come to appreciate the Ware's value. They may even become valued customers of mine."

"And how can you be so sure you can manipulate them?"

Vabion smiled. "Because they are idealists, while I am a pragmatist. That gives me the advantage. They will throw enormous resources into an act of charity, however misguided. I invest only in my own profit. And that is why I will inevitably win."

Lokog laughed and clapped Vabion on the back, staggering the Vanotli and earning a glare of irritation. "To victory!" the Klingon crowed.

Vabion stared out at the Ware, seeing power in it far beyond the raw force that Lokog craved. "Yes," he murmured. "Always."

August 22, 2165
Partnership planet Cotesc

When Reshthenar sh'Prenni was brought into the visitation area, she brightened at the sight of Malcolm Reed, cried his name, and ran over to clasp his shoulders firmly—hard enough to make him wince. "Forgive me," she said, letting go.

"I'm just so glad to see you. And I forget how little you are in person," she added, tousling his hair.

His urges to laugh and fidget were equally strong, so he gave in to them both. If anything, he was grateful that the Partnership did not forbid direct physical contact between prisoners and visitors, trusting the Ware's sensors to detect any contraband. "It's good to see you too, Thenar. I wanted to come much sooner, but—"

"The damn Partnership, I know. I've screamed at them for hours about my rights, and all I get are excuses."

"How's the rest of your crew?"

"They're fine. Well, they're in cells, but they're no worse off than I am." She gave his shoulders another squeeze. "Please tell me you're here to get us out."

Reed sighed. "Thenar . . . the reason we've taken so long to come here is that we've spent the better part of the past two weeks helping to provide emergency relief to Etrafso—the planet whose Ware you deactivated."

The Andorian captain stared at him. "Emergency? I know what they've claimed about the consequences there, but I took it for propaganda."

"I'm sorry," he told her. "But I've been there. Seen for myself, and heard the details from Kulef, who's been dealing with it even longer."

Her antennae folded back in alarm as she studied his expression. "Tell me."

So he did. It was at once a relief to unload the burden of the horrors he'd seen and an ordeal to force sh'Prenni to hear the full consequences of her actions. "Things are getting under control now," he finished. "Other Partnership worlds have provided relief supplies and evacuated the Nierl and Xavoth surv . . . survivors to safe environments. The Tyrellians have agreed to set up a regular supply line to help sustain the rest of Etrafso's population. It'll be some time before things are normalized there, but . . . at least the deaths have stopped."

It was some time before she spoke. "I thought . . . I knew losing the Ware would be a hardship, but I thought, let those spoiled, self-indulgent people have to work a little for the needs of life. It'll teach them character. Admiral Shran always taught me, it's only the things you struggle for that have any real value. He really drilled that in, since everything always came so easily to me." She shook her head, her antennae curling downward. "I was starting to think this was easy too, letting myself get careless. I should've investigated more closely before I acted."

Reed moved forward and laid a hand on her shoulder. "You thought you were helping them. We've all seen the damage the Ware has done."

She stared. "You think I don't know that, Malcolm? Of course this is ultimately the Ware's fault! One more atrocity to lay at the feet of its creators, when we find them." She paced the austere but spacious visiting area. "But I let myself get drawn into one more layer of their deceptions and manipulations. They've made their clients so dependent that you can't even free them without killing them! And I should have seen that. I should not have underestimated the enemy." Growling through her teeth, she spun and pounded the wall with one sharp, ferocious blow. The guard, one of the burly humanoid Monsof, stepped closer.

"Thenar," Reed cautioned in a soft voice. She turned, saw the guard, and gathered herself. The human continued: "I didn't come here only to give you bad news. The Partnership says you'll have a fair trial. And I'm to be your advocate. I'm working with their legal counsel to study their laws and prepare a defense. And *Endeavour*'s coming with a diplomatic team. They may be able to negotiate an agreement for your release."

Her antennae took on a skeptical twist. "And the Partnership swears they'll play fair—even while they cozy up to Vabion and Lokog. Do you believe them?"

"Two weeks ago, I would have said no. But now . . . I don't think they saw any other recourse. They need the Ware to survive, more than we ever could've anticipated."

"They're still addicts, Malcolm. And addicts will do anything if their supply is threatened." She took a deep, controlled breath. "How's *Vol'Rala*?"

"Still under impound. They won't let us see her."

"Well, that's something," she said. "I was afraid they'd just destroy her. The poor girl took an awful pounding from the Klingons, but she survived. I would've hated to think she'd end so ignominiously." She started pacing again. "Though I'm not much happier to think about *Vol'Rala* just sitting there somewhere, her wounds untended, with no one to keep her company."

"Who knew you were such a romantic?" Reed asked. "Though I suppose ships named *Enterprise* will do that to you."

"Well, it could be worse," she said. "The Klingons could've taken her as a prize ship. I'd have blown her cores myself before I let that happen."

She stopped pacing and faced Reed gravely. "Still . . . what matters most is my crew. If you're my lawyer, then my instructions to you are not to worry about me. I'll take responsibility for everything, just so long as they let my crew go free."

"Thenar, don't be noble. There may still be a way to get you out. Travis and *Pioneer* are still searching for the Ware's creators. If we find them, if we can prove their intentions are malevolent, maybe we can convince the Partnership you were acting in their defense."

Her piercing green eyes met his intently. "You think good faith matters to the dead? No, Malcolm. Whatever my intentions, my methods were reckless. My crew was just following my orders, but those orders were issued in excessive haste." She smirked. "Admiral Archer cautioned me once—he said I was paradoxical because I was a creature of impulse, yet I tended to act at warp speed. It confused me until I learned English better; the pun doesn't work in Andorii. Perhaps I got so distracted by the wordplay that I missed the underlying point."

Sh'Prenni moved closer, looming over Reed. "Now, though, I'm the distraction. You mustn't make this about me. Yes, find the Ware's creators, prove to the Partnership the trap they've fallen into. But do it for *them*, not for me. Convince them to free themselves. Convince them the Federation will help. Let me accept my fate as a show of good faith."

"I can't ask that of you, Thenar!"

"*I'm* asking it of *you*. If that's what it takes to save my crew *and* the Partnership, I'm willing to pay that price. Would you do any less?"

He met her gaze with sadness, but with the deepest of respect and admiration. "I haven't told you how honored I am to call you a friend."

She clasped his arms again. "You've shown me. Every day. It's been an honor to serve under you, Captain Reed. I only wish I could have been as fine a captain as you."

"We're well-matched as captains, Thenar," he told her. "Because we both refuse to give up on anyone under our command."

"No!" Ramnaf Breg lunged at sh'Prenni after the captain relayed the news about Etrafso to the rest of her crew, gathered together for their daily exercise session. Most of them were in Ware-gray tank tops and shorts, barely standing out from the institutional-white walls that surrounded the yard and the overcast sky above. The blue of their skin—and the orange of Breg's and the ruddy brown of Banerji's—provided the only color to the place.

But Breg's face now flushed bright red as Giered Charas and Zoanra zh'Vethris grabbed her arms and held her in place. "How could you?" the young Arkenite screamed at her captain. "I thought Starfleet were liberators! You made us mass murderers! Monsters!"

"Control yourself, child!" Charas barked. "Even in these rags, she is still your captain!"

"It's all right, Giered," she said. "She's just saying what a lot of us are thinking."

"But it . . . it was all a mistake," Hari Banerji said. "We couldn't have known. Could we?"

Breg whirled on him. "And you. You're as much to blame as she is! You made the shutdown code into a weapon. Something we could fire without thinking, without stopping to ask! You and your pinkskin impatience!"

"That's enough!" Charas roared. "No one insults Hari but me, have you got that?"

Breg slumped, her fury spent, and Banerji threw Charas a look of appreciation that the first officer did not acknowledge in any way. Zh'Vethris took the weeping Arkenite in hand and led her away to a more private corner, stroking her smooth-skinned head and kissing her gently.

"Banerji is right," Charas went on to the rest of the crew. "We are not to blame here. The Ware is a scourge to the galaxy. These Partnership people are its victims whether they admit it or not. Their dependence on it was their own mistake."

"Yes," Tavrithinn th'Cheen spoke up, stepping forward. Even in his drab exercise clothes, he carried himself with all the dignity of his clan. "Let us not forget, we are on a mission to defend the Federation against an unfeeling enemy. Any collateral damage falls into its ledger, not ours."

"How are we defending the Federation?" Silash ch'Gesrit countered, his engineer's skepticism fully engaged. "We're two moons' travel from the nearest Federation border. We're meddling in the affairs of total strangers."

"We are extending the benevolence of our protection to our neighbors."

"They didn't ask us to get involved."

"Enough," sh'Prenni said. "You're to stop thinking in terms of 'us' right now, and that's an order. I gave the commands. The responsibility of all of this, right or wrong, is mine."

They immediately gathered closer. "Don't ask us to abandon you, Captain, because we won't," Charas insisted. "We stand together or not at all."

"He's right, Thenar," Banerji said. "We're more than a crew. We're a family." He glanced sadly toward Breg. "Or a *sia lenthar*, as Ramnaf would say."

"I'm not sure she'd extend me that courtesy anymore," sh'Prenni told the elderly human. "Or that I deserve it. The impatience was mine. And so are the consequences."

Th'Cheen sighed uncomfortably. "If Zoanra weren't . . . otherwise occupied . . . I imagine she'd offer some pithy insight reminding us that we've survived worse together."

"Would she?" ch'Gesrit asked. "Considering that what we're enduring is trivial next to what we've inflicted?"

"I can still hear you!" zh'Vethris's voice carried loudly from across the yard. "And my pithy insight is to shut up, stop

fighting, and just hold on to each other! The rest will sort itself out in time! And we'll need each other no matter what
happens!"

Despite the incongruous roar in which it was delivered, the
young navigator's sentiment was hard to deny. The crew stood
together quietly, uneasily, for some time afterward.

But they stood together.

August 24, 2165
Nierl home system

Samuel Kirk stood on a plain of hardened lava, staring down
at a set of bone fragments half-embedded in the surface beside the boot of his EV suit. The fragments were in the rough
shape of a humanoid arm. A few dozen meters beyond, a jag-
ged chunk of wall, now gray with dust but no doubt white
underneath, jutted out of the ground like a misplaced grave
marker.

"The Manochai's bombardment was thorough," said
Tefcem var Skos, Senior Partner for the planet Etrafso. The
large-eyed, rodentlike Enlesri stood by Kirk in an EV suit that
barely came up to the chest of Valeria Williams, who stood
behind them both. "After all, Ware can self-repair from even
a small surviving portion, so they made sure to leave no fragments large enough. This moonlet was once entirely covered
in Ware habitations, supporting over a hundred thousand
Partners of half a dozen races. The Manochai did not stop
blasting until the surface was molten. Over the many rotations
that followed, as the surface cooled and hardened, fragments
blasted into space gradually re-accreted. Most sank into the
molten crust, or pulverized on impact once it had hardened.
But some . . ." He gazed wordlessly at the remains before them.

He did not need to say anything more about the near-featureless white globe that loomed above the horizon—actually thousands of kilometers below the captured asteroid on which they stood, orbited by the asteroid while orbiting a mighty Jovian in turn. The spherical moon had been the home-world of the Nierl—a larger version of Titan, with a thick crust of water ice and a methane-ethane atmosphere. Hundreds of millions of Nierl had lived on its surface in vast urban complexes made of Ware. Now the atmosphere was all but gone, the surface a nearly pure, smooth layer of ice—refrozen after the Manochai's bombardment had melted the planet's crust into an ocean. Planetary genocide had never looked so pristine.

"You are not the first to mistrust our peace with the Ware," var Skos went on after a time. "Others have decreed that the Ware must be exterminated for the good of all—all except those who rely upon it. The Manochai did not even let the populace evacuate, for our only ships were Ware. They would have done the same to all of us . . . had the Ware not manufactured enough drones to turn back their fleets at last." The lithe brachiator lifted his head in its compact white helmet. "I hear now that the Klingons conquered the Manochai—nearly wiped them out when they resisted, and turned the survivors into servitors. Only the first of the services they have done for us."

"The Klingons only serve themselves," Williams told him. "You'll learn that lesson the hard way if you aren't careful."

"Better their selfishness than the aggressive benevolence of you or the Manochai."

Var Skos clearly felt no love for the Federation. Kirk knew that Reed's orders were to attempt to persuade the Partnership of Starfleet's good intentions, but that was evidently a lost cause where this Senior Partner was concerned. His homeworld had suffered badly in the wake of *Vol'Rala*'s actions, however benevolent their intent.

Kirk had found it surprising that a Senior Partner of an entire planet, particularly one in the throes of a disaster, would be free to escort the *Pioneer* team like this. But apparently the Senior Partners were more like Federation councillors than chief executives, representing their planets in the Partnership's collective debating and decision-making process. Their Ware-based lifestyle was so automated that it required little hands-on attention as a rule. Of course, Etrafso's current emergency was another matter. But evidently var Skos was the subordinate half of a mated pair, speaking on behalf of Etrafso's real Senior Partner, his "overmate" Wylbet Skos. She had remained to tend to their world in its crisis while he served as her spokesperson abroad, representing Etrafso in the proceedings against *Vol'Rala*'s crew. He had volunteered to supervise *Pioneer*'s officers as they conducted their investigation for the defense.

Williams turned away from the grisly ejecta before them. "You've made your point, Partner. Are we done here?"

Var Skos glowered at her for a bit, but he could contrive no excuse not to lead them back to the Ware transport ship that had brought them to the moonlet. Williams took Kirk's arm, guiding him across the surface with care. His boots were magnetic, but he had little experience walking in gravity this low.

As they trudged carefully along arm in arm, Williams switched to a private comm channel and spoke far more softly than she needed to with vacuum surrounding them. "It's not guilt," she said.

"What?" In the context of the dreadful aftermath around them, it was initially unclear to Kirk what she was talking about.

"I'm not just taking an interest in you because I'm guilty about Rigel. I mean, I'm not guilty about Rigel. I mean . . ." Her sigh was a sharp burst of static from his speaker. "It's not about Rigel at all. It's about . . . the year since then. Keeping my distance, waiting for you to be ready to be friends again . . . it made me realize how much I missed having you around." She stopped walking and turned him by his shoulders until their eyes could meet through their helmet visors. "Sam . . . we just click, in a way it took me a long time to recognize because it was so . . . effortless. I'm used to a certain amount of drama and turbulence in my relationships, so I didn't quite realize what I was feeling until . . . until it went away.

"Sam . . . Oh, I couldn't have chosen a worse time to talk about this," she said, rolling her eyes. "Let's just say I really want to continue this conversation someplace where we can take our EV suits off."

Kirk winced. Once, this conversation would have been the stuff of his fantasies—present circumstances notwithstanding. Now, he hated that she'd made herself vulnerable to him when he had to let her down. "Val . . . it's kind of amazing to me that you feel that way. You're an amazing woman, and you're way out of my league."

"Don't say that. You're smart, and kind, and strong in ways I didn't understand before I met you. And you've got the sexiest—"

"Val." He closed his eyes. "You're also an armory officer, and you're very, very good at your job. And that job . . . sometimes it forces you to choose your duty over your personal feelings—your relationships. Like saving a stranger instead of a friend."

"Sam . . ."

"No, listen—it's not that I still blame you for that. It's

that . . . it made me understand that your duty will always come first. Val, I would love to be involved with you. I've wanted that since the first time we spoke. Probably sooner," he admitted. "But if I were . . . I'd never know when you might have to put someone else's safety ahead of us. And . . . I'd never know when you might have to risk your life . . . even lose your life . . . to save someone else."

He stepped away, pulling free of the anchor she provided. "I'm sorry, Val. I'm just not brave enough to take that kind of risk. I don't know if I could bear it."

Var Skos had finally noticed that they'd stopped. "Is something wrong?" his voice intruded on a separate channel.

Williams stared into Kirk's eyes a moment longer, then turned away sharply and switched back to the wider channel. "Nothing's wrong," she told him. "Minor misunderstanding. Let's just get the hell off this rock."

9

LANETH HAD THOUGHT this would be a bad day when she'd learned that the ship had run out of *qa'vIn* beans. The bitter, black brew they produced may have been an invention of the weakling humans, introduced to the Empire through the looting of Terran cargo ships, but Klingon agronomists had bred a far more potent strain of the beans, making them a stimulant worthy of a warrior when properly brewed. Yet today, Laneth and the rest of her twenty-five-Klingon crew had needed to settle for the instant stuff, which was nowhere near strong enough for warriors who needed to stay alert to danger. The entire crew had gone through the day surly and irritable . . . but only half as much as they should be.

That, she had thought, was the cost of being *QuchHa'* in today's Empire—forced to exist on the margins, to settle for limited and low-quality resources. Even crews in the service of the few powerful *QuchHa'* nobles, like her own patron General K'Vagh, needed to make do with the meager leavings cast aside by the *HemQuch* majority.

But now, as her ship convulsed and groaned around her, as plasma conduits burst and spewed a heady mix of fumes into the air, as her gunner lay dead atop the burning ruins of his console and Engineer Muqad struggled to reroute weapons control to Laneth's command throne, she knew that the cost of being *QuchHa'* was far dearer than she had realized. Her Bird-of-Prey and the small battle fleet it led were all that stood between the *QuchHa'* colony on Mempa VII and total obliteration. And it was beginning to look as if it might be a good day after all—a good day to die.

To be sure, there were better ways to die than as a near-defenseless sitting target. But even that could be an honorable end if the cause was worthy. The people of Mempa VII had done nothing to warrant annihilation. Councillor B'orel had encouraged their persecution and harrassment by *HemQuch* from the neighboring Mempa VIII colony in order to provoke retaliation, then had claimed that the Mempa VII colonists had launched an insurrection—even that they had conspired with the native *jeghpu'wI'* on Mempa II, using those frail bipeds' skill in genetics to engineer a new version of the Qu'Vat virus and turn all Klingons into *QuchHa'*. A lie, of course; if the Mempans' science had been capable of that, the *QuchHa'* would have used it to cure their affliction rather than spread it further. But B'orel's power on the Council was based on his exploitation of the Klingon majority's hate and fear toward the victims of the Qu'Vat mutation, and he hoped that he could win the chancellorship by rallying the Empire behind a war of extermination against them. Starting with Mempa VII, so that the evidence of his lies would be turned to glass and ash along with every populated area on the planet.

Laneth cursed Arbiter Daqel for his slowness in picking the new chancellor. The weakling claimed it was to allow fair consideration of all candidates, but it had only created more instability within the Empire as factions like B'orel's acted on their own to bolster their status. B'orel had even implicated

General K'Vagh in the alleged insurrection, scuttling her patron's bid for the chancellorship before he had even completed the declaration of his achievements in the *ja'chuq*—achievements that easily eclipsed B'orel's. And civilians like the Mempa colonists were paying the price for B'orel's political maneuvering.

It was the Klingon way not to fear death, but a pointless death raining down from above, based on a lie and delivered against those with no opportunity to defend themselves, was without honor for either side of the battle. By sparing the colonists to fight on, and more importantly by standing against the lying, dishonorable *HemQuch* who sought to annihilate them for selfish gain, Laneth and her crew would earn their own place in *Sto-Vo-Kor*.

At least, she hoped they would. She strove not to believe B'orel when he argued that the human taint within them would forever bar them from the fields of the honored dead. Surely his own actions proved he had little understanding of honor. But at least he was still a true Klingon.

No—she quashed the doubt within herself. If nothing else, Laneth felt an obligation toward the *QuchHa'* people. She had been one of the original subjects of Doctor Antaak's Augment experiment at the Qu'Vat colony, under K'Vagh's supervision. The idea of injecting herself with human DNA to become stronger had seemed ludicrous to her, even knowing that it was genetically augmented; but she had obeyed the general's orders and undergone the treatment. At first, the increase in strength, aggression, and sensory acuity had been heady, but the loss of her beautiful ridges and fangs had been a high price to pay. She had soon learned that there were deeper changes as well, for when she and the other four survivors of the experiment had attacked the

Starfleet vessel *Enterprise* to prevent its interference, Laneth had felt fear for the first time in her adult life. She had been sickened by the human taint within her—at first figuratively, then literally as the mutagenic virus had become deadly and nearly killed her and her brother Augments. When Antaak and his Denobulan consultant had finally devised a cure, by cruel fate it had stripped the five of them of their superior abilities, while leaving them and countless others with the taint of humanity upon their faces—and, she had believed, in their hearts.

In those first bleak months following the Augment crisis, Laneth would have agreed with the likes of B'orel that she and all the other victims of the mutation should be put out of their misery. She would have taken her own life if General K'Vagh had not forbidden it. Though K'Vagh had been made *QuchHa'* himself, a sacrifice he had made to save Laneth and millions more from the dishonor of death by disease, he had refused to compromise his own honor, becoming a relentless advocate for the *QuchHa'* under his command and all others like them on Qu'Vat, Mempa VII, and every other world ravaged by the virus. His own son Marab, whom Laneth had once scorned as weak for allowing himself to be beaten by *Enterprise*'s human crew, had died honorably in a battle against *HemQuch* bigots, proving that his heart was Klingon after all.

Marab's sacrifice had convinced Laneth that the weakness she had felt within her heart had been merely the result of her own fear that the human element within her would make her weak. K'Vagh had reminded her of the Sixth Precept of the *qeS'a'* and the words of Kahless that went with it: "All Klingons have weaknesses. Warriors know to hunt their weaknesses and cut them out." B'orel now twisted that very precept as his excuse to slaughter the *QuchHa'*, but Marab had shown Laneth what it truly meant: that it was the effort to destroy the weakness within her own heart that made her Klingon. Battle against others was merely a crucible to burn away the weaknesses within oneself.

Laneth took comfort in that thought as enemy fire continued to tear into her Bird-of-Prey, hoping that, by defending this colony, her fleet could prevent B'orel from gaining a victory that would propel him closer to the chancellorship.

At first, that had seemed an attainable goal. B'orel's commanders were dull-witted sorts employing typical, straightforward orbital bombardment tactics, parking themselves over the colony towns in forced synchronous orbits and sending down torrents of disruptor fire. This had made it easy enough to counter them, whether by striking at the sitting targets or moving beneath them to block their fire. Laneth's fleet had managed to take out half the *HemQuch* ships while losing only one of their own, and that one merely a five-person *Tajtiq*-class fighter of the type Laneth had commanded in that long-ago attack on *Enterprise*, back when all this had started.

Her hopes had been dashed when enemy reinforcements had arrived, thanks to B'orel's alliance with Ja'rod, son of Duras. Although his father had been disgraced and defeated by Archer of the selfsame *Enterprise*, Ja'rod had spent the subsequent years seeking to rebuild his fallen House's reputation through victory in whatever battle presented itself. He had managed to accrue enough wealth, lands, and glory through his conquests to make it likely that he could win a seat on the High Council, particularly if he had the patronage of the next chancellor. Ja'rod had come personally to join the attack on Mempa VII, and Laneth had found that, however much she might scorn his opportunism and *HemQuch* sense of entitlement, his battlefield victories were well-earned. His ships employed a more imaginative bombardment strategy, taking advantage of orbital dynamics to send torpedoes on spiral paths around the planet to strike from multiple directions, running the defenders ragged in their attempts to intercept the fire. Once B'orel's remaining ships had followed this lead, Laneth had seen no choice but to let the Mempan colonists endure some hits while her ships targeted the enemy fleet directly. Her brave *QuchHa'* had inflicted serious losses on the foe, yet at the cost of equal losses on their own side—and the enemy had more and larger ships to spare. A battle of attrition would inevitably be resolved in the foe's favor.

Laneth had lost most of her fleet now, and *Krim*'s own weapons were nearly silent, forcing her to block the enemy's fire with her ship's shields for as long as they lasted. It was little more than a token gesture . . . but a Klingon never retreated. The only ground she would let herself or her men fall back to was the endless battlefield of *Sto-Vo-Kor*.

She tried to take comfort in the thought that she had earned an honorable death, that she would soon be reunited with Marab and her father and brothers. But a trace of doubt lingered. She could not be sure what awaited her upon her death. All she could be sure of was that she was losing. She had failed in her mission to protect the colony. She may have failed to prevent B'orel's chancellorship and the extermination of her people. What comfort was honor in the face of that? What she needed was victory, and her last chance at that had been taken from her.

Along with a decent cup of *qa'vIn*.

She was just about to cut loose with a string of curses against the inevitable when a new tone sounded from the barely functioning tactical station. "Commander!" cried its operator Kholar, one of the few surviving personnel on the bridge. "A wave of new ships is incoming!"

"Theirs or ours?" Laneth demanded.

"I do not know, Commander! I do not recognize the configuration. They are small, but these energy readings . . . Odd . . . I read no life aboard!"

She stared. "They must be shielded."

"Not that I can detect. Commander, now they decelerate. The sheer force of it! It would crush a crew, even with our best dampers."

"Never mind that! What is their course?"

"They are closing . . ." Kholar gasped and straightened. "On the enemy fleet, Commander! They are opening fire!"

The main screen was cracked in two, so Laneth had to watch the tactical display over Kholar's shoulder as the strange, boxy gray ships unleashed powerful energies against the fleets of B'orel and Ja'rod, battering down their shields. Three *HemQuch* ships were blown from orbit before they could redirect their batteries from the planet to the new attackers. That put paid to the last of B'orel's forces, but Ja'rod's ships managed to return fire effectively, tearing large holes in the newcomer ships. But to Laneth's astonishment, the new ships seemed to repair themselves and continue the attack. More and more of Ja'rod's vessels were rendered unto dust, and Laneth found herself bitter that she could only watch this glorious battle—and hopeful that the newcomers were truly on her side, rather than some new invaders who would turn their attention against her next.

The battle was resolved when Ja'rod's flagship turned tail

and ran, vanishing into warp with one other survivor and lowering Laneth's opinion of the man enormously. So much for Klingons never retreating. Still, he had survived to fight more battles, which made him better off than Laneth had been a moment ago. After all, her fleet was holding its ground only because they had no means to do otherwise.

"Commander," Kholar said, "they are hailing."

She let out a breath. Hailing was not shooting. "Respond."

A *QuchHa'* visage appeared on the screen, but it was not one she knew. He had the long hair that Defense Force regulations no longer permitted *QuchHa'* males to wear, but it was scruffy and unkempt, as was the leather vest he wore instead of a military uniform. Behind him was a bridge that seemed to be that of an old corvette, probably decommissioned decades ago. *A privateer?* she wondered.

"*I am Captain Lokog,*" the Klingon said, offering no patronymic. "*I control the fleet that has come to your rescue. And in timely fashion, it seems.*"

She looked down her nose at him. "An earlier arrival would have been preferable, Captain. I am Commander Laneth, daughter of Garjud, in service to General K'Vagh."

"*Then I would like to speak with your general and offer him my services. I control many of these ships.*" Lokog leaned forward and smiled. "*And with them, we* QuchHa' *can conquer the Empire!*"

Laneth smiled back. Perhaps fate had sided with her after all.

August 27, 2165
U.S.S. Endeavour

T'Pol had been staring into her meditation flame for some moments before she realized that Hoshi Sato was giving her a puzzled look from its other side. The captain had invited her friend to sit with her so that they could discuss a matter of some delicacy, but she had fallen into silence thereafter.

"Forgive my unaccustomed hesitation, Hoshi," she said. "I have been uncertain how to broach this topic."

Sato looked uneasy, but replied, "Take your time."

"I have waited more than long enough. There is a secret that I and others have been keeping for a considerable amount of time—a classified matter that circumstances now require me to reveal. It is also . . . a personal matter. The reason I have waited this long to broach the subject was that it required consultation with a certain individual who . . . cannot be communicated with openly."

T'Pol suppressed a surge of frustration as she gazed at the meditation flame. For years, she had been able to commune telepathically with Trip during meditation, due to the unusually strong mental bond they had somehow forged as a consequence of their intimate relations during *Enterprise*'s mission to the Delphic Expanse. This ability to communicate across interstellar distances had saved both their lives on more than one occasion, and had facilitated their pursuit of a relationship despite their need to avoid open interaction. Trip had often said that his awareness of her in his mind was the primary thing that kept him emotionally stable in the course of his work for the secretive group that he called Section 31.

But three months ago, something had changed. V'Las had captured her and Archer and attempted to employ forced mind-melds to program them into doing his bidding. T'Pol had endured a similar mental assault years before, and the prospect of being subjected to another had been profoundly disturbing—terrifying, to be quite frank. She had reached out to Trip's mind, seeking comfort . . . and had been unable to make contact. This had not been unprecedented, given the intermittent nature of their connection; and she had been rescued soon thereafter, so she had given the matter no further thought. Yet in the weeks that followed, the bond had not resumed. She knew from *Pioneer*'s reports that Trip was alive and well, and the coded communications they had exchanged when the opportunity arose had given no hint of any problem. She had been reluctant to broach the issue overtly through such a detached method of correspondence, or to burden Trip with her concerns while he faced the crisis posed by the Ware. She had considered the possibility that *Pioneer*'s distance might be too great to allow their connection to form. Theory suggested that telepathy was based in quantum entanglement and thus independent of distance, but in practice, it seemed to become increasingly difficult as distance increased—at least in Vulcans, who were primarily touch telepaths.

Yet *Endeavour* had been drawing closer to *Pioneer* for two weeks now, ferrying one of the Federation's top diplomats, Ambassador Boda Jahlet of Rigel, to negotiate with the Partnership of Civilizations on behalf of *Vol'Rala*'s captain and crew. Thanks to Chief Engineer Romaine's creative efforts to boost *Endeavour*'s speed and Ensign Ortega's deft selection of the most expedient route, the starship was now more than halfway to the rendezvous point, within the range of distances that had allowed T'Pol to communicate with Tucker in the past. And still there was nothing. The loss of contact was becoming a source of concern for her. Could something Trip had experienced in Ware space have closed his mind to her— or made him turn away by choice?

At the moment, there was nothing she could do to address that question. She turned her thoughts back to the here and now. "I also hesitated for another reason. This revelation could be upsetting. I had hoped to think of a way to soften its impact for you."

Sato laughed nervously. "Whatever it is, you're just making it feel worse at this point. You should probably just tell me."

"Very well." She took a deep breath. "Hoshi . . . Trip Tucker is alive. We falsified his death a decade ago so that he could pursue a deep-cover mission in Romulan space. He is currently aboard *Pioneer* as the civilian engineering consultant Philip Collier."

The human's reaction was unexpected—a deep sigh of relief. "I knew it! Oh, and here I was worrying what terrible thing you were going to tell me."

T'Pol frowned. "You were aware that Mister Tucker was alive?"

"Well, I didn't exactly *know* . . . not in the sense of having proof, or anyone telling me. But I figured it out long ago."

The captain studied Sato, struck by all the ways this woman continued to surprise and impress her. "When did you realize the truth?"

"I guess it was at the Battle of Cheron. Remember how I recognized the coded transmissions from that agent calling himself Lazarus? Then I saw how—forgive me—how agitated you were about rescuing Lazarus from his escape pod."

"I need not forgive the truth," T'Pol admitted. "It is an accurate assessment."

"And Admiral—well, Commodore Archer seemed pretty intense about it too. So I realized Lazarus had to be someone important to both of you. You and he didn't really have a so-cial circle in common outside the *Enterprise* crew." She shrugged. "And the name 'Lazarus'——to someone like me, who thinks about words and their origins all the time, it indicated some-one who'd come back from the dead. And that brought some of the oddities about Commander Tucker's 'death' into focus for me. Not right away, but when I thought about it afterward, I saw how it all fell into place."

"Impressive deduction," T'Pol said. "I am relieved at your equanimity. When Commander Mayweather learned the truth, he was justifiably angry at the deception. It took him some time to come to terms with the situation."

Sato looked down at her lap, pausing to choose her words. "I was upset too. Hurt that I and so many others who cared about Trip were being lied to, made to grieve when they didn't have to. It felt very cruel." T'Pol could not dispute her words. "But over time, I came to think it must be even harder on Commander Tucker. And on you." She cleared her throat. Hoshi was one of T'Pol's closest friends, and was aware to some extent of the nature of her relationship with Charles Tucker before his ostensible death; but by the same token, she understood T'Pol's reluctance to discuss such matters. "I real-ized you wouldn't be doing this if there were another choice. That it must be for a good reason."

This time, T'Pol was less sure of her agreement. The rea-sons for Trip's continued affiliation with Section 31 were nebulous to her, and there were times when it appeared they were nebulous to Trip as well. But she did not wish to trouble Hoshi with those doubts.

"Why did you say nothing?" she asked. "Naturally, you would not publicly discuss classified information, but you could have broached the subject in private."

"It wasn't my place. I figured you must have had good reasons for keeping Commander Tucker's survival a secret. If you didn't want to talk to me about it, then it would've been an invasion of privacy to bring it up myself. Besides, I didn't really know, I just guessed. So it was better just to stay quiet and hope that, someday, the need for the secret would pass."

T'Pol pondered her words for the duration of a deep breath. "Unfortunately, that need has not passed. Mister Tucker's work is clandestine by nature, and it is important that we help him maintain his cover. Of those involved in this mission, only you, I, Malcolm, and Travis are privy to Philip Collier's true identity."

Sato frowned. "What about Elizabeth? She'd probably recognize him if she saw him again. And there are a few others aboard who worked with him on *Enterprise*. Plus, Ambassador Jahlet met him at the Coalition talks."

"It is preferable that we not reveal Trip's survival to more people than necessary. It may be possible to arrange duty rosters to prevent them from interacting directly. Or perhaps we can convince Lieutenant Cutler that there is simply an unusual resemblance between the two men. She was enlisted on *Enterprise* and did not interact with Trip as frequently as his fellow officers. As for the ambassador, she met him only as a member of a large group a decade ago. And it is unlikely they will have much need to interact."

They spent some time discussing their approach to maintaining Tucker's cover once the ships rendezvoused. T'Pol could tell that Sato was not happy about the situation. Still, sharing the truth with her had lifted a weight from them both. More than ever, she was grateful for Hoshi's friendship and support.

Though it still troubled her that Trip's support was so elusive.

August 29, 2165
U.S.S. Pioneer

"I hope you've been able to get more from the Partnership than just guilt trips, Sam," Travis Mayweather said to the young historian, whose sandy-haired visage was displayed on a wall monitor in *Pioneer*'s situation room. Captain Reed and Lieutenant Williams flanked Kirk on the screen, while Mayweather was joined around the situation table by Charles Tucker and science officer Rey Sangupta.

"I have, sir," Kirk replied. *"I've gathered every bit of data and lore I could find in the Partnership's records about their origins, the order in which their founding worlds received the Ware. That gives us a sense of the direction it originally came from."*

"But you couldn't find a reference to its origin?" Sangupta asked, a frown wrinkling his handsome bronze features. "The Partnership has been benefitting from the Ware for centuries. You'd think they'd have wanted to know who created it."

"They have looked. I've found references to a number of searches for the origin world. But they were never able to locate it. I'm doing my best to scan the records for some clue, but maybe that's a job for a science officer, Rey. Hopefully you can find something I've missed."

"There's something else, Travis," Reed put in. *"Apparently we aren't the only ones asking these questions. Just about everyone we've spoken to has told us that Daskel Vabion visited them first."*

Mayweather grimaced. "I knew it. He's still trying to crack the mysteries of the Ware for himself. I don't like the idea of him beating us to the answers. He's done enough damage without them."

"Don't worry, Captain Reed," Tucker added. "We're keeping an eye on Vabion's ship, thanks to a tracking program I installed in the long-range sensors. If he finds a lead before we do, we'll be able to follow him."

"That's good," Reed said. *"But following him may not be enough. I'd prefer it if you could beat him to it."*

"We'll do our best, sir," Sangupta affirmed, "but there are a lot of variables. The other task force ships have helped us piece together a pretty good map of the Ware's spread, but there are multiple loci, signs of the Ware being pushed back and then re-expanding. I've been running simulations, produced a few candidates for origin sites, but it'd take time to check them all out. And there's no way to know in advance if they're the original origins—so to speak—or more false alarms like the Pebru and the Partnership."

"If you have candidate sites, then I suggest you begin searching them. We'll keep looking on this end."

Mayweather saw Tucker flinch briefly. No doubt the engineer had been hoping to be on hand when T'Pol arrived with *Endeavour*. But he hid it quickly, thanks to his years of training in intelligence work. Mayweather could imagine how strong the emotion had to be for it to slip out. He sympathized, but he could do nothing about it. He needed Tucker's expertise on hand in case they found the origin world, and it might jeopardize Tucker's secret identity if he acknowledged the man's desire to wait for *Endeavour*.

Besides, there were bigger concerns. "I have to wonder, sir," Mayweather said to Reed, "if maybe the Partners aren't telling you all they know about the Ware's origins. After all, if we find its builders, that might give us the answers we need to stop the Ware."

"I thought of that," Kirk said. *"One of the first things you learn in studying history is to read defensively, to be skeptical of your sources. Lots of people lie, or have unconscious biases. But so far, the Partners seem to*

be remarkably forthright about their relationship with the Ware. Like they're determined to prove to us that they've got it licked, that we've been misreading the whole affair. They're so sure they have right on their side that I don't think they feel the need to hide anything."

"If you ask me," Tucker said, "those are usually the people you need to watch out for the most."

10

September 3, 2165
Mempa VII colony

"YOU EXPECT US TO HIDE behind machines?!" General K'Vagh loomed over Lokog, shouting in disapproval at the privateer's proposal. "True Klingon warriors fight our own battles!"

Lokog refused to let himself be intimidated by the general's bulk or his deep, roaring voice. After all, K'Vagh needed what he had to offer, even if the fat old veteran was loath to admit it. The very meeting room in which they stood, within the public hall of Mempa VII's most intact remaining city, survived only because of the commodity Lokog bargained with.

And the leading nobles of the *QuchHa'* resistance must have recognized that, for two of them had come all the way to this border world to meet with him. K'Vagh was one; the other was Kor, son of Kaltar—a proud, robust *QuchHa'* from a Great House, which he had renamed from the House of Kor to the House of Mur'Eq a decade ago, in order to remind others that he and his kin were direct descendants of the mighty Emperor Mur'Eq, no matter their current appearance. According to Captain Laneth, who stood nearby at the head of several of her officers, these two were among the staunchest advocates for *QuchHa'* standing and power within the Empire, Kor out of the nobility's sense of entitlement and K'Vagh out of devotion to the Klingons under his command (among whose number Laneth proudly counted herself). Both men recognized that their people were being slaughtered, that they had no hope of victory against the ridged majority without something to reorient the battlefield.

Knowing this, Lokog was able to meet K'Vagh's bluster with a confident smile. "With respect, General—how many battles do you personally lead? Was it not Laneth and her men," he went on, gesturing to the striking, bronze-haired female, "whom you sent to fight and die in your name?"

"Do you call me a coward?!"

"Of course not, General. I merely point out that not all battles are fought one-on-one. You cannot be everywhere, so you must strike at your enemies from a distance. You send Laneth to defend the colony. She sends torpedoes to hunt and kill its attackers. Ware drones are no different. They are simply another weapon to wield against our enemy. A weapon that will grant our people the victory that has been elusive until now."

Kor shook his head grimly, stroking his full, thick beard. "I do not like it. Yes, privateer, we send our soldiers to battle for us. But they are warriors like ourselves, with their own honor. By allowing them to spill their blood in noble combat, we grant them honor and thereby earn it ourselves. Mindless drones cannot win honor on a battlefield; they reduce combat from an art to a mere chore. If I send these machines to kill my foes while I sit back in comfort, how can I tell my boy Rynar that I have guarded honor above all?"

Laneth stepped forward. "That is easy to say, Lord. But B'orel and Ja'rod also talk of honor to justify their lies and their massacres. The *HemQuch* claim they have more honor than we do, claim that burning helpless farmers and infants from the safety of space is an act of honor, merely because they have the power to define honor in whatever way suits them."

Kor's eyes flashed. "You speak dangerously, woman."

K'Vagh growled. "Mind your tongue, son of Kaltar. Her title is captain." Despite his reflexive defense of his officer, the general seemed nearly as offended by her words as did Kor.

Laneth went on. "I recognize, Lord Kor, that it was not honor that saved this colony, any more than it was honor that nearly destroyed it. It was superior strength and ruthlessness. We were completely outmatched by the *HemQuch* forces—until they became outmatched by the Ware.

"Power, not honor, is what shapes our fates. Without power, without new weapons, the *QuchHa'* will not survive. These weapons Lokog provides will let us win a place of power for ourselves within the Empire. Perhaps even its rule. And then we will have the luxury of quibbling over honor."

Kor started forward, but K'Vagh's thickset arm held him back. "I know her words rankle. Her tongue has always been her sharpest blade. But its aim is true. Our people are not in a position to argue among ourselves. We need to be united in our goals if we are to earn survival. And we need whatever advantage we can gain. The *HemQuch* do not fight honorably, so they do not deserve the consideration of being fought honorably. Let us treat them as they treat us: as an obstacle to be swept aside. Then we can restore true honor to the Council and to Klingon society."

After some consideration, Kor nodded. "Very well. We shall employ this Ware. But I fear that if we grow too comfortable with winning by any means, then we may lose sight of our nobler principles."

"If you want to die for your principles, go ahead," Laneth told him. "I choose victory as my principle."

Her warriors backed her up in her call for victory: *"Qapla'! Qapla'!"* K'Vagh and finally Kor joined in the chant, but Lokog could tell they did so grudgingly.

For himself, Lokog thought that Laneth had the far wiser perspective. Honor was just a word, an excuse Klingons used for doing whatever they wished. He had lost his wealth, his ship, and his place in the Empire, forced to scrounge on the fringes as a pirate because of those who defined honor purely as a property of the bone structure of one's forehead. So what was honor to him? No—Lokog craved victory, just as Laneth did. And he had found, in his years on the fringes, that victory could be gained only by those willing to use any means at their disposal to win.

Maybe that should be the Klingon way from now on, Lokog thought, catching Laneth's eye and wondering what means would be necessary to conquer her.

September 7, 2165
U.S.S. Pioneer

"There you are, Collier," Olivia Akomo said as Charles Tucker entered *Pioneer*'s engineering lab. "I've been looking over the Partnership's software hacks."

Tucker found her parlance a bit old-fashioned, but he figured that was an occupational hazard of working for Willem Abramson—the current alias of a man Tucker knew to be far, far older than he appeared. *Poor Olivia,* he thought. *That's two of us whose real names she doesn't get to know.* "And?"

"And they seem pretty sound," the civilian engineer replied. "Based on what we've deciphered so far of the Ware's programming, these are pretty effective workarounds."

"As far as we can tell," Tucker countered. "We still haven't been able to break through to the Ware's kernel program—and neither has the Partnership. Whoever designed this stuff, they were fanatical about secrecy."

"Well, you should know."

"The point is, we don't know if the Ware's really being fooled or is just playing possum. Lulling the Partnership into a sense of complacency."

"For hundreds of years?"

"Nothing's more patient than a machine."

"Damn, you sound paranoid even for a spy."

He resisted the urge to glance around furtively, aware that they were alone. Akomo had necessarily been aware of his clandestine purpose from the beginning, when he had come to Abramson to request forged credentials as a member of his cybernetics firm and to solicit Akomo's expert assistance on the mission. He had never revealed the existence of Section 31 to her, but she knew he worked for some branch of Federation intelligence. Yet she had reliably kept his secret from *Pioneer*'s crew, despite her disapproval of his methods. Perhaps it was because they'd developed a good working relationship as fellow engineers.

"Try to think a little more optimistically," Akomo went on. "What if we're wasting our time trying to find the Ware's creators? Maybe we've found all the answers we need already. Maybe the Partnership found them for us—found a way to get all the benefits and luxuries the Ware provides without having to sacrifice a single life."

"People still have to sacrifice."

"A few months out of a lifetime. Sure, it doesn't sound pleasant, but neither does jury duty or paying taxes. There were countries in the past where citizens were required to serve in the military for a couple of years. One of the Martian colonies drafted random citizens into its legislature for a year, rather than let career politicians make the decisions. Is this really so much worse? Especially considering all it gives them in return?"

"It's not the same. None of those things is the same as having control of your mind taken away from you—being reduced to a cog in a machine, not even able to think for yourself. You saw what being forced back into the Ware did to Travis. How he and all the others took the first chance they could to get away from it."

"When they were forced, yes. Doing it by choice makes a huge difference."

"Not enough of one. There are better ways. Someday we'll have computers powerful enough to do all these amazing things without needing to enslave living minds. Maybe Abramson's neural circuitry'll make that happen. We just need to be patient enough to get there on our own."

Akomo shook her head and laughed. "Look at you—the champion of morality. Quite a change from the black-suited company man who skulked in the shadows and blackmailed my boss into giving his help."

Tucker winced. That had not been one of his finer moments—discovering the scientific miracle of a man who had lived for thousands of years and threatening his exposure to force him to cooperate. But it was not the first moral compromise he'd needed to make in the name of Federation security as Section 31 defined it, and he doubted it would be the last.

She studied him, tilting her close-shorn head. "That actually bothers you, doesn't it? Hm. Maybe you've been playing engineer so long that you're forgetting how to be a spy."

He thought about her words for quite some time. *Maybe. But is that such a bad thing?*

September 14, 2165
Partnership planet Avathox

T'Pol stood inside a Ware-manufactured environment suit, watching closely as a team of Xavoth worked to revive one of their people and remove her from her berth within a Ware central data core—while another team worked alongside them to prepare another Xavoth to take her place. Normally, T'Pol would not have entrusted herself to a life-support garment of Ware manufacture, but in this case, there had been no alternative; Starfleet EVA suits were inadequate to withstand the extreme heat, pressure, and acidity of the Xavoth homeworld's atmosphere. The conditions on Avathox were comparable to those of Venus in the Sol system, albeit with greater reserves of fluorine, sufficient to support the type of fluorocarbon-sulfur biology that was capable of thriving in these temperatures.

Alongside T'Pol were Captain Reed, his armory officer Lieutenant Williams, and one of Williams's security men, as well as Ambassador Boda Jahlet, a pale, craggy-featured Jelna-Rigelian woman who had shed her traditional mantle of wooden beads to fit into her own environment suit. Also present were two Senior Partners, the rodentlike brachiator Tefcem var Skos and the ratite avian Rinheith Chep, the latter of whom was accompanied by his hominid aide Fendob. All were similarly accoutered in Ware environment suits tailored to their distinct anatomies. Reed, for his part, had witnessed an equivalent exchange of processor volunteers weeks before, in less extreme conditions than this. But once *Endeavour* had arrived, T'Pol and Jahlet had insisted on seeing the procedure for themselves. According to Rinheith, the Avathox facility had been the most convenient one with a revival scheduled in the near term. When T'Pol's first officer, Thanien ch'Revash, had questioned the necessity of risking such hostile conditions, the Hurraait representative had reacted with surprise. Apparently the Partnership's citizens considered this kind of movement among extreme environments to be routine, facilitated by the advanced life-support technology the Ware provided for them. T'Pol had found that intriguing.

The Xavoth were a flying species, averaging nearly two meters long with torpedo-shaped bodies and stubby delta wings, more than sufficient for lift in this thick, buoyant carbon dioxide atmosphere. Three pairs of slender limbs, ending in three-digited appendages serviceable as both feet and hands as needed, descended from the underside of the body, able to fold flat against it in flight. They were among the more dexterous species within the Partnership, limited in technology more by their inhospitable environment than their anatomy. As T'Pol watched, two Xavoth experts, a doctor and an engineer, perched on their hindmost limbs while using their others to detach the neural interface and feeding tubes from the comatose Xavoth on the berth between them, an individual whose wings were wrapped tightly around its body and limbs so that it somewhat resembled an ear of Earth corn. Despite the volunteer's compactness, T'Pol recognized that the berth was larger and more ergonomic than the bare slabs she had observed thirteen years ago during her rescue of Travis Mayweather from the Ware repair station that had captured him. Also, the entire data core facility appeared more clean and inviting, allowing for the profoundly alien needs and aesthetics of the Xavoth. It was clearly a place that was visited routinely, unlike a typical Ware data core.

Even so, the Partnership technicians worked briskly and with an air of calm alertness. T'Pol could understand why. According to the task force logs as well as her own one-time experience, the Ware possessed vigorous physical and digital security systems to resist any form of tampering. Normally, any intrusion into a primary data core would be objected to strenuously by the automated systems. Anyone who attempted to access a core would be summarily beamed away, and any who circumvented that and attempted to remove the living processors would be met with aggressive retaliation upon their exit, pursued relentlessly until the liberated "components" had been retrieved. T'Pol knew this security was not infallible; she had personally disabled the repair station's transporters during Mayweather's rescue. But she also knew that the Ware was capable of self-repair. That the Partnership had managed to bypass or spoof the programming sufficiently to allow this exchange of volunteers at all, let alone maintain it on a continuous basis on more than a dozen worlds, was truly impressive. Yet the hushed, vigilant haste with which the technicians proceeded was a reminder that the underlying threat of the Ware had not been eliminated, only tempered. Jahlet noted this in more poetic terms: "Like trying to remove a cub from the bower of a sleeping raptor-wolf."

The thought prompted T'Pol to step closer to the new Xavoth volunteer, a female named Bexa-Xak. (All Xavoth she had met so far identified as female. T'Pol had not yet inquired about the apparent absence of males, aware it might be an offensive question.) "You are certain you wish to do this?" T'Pol asked.

The Xavoth had little in the way of a readable face; the species relied mainly on an echolocation node and chemo-sensor tendrils to perceive its environment, and had only small, nearsighted eyes on the underside of its forward tip. But T'Pol could recognize the assurance in Bexa-Xak's body language. "It is with pride that I offer myself for the benefit of my fellow Partners," she replied. "I have awaited this opportunity for years."

"And you are fully aware of what will happen to you? That your mind will be subordinated to a mechanism, your will and consciousness suppressed, your brain and body subjected to harmful stresses?"

Bexa-Xak turned toward her. "All my life, I have shared in the blessings the Ware gives us. When I nearly lost my first litter, the Ware healed me and ensured that they were born alive and healthy. A few months of my life are the least I can offer in repayment."

"Do you not at least wish to wait to ensure that Hakev-Tal is well before you take her place?" T'Pol continued, naming the volunteer currently being revived.

Rinheith Chep came alongside them—merely to get T'Pol's attention, since they could all hear one another clearly through their suit comms. Fendob remained where she was, though her eyes followed Rinheith's every move. "That is not an option," the Hurrait Partner told T'Pol. "As you know, the Ware is not designed to release its processors. Our ability to circumvent its security relies on the rapid replacement of re-awakened volunteers. We will need to install Bexa-Xak in the berth before we will be able to leave with Hakev-Tal."

"So you just expect her to trust that it'll be safe?" Valeria Williams asked.

"I do not." A brief shudder ruffled his downy orange feathers. "I offer myself as evidence. I was a volunteer for Ware service eight years ago. I did my term as a processor, contributed my brainpower to the operation of our society, and recovered without permanent harm."

"Before you became a Senior Partner?" T'Pol asked.

"In between my two terms in that role." Rinheith tilted

his birdlike head to peer at her sharply. "If you expected that the elites of our society exempted ourselves from the selection rolls, you were mistaken. We could not call ourselves Partners if we did not take on the responsibilities of that title." He glanced toward Bexa-Xak. "Or the risks."

"Yes," the Xavoth added. "I was informed of the risks when I volunteered, Captain T'Pol. There is a slight chance, even with the best screening, that I may emerge with damage to my neural conduits. There are even deaths—rarely, but they do happen.

"But it is not as if I am free from risk in my daily life," she went on. "At any time, I could be caught in an acid wind-storm or buried in a rock melt. I could be taken by a predator that got past the security drones. If anything, I will be safer in here, with my condition constantly monitored and doctors ready to assist me at any time."

"If we did not take this slight risk as individuals," Tefcem var Skos added, "then all our people would be deprived of the Ware's bounty, completely vulnerable to starvation, disease, predators, and ignorance. This is the fate that you would wish upon us. So do not pretend your compassion for our volunteers is so great. Not when you would attempt to instill fear in Bexa-Xak at the moment when she most needs reassurance."

T'Pol took his point and schooled herself to silence. The captain realized she had been provoked by an emotion—her distaste at the idea of mental invasion and control, a remnant of her recent ordeal in V'Las's custody. Yet Bexa-Xak's words made it very clear that she was submitting voluntarily. If T'Pol was concerned for the Xavoth's mental autonomy, then it was incumbent upon her to respect that choice. Whether the same choice would continue to be required for Partners in the fu-ture was a question that would not be resolved here.

The remainder of the procedure went smoothly. Once the doctor and technician were ready to awaken Hakev-Tal, they laid Bexa-Xak on an identical pallet and administered a sedative. When Hakev-Tal's neural implant was disengaged, the Ware sounded an alarm and an automated warning that "theft of primary data core components" would not be permitted. Jahlet, who had never heard a Ware warning announcement before, was startled; Williams and the guard grew more alert. But the transfer team took the repeating announcement in stride as they efficiently swapped out the two pallets and attached the neural implant to Bexa-Xak. A tense moment elapsed before the warning subsided, but the team had already begun the careful process of inserting the life-support tubes that would sustain the Xavoth during her months of service.

Rinheith and var Skos allowed T'Pol to scan Hakev-Tal's biosigns and neural activity, comparing them to the baseline scan she had taken of Bexa-Xak earlier. As far as she could tell, the recovering volunteer was awakening normally, still weak but with no signs of lasting damage. When Hakev-Tal spoke, it was to thank the Partners for taking care of her. Rinheith and var Skos did not allow the Starfleet personnel or Jahlet to speak to her directly, not wishing to confuse her, but Rinheith asked for their benefit: "How was the service period for you? Do you recall anything of your time within the Ware?"

"No," the Xavoth said after a moment's thought. "I drifted to sleep, and now I wake. I feel weak, though . . . as if I had flown halfway around the planet."

Rinheith issued what may have been a chuckle. "I would give much to know what that feels like, my friend," he said, shrugging to indicate the nonfunctional wings encased in his environment-suit sleeves. "But I have been where you are. They will take good care of you while you regain your strength."

While half the medical team remained to ensure Bexa-Xak's smooth transition, the other half led Hakev-Tal through the makeshift hatchway that the Xavoth engineers had managed to install in the bulkhead of the data core, taking care not to dislodge the sensor interference modules around its frame. "We should leave with them," Rinheith advised, "so that the breach does not remain open for too long."

Rinheith exited the core first, assisted by Fendob, but var Skos remained behind, watching the Federation contingent warily and exiting after the last of them. The party proceeded along a familiar, white-walled corridor, though the dense air created a reddish tinge in the near distance. Jahlet stroked the wall surface with a white-gloved hand. "Remarkable," she said. "That this material can withstand so many extremes of temperature and atmosphere. I thought Rigel unparalleled in the diversity of its environments and peoples; I see now how limited my perspective was."

"Indeed, the robustness of the construction material is extraordinary," T'Pol said, "particularly considering that this corrosive atmosphere would dissolve nearly all metals. The technology that created the Ware must have been formidable indeed." Meeting Jahlet's pale eyes, she could tell that the ambassador read her subtext: such technology would be difficult to counter.

But Jahlet turned her attention to Rinheith, in the evident hope that individuals could be more amenable to persuasion. "Partner Rinheith," the ambassador asked, "why did you not mention your term as a Ware processor before?"

The Hurraait's body language was difficult to read, due as much to his alien anatomy as to his heavy environment suit, but the interruption in his gait indicated that the question had provoked an emotional response. "It is not a pleasant thing to dwell on," he admitted. "We serve for the good of all Partners, but it is a strain upon the body and mind. My recovery was slow and difficult. And when I awoke, I learned that Gondob, the Monsof who had been my Hands since my earliest days, had died of old age." He extended a wing to brush Fendob's back. "Fendob, his daughter, was a great help and comfort during my recovery, but being required to miss his final days was the one sacrifice I wish the Ware had spared me from."

T'Pol noted the uneasy reactions of Reed and Williams. She gathered that they perceived the Monsof's service to the Hurraait as a form of slavery. But watching Rinheith and Fendob, T'Pol recognized that the Hurraait were as helpless without the Monsof's dexterity as the Monsof were without the Hurraait's intellect. If the Monsof had wished to escape or even dominate the Hurraait, they would have been physically capable of doing so with ease.

Perhaps Reed was aware of this as well, for his next words were otherwise directed. "You chastise us for lacking compassion. But is the Ware really so much better? So benevolent that it preys upon you, drains you to the death unless you trick it into letting you go? So merciful that you have to watch in fear at every moment that it might catch on to what you're doing and turn on you?"

They entered a lift, and Reed continued. "Have you really achieved a stable symbiosis with the Ware, or have you just found a way to appease a predator? You said it yourself, you'd be helpless without it. That gives it all the power. You may have found a way to make the best of a bad situation, but that doesn't mean there aren't better options. There are societies out there that would help you without demanding your mental subjugation in return."

"Your Federation?" var Skos countered as the lift began to rise.

"Yes," Jahlet replied simply.

Reed added: "Or the Tyrellians, the Menaik, other neighbors in this region."

"We have seen what our 'neighbors' think of us. The Manochai, the Guidons, the Silver Armada, all have sought to 'liberate' us from the Ware and reduce us to our former primitive existence, or total dependence upon them."

"How," T'Pol asked, "is total dependence upon the Ware any better?"

"Because the Ware is neutral. It is a mechanism, operating without volition or malice. It is a force of nature, one that gives and takes without prejudice."

"But what about the Ware's creators?" Reed countered. "They designed this system, its traps, its lures and deceptions. They set it loose upon the galaxy to prey on others."

"Then where are they? Why have they not come for us? We have never seen them. We have only seen races like the Silver Armada and the Federation."

"We aren't like those others. We want nothing from you beyond your participation as equals."

Exiting the lift brought them to the airlock where their atmospheric transport craft was docked. The Starfleet personnel had been reluctant to entrust themselves to the Ware transporters, and both T'Pol and Reed had been intrigued by the opportunity to explore a Venus-like environment, hence this more conventional mode of travel—if anything in these conditions could be called conventional.

"The Federation," Jahlet explained as they stepped into

the airlock, "is an alliance of diverse worlds joined in mutual interest. Multiple species cooperate and share knowledge and culture, much as you do here in the Partnership. Our societies are very much alike, with similar ideals. You would be welcomed as members of the Federation, and would share in its benefits equally, as my own Rigel system has done."

"So you say," var Skos replied. "And yet these others wear the same uniform as those who attacked our Ware without warning, without regard for the safety of the people of Sris and Etrafso and Rastish. Why should we expect more consideration from your state than any other?"

There was little to say in response to that, and little opportunity as the dense atmosphere was replaced with one suited to Minshara-class conditions, allowing the party to remove their environment suits. Rather than risk provoking the Partners further, the Federation party proceeded to the observation deck of their transport as it undocked from the data core facility.

Since the carbon dioxide atmosphere outside was considerably denser than the nitrogen-oxygen mix within, the vehicle was naturally buoyant and rose without the need for thrust. It was, T'Pol reflected, an elegant design. And the view outside was fascinating. It was difficult to see much through the thick, ruddy atmosphere, a fluid so dense that it warped the light and made the landscape appear concave, like the interior of a bowl. But T'Pol could see an elaborate Ware-built city extending in all directions around the data core, with thousands of delta-winged Xavoth flying effortlessly among the ziggurat-shaped structures. Most flying species expended considerable metabolic cost to stay airborne, which was why larger ones like the Hurraait often became flightless. But the

Xavoth were almost neutrally buoyant in their native atmosphere, flying as easily as an Earth dolphin swam.

The transport rose swiftly, and the cityscape was lost to view through the ruddy murk. Before long, the view was further obscured as they entered the dense clouds of sulfuric acid and sulfur dioxide that enswathed the Venus-like world. This was all they would see for several minutes.

"It is remarkable," T'Pol said to Reed during the lull. "In all my travels, I have never seen an environment like this with my own eyes, rather than through sensor telemetry." The Starfleet personnel and the ambassador were gathered together by the windows, while the Senior Partners sat at a Ware matter-replication table and ordered beverages. For them, this journey was routine.

"We've seen so many," Reed replied. "Hot planets, ice planets, ocean worlds . . . I'll give the Partnership this: the diversity they've achieved is staggering."

"It is the Vulcan ideal of Infinite Diversity in Infinite Combinations," T'Pol agreed, "achieved more fully than even the Federation has managed."

"Granted, though, these are not the kind of species you'd normally encounter in an interstellar civilization. The one thing that unites them is that they wouldn't fit in anywhere else."

"Indeed. I cannot deny that it is the Ware that made this alliance possible. It provides them ready transport to other worlds, grants translation between their languages, offers assistance to let them function in one another's gravities and atmospheres, and meets all their resource needs so they have nothing to fight over."

"Their biologies are so different," Ambassador Jahlet observed, "that most have no overlapping needs to begin with.

They would have had no reason to fight over resources or territory."

"Nor would they have even interacted, absent the Ware," T'Pol replied

"I wouldn't go that far," Reed objected. "Other races, like the Federation or the Tyrellians, would've contacted them in time. Interacted with them, traded with them."

"Would we? By Vulcan policy, these races would never have been contacted at all, due to their inability to create high technology of any kind, let alone warp drive. In time, the Federation may see the wisdom of adopting the same policy."

"Although," Jahlet countered, "many of us would rather see the Federation maintain the freedom to trade with prewarp worlds."

"But the members of the Partnership would have little to offer in trade, left to their own means."

Reed frowned. "It's not as if the Ware offers its services free of charge. It demands raw materials, refined products . . . and sentient lives."

"Even so," T'Pol replied, "it is difficult to deny that the Partnership has managed what no other civilization known to us has done—achieved a measure of symbiosis with the Ware, one that does not require the sacrifice of lives."

"Not always." Reed paced before the windows, beyond which the clouds seemed to be thinning, the light increasing. "But you know what they'll do to Thenar and her crew if they're found guilty. They'll be installed as Ware processors for the better part of their lives! Oh, the Senior Partners claim they'll be given periodic respites to 'mitigate' the neurological damage, but Doctor Liao is convinced it'll be enough to cause them permanent brain damage. And there's a nonzero chance it could be a death sentence!"

He took a deep breath that did little to calm him, then continued. "What the Partners don't seem to appreciate is that it isn't just their own well-being at risk. They have the Ware mollified, but not contained. Nothing's stopping it from spreading to other worlds, worlds that don't know the Partnership's tricks for holding it at bay."

"But their methods could be shared with other worlds. And if these beings could achieve so much, it suggests that we could devise a more comprehensive solution—a way to re-program the Ware so that its benefits would be available to the galaxy without the cost in lives."

"I have a hard time believing that's possible, T'Pol. The Ware is a weapon."

"Swords may be beaten into plowshares, Malcolm."

She stepped closer to the window as the transport broke through the clouds into brilliant sunlight. Above them, rapidly drawing nearer as the transport rose, was an enormous city floating in the sky—a collection of thousands of interconnected modules of gleaming gray-white Ware architecture, airborne islands linked by a network of bridges and buttresses. As with the Xavoth city below, its edges stretched far enough to be lost in atmospheric haze, even though T'Pol could see much farther through the clear air at these heights.

"Say what you will about the Ware," she said to Reed, "but it made this possible."

The city was named Zytheel, and it was home to the Hurraait, Enlesri, and other oxygen-breathing species that shared this world with the Xavoth. T'Pol knew that it was one of several aerial cities, others of which were adapted for the environmental needs of Nierl, Sris'si, and other exotic Partner races. Avathox was one of the Partnership's central worlds, home to Partners of every race in the alliance. The aquatic environment where the Sris'si lived needed antigravs to hover in the sky, but Zytheel's nitrogen-oxygen mix made it naturally buoyant in Avathox's atmosphere even at the Minshara-level temperatures and pressures found above the clouds, leaving the antigravs as a backup system only.

Once the transport docked, the Senior Partners allowed the Federation contingent to wander the city, observing the life and activity within it. As an explorer, T'Pol found it a fascinating opportunity, and she could tell that Jahlet, Reed, and even Williams and her subordinate found it so as well— though there was a somber undercurrent to it all, for they knew the Partners were showing them this to remind the Starfleet crew of what their colleagues on *Vol'Rala* had unwittingly destroyed.

While most of the interior architecture was the familiar white-walled Ware design, Zytheel's inhabitants had customized it to suit their needs—painting the walls, clearing out large interior spaces as parks and gardens, enriching the scenery with foliage and sculpture. One whole module of the city had been converted into an open grassland of the type where the Hurraait had evolved, and dozens of young Hurraait used it as a park, running through it and playing games that mimicked the hunting behavior of their forebears. All of it was done under the watchful eyes of their Monsof helpers; although there was no evident danger to the children here, each Hurraait was bonded from childhood with one of the hominid Monsof, who served as the ratite's "Hands" for the duration of the Monsof's shorter lifespan.

The Partnership had raised many questions that T'Pol was finding it difficult to resolve in her mind, making her wish for the counsel that had so often been available to her in the past. She had been looking forward to reuniting with Trip Tucker upon reaching Partnership space, hoping that together they could discern the reason for their inability to connect telepathically in recent months. But Trip was still aboard *Pioneer* as it probed deeper into the unknown in search of the Ware's elusive origin planet.

Finally, she could hold out no longer. When she and Reed stopped to appreciate the spectacular view from the peak of a narrow, arched crossover bridge between modules of the city—an eclectic cluster of modules in the near field, then nothing but blue sky and white clouds beyond as far as the eye could see—T'Pol took advantage of their momentary privacy to broach the issue. "How has our mutual friend been?"

Reed took her meaning instantly. "He's well. Getting back into engineering work agrees with him. There are times when he's almost his old self again—closer than I've seen him get in years, at any rate."

"Nothing has been troubling him unduly?"

"The Ware situation, of course. The threat to *Vol'Rala's* crew . . . the incident on Etrafso . . . the search for the Ware builders. But no more than the rest of us. If anything, I'd say his . . . isolation . . . has been to his advantage. He's not as close to sh'Prenni and the others as the rest of us. Concerned, certainly, but not as personally invested. And he's built up quite a thick skin over the past decade."

"I suppose he has," T'Pol replied. Could it be that he was schooling himself to such detachment over the lives lost and endangered that he had closed his mind to his bond with T'Pol? But that seemed unlikely. They had connected during other crisis situations in the past; and the loss of contact had occurred months ago, before Trip had encountered the Partnership.

Could it be, conversely, that he was too content? T'Pol

could imagine, even without Reed's words, how Trip would be revitalized by the opportunity to return to the kind of technical problem-solving and innovation he had loved so much aboard *Enterprise*. Cracking the technology of the Ware, devising a way to deactivate or contain it, was the kind of challenge that could keep him excited for months. Could it be that when he was fulfilled by his work, when he was not in need or distress, he felt no urge to reach out to T'Pol? Was their bond merely an emotional crutch to him?

And was her reaction to that prospect a sign that it was merely a crutch to her as well?

"T'Pol?" Reed was studying her with concern, and she realized with some abashment that she had allowed her emotions to show.

"I am fine, Malcolm."

"I don't blame you for missing him," Reed said, though she knew he had sensed something deeper in her reaction. She appreciated his polite fiction. "You know . . . my team has been managing fine for weeks without *Endeavour*. But *Pioneer* could surely use a hand in the search for the Ware builders. Why don't you take *Endeavour* and rendezvous with them?"

She met his eyes. "I appreciate the offer, Malcolm. But Admiral Archer sent *Endeavour* to assist you and Captain sh'Prenni. It would not be appropriate to base my choices on personal considerations."

"Finding the Ware's origins would assist us. It could be the key to this whole problem. And the rest of the task force is busy cleaning up Ware outside Partnership space. Travis and his people could really use the assistance of a *Columbia*-class starship."

T'Pol considered. Refusing a logical assignment to avoid the appearance of a personally motivated choice would itself be a personally motivated choice. "Very well," she agreed. "If you are confident your people can manage without a ship . . ."

"There's no shortage of transport drones available in the Partnership, I'll give them that much. It's an easier commute between worlds here than it is in the heart of the Federation."

"Then I shall leave Commander Thanien behind with a team to assist you, then take *Endeavour* to aid in the search."

"That will be fine." Reed gave her a tight smile. "Good luck, T'Pol," he said, meaning it on several levels.

She took his blessing in the spirit intended, but she did not believe in the human concept of luck. Outcomes were the result of a mix of choice, circumstance, and accident. It remained to be seen what circumstances she and Charles Tucker would face upon their reunion—and what choices they would make.

11

Samuel Kirk was glad that *Endeavour* had joined the task force. Its crew and *Pioneer*'s had worked well together during the Rigel mission last year. Not to mention that Captain T'Pol and Ambassador Jahlet were both accomplished diplomats, bettering the task force's chances of reaching some sort of accord with the Partnership and securing the *Vol'Rala* crew's freedom.

He was also glad to have the assistance of such a legendary linguist and first contact veteran as Hoshi Sato. It was no affront to his friend Grev to think so; while the amiable young Tellarite was a language prodigy in his own right, even he was in awe of Commander Sato and her uncanny intuitions into alien mindsets and methods of communication. Some of the Partnership's members, such as the Monsof and Sris'si, had very different ways of thinking and communicating than most humanoids. The Sris'si, for instance, not only perceived the world through echolocation rather than sight, but were a largely solitary predator species. With less social interaction than most sophonts, their intelligence was not filtered through language as strongly as most, their communication more through action. And the Monsof were at a far more basic level of linguistic processing than Federation humanoids, for all their intelligence in other respects. It was only through the shared benefits of the Ware that these races had been able to interact with the other Partnership species at all.

And yet Kirk was not ready to dismiss either species as having nothing to say. Both had experience with attacks by anti-Ware factions like the Silver Armada and the Manochai. The Monsof, like the Nierl, had lost their homeworld to a Manochai assault, leaving them as refugees that the Hurraait had taken in. It was Kirk's suspicion that those races' vehement hostility toward the Ware was due to prior experience. The Partnership scholars that Kirk had spoken to had insisted they knew nothing of the Ware's beginnings, but maybe there was some clue hidden in the accounts of the invasions. Conquering armies often left tales and records of their own behind in the lands they overran, if only to attempt to justify their conquests to their victims.

But drawing out the clues from one species' documentation of another species' accounting of itself was a tricky linguistic challenge, especially when the mediating cultures were as exotic as the Partners. Kirk hoped that Sato and Grev together could make a breakthrough that Grev alone could not.

When he returned to the two communications officers' study kiosk after going to get them coffee (for the Partnership's Ware had scanned *Pioneer*'s nutritional database weeks ago), Kirk found them laughing and gossiping instead. "Oh, Val hasn't given up," Grev was saying. "And she's not the type to try to make him jealous by pretending interest in someone else. She's just being his friend, same as always—though maybe a little more pointedly."

Kirk made himself known. "Aw, Grev, I've asked you not to gossip about me. Val and I aren't your personal soap opera."

"You just keep telling yourself that, Sam," Grev said,

patting his hand as he retrieved his cup of coffee. Sato laughed.

"Oh, marvelous," Kirk said. "Two communications officers who think my love life is funny. It'll be all over the fleet soon."

Sato's striking, dark eyes became sympathetic. "I'm sorry, Lieutenant. I don't mean any harm. I'm sure Grev doesn't either." Kirk nodded, chastened.

"Besides," Grev couldn't resist adding, "it's hardly fair to call it a love life, is it? And whose choice is that?" He sipped the coffee. "Oh, Sam, this is mocha! I wanted hazelnut. Be right back."

He left the two humans alone, an uncomfortable silence in his wake. "You know," Sato began after a moment, then broke off.

"What?"

"It's not my place."

"That didn't stop you when I wasn't in the room." His expression was sardonic, but his tone softened the words.

The older woman sighed. "I just think you're making this harder for yourself than it has to be. I mean, look at Grev. He's obviously got a crush on you, and even he's trying to push you and Val together. Doesn't that tell you something?"

Kirk blushed. "Honestly, sometimes I wish I *could* return Grev's interest. It'd be a lot simpler. But . . ." He fidgeted. "Don't ever tell him I said this . . . but I just can't find a way to see Tellarites as attractive."

Sato pursed her lips thoughtfully. "I dunno, I think he's kind of cute." Kirk chuckled. "But this isn't about Grev. I mean . . ." To his surprise, she smacked his arm with the back of her hand. "What is *wrong* with you? I've seen Val Williams. She's gorgeous. She's *really* athletic. She's smart, she's fearless—and she likes you. How are you not okay with that?"

He slumped into a vacant seat. "I know. She's . . . I thought she was totally out of my league. For a woman like that—for her most of all to be interested in me . . . it's a dream come true. But since Grev told you everything else, I assume you know the problem."

"You mean the fact that she's an armory officer. That she has to risk her life for others and you're afraid you might lose her."

"Yeah, basically."

"Which means you're an idiot."

He stared at her. "Wow. Not the kind of diplomacy I expected from the great communicator."

"Screw diplomacy. This is first-hand experience." Sato leaned forward. "Sam, did you know I'm engaged to be married?"

He blinked. "Oh yeah, I heard Commander Mayweather talking about it. Um, congratulations."

"Thanks. Do you know who I'm getting married *to*?"

"Just that he recently retired from your crew."

"Takashi Kimura. Until three months ago, he was *Endeavour*'s armory officer."

Kirk took that in. "Oh."

"Yes, 'Oh.' He risked himself for me, for the crew, for total strangers on a regular basis. And it cost him," she went on more solemnly. "On Vulcan, when V'Las's rebels set off that explosion in the Irinthar Mountains . . . Takashi was there. He was badly injured. He lost an arm . . ." She blinked, her eyes moist. "He suffered brain damage. Impairment of language skills, fine motor control, the ability to plan and anticipate . . . Obviously, it ended his Starfleet career."

"I'm so sorry."

She held his gaze frankly. "Don't be sorry for me. I have

what you don't. I have his love. I have every day we shared together . . . and every day we have yet to come, whatever happens. And whatever he's lost, I take comfort knowing that he still has me. We didn't get engaged until after he was hurt. Until we realized what we might lose if we didn't seize every chance life gave us."

Kirk spent quite some time absorbing her words. "It's just . . . so frightening. The risk of losing her if I let myself . . . I don't know if I could bear that."

"Here's the thing, though: It's not just about you." Sato placed her hand on his wrist. "Takashi put himself at risk because he's the most selfless man I know. And his selflessness, his willingness to take risks out of love for others, is what inspired me to be able to take those risks too. His sacrifice showed me that risking yourself for others is what love is all about. And you lose far more by avoiding that risk than you do by taking it."

Kirk was silent for a long while after that. She had left him with much to consider.

September 17, 2165
Beta Lankal system

Lokog laughed as he and Laneth stared through the space station's viewport at the cloud of debris slowly dissipating into the orbital space beyond. That debris was all that remained of the Imperial fleet that had defended this station and held this system—a system that was now in *QuchHa'* hands. "And all thanks to my mighty drone fleet," Lokog declared, placing an arm around Laneth's shoulders. "Do you not find my conquests impressive, my dear?"

He leaned in toward her, but she slapped him forcefully

across the cheek, sending him staggering. She gave him a look of disgust as he regained his footing. "Do not think you are entitled to me merely because I find your services useful, privateer scum."

Tasting blood in his mouth, Lokog burned with fury at the humiliation. Of course he was entitled to her! She would have died if he hadn't saved her. That put her in his debt, and he intended to collect. The high-born Laneth probably expected educated suitors who would woo her with love poetry, but he preferred a more basic form of conquest. After all, what prize was sweeter than one wrested from an opponent by force? And the arrogant bitch needed to be taught a lesson.

Moments later, though, his attempt at her forceful edification ended with Lokog coming to his senses on the floor against the viewport, his head aching fiercely and his right shoulder perhaps mildly dislocated. Laneth looked down at him with more scorn than anger. "Lowly pirate. You think to pit yourself against Defense Force training?"

But anger came soon enough, from General K'Vagh as he arrived in response to the disruption. K'Vagh grabbed Lokog by the front of his leather vest and yanked him upright. "Filthy marauder! You think to use my finest soldier as though she were a common whore? I should tear you limb from limb."

Lokog found the strength to laugh. "No doubt you should, General. But then who would sell you more drones so that you could score victories like this?" He gestured around at the captured station with his one good arm.

The burly general growled and let him go. "Curse your drones—and the pirates who direct them. The Imperial forces have caught on that they need to take out the command ships. And your men lack the strategic skills to guard those ships. I just heard from Kor: his forces have lost a major engagement near the Ghahak system."

Lokog waved it off. "Ghahak is minor. We mined it out decades ago."

"It is not Ghahak that matters. What matters is that the man you had controlling that contingent of drones allowed himself to be taken alive! Now the Imperials have a prisoner they can interrogate! They will learn of the Ware and its source."

"Well, then," Lokog replied, "you need me to get you more Ware. For the agreed-upon price, of course."

A low rumble sounded in K'Vagh's throat. "Fine. Your payment will be arranged." He loomed over Lokog. "But I recommend you return to the source of the Ware and prepare the new shipment personally. In fact, you should remain there to oversee further deliveries."

"Just so long as the money keeps coming," Lokog replied. "And so long as I still get my title once you control the High Council."

Laneth looked him over pityingly. "You may buy your way into a title . . . but do not imagine that anything could make you noble."

September 19, 2165
Qam-Chee, the First City, Qo'noS

At last, Ja'rod had achieved his ambition to stand within the High Council Chamber. True, he was here merely as a visitor, not yet a councillor. But the achievement that had brought him here today might well ensure his ascension to a Council seat in the near future.

For weeks now, the *QuchHa'* had been using their infernal robot fleets to strike against Imperial forces and installations.

The cowards kept their distance from battle, like the humans whose taint they carried, while allowing the boxy gray drones to do the killing for them. The robots lacked the fire and imagination of true warriors, but their sheer numbers, their great maneuverability, and their ability to repair themselves made them a formidable threat nonetheless. Many true Klingons had lost their lives, and several colonies and strategic locations had fallen under *QuchHa'* control, including the Mempa, Da'Kel, Qu'Vat, and Beta Lankal systems. The supply lines to the farming and mining colonies in the Pheben and Narendra systems had been interrupted, costing the core worlds wealth and tribute.

The one benefit of this scourge was that it had dulled the conflict between the various *HemQuch* factions vying for the chancellorship, as they stood together against their common foe. Even so, arguments raged between those who wished to see the *QuchHa'* exterminated once and for all, with Councillor B'orel as their leader, and those who argued that the flat-headed ones had proven their will to fight and should be accepted once again as true Klingons, as Councillor Alejdar advocated. One would not expect a female's weak ideas to be given consideration, but Alejdar had the favor of Councillor Khorkal—the oldest contender for the chancellorship, but the one who had cultivated the greatest number of political allies and supporters, and thus not an easy foe to overcome. And the tediously intellectual Arbiter Deqan had dragged out the *ja'chuq* for a *jar* and a half now, insisting that all eligible contenders must proclaim their deeds before the council—even those whose duties on the battlefield kept them from reporting in. Thus, the Empire remained divided, the Imperial fleet held back from decisive action. Ja'rod hoped his accomplishment would change that.

It was his patron, Councillor Ramnok, who had brought him here to present his prisoner to the High Council. Ramnok was a fierce warrior who had earned his seat through multiple successful conquests and victory in several duels. The glory to be won in combat meant everything to him, as it did to Ja'rod. But he did not lack for rhetorical fervor either. "This is the key to our victory," the tall, bright-eyed Ramnok intoned before the Council now. "At last, Captain Ja'rod has done what no other has managed to do. He broke through the lines of the mindless drone ships at Ghahak, tracked down the renegade vessel that controlled them, and captured its master for interrogation. You see what remains of that one here."

That was Ja'rod's cue. He strode forth proudly, dragging the chained *QuchHa'* privateer alongside him, then shoving the man to the hard stone floor of the smoky chamber. "My councillors," he said. "This . . . creature . . . calls himself Klorek. He is a pirate and a coward. He broke easily under my interrogation."

Khorkal stepped forward to study the man. "This privateer is one of those who provided the technology to the insurrectionists?" the stately, gray-haired councillor asked.

Ja'rod kicked his prisoner. "Answer him."

Klorek winced and spoke in fearful tones. "The machines are called the Ware," he said. "They come from unconquered space, beyond the Kromnoth sector. They are widespread there. Many worlds use them."

"How did you obtain them?" asked Khorkal.

"We were approached . . . by an alien named Vabion. He is a merchant and an engineer, and he learned some of the Ware's secrets . . . with help from Starfleet."

Clamor rang through the high-roofed, echoing hall as the

councillors reacted. Councillor B'orel's voice rose above the others. "Starfleet? Do you say the Federation is behind these abominations?"

"I do not know," Klorek said. "Lokog—our leader—helped Vabion escape from Starfleet. They were working with him, but then they betrayed him. Or he betrayed them. I do not know. But Starfleet is moving against worlds that use the Ware, shutting it down, leaving them defenseless. Vabion made a deal with a group of worlds there—they give us the drones in exchange for our protection against Starfleet."

"So Starfleet is against the Ware," said Councillor Alejdar. "This agrees with the reports from our spies in the Federation."

"For, against, it does not matter!" Ramnok cried. "Once again, the humans meddle in affairs they do not understand. They assume they are wiser and better than the rest and entitled to tell others how to live! And the consequences once again descend upon us!" Other councillors in his faction cheered his words, emboldening him to speak further. "I say we have tolerated their interference long enough. They have grown too powerful, too bold, with this new union of theirs. Now they expand toward the Kromnoth sector, spreading their influence. We must not sit idly by and allow this!"

"Do you propose war?" Khorkal boomed.

"I do! A war we should have waged years ago! It was a black day for the Empire when the Federation formed, joining our Vulcan, Andorian, and human foes into one larger force." Councillors muttered in agreement. "Now they grow ever stronger, taking Rigel and others, expanding in our direction! We must no longer tolerate this threat! It is time we subjugated them once and for all like the *jeghpu'wI'* they are!" His supporters roared.

"This is nothing you have not said many times," Khorkal replied. "But we already fight a war on two fronts. The insurrectionists undermine us from within, and now the privateers and their drones besiege us from without. We cannot afford to divide our focus with yet another war."

Ja'rod dared to speak. "We cannot afford not to, my lord. Starfleet has an entire fleet in the region beyond Kromnoth! They expand into territory we had planned to conquer. They will take those worlds from us if we do not stop them!"

Ramnok came to his support. "Ja'rod is right! If the Federation succeeds there, they will have us in a pincer. Soon enough they will surround us if we do not stop them!"

"Choose your enemies well, Ramnok," said Alejdar. "It is the first of Kahless's precepts for a reason. Consider: We stand against the Ware, and so does the Federation. More, they appear to have the means to control or destroy it. Would it not be wiser to ally against a common enemy?"

B'orel replied with disgust, his voice trampling over her last few words. "Wisdom is an excuse for the cowardice of a female! These Ware are mere machines, a minor nuisance. The human poison that infects us is the real threat! Without the humans, there would be no *QuchHa'*, no insurrection, no privateer alliance with these Ware worlds."

"Then let us plan against them wisely," Khorkal advised. "Deal with the threat at hand so that we can then confront the Federation with all our strength."

"And let them grow stronger while we wait!" Ramnok countered. "That is the strategy of a weakling. Warriors do not win honor by letting fights go unfought!"

"Nor do they win it by rushing recklessly into every fight that presents itself! Honorable war is that which benefits and enriches the Empire. Not that which benefits personal glory at the Empire's expense!"

"You only fear this war because you know you are too weak to lead us to victory, old man! Step aside and let a true warrior lead!"

Khorkal took a heavy step forward. "If you think me a coward, step forth now and test my courage!"

"I will!" Ramnok advanced.

Ja'rod thrilled at the prospect of witnessing such a high-level duel, but Deqan spoiled it by stepping between the councillors. "This is out of order!" the arbiter declared. "There are still other oustanding contenders for the chancellorship. Not all have completed the *ja'chuq* and proven their case, and I have not yet selected the final two contenders. It is not your place to select yourselves!"

"Outrageous!" B'orel exclaimed. "You delay interminably with these arbitrary rulings."

"Let me remind the esteemed councillor that his own accusations against General K'Vagh required the suspension of the *ja'chuq* during the investigation. In the wake of his disqualification, new contenders have come forth, and all are entitled to declare their—"

"To Gre'thor with your prattling excuses, scholar! You leave us without a leader at our time of greatest crisis! Stand aside and let true warriors resolve this!"

Ja'rod could see that many councillors sympathized with B'orel. Deqan was an unpopular choice for Arbiter of Succession, the last of Chancellor M'Rek's many unpopular decisions. He was a relic of the old days, before the warrior caste had risen to its rightful place and seized control of the High

Council. A scholar and diplomat by training, he had remained on the Council through some fluke of politics, and M'Rek had chosen the doddering fool as his arbiter on the basis of Deqan's complete lack of ambition, seeing him as a neutral party who could not be swayed to favor one contender over the rest. But he had chosen too well in that regard, for Deqan seemed to favor no one at all.

Still, as little respect as the other councillors may have had for the lone non-warrior among them, they had no hate for him either; he had been a fixture of the High Council for decades and had forged many alliances and astonishingly few enmities in that time. Moreover, the councillors respected the traditions of succession, and challenging an arbiter was a reckless move. B'orel found that no other voices rose to his support. Sullenly, he stepped back and held his silence.

But Ja'rod saw his chance. "My councillors," he began, kicking the prisoner Klorek. "I have interrogated this one not merely about the Ware, but about the Starfleet armada in the sector. It includes at least five Andorian warships—a significant portion of their fleet, weakening their core defenses. One of those warships has already been overpowered and captured by the privateers and mercenaries in service to the Ware worlds. Klorek has given us details on their weapons and tactics. We know they can be beaten, and we know how. Speaking for the commanders of the Fleet, my lords . . . we do not fear battle with the Federation. We welcome it."

The councillors in Ramnok's and B'orel's camps shouted in solidarity with his words. Ja'rod smiled as he realized that several of Khorkal's supporters did the same. His speech had struck the target: though Khorkal and Alejdar still resisted the idea of war with the Federation, they did not wish to appear weak or cowardly in the eyes of their supporters, lest it weaken Khorkal's bid for the chancellor's throne.

The war was as good as begun.

September 20, 2165
U.S.S. Pioneer

"So you have lost Vabion's ship?"

T'Pol stood with Travis Mayweather, Charles Tucker, and Reynaldo Sangupta around *Pioneer*'s situation table. So far, she had not had the opportunity to spend time alone with Tucker, so they had been unable to acknowledge each other with anything more than subtle glances while they maintained the pretense of being strangers. Tucker played his Philip Collier role with the ease of long practice, and without their mental bond, she could read nothing from him but what he showed on the surface. It was possible, she admitted, that her chastisement of Tucker had been harsher than was warranted.

Indeed, Tucker bristled, though how much of that came from him and how much from "Collier" was unclear. "Oh, we know exactly where his ship is, Captain T'Pol. The problem is, he isn't on it. From what we can tell, he left his Ware command ship behind and took off in one of the Klingon privateers."

Sangupta smiled. "But the good news, ma'am, is that we're pretty sure we know where he's going."

T'Pol raised a brow. "Explain."

"You see, I got to thinking," the cocky young science officer continued. "The Partnership have searched for the Ware's builders before, but never found them. Why is that? They've had centuries to look. So it occurred to me: What if it's somewhere they *couldn't* go? Somewhere they wouldn't be allowed to get near?"

Mayweather picked up the thread. "The Partners have told us about the civilizations that have attacked them for using Ware. The Manochai, the Silver Armada, and so on. They've all either attacked the Partnership and been driven back to their own space, or have fought off attempts by the Partnership, or the Pebru, to expand into their space. That means there are territories the Partnership has never been to. Odds are, the Ware's builders come from one of those."

T'Pol frowned. "Logically, if these powers oppose the Ware so fiercely, they would not tolerate the Ware's builders operating in their space."

"They could be in between the Partnership and the builders," Sangupta suggested. "Or maybe the builders are strong enough to hold them off, so they have to pick on weaker groups like the Partnership instead."

Tucker added, "And past experience with the Ware could explain why they're so hostile to it."

"Logical," T'Pol granted, holding Tucker's gaze for a moment longer than necessary. "But there have been multiple attackers in the Partnership's history. How does this tell us Vabion's destination?"

"Process of elimination," Sangupta said. "The Manochai were conquered by the Klingons. Not only does that mean we'd be out of luck if they *were* in the right direction, but they probably aren't, because as far as we can tell, the Klingons have never heard of the Ware until recently."

"True," the captain agreed, reflecting on the intelligence reports Admiral Archer had sent her over the past few weeks.

"We can rule out the Guidon Pontificate," Sangupta went

on, "because they got their Ware from the Partnership in the first place, back before the Partners realized it preyed on living beings. Apparently it was the Guidons who discovered that and, um, filed some pretty aggressive customer complaints about it." He gestured to the star chart on the situation table. "And there's this other group called the Reehansa, or something like that, but they came from way over here, near Romulan space, which is the wrong direction." T'Pol glanced toward Tucker, but he showed no outward reaction to the Romulan connection.

"So that just leaves the Silver Armada." The science officer zoomed the display in on the region of the map marked off with their approximate borders. "At least, that's what they call their warfleet. The Partnership never really got their name beyond that. They're absolutely fanatical in their hatred of the Ware. Reportedly they aren't xenophobic as a rule, or even particularly territorial, so long as you're flesh and blood. But try to bring even a single piece of Ware-made technology into their space, and the Armada will descend on you with a fiery vengeance. As the Partnership found out when they tried to make first contact two hundred and seventy years ago."

"So this civilization was already well acquainted with the threat of the Ware," T'Pol said. "Suggesting either that they discovered the threat promptly through happenstance, as we did on *Enterprise*, or—more likely—that they had a long enough prior acquaintance with the technology to accumulate evidence of its rapacious tendencies."

"And," Tucker added, "that they'd suffered enough damage from it to take it very personally."

She turned to Sangupta. "But you say the Armada is not hostile otherwise."

"As a rule, no." He smiled. "Which means that if someone went into their space in, oh, a Klingon privateer ship, they could probably get in with no problem."

"Vabion thinks he's found something," Mayweather said. "We need to find it too."

"I concur with your analysis," T'Pol said, "and your plan of action, Mister Mayweather. *Endeavour* and *Pioneer* will proceed to Silver Armada space together. Assuming the Armada grants us passage, we should be able to handle a single Klingon ship."

Mayweather grinned. "It's a pleasure to serve alongside you again, Captain."

"It is agreeable for me as well, Travis."

She took care not to look at Tucker as she said it.

It was not difficult for T'Pol to arrange a private meeting with Trip Tucker. After the briefing on the bridge, she requested that "Philip Collier" bring her up to speed on his analysis of the Ware's operating system and his attempts to penetrate it. In turn, he suggested a meeting in his quarters to avoid disturbing the work of his associates in the engineering lab. It may have seemed slightly unusual to some, but few humans would expect anything but professional behavior from a Vulcan captain.

In an archaic human gesture of courtesy, Trip allowed her to enter first. She turned as the doors closed behind him, intending to ask the question that had been preoccupying her for months. Yet he spoke before she could, clasping her shoulders in concern. "T'Pol, is anything wrong? Have you been okay? I've been tryin' for months to reach you in my mind, and there was nothing."

Her eyes widened in surprise even as she relaxed into his

grip. They shared an embrace for several moments before she said, "I had intended to ask you the same question."

He pulled back to meet her gaze, frowning. "Then nothing's been wrong on your end? Medically, I mean? Um, neurologically?"

Given her history with Pa'nar Syndrome and Trellium-D poisoning, his concern was understandable. She spoke calmingly. "I am in excellent physical health, Trip. I had been concerned for *your* welfare. Your reports, and Malcolm's, indicated you were physically well, but I wondered if, perhaps, something was . . . preoccupying you unduly."

"You mean, something upsetting me about the mission? No." He chuckled. "Actually, bein' back in the saddle again, bein' an engineer . . . it feels great."

She pulled back slightly. "Then perhaps that has been the issue. If you felt no need to reach out to me——"

Trip stared in disbelief. "Are you kidding? T'Pol, I've been missing you every day. Every chance I get, I've been trying to reach out to your mind, make contact. I miss it."

He stroked her hair, and she raised her hand to touch his. "As do I. There have been times when your presence in my mind would have been most reassuring."

He smiled. "Well, I'm here now. Maybe . . . maybe we've just been apart too long. Maybe we just need a jumpstart." His fingers pressed a bit more firmly against her temple. "Know what I mean?"

She did. With both eagerness and trepidation, T'Pol raised her hands to his temples, found the neurological contact points, and opened herself to the meld.

Yet nothing happened. In the past, they had been so closely connected that their melds had begun almost effortlessly. Considering that they might be out of practice, she focused her mind and attempted the standard mantra. "My mind to your mind. Your thoughts to my thoughts. Our minds are merging . . . our minds are becoming . . . one."

Yet reality did not conform to the words. Try as she might, she was unable to engage the meld. "What could be wrong?" Trip asked. "Could it be something medical? Something wrong with one of us?"

"Difficult to say. Unfortunately, Phlox is not available to consult."

"Yeah, and Doctor Lucas might recognize me from when we met on Sauria a while back."

"Not to mention that we would need to explain the nature of our relationship. I assume the same goes for Doctor Liao."

"Right. I guess we need to try to figure this out on our own." He began to pace. "When did this start? When was the last time you sensed me in your mind?"

She thought back. "Over three and a half months ago. Late May, I would say."

"Hmm, I can't remember as well as you. I was kind of busy dealing with raiding Ware stations and such. But that seems about right. It took me a while to realize we weren't connecting, though. It does come and go sometimes. What makes you so sure?"

T'Pol lowered her eyes. "I became acutely aware of your absence in my mind on the third of June. That was when Admiral Archer and I had been abducted by V'Las."

He grimaced in sympathy. "That's right. He was gonna force a meld on you, wasn't he? Damn him . . . I was furious when I heard about it."

She brushed her fingers across his in appreciation for his concern. "It was a traumatic moment for me," she acknowledged. "I reached out to you for support . . . for comfort. I hoped that . . . if the worst happened . . . I could take solace in your mental presence."

"Oh, God . . . I'm so sorry I wasn't there for you."

She showed her appreciation with her eyes. "Fortunately, it proved unnecessary, for I was rescued soon thereafter. Still, my inability to reach you troubled me . . . especially when it continued thereafter."

He furrowed his brow. "And that's when it began?"

"To the best of my ability to determine." She studied him. "You are suggesting that V'Las's attack was the trigger. That my distress at the prospect of a forced meld caused me to erect some form of mental block."

"Could that be it? That you raised some kind of psychic deflector shield and now you can't turn it off?"

"I am not sure I would phrase it that way, but it is possible."

He smiled. "The hell with phrasing. The point is, if it's just a mental block, then it's temporary! We just need to figure out how to lower your shields."

Now she began to pace. "I am not so sure," she said after several moments' thought. "I admit, I had not given this adequate consideration . . . because I had been concerned that the problem originated on your end."

"Like, you thought I wasn't interested in you anymore? T'Pol, don't be ridiculous!"

She looked at him sidelong. "Can you really say you had no such doubts about my loyalties?"

Trip blushed. "I guess . . . insecurity comes with the territory."

"In any event, now that I consider the prospect that the problem originates in my mind . . . I am not convinced it is temporary."

"Why not?"

She came close to him again, touching his hand. "Trip . . . what we have shared this past dozen years is far from typical. Normally, Vulcans require direct physical contact to join minds. Sensing a bondmate's thoughts or reactions over a distance is not uncommon, but the kind of full sensory communication we have experienced is exceptional in the history of Vulcan telepathy. I did not know this at first, as the study of the telepathic sciences was suppressed under the High Command, and it has taken years for Vulcan scholarship to rediscover forgotten knowledge. My recent visit to Vulcan gave me the opportunity to review the latest literature, and it has made me aware of how anomalous our bond was."

He stared at her for a long moment. "'Was.' Are you saying you don't think it's coming back?"

"I don't know, Trip. I cannot be sure what made our bond possible in the first place. It may be that the Trellium-D damage I sustained to my mental barriers in the Delphic Expanse left my mind more open to a telepathic link. Or the space-time anomalies in the Expanse may have enabled an atypically strong entanglement to form between us. Whatever the cause, it was the exception, not the norm. It may have been wrong to expect it to last forever. Trip . . . we must consider the possibility that our ability to communicate telepathically over a distance may never return."

Tucker looked stunned as he absorbed her words. "Then . . . what does that mean for us?" he finally asked. "We spend so much time apart . . . we *have* to. Moments alone like this are so hard to arrange. I've depended so much on your voice in my head, your image and touch in my mind to keep me going. Without you as my anchor . . . I'm not sure I *can* keep going."

T'Pol looked at him for several moments . . . then rose and began to disrobe efficiently. "That is something we will face in the future. For now, we are together. Nothing stands between us. Let us make the most of that opportunity."

She was nude by the time she finished speaking. He gazed at her in admiration and longing, a gaze that brought her surprising comfort and pleasure. Though it brought her more pleasure when he began to remove his own clothing.

12

"I'M GLAD YOU FINALLY changed your mind, Dad," Vaneel said as she and Phlox approached the prison where Mettus was currently confined. "I know it was hard for you."

The doctor gave a rueful sigh. "Not nearly as hard as it must have been for you," he admitted to his daughter. "To forgive the man who killed your father-in-law . . ." He shook his head. "I imagine it must have been difficult to persuade Pehle."

"Pehle isn't a vindictive man," Vaneel said. "That's part of why I love him. And he understood once he realized . . . I don't forgive the act." Her voice was more subdued, more bitter, than he could ever remember hearing it. "What Mettus did . . . it was something he can never truly make amends for."

"But he is still family," Phlox replied after a moment, reiterating the words she had spoken to him on so many occasions over the past few weeks, while the Curia and the judiciary had wrangled over how to deal with Mettus's crimes against Denobulan nationals so as to clear the way for his extradition to Antar. "If we renounce that completely, we become no better than the person he has become."

"Exactly," Vaneel said. "In the hearing, even through my anger and pain . . . I couldn't help feeling pity toward

Mettus when I heard how those monsters had twisted his mind. Yes, it was his choice to accept those lies. And it was his choice to pull the trigger, no matter what excuses he makes." Mettus claimed that he had lost his nerve and pulled his aim away from Pehle at the last instant, not realizing that Sohon would leap into his redirected line of fire. In his version of events, Sohon's own recklessness had gotten him killed and sabotaged Mettus's attempt to show mercy. "He is guilty. But . . . he needs to accept his guilt before he can have a chance to heal. Those lunatics have spent years convincing him to blame everything on others. The government just wants to make an example of him to calm the Antarans."

"Meaning that only his family has a chance to help him face his own guilt," Phlox said, almost amused at her intensity. "I know. You don't need to convince me again."

Vaneel blushed. "I do let my passions run away with me, don't I?"

"Never stop letting them, my dear. They've changed so many minds. They changed mine, or I would never have come here. So if anyone has a chance of getting through to that boy, it's you."

"I've tried, believe me. But I'm not at the root of his issues. Fathers . . . well. They shape us in ways we can't escape, whether we admit it or not."

Phlox cleared his throat. "Mettus rejected everything I ever tried to teach him."

"Yes. And maybe if you and he can figure out *why* he felt that need——"

Vaneel didn't get to complete her thought, for just then, a massive explosion blasted out a wall of the prison before them. Phlox reflexively pushed Vaneel to the ground and lay atop her, though they were far enough away to avoid shrapnel. But he heard weapons fire and shouts emerging from the hole in the wall, so he kept her head down over her protests. "What's going on? I want to see!"

It took some effort to draw her away from the scene and persuade her to return home. Once he'd done so, he headed back toward the prison, where numerous police skimmers and ambulances had descended on the grounds. He presented himself to the head of the police unit, a middle-aged male lieutenant named Deemal, and offered his medical services to assist with the wounded. "What happened here?" he asked as the lieutenant led him to the triage site.

"According to the prison guards," Deemal said, "a band of Antarans fought their way in."

"Antarans? Were they military?"

"From the descriptions, no, but we're still assessing the situation."

"Lieutenant, my son Mettus is in this prison for killing a prominent Antaran. This is surely some form of retaliation. I need to know if Mettus is all right." As he said those words, he wasn't entirely sure how much the answer mattered to him. He might find out when it came.

Deemal promised to look into it, but tending to the injured prison guards came first. Phlox worked with the emergency crews and the prison doctors for the next hour, stabilizing the few serious cases and treating the minor injuries of the remaining guards.

But when he was done, Deemal was there. "Come with me."

He led Phlox toward the prison's security office. "Doctor, the visual records confirm it: the raiders have taken your son with them."

"But why? Where are they now?"

"Gone. We tracked their skimmer, but when we intercepted it, the craft was empty. Apparently a ship in orbit used a transporter device and went to warp before we could stop them." Phlox could not formulate a response as he struggled to process the information. "As for the why," the lieutenant went on, "well, we captured one of them. Let's see what he can tell us."

The captured Antaran was dressed in a drab green uniform different in detail but similar in effect to the outfits worn by Mettus's hate group. The prison warden, a stocky, brown-skinned woman named Vunim, stepped away from her questioning of the man and approached Phlox as he entered with the lieutenant. "Doctor Phlox," Vunim said. "I fear this is not the way I had wanted your visit to go."

"Of course, Warden. Has this man told you anything about the raiders?"

"We can't get him to stop," Vunim replied. "He's a proud fanatic, just like Mettus and his cronies. The Antarans have their own hate groups, which I suppose comes as no surprise."

"Of course we hate you!" the captive cried. "Lying monsters, you talk of peace and then murder our leaders! You think we would trust you to punish Sohon Retab's murderer? We have taken him to Antar for a *real* trial!"

Phlox stepped forward to face the Antaran. "You're lying. I know the Antaran government would never sanction such an action."

The raider scoffed. "You think we would get justice from the appeasers of the Reformist Party? No—the assassin Mettus will be tried by the True Sons of Antar. Only we can ensure that justice is done."

Phlox stared at the man in dread. His throat was tight as he spoke. "And I suppose the verdict is already decided."

"The only verdict there can be for any Denobulan!" The

raider grinned as if he were the captor and not the captive. "The sentence will be a very slow death."

September 26, 2165
Starfleet Headquarters, San Francisco

". . . And the government refuses to take any action," Doctor Phlox said on Archer's office monitor, *"either to mount a rescue mission or even apply diplomatic pressure. Relations with Antar are still tenuous after Sohon's death, and they're afraid that intervening on behalf of his murderer would send the wrong message."* The physician grimaced. *"I tried to persuade them that exercising compassion on behalf of every individual without prejudice would send the best possible message about Denobula's intentions, but they would hear none of it. I won't be getting any assistance from the Curia."*

Archer met his old friend's eyes regretfully. "I'm sorry, Phlox. I can only imagine what you must be going through. But I'm afraid there's not much I can do either."

"You're an influential Federation official. If you spoke to the Antaran government—"

"It's not my place. Antar isn't a Federation member, and I don't need to remind you, neither is Denobula."

"You could still get involved as a negotiator."

"If both sides wanted me to. And the only one who does, it seems, is you. As your friend, Phlox, I'd love to help. But as a Starfleet chief of staff, I just don't have the luxury. We're already stretched thin with everything that's happening. I have a dozen things to juggle—I'm overdue for a Joint Chiefs meeting as it is." At least Alrond was no longer a problem; the new governor had officially renewed the colony's allegiance to the Andorian Empire and the Federation weeks ago, and efforts to rebuild the planet's damaged cities and communities were proceeding apace.

Phlox nodded sadly. *"I understand. I'm grateful you made time for me at all, Admiral. Perhaps I shouldn't have tried to impose on my relationship with you and Starfleet. I'm not technically in your service at the moment."*

Archer had a thought. "You know . . . we're not the only interstellar organization you have a relationship with."

A moment later, Phlox brightened. *"You're quite right, Admiral. That might be exactly what I need."*

"Good luck, Phlox."

He had to sign off quickly, gathering his data slates and rushing out of his office. Archer hoped no other crises would erupt between there and the meeting.

So naturally, Marcus Williams chose that moment to come up to him in the corridor and announce, "It's finally happened."

Studying his aide's face, Archer wasn't immediately sure what he was referring to. The Klingons were amassing troops on their near border; had they struck sooner than expected? Had the Partnership delivered a verdict against Captain sh'Prenni? Had T'Pol and Malcolm found a way to stop the Ware once and for all?

But Williams didn't leave Archer hanging long. "Maltuvis has launched his conquest of Sauria," the big man said. "He's deployed a fleet of spacecraft around the planet to bombard the remaining holdouts. Demanded they surrender or he'll blast them all from orbit."

Archer stared. "A fleet of ships? Three years ago, the Saurians could barely launch a pressurized tin can into orbit."

"Well, they are a very inventive people."

"Not that inventive. I'll bet you a month's pay Maltuvis had Orion help."

"No bet, Admiral. The question is, how to prove it?"

Archer sighed. "And what do we do about it if we can? We've got other things on our plate at the moment."

"Don't we always?"

Archer didn't need to respond, since the very existence of this meeting was answer enough. As they entered the conference room, a bright, open chamber with a wall of windows looking out on San Francisco Bay, Archer saw he was the last chief of staff to arrive. Arrayed around the table were his fellow chiefs of Starfleet's various divisions: Admiral Shran of Andoria; Fleet Commander T'Viri of Vulcan; Admiral Flar of Tellar; and Admiral Osman of Alpha Centauri. Defense Commissioner sh'Mirrin also sat in on the meeting.

Greeting his colleagues, Archer took a seat next to Shran. The windows were behind him, so he wouldn't even have the view to cheer him up. And the news was indeed grim. "All our analysts agree," Commissioner sh'Mirrin finished after she brought the gathered chiefs up to speed. "The Klingons aren't waiting. Despite their internal strife, they're readying for an attack on a Federation outpost. We don't yet know which one, so we need ships in position to guard the whole border area."

"I have assessed our fleet distribution," T'Viri put in. She operated the table controls to put a tactical chart on the three-sided viewer in the table's center. "This would be the most efficient reallocation of available vessels." Archer noted that the plan included the approval of Admiral Narsu's request to transfer *Essex* to his command out of Starbase 12—which meant that the mystery of Theta Cygni XII would have to go unsolved a while longer. No doubt Captain Shumar would be disappointed, but if any Theta Cygnian refugees had escaped the planet at all, their fate was not immediately at stake. Like any Starfleet officer—like Archer on that terrible day when the

Xindi weapon had burned a swath across the Earth—Shumar knew that exploration must be set aside when the defense of his home demanded it.

Shran frowned as he studied the display. "That would mean pulling ships away from the border of Ware space. We need those assets there if our task force requires assistance liberating Captain sh'Prenni and her crew."

"We can't just invade another nation if their verdict doesn't go the way we want," Archer protested. "I want sh'Prenni out as much as you do, but we have to do it the right way, or we're no better than the Klingons."

"And 'the right way' is just to let others carry out whatever injustices they want? I don't hear you saying that where the Saurians are concerned."

"I don't want to invade them either. Not even now." He filled the others in on Williams's news. "Things only got that bad on Sauria *because* of our rush to make contact with a society that wasn't ready for the impact we'd make."

"Which has nothing to do with the Partnership!" Shran cried. "They've been spacegoing for centuries. They've interfered with plenty of other cultures. Now they're messing with ours, and a friend of mine is about to pay the price!"

Archer held his tongue. This was not the place to rehash the argument they'd been having for weeks. Matters had not been this tense between Archer and Shran since before the Federation was founded. But Archer could hardly blame Shran for his concern for his protégée. It would be petty to remind him that sh'Prenni would never have been in this mess if she hadn't recklessly interfered in a culture she didn't understand.

Commissioner sh'Mirrin filled the silence. "No one here is happy about the Saurian situation, Jon. But we have our own invasion threat to consider. You know that if we need to ramp up production to wartime levels, we'll need Sauria's resources, even if we have to hold our noses while shaking the hand of the person who provides them."

"After all," Admiral Flar put in, "if we stop buying Maltuvis's dilithium, he'll just sell it to the Klingons, and then where will we be?"

"These are matters for debate in the Commission and the Council," said T'Viri. "We should focus our attention on matters of logistics and strategy."

"Quite right," sh'Mirrin said. "To that end, Alexis, how do we stand on new ship construction? Even with the reallocations T'Viri suggests, we're thin on the Klingon front. And the grim reality is that we're likely to become thinner if a war starts. We'll need to ramp up production."

The discussion turned to construction timetables and starship specifications for a while. The next new *Columbia*-class ship was still months from completion, but new waves of *Intrepid*-class light cruisers and delta-shaped *Ganges*-class frigates were also under construction as part of Archer and Osman's fleet modernization plan. While not the most cutting-edge designs, they were more advanced and versatile than the favored wartime classes of Samuel Gardner, Archer's predecessor as UESPA chief of staff. Gardner was the warhorse who'd pushed the mass manufacture of the old, basic *Daedalus*- and *Marshall*-class ships during the Earth-Romulan War, favoring speed of construction and—frankly— disposability over the innovation and flexibility of the multi-purpose vessels Archer preferred. Yet Archer now feared the looming Klingon conflict could scuttle his modernization plan and force the fleet back into Gardner's military mode. There was already pressure to abandon the *Ceres*-class construction plans in favor of the more combat-oriented *Poseidon* class, and to reconvert the surviving *Daedalus*-class ships into troop transports if war broke out again. The Andorian Guard, meanwhile, seemed content to stick with its tried and true *Kumari* and *Sevaijen* classes.

Still, Archer couldn't help considering the resources that would be needed to build and power those ships, and where those resources would need to come from. He had to make one more try to offer alternatives to bankrolling Maltuvis's dictatorship. "I think we should intensify efforts to upgrade Rigel's shipbuilding facilities to Starfleet specs," Archer suggested. "Aside from their technical expertise, they have access to multiple sources of dilithium and rare metals."

"That's true," Osman agreed. "There's also the Vegan debris disk and our trade deal with the Vissians." The jovial Centaurian looked up from her data slate, her dark eyes piercing. "But I can't order up a dilithium-rich planet on request. And Flar's right—better we get Maltuvis's minerals than the Klingons do."

"I just don't like the idea of throwing innocent Saurians to the wolves to benefit ourselves."

Osman pondered. "Well, who knows? Maybe Captain Reed's task force will crack the Ware's programming soon and find a way to bring it under our control. Imagine having a whole armada of drone warships to take on the Klingons."

"*If* we could make them work without enslaving sentient beings in the process. And *if* the technology could be trusted not to turn on us. I tried trusting it once, thank you."

Shran looked at him askance. "Would you rather trust Maltuvis? There are no ideal solutions here, Jonathan. You should've learned that by now. When the galaxy is falling down around you, you have to prioritize whom to save. You look to your own first and let the rest take care of themselves."

"Sauria is one world," T'Viri said. "The equation is simple. The needs of the many outweigh the needs of the few."

Archer kept his peace, recognizing that he had no sound alternatives to offer. Still, he couldn't help wondering: *How many times do we have to sacrifice the few before they outnumber the many?*

September 28, 2165
U.S.S. Endeavour, Silver Armada border

The Silver Armada's border patrol ships were considerably less polished in appearance than Travis Mayweather had expected from the name. They were a ragtag assortment of older ships apparently cobbled together from mismatched pieces with little regard for aesthetics. But they were abundant and quite heavily armed, so Mayweather had no doubt of their ability to prevent any unwelcome ship from entering their territory. *Pioneer* and *Endeavour* had been confronted on their approach by four Armada ships and required to submit to a thorough inspection to ensure they were Ware-free. Mayweather and T'Pol had offered no resistance, and they had been greeted with hospitality once their lack of Ware and their agenda toward it had been established.

The species operating the Armada came from a planet they called Pegenor, a superterrestrial world with high gravity and a dense atmosphere that was mostly nitrogen and oxygen, but thickly laden with carbon dioxide and volcanic gases. They had been able to breathe the atmosphere aboard the Starfleet ships with only the occasional whiff from breathing tubes built into their uniforms, though a visit in the other direction would have required full EV suits. The Pegenoi were oversized near-humanoids with heavy, elephantine feet, scaly blue-gray skin, and stocky, apish bodies that could barely fit through some of the tighter hatchways aboard the Starfleet ships. But they conducted their inspections diligently nonetheless, determined to keep the Ware out of their space at all costs.

According to Captain Garaver, the Pegenoi female who led this interceptor group, their species was one of multiple races in the region that had been former clients of the Ware, and the only one that had managed to maintain a space fleet following the societal collapse that had resulted from its spread and the ensuing wars to purge it from their territory. "The Ware drained so many of our resources and our great minds before we rose against it," Garaver told Mayweather and T'Pol, "and we expended so many more in the battles that followed. Many of our neighbors had forgotten how to create or invent without the Ware, and collapsed back to the primitive when it was gone. Some were happy to revert to a more basic existence, free of machines. Others still struggle and need help, but our resources are stretched thin by the effort to guard our space. This is why we welcome trade with any who are free of Ware."

"Societies fitting that description seem uncommon in this sector of space," T'Pol observed.

"The Ware infests this region," Garaver answered solemnly. "Ever spreading on its own, manipulating its victims into spreading it as well. We must guard relentlessly against reinfection. But we do not have the resources left to take our battle wider. Your own success against the Ware is a great victory. You must share your method with us."

"Our method is only partially effective," T'Pol replied, remaining noncommittal. "Our goal has been to locate the Ware's original creators in hopes of gaining insight into its fundamental nature and purpose."

"Which is why we need to know about the other ship that

entered your space four days ago," Mayweather added. "The man aboard that ship is also seeking the Ware's creators, but he wants to exploit the Ware for his own gain, not stop it."

Garaver took a thoughtful suck on her breathing tube. "Yes, we thought as much when we spoke to him, despite his claims," the massively built captain said. "That is why we told him what he sought to know."

Mayweather frowned. "Excuse me, there may be a translation problem. Did you mean you *didn't* tell him what he wanted to know?"

Garaver smiled. "I mean that we told him exactly where to find his answers. The origin world of the Ware. It is here, in our space. And we will be happy to take you there."

September 30, 2165
Ware origin world

They found Daskel Vabion alone in the single intact structure left on the planet. All around, the world was a barren, irradiated ruin, without enough oxygen to sustain life. This temple had been built by the world's last survivors, and now that they were gone, the Pegenoi maintained it and supplied it with oxygen for the benefit of visitors.

Vabion's Klingon escorts had left days ago, finding nothing for them here, but the Vanotli industrialist had remained, combing through the historical records and relics left behind, with the assistance of a text translation device the Pegenoi had lent him. The device contained the Ware's translation database, the one piece of Ware code the Pegenoi suffered to exist in their space—for naturally it contained the languages of the Ware's creators, and theirs was a story that the Pegenoi wanted the seekers of the Ware's origins to learn. Mayweather had not

understood why until he saw the look of desolation on Vabion's gaunt face.

"The Ware's creators were not one race," the Vanotli genius
explained to the Starfleet landing party, readily sharing his dis-
coveries once he recognized that misery loved company. His
listeners included Mayweather, T'Pol, Tucker, and Sangupta as
well as Captain Garaver and a pair of *Endeavour* security guards.
"They were a corporation—an industrial giant within a trading network of four disparate races. They assembled knowledge and talent from all four civilizations, combining their
areas of skill and expertise to advance their technology. They
developed goods and services that could be adapted for sale
on worlds with exotic environments—not only the two within
their own community, but others among the worlds farther re-
moved with whom they began to trade, including the Pegenoi.

"Their goal was to provide the finest in customer service—
the most advanced technologies, the most adaptive and reliable
systems, the most authentic replications of any desired goods.
In order to reach new markets, the systems had to be able
to scan any species' biological and environmental needs and
quickly adjust. The computers had to be sophisticated enough
to translate any language in moments. They even made the
technology self-repairing, so it would be more reliable than
what their competitors could provide. After all, they profited
from the material goods paid in return for the Ware's products
and services, and in the licensing fees paid for the use of their
proprietary replication patterns. The Ware was a base invest-
ment that would repay itself over the long term; hence, it was
designed for endurance rather than obsolescence."

"So what happened?" Tucker interposed. "It demanded so
much computing power that they needed to start kidnapping
people to use their brains?"

Vabion smirked. "On the contrary. The Ware Corporation—let us call them that for simplicity—devised the most advanced and powerful computers in the entire sector. Electronic brains more than capable of handling the requirements of the system, operating entirely without the assistance of living beings—either from without or from within."

Mayweather shook his head. "That doesn't make sense. This is just one more of your lies."

"To what end, Mister Mayweather? If anything, it makes tragically perfect sense. You see, the computers they built were so efficient, so adaptable, so self-sufficient that the corporation's need for live employees diminished. They were able to save a great deal of money by laying off their workforce and relying on the Ware to manage itself. They even programmed it to market and distribute itself, to recruit new consumers in other star systems."

Mayweather was still skeptical. "And what, it suddenly came to life and started to eat them?"

There was a quality of sadness to Vabion's chuckle, as well as a touch of hysteria. "Again, you're looking at it from entirely the wrong direction. The problem is not that it gained self-awareness. The problem is that, despite all its power and versatility, it remained resolutely dumb." He paused. "But I am getting ahead of the story.

"No, the guiding intelligence remained the Ware Corporation. Which, like any corporation, sought to maximize its profits. Naturally they had competition, and naturally there were corporate spies attempting to penetrate their secrets. They designed the Ware to resist all attempts to parse its programming. They became utterly fanatical about preserving their monopoly on its technology—so that they could monopolize all technology, all industry. They sought to buy out their competitors or drive them out of business. They used their influence to control legislators and amend the laws in their favor. They even bought up the educational institutions so that they could ensure no one but their employees had the knowledge to develop technologies that could compete with the Ware." He shrugged. "Basically, the same things I did on Vanot. Just good business, you know."

When he paused, Garaver spoke. "Meanwhile, the Ware's client worlds became more dependent. We could get everything we needed made for us, so fewer of us bothered to learn the skills necessary to fend for ourselves. Some worlds were raised from basic agriculture or hunting lifestyles. They became spacefaring peoples without even understanding basic physics or engineering."

"For decades, the corporation monopolized higher learning," Vabion continued. "But the executives themselves had become so reliant on the amazing computers of the Ware that they grew lazy and thoughtless. In time, they began to ask: 'Why do we spend money teaching scientists and engineers when the Ware can make all we need? Why not shut down the universities and put that money in our own pockets?' Their experts warned that this was dangerous. The computers at the heart of the Ware were the one thing that could not be easily replicated, for they were so complex, so fragile. But the executives had grown up pampered by the Ware. They could not believe it was capable of failure. And so they closed the schools and left the fate of the Ware entirely up to the Ware."

T'Pol raised a brow. "And the Ware was designed to be adaptive. To repair itself using the available resources."

"Exactly!" Vabion spun toward her and gestured sharply with a bony finger. "That was its imperative. To maintain its ability to provide service. But it did not *understand* service. It

had no consciousness, no judgment, only mindless imperatives. It knew it had to go through the motions of serving its
customers at all costs, but it did not know what service was *for*.
It enacted its function as an end in itself, oblivious to the consequences to the people it was attempting to 'serve.'"

"Now you're contradicting yourself," Mayweather declared.
"How could it be so sophisticated but have no intelligence?"

Surprisingly, Vabion replied without the condescension
Mayweather had learned to expect, appearing simply thoughtful. "Intelligence is a specialized form of processing. It is not
something you gain merely by putting a billion adding machines together. The system needs to be designed in a specific
way, a network analogous to a living mind."

"He's right, sir," Rey Sangupta said with a hint of apology.
"Consciousness is a special kind of neurological architecture.
A network of complex feedback loops that make a mind aware
of its own activity, able to modify and direct that activity. In a
way, a conscious mind is like a simulation constructed by the
brain—a simulation of *itself*, so that it can take its own activity
and attention into account in its own calculations and adjust
itself accordingly. It's crazily complex. It's something nobody's
ever been able to reproduce in a machine."

"Not that we know of, anyway," Tucker added, but he declined to elaborate.

"For all its enormous complexity," Vabion went on, "the
Ware lacked that perception of itself, that ability to understand its own activity. It continued to operate on pure instinct, so to speak. And so, when its central processors began
to break down, when there were no longer engineers with the
knowledge to replace them, it acted unthinkingly on its programmed imperative: Adapt. Correct. Repair using whatever
resources were suitable. As it spread from world to world, it

had needed to learn how to adapt unusual materials and resources to fill its requirements."

"And at some point," T'Pol said in a hushed voice, "it calculated that sentient brains would be a suitable substitute for its original processors."

"Yes," Garaver said. "At first, it openly abducted people who came in for medical treatment. This was seen as a malfunction, and the Ware in question was dismantled. But it was designed to be adaptive. It could evolve its programming through trial and error. It learned to take victims in secret. But still we knew they were disappearing, and eventually we found out why. That was when the Pegenoi began to fight off the Ware. But it still adapted. Ware in other systems was networked with ours and learned of the failure of its new method. Eventually, it evolved a defense."

"Replicating exact duplicates of its victims," Mayweather said. "Faking their deaths."

"Exactly."

"But how? How could something mindless be so . . . so devious?" The first officer was no longer sure what to think. He might believe that Vabion was hiding the true identity of the Ware builders to hoard their secrets for himself, but why would the Pegenoi be complicit?

"That's evolution for you," Sangupta said. "Insects don't decide to make themselves look like flowers to hide from predators. Spiders don't design or engineer their elaborate webs. They just randomly mutate until they happen upon a modification that does something useful, and then modify it more and more until it gets more and more useful. They don't need a driving will behind it, because it's success or failure that determines what survives and what doesn't. Evolution selects for solutions that work, which is why it so often looks the same as conscious planning. And if it operates long enough, it can produce some incredibly intricate results."

Vabion turned to Tucker. "If you think about it, Mister Collier, this explains many of the anomalies your engineering team had noted about the Ware. Why would a system designed to prey on living beings have such makeshift attack mechanisms? Why do the stations have no means to prevent their captives' recovery except by repurposing their teleportation, repair, replication, and life-support machinery to attack liberators? Why do they have no defenses inside their primary data cores? Certainly they have battleships; that was one of the products the Ware Corporation had designed and made available to their customers. But the trading posts, the repair stations, the planetary industrial hubs—these were not designed to be predatory systems. They adapted to become that as a means of survival, modifying their existing systems to serve this new purpose." He shook his head, laughing. "Really, I'm disappointed in myself that I didn't see it sooner. I assumed there was simply some alien logic behind it. I should have realized that even alien logic must be distinguishable from randomness."

His point was hard to deny. Mayweather did recall hearing several of *Pioneer*'s engineers raise some of the same questions.

But he resisted accepting the truth. It would mean that, ultimately, there was no one to blame for what the Ware had done to him and to so many others. No one to be angry at. Just machines that had been built too well and depended on too much.

"So . . . what happened to the builders?" he finally asked, no longer confronting Vabion but simply asking. "How did this planet end up . . . like this?"

Garaver answered that question. "By the time we came to destroy their Ware . . . there was little of them left. The mindless Ware, in its hunger for resources to fuel its growth, had impoverished them. It could no longer provide for them, and they no longer knew how to do it for themselves. It did not care that they starved—only that they could not pay." She lowered her massive, scaled head. "They had turned on each other in fearsome wars over what resources remained. There were few of them left when we finally discovered this world. And those few willingly sacrificed their own children to the Ware in exchange for food and possessions. We freed all we could, then we devastated the Ware. But the damage was done. The survivors had few subsistence skills, and we had few resources to spare for them, for we had lost so much in our own fight with the Ware." She cleared her throat with a timpani rumble. "Ultimately, all we could do was help the last survivors build this temple to history—to preserve the truth of the Ware as a caution for those tempted by its power."

Vabion's deep voice erupted into laughter. "Such a cruel benevolence on their part. The prize I have sought . . . everything I have worked for . . . nothing but dust."

"Then there is nothing in the temple's records," T'Pol asked, "that would enable us to decipher or modify the Ware's kernel program?"

The Vanotli stared at her. "The kernel? Oh, I could probably extrapolate some fragments of its architecture and coding from the surviving documentation, but that is not the point. Don't you see?"

"I think I do," Mayweather said, drawing Vabion's gaze. "You said it yourself: The Ware Corporation did the same things you did. Pursued profit and control above everything else. And when they got everything they'd been working for . . . they had nothing."

He should have felt satisfied to say it—should have

delivered the words in self-righteous anger, condemning Vabion for his sins. But he couldn't bring himself to do so. The man just looked so grateful that he understood.

October 2, 2165
U.S.S. Pioneer

"This is a problem," Malcolm Reed said over subspace, his goateed image displayed on the bridge's main viewer. T'Pol, Mayweather, Tucker, and Olivia Akomo were gathered around Reed's empty command chair as they consulted with him on their findings. *"If we could have proven that the Ware was unleashed with malicious intent, then maybe we could've persuaded the Partnership that sh'Prenni was acting in their defense."*

"Instead," T'Pol observed, "the Ware acts with no intent of any kind. Its harm is accidental, the consequence of an untended autonomous system acting out its programmed imperatives. The Partnership could validly argue that they have merely taken possession of an abandoned technology and adapted it to a more constructive use."

"But are we really sure of this?" Reed probed. *"I mean, the story came from Vabion. Can we trust his version of events?"*

Tucker hated to let his friend down, but he had no choice. "The records are there in the temple, Captain. We spent a whole day going over them to verify their authenticity. And we have the Pegenoi's account to corroborate it. The Ware almost destroyed their civilization. It did destroy their neighbors. They have no reason to want to protect its creators."

"No chance they could be its creators?"

"With the hodgepodge tech their fleet's made out of?" Tucker shook his head. "No. The only thing that's kept the Silver Armada flying this long is sheer desperation."

Reed huffed a breath. *"So where does this leave us? We can't keep trying to shut down the Ware, because countless lives in the Partnership depend on it. But we can't just stop, because others like the Pegenoi are still in danger from it. Even if we shut the Ware down everywhere else, the Partnership's Ware could still pose a reinfection risk if it ever gets out of their control. Besides, if we acknowledge the legitimacy of their use of the Ware, we might as well be declaring* Vol'Rala's *crew guilty."*

The agent in Tucker had been trained to keep his cards close to the vest, to avoid voicing an idea until he'd worked out all the angles and ramifications, and even then to conceal as much of his true intent as possible. Yet the engineer in him won out, and he found himself speaking almost as soon as the idea came to him. "Maybe there's another way."

T'Pol turned to him. "Mister Collier?"

"We've found what we were looking for—the origin point of the Ware. There's not much left down there, no specific records of the Ware's kernel codebase or system calls. But there are bits and pieces that could give us insights into how its creators thought, what software architecture and molecular engineering principles they used. We might be able to find the key in that."

Mayweather looked at him askance. "That's what Vabion said. You're not trusting him, are you?"

"We know he's a genius, Travis. He's helped us before, when it was in his interests. And this is what he's been searching for ever since the first pieces of Ware fell out of Vanot's sky."

"And now he's seen it was all for nothing. It's broken him. There's no telling what he might do next. He could try to destroy himself, and maybe drag us down with him."

"He's not a movie villain, Travis. I know you like to see things in terms of right and wrong, but some people are pragmatists. They do whatever they think they have to if it'll get the job done. If what they've been doing doesn't work, they try something else. I think Vabion's smart enough to adapt. And he might be smart enough to help us discover something we need."

"Need to do what?" Reed insisted.

"To *change* the Ware," Tucker said. "Setting aside his methods, Vabion had the right idea. The Ware's broken. It uses living minds because it's malfunctioned and it's the only way it knows to fix itself. What we need to do is come up with a smarter fix. Re-engineer the Ware so it doesn't have to rely on living brains.

"Just think what that would mean for the Partnership. Not only would they no longer have to submit themselves to the Ware's brain drain just to survive, but they wouldn't have to live in fear of their neighbors anymore. Because the Ware would no longer be a threat to the Pegenoi or the Guidon or anyone else." He grinned. "Offering that to the Partnership would give us a hell of a lot of leverage. It'd be worth granting immunity to sh'Prenni and her crew, don't you think?"

While Reed pondered the idea, T'Pol addressed Tucker. "It is an intriguing notion, Mister Collier. But as we have learned, the operation of the Ware relies on extremely advanced computer systems, comparable in complexity to the living brain, if not in cognitive ability. Neither our technology nor Vabion's is adequate to the task of re-creating such systems."

"That's where I come in," Olivia Akomo spoke up. "Or rather, Abramson Industries. We've been working on a prototype bioneural technology—computer circuits that incorporate organic nerve tissue and function analogously to a living neural network. A bioneural computer could take the place of the living brains the Ware uses now, rivaling their processing efficiency and flexibility. What's more, they could give us the kind of interface that Mister Mayweather gained when Vabion put him into the Ware back in Pebru space." Travis grimaced at the reminder, but he was listening with interest. "He and the other sleepers gained root access because they were *part* of the core itself. We haven't been able to replicate that yet, but maybe, with the right kind of bioneural processor, we could achieve it. And that would not only let us replace living brains with synthetic processors, but could let us bypass the Ware's kernel security and reprogram it however we wished."

"What would you require to achieve this?" T'Pol asked.

"As quickly as possible?" Reed added.

"A subspace link to Willem Abramson," Akomo said. "It would take a genius of his level to pull this off."

Mayweather frowned. "Unless he were actually here, able to work with the Ware firsthand, there's only so much he could do." Looking like he hated himself for saying it, he went on, "What about the computer genius we already have on hand?"

Akomo traded a look with Tucker, who nodded in agreement. "You're right, Travis," Tucker said apologetically. "Vabion's got more experience studying Ware architecture than any of us. Certainly no one in the Partnership could understand it as well, since they had no science or technology before it came along. Vabion's the greatest Ware expert we have. We need him."

"All right," Reed said. *"But I'm not convinced he's the only one who can help. Hari Banerji made some valuable breakthroughs of his own. If the ambassador and I can convince the Senior Partners that we need him on this, they may let him out to assist you."*

"I'd be glad for the sweet old guy's help," Tucker affirmed. "But you think the Partners would go for it?"

"They pardoned Vabion when he offered them something in return. Hopefully we can turn that to our favor."

"Then it seems we have a plan," T'Pol said. "Proceed, Mister Collier."

Tucker met her eyes, wishing he could convey his gratitude telepathically, hoping she could at least read it in his expression. The fate of many worlds and countless lives was in his hands—but it depended on his ability to solve an engineering problem, rather than his capacity to deceive, manipulate, and exploit one group for the benefit of another.

It felt like old times again, and he couldn't be happier.

13

October 3, 2165
Qam-Chee, the First City, Qo'noS

WORIK STARED IN MIXED awe and confusion at the orders his kinsman had just handed to him. "I am deeply honored, Grand-Uncle Deqan," the young Klingon said. "I never thought to earn a captaincy so soon. If ever," he admitted. "And *Gantin* is a fine Bird-of-Prey, honorably named. But . . . the Federation front? When war is looming? I did not think you approved."

The elderly councillor gazed out the window at the nighttime fires of the First City, letting out a heavy sigh. "There is much happening now of which I do not approve. So I am myself forced to do things of which I would not normally approve. Such as using my influence to arrange your assignment to such a treacherous post. You have my apologies, kinsman."

Worik was less concerned for his own future than for his elder kinsman's honor. "But as the arbiter, is it not your place to remain detached?"

"When the Empire is threatened by the madness of its leaders, I can remain detached no longer. Even the warrior caste once understood that war, like any weapon, must be wielded with discipline and restraint, lest it turn on the wielder. But now it has become a fetish for them, a way to boast and bluster and prove their manhood. They play at it like children playing with firelighters, and they do not care how much they burn so long as they can thrill at the sight of the flames."

"But surely councillors like Khorkal . . ." Worik began. He trailed off, for these were matters above his station.

"Khorkal's position is too weak. The insurrection has made everyone angry and afraid, and the rhetoric of the militants and the bigots inflames them. No one is willing to risk appearing timid and losing political standing."

"But you are the arbiter. Can you not simply disqualify the more dangerous candidates?"

Deqan was rarely prone to violence, but he whirled on Worik with anger. "I will not debase my sacred duties!" He took a breath and went on more calmly. "I must remain neutral in this. I must uphold the system, trust in it, if I have any hope of its preservation."

"Of course. I ask forgiveness."

"I cannot blame you," Deqan admitted. "I have bent the rules to give you *Gantin*. But I must draw the line somewhere."

Worik shook his head, still confused. "Why give me *Gantin* at all, then?"

Deqan moved behind his understated but elegant antique desk and sank into his seat, which creaked under even his unimpressive weight. "Because I need someone I can trust on the Federation front. I may not be able to prevent the Council from authorizing an attack, but at least I can place a kinsman in a position from which he might be able to take meaningful action on the Empire's behalf."

Worik straightened in his own seat. "I understand, Grand-Uncle."

Deqan met his gaze, and Worik could see the profound grief within his kinsman's eyes. "I fear you do not—yet. For the action I have in mind . . . will require a great sacrifice from you, my kinsman. I only pray that you will be able to forgive me for it."

October 4, 2165
Partnership planet Cotesc

Rinheith Chep ran.

It was what he always did, given the opportunity, when faced with a difficult decision. He would go out onto the plains of Rastish—or a substitute, like the parkland that surrounded him now, just outside Cotesc's towering capital city—and run with all his might, hoping to stalk and overtake a solution as he would with prey. The local parkland was not as well-suited for his thinking as the plains of home; it was a bit too well manicured, its game too small and tame, its gravity a touch too light. But it was all he had.

No; he had Fendob too. The loyal Monsof had run alongside him as long as she could, her own legs nearly as well-adapted for the task as his own; but that ungainly vertical body inevitably slowed her down, and soon she was falling behind and panting profusely. He did not slow his own run, though; he knew she would catch up to him once he rested.

Indeed, once he stopped to rehydrate at a just too perfectly positioned pool under a just slightly too symmetrical set of parasol trees, it was not long before Fendob staggered up, sank to her hands and knees, and dunked her head into the pool to cool off. Once she was ready, she crawled over to where he crouched beneath a parasol tree and plunked herself down next to him, leaning against his downy flank. He wrapped a wing around her hirsute shoulders, glad it was useful for that, at least.

"I do not know what to do, my Hands," he said to her, not

expecting a reply. "I had hoped to find answers here, but they are more elusive than *yurhaath* with newborn chicks."

The Federation ambassador and Captain Reed had both made eloquent cases for their proposal to experiment with the Ware, to attempt to modify its construction and programming and create a substitute for the living brains it now required. For all Rinheith knew, they had the technology to achieve it. After all, the Partnership had no science or engineering knowledge beyond what the Ware itself had given them, so few within it could assess what technical skills other civilizations might have. On the other hand, as Tefcem var Skos had pointed out during the Senior Partners' assembly, other advanced races like the Manochai had failed to reprogram the Ware, resorting instead to raw destruction. But Rinheith wondered if that had been more a matter of will than knowledge. The Federation representatives, as difficult as it was to believe in the wake of sh'Prenni's crime against Etrafso, appeared genuinely reluctant to accept brute force as a solution. Had others merely given up too soon?

Yet how could he even contemplate making such a change to the source of the Partnership's bounty, the key to its very existence? Did others have the right to demand that the Partnership change what it was in order to satisfy their convenience?

Rinheith shook his neck and wings in frustration. "You know, I really thought Tefcem would be the deciding vote. He hates the Starfleet people so much for what they did to Etrafso. I thought he would tip the scales against this mad plan." Fendob looked up at him with a question in her big, dewy eyes. "I had forgotten that he merely speaks for Wylbet. I wonder if he argued with her—in private, of course. I wonder if it's even possible for an Enlesri undermate to challenge his overmate. I never would have considered the possibility until I saw how much Tefcem hated relaying Wylbet's wishes." Naturally, no one had ever heard a female Enlesri speak except through one of her undermates. Their males were the only ones with vocal cords. Rinheith wasn't even sure how the Enlesri's silent communication worked. He could probably ask the Ware to show him their medical data, but he doubted he would understand the information.

"Etrafso. Better," Fendob said.

"Yes, I suppose. The Tyrellians have been most generous. Obtaining the technology we need without having to volunteer our brains and bodies in service . . . I can see the allure." He shuddered. Fendob tensed in concern, laying solicitous hands on him, peering at him with a clinician's gaze. Rinheith chuckled. "I am well, pretty lady. Merely a memory." His beak mandibles clacked together with tension. "Volunteering . . . it is an ordeal. It took something from me that I am not sure I will ever get back. And not only the loss of your father, my dear Hands. Something deeper, inside me. The cost is more than we like to speak of, for we have never had a choice but to accept it.

"And yet . . . now we may have a choice. Naturally that would make us question—and wonder."

"Armada," Fendob pointed out.

"Yes, I saw how Captain Garaver's words affected the assembly. Perhaps she was sincere about the Silver Armada ending its attacks if the Ware no longer posed a threat to them. Perhaps no one would try to attack us anymore simply for using the Ware. It could make us safer." He clacked his beak again. "But I do not like the idea of making such a decision on the basis of fear. It felt as if they were threatening us to change our ways or face retribution." He hesitated. "Perhaps that is unfair to Garaver. She sounded sincere. But it was the implication, whether she realized it or not."

Needing to pace, Rinheith rose, gesturing to Fendob that she need not follow. He raised his voice so she could hear him as he circled the small pond. "But what would we be giving up? These aliens—their technology is not as advanced, nor as versatile as the Ware. They have no experience with the needs of Nierl or Xavoth or Krutuvub. They do not even have matter replication."

"Ware. Fix."

"Yes, of course, my dear. If they do reprogram the Ware, it would still provide all the same benefits—or so they say. But they are beneath its level. Who is to say their computers will be as advanced as the ones they claim the Ware originally had? Without living brains to enhance it, how much less flexible and powerful will the Ware become? Is it worth sacrificing our standard of living to end volunteer service? Yes, that would spare some few of us a traumatic experience, maybe even spare a tinier few from brain damage or death. But it would diminish the benefits of civilization for all of us. Is it right to ask all to get by with less so that a few may be spared?

"Because Partner Chouerd is right," he said, evoking the Nierl Senior Partner who had spoken so eloquently in the debate that had provoked his run. "The sacrifice that we make as volunteers reminds us of our obligation to place the greater good above our own convenience. If we could have everything we wanted without cost, without personal hardship, how would we appreciate the value of what we gain from the Ware? How would we recognize the importance of the community and our commitments to it? We are Partners. That cooperation is core to our very identity!" He caught the inquisitive look in Fendob's eyes and stopped pacing, holding her gaze. "Yes. Yes, sweet one, that is what I believe. I *have* to."

She clapped a hand against her chest. "Partner."

"Yes, Partner Sorbod's vote surprised me." The Monsof Senior Partner usually followed Rinheith's lead, but in this case, Sorbod had unhesitatingly indicated his support for Jahlet and Reed's proposal to modify the Ware. "Surely if anyone appreciates the value of service and submission, it is your people. You have always been loyal and giving beyond measure."

Fendob stood and placed herself before him with a few long-legged strides. She reached out her hands before her, palms raised and cupped helpfully. "Service," she said, smiling warmly and nodding.

Then her body language changed. Her arms fell limply to her sides. She slumped, shoulders sagging and head lolling, and her eyes closed. And yet her pose was rigid, tense, as if confined and afraid. He recognized the essence of her pose, feeling it on the level of visceral memory, even before she said "Volunteer" in a tone of profound dismay.

Finally, she reached out to Rinheith, stroked his head in sympathy, and said "Volunteer" once more with tears in her eyes.

He stared at her for a long time. "I never realized," he said at last. "Oh, I have been such a fool. What would I do without your wisdom?" He nodded. "You are right. They are not the same thing at all. There must be a better way. I will break the tie. Starfleet will have their chance to change the Ware."

Fendob hugged him tightly, and he returned it as best he could. Then, as he always did at the end of these runs, he let his weary Hands climb on his back and carried her all the way back to the city.

October 6, 2165

Daskel Vabion and Willem Abramson had hit it off with disquieting ease, in Travis Mayweather's view, once the latter had been brought into the engineering team's discussions over subspace relay. Abramson was one of the greatest technological geniuses of the Federation, a pioneer in prototype robotic technologies that had the potential to revolutionize civilization. The idea that Vabion's intelligence was sufficient to impress him made Mayweather sick to his stomach. When he'd said as much to Charles Tucker, the engineer had shaken his red-bearded head and replied, "Travis, you don't know the hundredth of it."

Still, Abramson's input had paid off, and his experimental bioneural circuitry did seem to have the potential to do everything Olivia Akomo had promised. Akomo and her team had not brought any of the valuable experimental compound with them on the mission, but she proposed that the Ware could replicate the substance as long as it had the molecular pattern data uploaded into it. At first, that had seemed unlikely, given that the Ware's replication systems were incapable of synthesizing living tissue. But Vabion had concluded that the problem was one of resolution. Although the replicator mechanism was based on the transporter principle, it needed to process data at a lower, less memory-intensive resolution in order to store the patterns of countless different foodstuffs, instruments, and the like. This introduced assembly errors sufficient to prevent the intricate processes of life and consciousness from operating, like a more drastic version of the subtle reassembly errors that had led to Federation transporter technology being declared unsafe for routine use.

However, since a transporter only needed to store a

pattern temporarily, it could operate at sufficient resolution to record the detailed quantum state of every particle and thereby reassemble a viable living organism. The Ware's transporters did so with even greater fidelity than the Federation model. Vabion had thus proposed interfacing the Ware's replicator and transporter systems, using the latter in place of the assembly systems of the former and thus allowing the replication of viable, live bioneural tissues. The method would not be able to reproduce an entire living being, but the bioneural circuits were simple enough synthetics that Abramson agreed the principle was sound. Impressed by Vabion's ingenuity, and prompted by urging from his apprentice Akomo, the grayhaired industrialist had reluctantly consented to share his proprietary data—though only after getting a guarantee from the Partnership that he would be paid royalties for every use of the pattern.

Still, the bioneural circuitry was just the raw material. Tucker's team would need to design a mechanism that would integrate into a Ware data core in place of a living brain, as well as a delivery system to enable its spread throughout the Ware network.

And that was why Mayweather was here on Cotesc alongside Captain Reed, attempting to convince the Senior Partners to reconsider their refusal to release Hari Banerji. "This is absurd," Tefcem var Skos complained. "We have already convinced the judicial council to delay the *Vol'Rala* crew's trial to allow you time to familiarize yourselves with Partnership law and custom and to negotiate a diplomatic agreement. Now you ask us to intervene once again and have one of the defendants released?"

"You already agreed to release Vabion in exchange for his help," Reed countered.

"Vabion left us with no choice. His freedom was the price for his protection—from you."

Mayweather spoke up. "This could protect you, too," he said. "Our engineers have an idea for a way to unify the conversion process—not only use the Ware to replicate the bioneural replacement circuitry, but to program it to automatically install those circuits and remove the sleepers all at once. Commander Banerji's the one who devised the means to interface remotely with the data cores and override their commands. We need his expertise."

"Why?" asked Chouerd, the Nierl Senior Partner, from within the hovering environmental capsule it occupied. "We already have the ability to enter the cores and awaken the sleepers. We do not need such an indulgence."

"But others don't have that ability," Mayweather went on. "Other nations out there still fear the Ware, and they're a threat to you because of it. If we can find a solution that works for them as well as you, one that makes the Ware harmless and useful for everyone, then their danger to you would be over. And wouldn't that be a far better form of protection that hiring a bunch of Klingon mercenaries?"

Rinheith and others seemed swayed, but var Skos still resisted. "You demand too many indulgences. We have already given you license to conduct your experiments on the Etrafsoan Ware, in exchange for your commitment to reactivate it. You have yet to deliver on that promise."

"Because we can't," Reed told him, "without putting living people in there. We know you have volunteers ready and waiting, but we just aren't ethically comfortable with using people in that way. Especially when we're so close to finding a better alternative."

After giving Reed a querying look and getting a subtle nod

in return, Mayweather stepped closer to the wide, curved table that the Senior Partners sat (or floated) around. "I understand that you have reason to resent Banerji, and sh'Prenni, and the others. I know resentment. Vabion and I have a history. He kidnapped me and my friends, threatened the life of a woman I cared about to force me to cooperate, and made me relive one of the most frightening experiences of my life by putting me back into the Ware against my will. And he did all that deliberately, purely for his personal gain. But I'm willing to put that aside and work with him now, because we need his skills to make this happen. And," he confessed, "because I'm willing to believe that maybe, just maybe, his discovery of the truth about the Ware has changed him, given him a chance at repentance.

"Hari Banerji, on the other hand, is a man who was only trying to help you—who made a mistake because he didn't understand the situation. I know he'd want nothing more than to make amends for that—not because he'll get something from you in return, but because it's the right thing to do. Why not give him that chance?"

The Partners deliberated, and finally cast their votes in the affirmative. "We will intervene on Doctor Banerji's behalf," Rinheith stated. "But our indulgence has its limits. If we do not begin to see positive results from these licenses you have demanded, there will have to be consequences."

Reed locked eyes with all the Partners in turn (those who had eyes) and spoke with solemn sincerity. "The Federation will not let you down. I promise you that."

Mayweather suppressed a frown at the captain's words. He had made a similar promise of his own when this had started, guaranteeing a liberated Menaik that she was safe from the Ware; but he had ultimately been helpless to prevent her recapture. Time and again, the Ware had proven to be a more intractable challenge than anyone had expected. Mayweather only hoped that Reed was not promising more than the Federation could deliver.

October 7, 2165
Partnership border outpost

Lokog finished off his latest stein of replicated bloodwine and tossed it against the boring white wall of the Ware station's so-called recreation area. "To Gre'thor with K'Vagh and all his nobles," he growled, not for anywhere near the first time. "They're no better than the *HemQuch*. Looking down on me, treating me like their servant, even though they're as deformed as the rest of us."

Next to him, Captain Korok gave a warning growl, though it was halfhearted. Korok was *HemQuch* himself, but he was a commoner like Lokog, a raider and mercenary with no loyalty save profit and no love for the nobility. Lokog suspected that Korok thought himself better than the *QuchHa'* who made up the bulk of Lokog's mercenary fleet, but if so, he had kept it to himself. After all, Korok was the captain who had once let himself be beaten by a group of backward, unarmed deuterium miners on Yeq. That planet had been a rare prize—a planet where gaseous deuterium was concentrated in underground pockets as a decay product of celebium, enabling it to be easily collected and purified, rather than existing in trace quantities that had to be meticulously sifted out of water or interstellar hydrogen. It had been just the thing for those who operated on the fringes and preferred to avoid the normal supply lines. Moreover, the alien miners who had settled there had been placid and easily intimidated

into compliance—or so it had seemed until they had somehow developed the backbone and the strategic skills to drive
Korok and his men away in humiliating retreat. Korok insisted to this day that some third party must have trained the
colonists, but he had never been able to prove it. In the thirteen years since, he had been a laughingstock even among his
fellow privateers and outcasts. So he had come along readily
enough when Lokog had put out the call for mercenaries to
defend the Partnership's borders in exchange for the drones
now conquering the Empire.

"They forget that they need me," Lokog went on. "Without my drones, their heads would be trophies on the High
Council's wall by now!"

"High Council, rebels, who cares?" Korok complained.
"We're way out here playing border guards for *Ha'DIbaH*. The
khest'n things don't even qualify as *jeghpu'wI'*."

"Why should you mind?" Lokog countered. "Makes them
all the easier to push around. You should appreciate that—
they're just your speed!"

Korok snarled and threw his half-empty stein at Lokog.
But he was too drunk to throw straight, and the clean miss
wasn't sufficient provocation to start a fight they were both too
drunk to bother with. Instead, the ridge-headed, long-haired
Klingon pounded the table and ordered, "More bloodwine!"
He only got a warning buzz from the table until he remembered to pull his hand away from the platform on which the
new stein materialized. It would have served him right, Lokog
thought, if the infernal mechanism had beamed away his hand
instead. It would certainly have been funnier.

"Is drinking all you know how to do?" asked the third
mercenary in the room. Umplor was a Balduk, a large, canine-
featured biped with pitted black skin and a long white mane.

He sat alone at his table, due as much to his fierce territorial instincts as to his sheer girth, about equally fat and muscle, which left little room for company. "You're boring me."

"That's exactly the problem," Korok replied. "It's boring here. There aren't even any decent females in this Partnership."

"There are those hairy ones," Umplor said. "The big birds' pets. I like the looks of them."

The Klingons grimaced. "Little more than apes," Korok said.

"I asked the birds to give me one," Lokog admitted, drawing a stare from Korok. "What? I was as bored as you. And I thought they were bred for service, after all. For some reason, the birds said no." He harumphed. "They'll use their bodies to power the Ware, sure enough, but for a bit of fun? No!"

"Hey, hold on," Umplor said, scratching his protruberant brow. "The command drones need people in the machines, right?" Lokog grunted an affirmative. "But the Partners, they're all about volunteering and making sure people don't die in the machines. They aren't just giving you brain-slaves to die in battle, are they?"

"No," Lokog said. "Vabion and I took a few Pebru captives to serve the first couple of drones we captured. For the rest, we've fed them the servitors and slaves from our own ships— and by now, there are probably a few *HemQuch* inside the things, guiding them to kill others of their kind." He laughed. "A fitting fate for all the nobles! When we're done, they'll still be running the Empire—from inside the machinery!"

His laughter was interrupted by a call from Ghopmoq aboard *SuD Qav*. *"Captain Lokog! We're reading multiple ships emerging from warp, heading this way!"*

"Starfleet?" Lokog asked. He wouldn't have expected them to make an aggressive move while trying to negotiate with the

Partnership. He hadn't given them that much credit for deviousness.

"No, sir. Klingon! It's the Defense Force!"

Lokog shot to his feet. His bloodwine-laden circulatory fluids were slow to follow his brain upward, so he reeled, almost falling until Umplor caught and steadied him. Trying to regain his command dignity, Lokog strode forward and yelled, "To the ships!" Korok started to raise his stein and repeat the cry, then realized it was not a toast and clambered from his seat, tossing the stein aside.

Once aboard *SuD Qav*'s bridge, Lokog ordered Krugt to cast off from the Ware station. Then he studied the tactical plot of the incoming Imperial ships, puzzling over how they had gotten past the multiple lines of Ware drones between the Empire and here.

The drones, he remembered, whose delivery he'd been delaying to make K'Vagh sweat.

All right, so that may have been a factor. But still, the drones that were on hand should have been enough to hold them at bay.

Unless they made an end run around the drones and came at the Partnership from a different direction. Which could be why it had taken so long for them to get here. The bulk of the fleet must surely be busy with the uprising, but a few ships could have gotten through as an expeditionary probe to size up the Partnership as a threat . . . maybe just to posture and intimidate them. "How many ships?" he asked.

Ghopmoq was slow to answer. Was he counting on his fingers? "Fourteen, Captain."

Lokog staggered. Then he ran to study the readouts over Ghopmoq's shoulder. Yes, fourteen ships—and more than half were battlecruisers. This was a whole armada.

"They're making challenge!" Ghopmoq said.

"Let's hear it."

The channel opened, and a heavy-browed young *HemQuch* appeared on the screen. *"This is General Ja'rod, commanding the Imperial invasion fleet. You are all under arrest for high treason against the Klingon Empire. You may surrender like the dishonorable dogs you are . . . or you may attempt to reclaim your honor by dying in battle. Choose well—and choose quickly."*

"Captain," Ghopmoq said, "I'm getting hails from Bakokh's squadron and M'Tar's—there are Imperial fleets attacking their positions as well! This is a full invasion!"

Lokog's breathing quickened, and he tried to get it under control. "Get me the other squadron captains."

"I have Korok and the two Balduk ships," the sensor officer reported a moment later. "The others . . . they have already retreated." He threw Lokog an imploring look, as if hoping to hear the same order.

"Flee, you cowards!" Korok was shouting drunkenly when he appeared in one segment of the screen. *"Lokog, order them back to die like men!"*

"We . . . we should regroup," Lokog replied. "Gather more ships to . . . to make a stronger stand."

"No," Korok insisted. *"Never again will I be forced into retreat!"*

"These are not a handful of miners, you fool! These are the Empire's finest warriors!"

"I will not be remembered as a coward!" Korok closed the channel with a forceful snap.

"We will go nowhere either," Umplor said. *"We are Balduk! We will stand our ground, even if we must be buried beneath it!"* He gave a howling battle cry, which the other Balduk captain echoed.

"The other ships are engaging the Imperial fleet," reported the gunner, Kalun.

Lokog watched the screen a moment longer as return fire

began to blast through the fools' shields. "Good. Let them buy us time." *Who cares how I'm remembered, if I'm not around to know it? Let the nobles kill each other over honor—I fight to survive.* "Get us out of here," he cried even as Korok's ship was blown into a cloud of debris. "Do it now!"

14

LIEUTENANT D'KHUR HAD QUESTIONED Worik's strategy at every turn. "It is reckless," the warrior-caste officer had insisted, "to sabotage a Starfleet listening station. They must surely monitor them closely. We could alert them to our impending invasion." Worik had insisted that it was worth the risk to blind the Federation to internal Klingon communications.

D'Khur had objected even more fiercely upon learning of Worik's full plan—not merely to disable the communications relay that Starfleet used to spy on the Empire, but to install a signal interceptor that would feed it false communications, the better to mislead the Federation. "The modifications will take too long! If Starfleet detects the signal interruption, a warship could arrive before we finish!"

Worik had asked if D'Khur feared the prospect of battle, shaming him into silence. But the captain knew it was only a matter of time before the lieutenant challenged his competence and fought him for command of *Gantin*, a command D'Khur had been slated for before Worik was promoted above him.

After all, Worik knew that D'Khur was entirely right. He only hoped the proof of that would come before D'Khur decided to kill him at last.

Fortunately, Starfleet's response time lived up to D'Khur's warnings. *Gantin* had barely left the station when a sphere-prowed, cylinder-bodied Starfleet vessel interposed itself in their path. Worik recognized it as a *Daedalus*-class warship, the kind that had formed the backbone of the Earth fleet during the war with the Romulans. The *Raptor*-class *Gantin*, a compact Bird-of-Prey variant with only a dozen men in its crew, was entirely outmatched. The human who appeared on the viewscreen to issue his challenge appeared strong and stalwart as well. *"This is Captain Bryce Shumar of the* United Starship Essex," he announced. *"Surrender at once or be destroyed."* Shumar did not speak with fury, but he did not need to; it was clear from his eyes that he would make good on that threat. This was a man who had seen many battles and would not shrink from another.

Still, Worik had to make it look good. "Battle stations!" he cried. "Strike them hard!"

D'Khur and the crew fought well, not caring that they had no hope of victory. All that mattered to them was being true to the precepts of a warrior—to strike quickly or strike not, to face the enemy and reveal one's true self in combat, to seek adversity and destroy weakness . . . and most of all, to choose death over chains and to die standing up.

That was what made it so hard for Worik to betray them—even if, by doing so, he was honoring two of Kahless's most important precepts, the first and last: to choose one's enemies well and to guard honor above all. He may not have been warrior caste like his crew, but he shared their belief in the *qeS'a'*, and he acted now for the Empire's honor, even at the cost of his own.

And so it was that Worik exploited his crew's lust for battle to lure them into recklessness, attacking when evasion would be wiser and leaving *Gantin* open to crippling blows from *Essex*'s phase cannons and torpedoes. D'Khur was killed when a surge of phased energy penetrated *Gantin*'s failing shields and blew out a plasma circuit behind his station. Worik was glad that the first officer had been spared the ignominy that was to follow.

Soon, *Gantin* was crippled and helpless before *Essex*, and Shumar appeared again on the cracked viewscreen. Warrior or no, he proved himself human by declaring: *"I give you one last chance to surrender your vessel and spare your crew. There is no need for anyone else to die."* Worik wondered how many of Shumar's crew had been lost. Not too many to close his mind, Worik hoped.

The engineer placed his hand upon the control that would detonate the warp reactor. "I stand ready, Captain," the veteran soldier announced with pride. The blast might not be enough to destroy *Essex* at its current range, but it would ensure the crew's honor and their place in *Sto-Vo-Kor.*

It was the hardest thing Worik had ever done to open a return channel to Shumar and accept his offer of surrender.

U.S.S. *Essex* NCC-173

Shumar's security officer, Morgan Kelly, was a tall, strongly built female whose dark skin and unflinching manner would have let her pass easily as a *QuchHa'* Klingon. She and Shumar questioned Worik relentlessly about the purpose behind *Gantin*'s mission, looming over him in *Essex*'s compact brig while more guards stood by outside the grilled door. They pressed him to reveal whether his sabotage signaled an imminent Klingon invasion, and if so, where and when it would occur. Worik held out for more than an hour, not wishing to risk their disbelief by giving in too easily.

Finally, Kelly gave him an opening. "You understand what's going to happen to you and your crew, don't you?" she asked in a rough contralto voice that Worik had grown to find quite attractive. "You will rot in a Federation prison for the rest of your lives. All of you. But if you cooperate, things would go better for you. You could still see your homes again before you die."

Worik took his time before answering. The reluctance in his voice was genuine, but hopefully he masked the true reasons for it. "Let them go," he said.

"What?"

"My crew merely did as I commanded. I am the one responsible for the sabotage. Let them return home in *Gantin*. Let them escape the dishonor of letting a warship fall into enemy hands. And you can have me . . . and my cooperation. I will answer your questions if you set them free."

Shumar leaned in closer. "Your crew are enemy soldiers captured in an act of sabotage. We can't just let them go with a slap on the wrist."

"You can if it lets you save an entire Starfleet outpost."

That got their attention. "What outpost? Where?"

"That is my price," Worik told them, crossing his arms. "Send my crew home, and I will answer."

Kelly narrowed her eyes, studying him. "Why? Why would a Klingon captain surrender at all, let alone ask mercy for his crew? I thought you guys longed to die in battle."

He looked at her through hooded eyes. "That is what our leaders teach us we should do. But we still know fear and pain. I saw my first officer die before me—an officer you killed, Lieutenant Kelly."

"You attacked us first. You killed our helmsman and two engineers."

"I know. But whoever started the fight, we all die the same. I do not wish to see more Klingons die for a pointless war. My men deserve better." He grimaced. "They will call me a coward for this," he said. "They will see that my name is damned for all time. But they will not die for no reason, or share in my dishonor."

It was at most a partial truth. Even if they were sent home, his men were as good as dead. As honorable warriors, they would be compelled to commit *Mauk-to'Vor* to cleanse themselves and their families of the shame that Worik had inflicted upon them. They would believe—and the songs of history would record—that Worik had dishonored them by placing their lives above the good of the Empire. They would never know that he had done just the opposite.

But the Earthers did not think like Klingons. To earn their belief, he had to give them a reason for his betrayal that made sense in their terms. He had to make it seem he shared their morality, offering them the opportunity to save lives as an incentive to accept the truth he told them.

Shumar examined him closely. "*Are* you a coward, Captain Worik? Would you lie to us merely to spare your crew?"

Worik held his gaze without wavering. "If courage means being willing to throw away the lives of my crew in an unnecessary war, then I will embrace the mantle of a coward. And I will tell you where and when the attack will be, so that you may save hundreds of lives on your side . . . and perhaps millions more on both."

He saw that Shumar was ready to believe him, and his damnation by Klingon history was assured. But this was how it had to be. He had to take the stain of this treason on himself alone, in order to spare his family—most of all Deqan, whose position in the High Council must not be compromised.

Worik's act would help the Federation gird itself against invasion, but that might not be enough to avert the war by itself. Something more would be needed, and Deqan had to be in position to make it happen.

Hoping devoutly that Deqan knew what he was doing, Worik began to speak treason against the Empire.

Starfleet Headquarters, San Francisco

"According to Captain Worik," Shumar reported over the monitor in Jonathan Archer's office, *"the first strike in the Klingon invasion will be against the Starfleet outpost on Ardan Four. It will be a swift, surgical attack by at least three warships, and it will come within the week, Worik estimates."*

"Ardan Four," Archer repeated, sipping his herbal tea; it was too late in the day for coffee. "And you find his intelligence credible?" Even as he asked, he realized that an officer of Shumar's experience would not call for help just two days after beginning his border patrol unless something were genuinely wrong.

"Ardan makes sense as a target, sir. It's our strongest fortification in that sector of the buffer space between Federation and Empire, a key resupply and refueling depot for the border patrol and the exploratory fleet. And it's strategically positioned to be a foothold for an invasion force."

"All true," the admiral replied, "but there are other targets just as good. What if this Captain Worik is sending us on a wild-goose chase?"

Shumar grew solemn. *"Worik surrendered this information reluctantly, and at great personal cost to his honor. He's basically damned himself in the eyes of his people and his family to tell us this. At the very least, it's worth taking seriously. And if I may, sir, given the report that they plan a surgical strike, it wouldn't require that great a diversion of resources to safeguard against it."*

It was a bit brazen of Shumar to offer such unsolicited advice to his superior officer. Archer knew that Shumar disagreed with him on a variety of issues, most of all on the question of non-interference. But Shumar had accrued an admirable record in the Romulan War, and he took more readily to military matters than Archer ever had. The admiral was not averse to taking his advice.

Heaven knew, he had enough bad news to deal with already. The latest reports from T'Pol and Reed had been disheartening; solving the mystery of the Ware's origins had brought them no closer to negotiating leniency for *Vol'Rala*'s crew. Tucker's proposal to attempt re-engineering the Ware with Willem Abramson's help was promising, but there was no guarantee it would work.

Meanwhile, Maltuvis was still tearing through the opposition on Sauria; only two major states had yet to surrender to his conquests, and their aerial defenses were inadequate to stand against the space-capable fleet he now possessed. Archer had tasked Starfleet Intelligence with finding evidence that could expose the dictator's Orion backers, in the hopes that it would undermine his "Sauria for the Saurians" rhetoric and give political ammunition to the opposition; but the Three Sisters, heads of the Orion Syndicate, seemed to have been working on their subtlety following the defeat of their attempts to infiltrate and undermine the Federation. Proof remained elusive, and Maltuvis still had leverage over the Federation as long as the threat of war with the Klingons remained.

Which meant that if there was any chance of heading off that war before it started, Archer had to seize it. "All right, Captain. It's your collar, so it's your mission. Get *Essex* to the Ardan system and set a trap for the invaders. *Docana* and *Atlirith* are in the sector—I'll ask Shran to divert them to meet you there."

"Very good, Admiral. If that's all . . ."

"One more thing—I'll talk to Admiral Narsu about sending a ship to transfer your prisoner to Starbase Twelve. We wouldn't be very good hosts if we took a cooperating prisoner into a war zone."

"Indeed not, sir. I had planned to contact the admiral myself."

"Then I'll let you go ahead with that, Bryce. How are you enjoying having Uttan as your commanding officer, by the way?"

"A bit odd, sir, after fighting side by side so long in the war. But some of us are more comfortable behind a desk than others. He's doing a fine job of it, sir."

"Good to hear. Archer out."

The screen blanked, and Archer shook his head. *Some more comfortable behind a desk than others. I just wish I were one of them.* He signaled the outer office. "Marcus, get me Admiral Shran as soon as you can." He sighed. "And have the yeoman bring me some coffee."

October 9, 2165
Ware orbital station, Etrafso system

"They want us to stop?" Hari Banerji asked in mildly cross befuddlement, which was as close as he ever seemed to come to anger. "But I've only just begun working!"

Vol'Rala's aging human science officer was crouched beside the Ware station's primary data core along with Tucker, Akomo, Vabion, and T'Pol, the latter of whom had just arrived from *Endeavour* to deliver the message from the Senior Partners. "According to the Partners," T'Pol told the engineering team, "the Klingon invasion takes priority. They request that we join in the border defense efforts rather than continuing our work here. Their drone fleets are defending their borders as well as they are able, with assistance from that portion of the mercenary fleet that has not retreated in the face of the Klingon armada. But the Klingons have gained experience in combatting Ware fleets and have adapted to their weaknesses."

"Tell the Partners that that is precisely why we must continue," Vabion told her, his cool, haughty manner restored now that he had a challenge to focus him. "This bioneural interface will give us the same root access that Mister Mayweather had when I installed him into the Pebru system." Tucker suppressed a grimace at the reminder. "It will enable us, or the Partnership, to modify the Ware's kernel functions and overcome the limitations of its drones' combat strategies. That will do more for the Partnership's defense than adding another handful of starships to the border fleet."

T'Pol looked to Tucker. "Do you agree with his assessment, Mister Collier?"

Tucker could see the reasoning for her question. Root-user access to the Ware's core programming had been Vabion's Holy Grail, and now it was within his reach. Had the revelations on the Ware origin world really cured him of his craving for power and profit at all costs, or was he falling back into his old patterns?

Vabion noted Tucker's gaze on him. "I know what you're thinking. That I'd do anything to solve this problem. And you're right—I'm not doing this out of compassion, though I agree that the conquest of this civilization by Klingons would be unfortunate, if the rest of them are anything like Mister Lokog and his crew. But I have nothing at stake here except the intellectual challenge. I have been pursuing the answer to this question for five years, and it has eluded me. All I want is the satisfaction of perfecting the solution. So I have nothing to gain here unless that solution is valid. I have no incentive to mislead you about our chances of success."

"I think we can do it," Akomo said. "The bioneural replication worked like a charm. We've got viable neural circuitry and the kernel's accepting its root privileges. It's just a matter of working out the programming to make the process self-sustaining—to enable the Ware to repair and replenish its own bioneural tissues."

"After all," Banerji added, "the replication of live tissue does require enormous processing power. It would take something as intricate as the neural tissue itself to replicate the tissue itself on a sustainable basis. Really rather elegant, wouldn't you say?"

"And the delivery system?" T'Pol asked him. "In order to upgrade the combat drones, we would need the capability to broadcast the necessary modifications remotely."

Banerji chuckled. "Don't you worry, Captain T'Pol. I have some ideas about that."

"Tell the Partners we'll make it work," Tucker told her. "We just need time to put the pieces together."

She held his gaze coolly. "The Partnership has little time to spare. I will do what I can to persuade them. But I recommend you work quickly."

Tucker smiled. "You know me. I always work best under pressure."

October 10, 2165
Qam-Chee, the First City, Qo'noS

Khorkal stormed into the High Council chamber with unwonted fury. Other councillors used such histrionics as a matter of routine, but Khorkal was generally a bastion of discipline and reserve, saving his bursts of rage for when they were truly needed. So his rage immediately drew the attention of the full Council. "The Menvoq system has fallen to the rebels and their drones!" Khorkal roared. "They are now within two days' warp of the homeworld itself!"

Councillor Ramnok strode forth to confront him on the debate floor. "The *QuchHa'* will never penetrate the home system's defenses."

"They should never have penetrated as far as Menvoq! But you and B'orel have spread out the fleet in too many directions, leaving our core worlds vulnerable. Now the rebels control one of our key manufacturing hubs! They will only grow stronger so long as they hold it, and we will grow weaker."

B'orel loped forward, acting unconcerned. "The half-breeds are nothing without their robot ships. Ja'rod's fleet is dealing with the source of that annoyance even now."

"And our warriors have the measure of the machines," Ramnok added. "They are limited, predictable. Distract the drones sufficiently and the command ships fall."

"And how many ships and warriors do we sacrifice for every 'distraction'?" asked Khorkal. "Victory over the drones is achievable, but it is costly, and they are many."

Khorkal's ally, Councillor Alejdar, glided forth to join him. "And do not underestimate the *QuchHa'*," she advised. "Generals K'Vagh and Kor were acclaimed as fine strategists before their mutation. They have not lost their wits along with their beauty. They use the drones to create their own distractions, then strike at our weakest points with their battleships. That is how Menvoq fell."

"If we wish to fight the drones both here and at their source," Khorkal intoned, "we must concentrate our efforts.

We have already lost one ship and its crew to this premature war with the Federation, and now you divert dozens more from where they are most needed! The Federation can wait."

"Wait?" Ramnok cried. "When we are on the verge of tearing a hole in their defenses? Their own fleet is divided; we expect to engage and destroy their ships in Ware space any day now. We must be ready to strike at their borders at the same time, before they can gather themselves."

"Do you not hear your own folly?" Khorkal demanded. "You call their division a fatal weakness, yet deny it is a weakness in our own fleet!"

"Because we are Klingons! Our strength is measured not in numbers, but in will! Four thousand throats—"

"May be slit in one night, yes," Alejdar interrupted with a roll of her eyes. "But the key word is 'night.' Krim bided his time and waited to begin his run until he had the advantage. Tygrak failed before him because he attempted to overpower the citadel's defenses by main force."

"The Second Precept says to strike quickly or strike not!"

"Quickly, yes, but at the right moment. The Precept teaches decisiveness, not reckless haste."

B'orel growled, perhaps disturbed to see how many councillors appeared to be swayed by Khorkal's and Alejdar's words. "This endless debate is a waste of time!" he exclaimed. "It is the lack of a firm hand leading the Empire that is the true source of our troubles." He strode over to Councillor Deqan, who had stood watching the debate silently, as he always did. "This *ja'chuq* has dragged out for two *jar* with no resolution in sight! It is your indecisiveness, scholar, that has left us vulnerable to dissent from within and attack from without." The other councillors in his faction voiced their support for his charge. "I say it is time! We have all recited our deeds to prove our worthiness to lead. We prove it even now as we wage war for the survival and purity of the Empire. It is long past time to choose! Pick the two worthiest and let us fight for the chancellor's robes at long last!"

Even many of Khorkal's supporters joined in the cheering at his words, no doubt believing that their candidate would surely win. Deqan considered the situation carefully. Khorkal had long been a powerful warrior, true, but B'orel and Ramnok were younger, hungrier. And Deqan did not share the warrior caste's conviction that the best fighter was automatically the best leader.

But he had studied the rules of arbitership carefully, and they gave him an option. "Very well," he declared. "I will now choose the final candidates to succeed M'Rek, as laid down in the traditions of our people." A hush fell over the Council chamber. "Khorkal, Ramnok, come forward!"

B'orel looked frustrated not to be chosen himself. Deqan would have preferred to choose him; his main asset was fanatical bigotry, which was not enough to assure his victory over Khorkal's experience and judgment. But Deqan could only permit himself to bend the rules so far; he was compelled to choose the two worthiest candidates, and Ramnok had done more to distinguish himself in battle and in politics—enough to pose a serious challenge to Khorkal.

Yet there was one last card Deqan could play, and he used it as the two named challengers stepped toward him . . . and as a frustrated B'orel slinked back into the watching crowd. "Wait!" he intoned before the challengers began to attack each other. "As Arbiter of Succession, I am empowered to choose the nature of the final challenge." The councillors muttered uneasily, surprised at this turn of events. "And my choice," Deqan continued, loudly enough to override them, "is that the chancellor's mantle shall go to whichever of these men succeeds in ending the *QuchHa'* uprising and the threat of the Ware!"

"What?" Ramnok cried while the councillors roared in outrage. "The Rite of Succession has ended with mortal combat ever since the warrior caste came to power! Do not think you can turn back history so easily, man of books."

"We *are* in a state of mortal combat already," Deqan told him. "We fight for the life of the Klingon Empire. As Councillor B'orel just said, that is how the contenders truly prove their worth. And he is right. Whether you or Khorkal can wield a *bat'leth* is not in dispute; you have both proven yourselves as great warriors. But it is the blade of leadership that will decide this combat and the future of the Klingon people. So that is the weapon you must prove yourselves worthy to wield." He was grateful to B'orel for his choice of words. By granting him the credit for the suggestion, Deqan made it more difficult for B'orel's faction, or Ramnok's equally militant one, to reject his choice.

Still, Ramnok protested. "How is that different from the state we were in before?"

"The difference, Councillor, is that the battle lines have now been clearly drawn. The endgame has begun. Will you complain at the shape of the battlefield, or will you act? That is your first test of leadership."

Ramnok glared at him murderously. Khorkal merely stood by, as stalwart and silent as the statues in the Hall of Warriors. Seeing this, Ramnok schooled himself to calm acceptance. "Very well," he replied. "Soon my fleets will triumph against our external foes, and then we will root out the cancer of rebellion within. What does Khorkal have to offer save words of warning and disapproval, and the philosophy of a female? My actions will prove my leadership."

"Now who relies on words?" Khorkal asked. "Let the final combat begin." And he turned and strode from the chamber, Alejdar in his wake. Not wishing to seem less decisive, Ramnok hastened to follow him out, barking orders at his supporters.

Deqan sighed heavily as he watched them leave. Were these the Empire's only choices? A disciplined warrior and a reckless warrior? How long could a nation endure when dedicated entirely to war?

Still, the lesser of two evils was plain to see. Deqan had done all he could, even sacrificed the honor of his own kinsman, to give reason a fighting chance. The rest was out of his hands.

15

IT WAS A RELIEF for Phlox to stand in the offices of Antar's Central Investigation Bureau at last. The Interspecies Medical Exchange had been most cooperative in permitting him to divert the medical vessel *Ronuas* to transport him to Antar, but it had still taken substantially longer than he had become accustomed to aboard *Endeavour*. During the trip, Phlox had experienced a rare bout of impatience, despite his efforts to reassure himself that the Antaran renegades' ship was probably even slower than *Ronuas*. He hoped he would still have at least a modest headstart over them.

But that was contingent on the cooperation of Golouv Ruehn, the heavyset, middle-aged Antaran woman who led the CIB. When Phlox was shown into her spare, wood-paneled office, he found her conferring with a lighter-haired, somewhat older man. "Doctor Phlox," Ruehn greeted him, rising and folding her hands in welcome, a gesture the man matched. Phlox returned it himself, grateful that Antarans did not insist on physical contact in their greetings. "Welcome. This is Mathas Kajel, our Undersecretary for External Affairs."

"Doctor," Kajel said. "Let me just express my appreciation for all the Interspecies Medical Exchange has done for Antar."

"Thank you, Undersecretary, Director. But I trust you'll

understand that my business is rather urgent and I have little time for the usual niceties."

"Of course," Ruehn said, seeming more comfortable with his preference for efficiency than Kajel was. "Have a seat."

She resumed her place behind her desk and Phlox took the offered chair before it, with the undersecretary then taking the adjacent seat. "Yes, the attack upon Denobulan soil by this group of traditionalist extremists was simply unconscionable," Kajel said. "Naturally the government of Antar condemns it in the strongest possible terms."

"Yes, thank you, but my interest is not in what they have already done, but in what they plan to do next. The captured raider said they intend to put my son Mettus on trial, with his execution already predetermined. I presume the trial will be held once they bring Mettus onto Antar, which could be any day now."

Ruehn and Kajel exchanged a look. "That fits with the chatter we've been hearing from the True Sons of Antar," Ruehn said.

"Their name, not ours," Kajel added, earning an annoyed glance from the director.

"They've been promoting this so-called trial on some of the darker channels of our data network," Ruehn continued. "They intend to broadcast it publicly so, in their words, the whole of Antar will see the true crimes of the Denobulan people."

Kajel grimaced. "As if we didn't already feel the pain of what that man did. Sohon Retab was a good friend of mine. I grew up with his wife in the Vemton District."

"Your grief is entirely understandable," Phlox said, a bit tensely. "But I trust you do not endorse this group's actions in any way."

"Of course not," Kajel said. "They're relics of the past—ideologues who still buy into the destructive lies of the old corporate regime. And of course we want to make it very clear that the government does not support renewed hostility toward Denobula."

"We are strongly motivated to bring them to justice," Ruehn put in.

"That's excellent," said Phlox. "May I ask what plans you have in place to ensure the rescue of their captive?"

Again, the officials exchanged an uneasy look. "Doctor," Ruehn began, "it was our understanding that you had repudiated Mettus and his actions."

"Of course I repudiate his actions. But whatever he has done, he is my son. I cannot disregard the obligation that creates."

Her features grew harder, more withdrawn. "I understand, Doctor. But we have our own obligations to consider—our own priorities."

"All due respect to your family ties, Doctor," Kajel said. "I'm a father myself. But your son murdered one of our most admired leaders. He turned one of my oldest and dearest friends into a widow. He can't be a priority in this operation. Not his rescue—not even his safety."

Phlox looked back and forth at them, sensing something between the lines. "What are you saying? As Mettus's father, I'm entitled to know."

Ruehn folded her hands. "Doctor, these people are elusive, insidious. They rarely emerge from hiding, making them difficult to track down. You have to understand that the impending trial offers a rare opportunity. No doubt the trial and . . . sentencing . . . will be recorded and released online. It will be broadcast more widely than any of their prior communications. And that will give us an unprecedented chance to trace the source of the upload and track down the True Sons' leadership."

The doctor was aghast. "You say it'll be recorded. You mean that by the time they release the broadcast . . . Mettus will have been executed already."

"We have little choice, Doctor. There is much more at stake here than Mettus. The True Sons' leader will surely want to release and preface this broadcast himself. Waiting for its release will give us an opportunity to bring down the very head of the group, not just the cell that's bringing in your son."

Phlox jumped on that. "Does that mean that you *could* locate and raid that cell before Mettus is executed? That you're *choosing* not to?"

"In order to strike a larger blow," Kajel insisted, confirming Phlox's guess. "I understand your concern for your son—but frankly, he doesn't deserve it. Our consideration is for the countless other sons and daughters who would suffer if the so-called True Sons further undermine the peace between Antar and Denobula—or inflame the traditionalists who want to undo the Great Reform. I hope you can set aside your personal feelings enough to recognize the importance of averting that kind of violence."

Phlox examined the man silently for a long moment before speaking. "Director Kajel. I am a medical man. I am well-trained in setting aside personal considerations in the name of my professional responsibilities." Kajel looked pleased—until the doctor continued. "And it is in my professional capacity as a representative of the Interspecies Medical Exchange that I must protest this plan. The IME would not look kindly on using any sapient being, even a convicted criminal, as a sacrificial victim in a political game. Knowingly throwing away a life that you have the ability to save is callous and unethical in the extreme, regardless of the desirability of the ends. It runs counter to the principles on which the IME was founded.

"So I caution you: If you proceed with this plan, and Mettus dies, I can guarantee that it will earn you a negative report from the IME's sentient rights panel. Such a report could have an unwelcome impact on your future trade relations with other IME signatories, such as the Federation."

Kajel met his gaze with disgust. "Outrageous. That you'd be willing to abuse your IME ties in such a way. Your son murdered a friend of mine!"

"As you have repeatedly reminded me. But I considered Sohon Retab a friend as well. In the brief time I was granted to know him, I came to value him as a man of enormous integrity, decency, and compassion. He died striving to save *his* son and several other innocent people, including myself. I owe him an enormous debt. And that is why I cannot endorse this unethical plan. I cannot believe Sohon Retab would wish anything so vindictive done in his name."

Even the more reserved Ruehn was looking offended now. "And what your son did doesn't matter to you?"

"Director, I despise what my son did, and I believe firmly that he should face justice for his crimes. But it must be justice achieved through legitimate means, as decided by the rightful institutions of society. Not a mockery of law performed as an excuse for an act of political assassination. Not a propagandistic endorsement of the violence that our peoples have spent three centuries trying to move beyond.

"Mettus's act of violence was reprehensible, yes. But we must counter violence with civilization, not with further violence. That is the only way we can ever transcend it."

Phlox took a deep breath. "And yes . . . I am personally

invested in this. Mettus is my son, and I cannot help but love him. But I believe the only way I have any hope to change my son is by setting an example of a better way to live, not by sinking to his level. Tell me: Can the government of a world trying to outgrow the sins of its past do any less?"

Ruehn spread her hands imploringly. "We have a chance to take them all down."

"To arrest a few people. People whose ideas will live on to infect others. It's the ideas themselves that must be fought— that must be cancelled out by demonstrating that there is a better way."

The two Antarans were silent for a time. Finally, Kajel spoke softly. "Sohon would not have wanted vengeance."

Ruehn reached over to her desk console and began entering commands. "Here's what we have on the cell that has your son. Their native districts, known movements, and so on. If we correlate them with their intercepted posts and messages, we may be able to predict a likely location for the trial. It will at least give us a chance to prevent the execution."

Phlox sagged in relief, feeling as drained as if he'd just free-climbed a sheer mountain face. Was this how it was for Jonathan Archer when his words had to make the difference between life and death?

No, he answered himself easily. *Because Jonathan Archer is not a father.*

October 13, 2165
U.S.S. Pioneer, Etrafso system

It felt good to Malcolm Reed to sit in his command chair again—though he judged Travis Mayweather to have done an excellent job filling it in his absence. Mayweather (along with T'Pol, admittedly) had overseen the crew's efforts to analyze and reprogram the Ware. Reed had merely shown up in time to see that difficult and inspired work put into effect. Yet *Pioneer*'s first officer had readily handed the responsibility for the final order back to Reed. "You speak for all of us, sir," he had said.

"And many more," Reed had replied, his thoughts focusing on sh'Prenni and her crew.

Now he nodded to Tucker, who manned the engineering station with Olivia Akomo and Daskel Vabion looking on. Across the bridge, Rey Sangupta had ceded the science station seat to Hari Banerji, standing by the older man's shoulder. "Are you ready?" the captain asked.

"As we'll ever be," Tucker replied.

At Reed's right shoulder, Senior Partner var Skos let out an uneasy chirp. "This had better work," the diminutive Enlesri warned.

"Believe me, we want that as much as you," Mayweather told him.

Reed nodded at Tucker. "Transmit the signal."

Tucker activated the command sequence that broadcast a powerful, intricate signal into the primary data core of the orbital station on the viewer—a station that already had a temporary bioneural interface installed, but only enough to provide power and a simulation of a live sleeper in order for the signal to do its work. "Okay, it's reacting as simulated," Akomo said. "The bypass commands are getting through . . . the replication systems are engaging. Laying down the modified pathways to the transporter coils . . . Yes! Now the bioneural pattern is uploading . . . the circuits are growing in."

"Reading a power fluctuation," Banerji advised.

"Noted. We expected that around now. The new circuits should begin to compensate any moment."

"Yes," Banerji said. "Power stabilizing—no, intensifying! The station is entering full-power mode!"

"At last," var Skos breathed, though Reed could not be sure whether he was impatient or astounded.

"And how about that?" Banerji went on. "Our simulated volunteer has been beamed out of the data core and materialized safe and sound in the medical bay." He chuckled. "I imagine the biosensors won't know what to make of our little surrogate brain."

"Is the station operational?" the Senior Partner pressed. "Try approaching. See if it responds."

"Be patient, Partner," Reed suggested. "We've just given your station a brain transplant. It'll need some time to find its bearings."

"To be sure," Banerji put in. "Yes, the temperature, gravity, and atmosphere are fluctuating wildly. Although the medical bay seems to be spared, luckily for our fake fellow. But the system is feeling its way toward a new equilibrium as the altered pathways finish growing in. Let's not confuse it with new sensory input."

The Enlesri spokesperson fidgeted for several moments. "How much longer?" he finally asked.

Tucker replied, "The pathway formation should be slowing down by now. Just a couple more minutes."

Akomo frowned, studying the readouts. "Wait. The replicator and transporter activity . . . they're increasing. Power's still surging."

"What?" Tucker studied the console intently. "That shouldn't be happening."

"What is wrong?" var Skos snapped.

"Please, Senior Partner," Reed cautioned. "Let them work."

"Materialization activity still increasing," Tucker reported.

"No," Akomo realized. "It's dematerialization! The station is disintegrating parts of itself!"

"Send the abort command," the chief engineer ordered.

Akomo tried, then shook her head. "Nothing. If anything, it's getting worse."

Events soon outraced any verbal report. Reed watched in disbelief as the large gray station orbiting beside *Pioneer* began to tear itself apart. The repair arms and cutting tools in its docking bays began to turn on its own structure, cutting and dismembering the docking structures themselves and their connective pylons, even as increasingly large pieces of the station were simply beamed into nonexistence. "Power system shielding is beginning to fail!" Banerji cried.

"Regina, pull us back!" Reed ordered. Ensign Tallarico fired the thrusters and pushed *Pioneer* away from the station. They had barely managed to make it to a safe distance when the dissolving structure finally reached its breaking point. The explosion was less forceful than Reed had feared—perhaps because the station was already half-disintegrated, offering no resistance to amplify the blast. But it was just as thorough either way. Where an advanced space station had orbited a mere minute before, there was now nothing but an expanding cloud of debris.

Tefcem var Skos stared dumbstruck for several moments before he finally gathered himself. "What . . . happened?" he asked with tight control.

His shocked delay had given Tucker time to study the readings. "The bioneural implants . . . we thought we'd developed a workaround for the Ware's immune system. Convinced it to accept the new circuitry as part of its own system. It should've integrated."

"Instead," Banerji said, "our program modification seems to have triggered, well, an autoimmune response. We confused the Ware's identification of self and other, and it essentially rejected itself."

Vabion gave a cold chuckle. "We underestimated the sheer paranoia of the Ware's original programmers. We thought that blurring self and other would cause it to accept the alien wetware and software as part of itself. Instead, its vehement rejection of anything outside its parameters won out, as we should have anticipated it would. And so it destroyed indiscriminately."

"My God," Mayweather said. "Four months ago, we would've welcomed this. It's the perfect anti-Ware weapon. But now . . ."

"Too perfect," Reed pointed out. "A reaction like this would kill any sleepers before they could be rescued."

"This is a disaster!" var Skos cried. "Look what you would unleash upon us! If this station had been active and networked with the rest of the Ware, you would have doomed us all!"

"Now, hold on," Tucker cautioned. "This was just our first trial. The whole reason we tested it here was to make sure any mistakes *wouldn't* spread beyond the one station. We have a pretty good idea what went wrong—we just need to find a way to compensate for it."

"And if you cannot? The Klingons continue to drive closer to the core worlds every day."

"And *Endeavour* is heading to intercept them," Reed told him. "With luck, Captain T'Pol can negotiate a cease-fire. Failing that . . . we're prepared to bring in the rest of the task force in your defense."

It was the least they could do, Reed thought, given how much damage they'd done already. Normally, he would think twice about taking an action that the Klingons would surely interpret as a declaration of war. But the Klingons, it seemed, had already declared war on both the Federation and the Partnership. If anything, an alliance with the Ware-based civilization could be necessary for the Federation's survival—*if* they could find a way to reprogram the Ware without destroying it.

Reed gazed at the now-diffuse cloud of debris on the viewscreen. *Whatever happens,* he declared to himself, *we must not let this weapon fall into Klingon hands.*

U.S.S. Essex, orbiting Ardan IV

It was fortunate, thought Bryce Shumar, that *Essex* had transferred to Admiral Narsu's command so recently. The shift from exploration to a more defensive footing entailed reassignments for much of the crew, as scientific specialists were rotated out in favor of more security, armory, engineering, and medical personnel. The scientists had already disembarked at Starbase 12 once *Essex* had reported there, but the bulk of the new combat crew had yet to arrive, leaving the ship with a lean 116-person complement, just over half the maximum a *Daedalus*-class vessel could support.

Which made *Essex* the ideal ship for handling the evacuation of the Starfleet outpost on Ardan IV. The outpost, a fortress-like ground installation located near the planet's modest but useful dilithium deposits, had a staff of two hundred and twenty Andorians, Tellarites, Arkenites, and humans. They would be in close quarters even by the standards of *Essex*'s tightly packed barracks, but the ship could support them for long enough to return them to Starbase 12.

Or it would have, at any rate, had the Klingons not had the singularly ill manners to begin their attack on the planet while *Essex* was still in the middle of the evacuation and thus unable to break orbit to engage the enemy. "Three of them," Lieutenant Commander Mullen announced from the science station. "Two D-five class battlecruisers, one standard Bird-of-Prey."

"Three of them, three of us," Commander Caroline Paris said from the helm station, which the redheaded first officer had chosen to take over personally in the wake of Ensign Ling's death in the battle with *Gantin*. "That seems fair."

"It'd be more fair if we could get in the fight," Morgan Kelly replied from tactical, sounding frustrated.

"Our responsibility is the safety of the outpost personnel," Shumar reminded her. "Trust our Andorian colleagues to handle the rest."

"Yes, sir," Kelly said, not particularly mollified. Kelly had never liked being left out of the action, even when Shumar had been acquainted with her back during the Romulan War—although Morgan Kelly had been a "him" at the time, at least anatomically. Her sex reassignment following the war had left her more comfortable with herself, but that had paradoxically made her even more aggressive than before.

But the Andorian Guard provided more than enough aggressiveness to go around. *Docana* and *Atlirith* soared ahead into the Klingons' path, making them scatter. Over the open comm channel, Shumar heard the voice of *Docana*'s commanding officer, Senthofar ch'Menlich, issuing a warning, which the Klingons responded to with disruptor cannons and torpedoes. The two *Kumari*-class starships returned fire, and the viewscreen's false-color enhancement turned the space between the five ships into a flickering, shifting cat's cradle of green and blue threads, amplified far beyond what the naked eye could see at this range.

Shumar followed the progression of the fight tensely, hoping ch'Menlich and *Atlirith*'s Captain sh'Retsu could succeed at preventing the Klingon ships from slipping past to come at *Essex* or the evacuation shuttles still rising from the surface. But they were two against three, and open space was not much of a bottleneck. All that the Andorians could do was to bombard the Klingons heavily in hopes of disabling or (if necessary) destroying them before they could break past for the outpost.

But *Atlirith* took a serious hit to its port wing cannon from one of the battlecruisers, leaving a gap in their firing pattern that the Bird-of-Prey took advantage of. The compact, pudgy-looking warship followed a wide arc that took it past the battle and in toward the planet. "They're vectoring in on the escape shuttles," Mullen warned.

"Caroline," Shumar ordered, "bring us down closer to the shuttles. Brush the atmosphere if you have to—we're due for a new paint job anyway."

"I want racing stripes this time," Paris bantered back. "Or maybe flames."

"I'd rather you avoid any flames at the moment, if you don't mind."

"Right, take all the fun out of it."

"Kelly, a spread of torpedoes at the Bird-of-Prey. Lock phase cannons and fire as soon as it's in range."

"Aye, sir!" The deck shook five times in quick succession as the torpedoes burst from *Essex*'s tubes. Their engines flared brightly as they homed in on their target, needing little amplification to be seen. Shumar often thought torpedoes could do their jobs better if they were less easily detectable, but starships moved so swiftly that a torpedo without active thrusters would be as useless as a cannonball. Thus, there was little that could be done to prevent the Bird-of-Prey from targeting the incoming torpedoes, other than relying on their high velocity and the lag time of light-speed sensors to throw off the Klingons' aim. The bulbous, winged vessel managed to pick off only two torpedoes before two others struck its shields. The fifth was a clean miss, its thrusters unable to bend its course enough to strike home.

"Its shields are weakened," Kelly reported, "but still online. Reading damage to starboard wing power relays and forward hull plating."

"Not good enough. Take out their weapons before they get in range of those shuttles."

Kelly kept firing, but the Klingons must have improved their shields and hull armor in the few years since their last battle against Starfleet, since the Bird-of-Prey kept coming. "How many shuttles left?" Shumar asked Steven Mullen.

"Three," the science officer replied. "One is on final approach now."

That left two shuttles with at least twenty persons each. Shumar could only watch in dismay as the compact but powerful warship came into range and unleashed green fire toward both *Essex* and the defenseless shuttles below. *Where is their precious honor now?* he wondered.

"The leading shuttle's hit!" Mullen cried. "Their propulsion's down . . . they're losing altitude."

"Can we get a tractor beam on them?" Shumar asked as disruptors continued to pound against the shields.

"Not yet," Paris said, setting her jaw. A moment later, *Essex* swerved and headed downward into the atmosphere, a dull and intensifying roar replacing the thud of the disruptors. Perhaps the Klingons had simply been too surprised to keep firing.

"The other shuttle, sir!" Kelly reminded him.

Nothing for it now. "Advise them to take evasive action," he ordered Miguel Avila at communications. "Kelly, keep the Bird-of-Prey busy as best you can."

Essex continued to shudder and thrum still harder as it descended. Shumar could see licks of red-orange plasma dancing across the viewscreen. "Careful, Commander. You do remember we're not built to handle atmosphere, I trust."

"I prefer to think the atmosphere isn't built to handle us," Paris replied. She blinked. "I have no idea what that means, but it sure sounds good."

"Range to shuttle?" Shumar asked.

"Still outside tractor beam range, sir," Kelly replied, working her console intently. Then she grinned, her teeth clenched. "But I've got the tractor beam on it anyway!"

"Morgan?" Paris asked. "Did you just void our warranty?"

The Klingons chose that moment to resume firing, and Paris was all business again. "Pull them in, fast," she ordered, rotating the ship to put its spherical prow in the Klingons' line of fire. Kelly cut loose with all four forward phase cannons and both torpedo tubes while Mullen took over the tractor beam operation, guiding the damaged shuttle into the aft bay.

"The Bird-of-Prey's breaking off to pursue the other shuttle, Captain," Kelly announced.

Shumar could hear a distant shriek of atmosphere beyond the hull as Paris fired the thrusters to bank the ship around. "I

296   **Christopher L. Bennett**

can't get us there in time, not with this drag," she said. "Anyone got an idea?"

Kelly snapped her fingers. "I can blind their sensors!"

"How?" Shumar asked.

"Artificial aurora, sir. A diffuse burst from the phasers, directed above the shuttle."

Shumar did a double take. "Phasers?"

Kelly blushed. "Pardon the slang, sir. Phase cannons."

Shumar nodded. "Do it. Quickly."

Moments later, beams of phased nadion energy sprang forth from the ship, exciting the nitrogen in their path to blue luminescence. Shumar could not tell from this angle, but he knew the beams must be spreading out with distance, and soon they created a burst of shimmering, rippling curtains of blue and green light, splashing out across the atmosphere like luminescent dye poured in a pool. It was surely the most beautiful combat tactic Shumar had ever seen.

Paris smiled. "Phasers. I like it."

Kelly shrugged. "Easier to say."

The auroral interference blinded the Klingons' sensors long enough to let *Essex* rendezvous with the last shuttle, though a few of their random potshots came uncomfortably close to both craft. But finally the last evacuees were aboard *Essex*, the planet emptied of all but its primitive indigenous life.

"Which still leaves one problem," Paris pointed out. "Getting them all out of a war zone."

"Sh'Retsu here," came the voice of *Atlirith*'s captain. *"We've destroyed one battlecruiser. We're coming in to lend you support. You see to the evacuees; we'll ensure the base is held."*

"Very good, Molsetev," Shumar replied. "But we could use some assistance getting this Bird-of-Prey off our tail."

"*Should be easy,*" interposed ch'Menlich from *Docana*. "*We've taken out the other cruiser's warp drive and weapons. A single Bird-of-Prey will be short work.*"

Shumar worried whenever victory over a Klingon seemed easy. As it turned out, his concerns were well-founded. As the two *Kumari*-class vessels moved in to trap the smaller Klingon ship between them and *Essex*, the surviving D5-class cruiser suddenly accelerated toward Ardan IV. "Sir!" Mullen cried. "It's on a collision course with the planet!"

Even as he spoke, the Bird-of-Prey fired a spread of disruptor bolts at *Essex* and broke past it, also diving planetward. "They're targeting the dilithium mine!" Kelly warned.

"All ships, retreat to a safe distance!" Shumar ordered.

Perhaps that was an excess of caution, given the modest size of the planet's dilithium deposits. Still, he had no desire to be anywhere close to the sight that filled the viewscreen mere moments later. Two blinding flashes of light erupted on the surface in quick succession as the antimatter cores of two Klingon warships detonated, the atmosphere intensifying the blast effects enormously. That would have been bad enough . . . but then the dilithium began to ignite.

"Mary, Mother of God," Kelly breathed, crossing herself. "It's Coridan all over again."

Mullen swallowed. "On a smaller scale . . . but . . . yeah."

Within minutes, much of the planet's surface was obscured beneath a spreading, rubicund cloud of dust, flickering with electric discharges and underlit by the glow of the molten surface. "It won't be long until the cloud covers the entire planet," Mullen said. "The heavy metals . . . the radiation . . . I doubt much of the indigenous life will survive, except in the ocean depths." He shook his head. "All those species . . . we were only just starting to learn about them."

"My God, what were the Klingons thinking?" Paris grated. "I've seen some sore losers, but this?"

Shumar put his hand on her shoulder briefly. "They were thinking that if they couldn't make Ardan Four a foothold, they'd at least make sure we wouldn't have it either. Or its dilithium, or the supplies and repair materials for our fleet." He exhaled heavily through his nose, ruffling his mustache. "They wanted to weaken our border, and they've succeeded, though not as much as they'd planned.

"We'd hoped that stopping this attack would avert a war," Shumar went on. "But I think it's safe to say the war has just begun."

October 14, 2165
U.S.S. Pioneer

Charles Tucker sipped his cold coffee, idly praying that this latest dose of caffeine would fire up the right neurons to give him the key insight he needed. His hopes buoyed more substantially when Olivia Akomo entered the engineering lab. "Good, you're still awake," he said. "I could use a fresh set of eyes. I've been going over this code for hours, trying to see a way we can fix the autoimmunity problem. Maybe you can find a new angle."

Akomo's dark eyes studied him for a time before she replied. "Are you sure the autoimmunity reaction is a problem? Maybe it's the solution."

He gave her a sour look. "There are a lot of people in the Partnership who wouldn't see it that way."

"Is that really our responsibility, Phil?" He blinked at the name. He was too practiced in the use of his Philip Collier alias to have trouble recognizing it, but it was surprising to hear Akomo address him so familiarly. "Don't we have a greater responsibility to the Federation?"

"What are you saying?"

She moved closer to the worktable, leaning in over him. "I'm saying the Klingons have already destroyed Ardan Four. They're about to invade the Federation, because they blame us for the Partnership giving Ware to their own rebels. But what if we could offer them a solution to the Ware problem? A way to destroy it once and for all, in exchange for the Klingons calling off the invasion?"

Tucker rubbed the bridge of his nose, still a bit surprised to feel the bump that had been surgically added to it as part of his disguise. "I thought of that. Of course I did. But you know it's not that simple. Those rebels are an oppressed minority, one we had a hand in creating in the first place."

"And that makes us responsible for them? Hell, that's just one more reason the Empire wants to destroy us!"

"It means it'd be a pretty rotten move to throw them in front of a hovertrain for our convenience."

"It's not like they have any less reason to want us dead."

"And what about the Partnership? You know the Klingons wouldn't stop with their rebels. Give them a way to disintegrate the Ware and the invasion would be over in days. The *Partnership* would be over."

"They're the ones who made a deal with the rebels."

"And that means they deserve to be conquered?"

"It means they're not our priority. We serve the Federation first."

"At others' expense?" He shook his head. "You sound like my bosses back home."

She glanced away, shifting her weight. "Yeah, well, there's a reason for that."

Even bleary and sleep-deprived as he was, he caught on to her meaning and shot to his feet. "You're working for the Section?" Her silence was confirmation enough. "How long?"

She sighed. "Only recently. I was contacted by your Mister Harris over subspace. You know he has ways to do that undetected."

"I know a lot about the way he operates."

"And he knows you aren't happy when it gets morally edgy, like it did on Sauria. So once he saw the way things were heading with the Partnership and the Klingons, he decided you needed a backstop. Someone to remind you of your responsibilities to the Federation in case the shades got a little too gray." She gave an abashed sigh. "I didn't like what he was selling. Not at first. But there's more to consider here. There's all we've learned about the Ware. Advanced technology and medicine that could do miracles for the Federation. Solve our transporter problem, give us matter replication—"

"Sure, except what good is it if the Klingons can disintegrate it with the push of a button?"

"I know, I know. But the situation has changed. New technologies won't benefit us if the Klingons destroy us first. I was willing to do almost anything to crack these secrets—"

"Just like Vabion."

"No! He wanted it for personal glory. I wanted it for the good it would do my family, my community, my Federation. That was worth bending a few rules, making a few compromises. And if I have to sacrifice all this technology for their survival, then that's worth it too."

He stared at her. "Your community. Your Federation. You think that's just about places and things? What about the ideas that built the Federation? People and species overcoming their differences to build a peaceful, cooperative society. That's what the Partnership is! They represent everything we stand for. They've built something amazing here, something we can learn so much from. Give the Klingons the means to destroy the Ware and most of these races will lose all their technology, go back to living like animals, lose everything they've achieved. Assuming the Klingons don't just kill them all out of revenge!

"Is that defending the Federation, Olivia? Or is it destroying everything we are?"

"Fine words, Mister Collier. Grand ideals. But they won't matter much to the millions of people who'll be in the Klingons' way when they make their push for Earth and Vulcan. Like my sister who lives on Deneva, with her husband and two kids. What am I defending if I let my sister die?"

Tucker stared at her. He wondered how much Harris had told her about his true identity and past. Was she deliberately playing on the memory of his own sister's death in the Xindi attack? Was she capable of such a low blow? Or had Harris merely studied her history and personality and predicted that she would be the optimal psychological tool with which to goad Tucker?

Either way, it had an impact. He did know all too well, even after so many years and changes of identity, what it was like to lose family to an arbitrary act of destruction. He couldn't easily set that aside in the name of an abstract principle.

But if he didn't, then all the good people he'd met here in the Partnership would probably suffer that same loss. How could he choose one over the other?

Maybe, he realized, it was a false choice. "There might be a third option," he told her. "All we need is to crack this problem, find the solution we wanted all along. If we could control the Ware without destroying it, then we *and* the Partnership could work together to stop the rebel attacks on the Empire. That should be enough to head off an invasion of the Federation."

She shook her head. "We don't know how long it'll take to find a solution. You saw what rushing led to the first time. The Klingons are gearing up to strike now."

"But we can tell them—the Section can tell them, through Starfleet, that we're close to a solution. Use that as a negotiating tactic, offer it in exchange for their backing down."

"That won't work. Not against Klingons."

"We don't know that! Sure, Klingons are angry and bluster a lot, but they aren't stupid. We just have to convince them we have something they need, and that'll give us leverage."

"It's too risky."

"Everything is risky. Even with your—with Harris's plan, there's no guarantee the Klingons wouldn't turn on us anyway once they were done with the Partnership. So let's not throw away our principles before we have to. Sure, sometimes there's no other choice, but the Section is supposed to be a last resort. Our responsibility is to do *nothing* until we're sure that every other possibility's been exhausted.

"So let's at least try it my way first. If the Klingons don't go for it . . ." He sighed heavily. "Then we can talk about more extreme options."

Akomo pressed her lips together and considered his words for a time. "Fine," she agreed. "I'll go along with your recommendation—for now. But you'd better hope you can be as convincing to Harris."

"You let me deal with Harris," he said. "I've got practice."

She gave him a sidelong look. "Yeah? And how well has that worked out for you before?"

16

IN ANCIENT TIMES, Enphera had been one of the cradles
of Antaran civilization. Its dwellers had perfected agriculture in the flood plain formed by its three great rivers, built
sprawling cities from the local wood and clay, and quar-
ried great stones from the nearby mountains to erect massive statues and temples in honor of their fertility gods and
goddesses. In modern times, Enphera was a blasted ruin.
Dry, barren mud flats stretched clear to the horizon, and
fragments of the once-great statues lay scattered about the
foothills, whose already uneven landscape was broken further by dozens of sizeable impact craters and a scattering
of smaller ones.

As Doctor Phlox peered over the fragmented torso of a
once-revered deity, he saw that one of the large craters—the
result of an impact that had blasted through the roof and
two floors of an underground temple complex and converted
it into a sort of natural amphitheater—was now occupied by
a dozen or so Antarans in olive drab. They had cleared away
much of the accumulated sand and dust and assembled the
surviving slabs of granite and sandstone into a facsimile of
a courtroom . . . with a young Denobulan man held in irons
before the bench as a self-appointed prosecutor declaimed the
case against him.

Golouv Ruehn tugged at Phlox's sleeve, prompting him to lower his head again. "You've seen them, Doctor. Don't let them see you."

"They have Mettus," he said. "The trial is already underway. Given that the verdict is already decided, I doubt we have much time."

"Don't be so sure, sir. These lunatics like to talk. See those cameras all around? They need to justify their atrocities to themselves as much as to their listeners."

"But why wait? Surely you have the proof you need to arrest them."

"Yes, and they have sentries around the ruins. We need to get our people into position to take them all down at once. Otherwise lives could be lost. You and your friends don't want that, do you?"

Phlox conceded her point, glancing at the other members of the five-person IME combat-medicine team he had insisted on bringing to the raid as a justification for his own presence. He prayed their services would not be needed.

"Here," Ruehn said, handing him a spare earpiece of the sort her CIB officers were using. "We've got audio surveillance on them. It sounds like it'll be a while before Bokal is done speaking."

Phlox took the earpiece and put it in with some trepidation. Fintar Bokal, he remembered, was the leader of this cell of the True Sons of Antar. (Phlox had wondered why no true daughters were included.) He was a young man, younger than Mettus, and he spoke with the self-assured arrogance of youth. *". . . these Denobulans call us a threat to their purity, their ecology. But the truth of things is evident all around us, here in the ruins of our great Enpheran forebears. This historic site stood for thousands of years, revered and preserved by countless generations of Antarans. Yet the Denobulans did not care! They called us the ravagers of their world, but it was they, in their vindictiveness, who targeted our oldest and greatest ruins, the remains of our first civilization, and bombed them into rubble, destroying much of our priceless cultural heritage."*

"Oh, please." Ruehn shook her head. "It was the corporate state's fault as much as anyone's, building their space command headquarters so close to the ruins. It's not like they cared so much about history—they were the ones who dried the rivers and turned this place into a desert." She wrinkled her nose. "Hmf. Not to mention that Enphera was only our second or third civilization. But it's not only Denobulans these people hate. As far as Bokal's concerned, only his own ancestors count as civilized."

"I see little sign of civilized behavior so far," Phlox said.

But Bokal's rant was interrupted as another True Son came up to him and whispered in his ear. *"Ah,"* the fanatics' leader said. *"I gather that a vehicle has been spotted nearby. Probably the puppet regime's stormtroopers coming to silence our truth."* Phlox peered around the edge of the broken statue for a better view. *"I had hoped to give a fuller accounting of the crimes of this Denobulan—of all Denobulans. Now we must cut these proceedings short. But Mettus-sollexx-oortann's crimes speak for themselves. The guilt of all Denobulans is carved into the stone around us! So let us expedite justice."* He pulled out his sidearm and placed it against Mettus's head. *"This will make our statement as effectively as anything I could say!"*

Phlox was in motion before he even realized what he was doing—and before Ruehn and her men could stop him. "No, we're not ready!" he heard her whisper sharply behind him.

He crouched behind a low rise to put some distance between himself and Ruehn's team, acting instinctively to shield them from harm as a result of his actions. He only prayed he would have time. Mercifully, he heard Bokal taunt Mettus: *"Does the guilty party wish to cleanse his soul with a confession before I send it on its way?"*

"The only guilt I feel," Mettus snarled, *"is for my failure to kill every last one of you!"*

"Oh, Mettus," Phlox muttered, shaking his head.

Bokal made an inarticulate noise. *"Here, Denobulan. Let me demonstrate how it's done."*

"Wait!" Phlox shouted at the top of his lungs, popping up into view. At the last second, he remembered to remove the police earpiece from his auditory canal and toss it into the rocks. "Don't shoot!" he hollered. "I'm alone! I'm unarmed! I'm a doctor!"

He continued in that vein until two of the green-suited bigots arrived to hold him at gunpoint and drag him down before Bokal. Mettus stared at him in shock and disbelief.

"Another Denobulan?" Bokal asked, his voice deeper and harsher without the earpiece's modulation. "Who are you? Who is with you?"

"There's only me, sir. My name is Phlox. I am Mettus's father."

"That was your vehicle we spotted?"

"Yes. Yes, there's only me. I tried to get help," he babbled purposefully. "Tried to convince my government, your government, the IME, even Starfleet, but none of them would lift a finger!" He didn't need to reach very deep to feign frustration. "So I came alone. I had to do something."

"How did you find us, then, if you had no help?"

"I am a medical officer aboard a Federation starship," he extemporized. "I have access to the most advanced biosensors in the quadrant. You don't think I wouldn't be able to track my own son's DNA, do you?" Given how xenophobic Bokal and his men were, Phlox doubted they knew enough about Starfleet technology to see through his lie.

After a moment's contemplation, Bokal laughed. "And naturally the Denobulans would not help you find your son. It is well known that Denobulans do not value their families the way Antarans do. You do not commit yourselves to a single mate, a single set of children. You spread your seed promiscuously, even within your own sex. You live your lives with no ties or commitments."

"I'm here, aren't I?" Phlox snapped. "I've crossed dozens of light-years and trudged through a desert to find my son. If not to rescue him . . ." He held Mettus's eyes. "Then at least to be with him one last time. To say the things I should've said long ago."

Bokal paced around him. "You want to speak, *Doctor?* Very well—speak! Address this tribunal. Confess your crimes as a Denobulan—so that all will know the reason for your impending execution."

Any time now, Director Ruehn! Phlox thought. But there was still no movement from the rocks. He hoped he hadn't complicated matters by providing the True Sons with a hostage whose life actually meant something to the Antaran government. Not that he'd had much choice.

But his years working with Starfleet had been nothing if not an education in adaptability. "All right," he said. "You want a confession? Very well. I can certainly do that.

"My people are not blameless in the dark history between our worlds. When your people came to Denobula, when you arranged for mining rights and drew on our resources, we came to believe you were despoiling our world. Rather than work with you to develop more sustainable practices, we violated our agreements and provoked you to retaliate. We came to see your very presence on our world as a source of pollution and expelled you by force. Matters escalated on both sides until we became convinced you were a threat that had to be contained at the source—leading to tragedies like the bombardment that destroyed these ruins and the famine that killed so many of your people. We have lived with the guilt of those crimes for centuries, as your people have lived with the guilt for the massacre at Zenubex and the burning of the Gintoril rainforest."

"Do not taint your confession with lies."

Phlox ignored him, fixing his gaze upon Mettus. "All of us, Denobulan and Antaran alike, bear some share of guilt for the centuries of enmity between our peoples and the mutual damage it has done. Our alienation . . . our refusal to communicate, to bend, to listen to each other for so long . . . all it has done is to create a rift that festered and made the divide even worse.

"Yes, I am guilty of that," he went on, holding his son's eyes. "I confess that guilt freely. I must. We all must. Because it is only by admitting our own mistakes, our own failings . . . that we can begin to forgive others." Mettus's expression hardened and he turned away. "I don't suggest that those wrongs should be forgotten," Phlox insisted to him. "Nor should they be excused. The pain, the harm they caused was very real, and nothing can change that. But that's not what forgiveness is about. Forgiveness is about healing. It doesn't erase the damage of the past, but it lets us begin to move beyond it. Clinging to resentment and blame and bitterness only perpetuates the pain . . . and creates a cycle of new wrongs and ever-worsening pain. Forgiveness is the only way to break that cycle."

Bokal sneered and opened his mouth to speak, but Mettus beat him to it. "Just get this torture over with already! I can't listen to any more!"

"Very well," Bokal intoned, signaling his men to drag Phlox over near Mettus and force them both to their knees.

It was to Phlox's very great relief when the sounds of stun pistols and fisticuffs descended from all around the rim of the crater. The CIB forces finally erupted into view and poured over the edges, descending toward the group below. The True Sons hunkered down behind pieces of rubble and began firing on the security forces, who fired back.

But Bokal was bent on his own goals. Leaving his men to handle the attack, he raised his weapon and aimed it at Mettus.

Phlox gave no thought to the ironic symmetry as he flung himself bodily in the path of the plasma bolt fired toward his son.

Phlox awoke to find himself under both a medical tent and the care of Doctor Turim, one of the Tiburonian physicians in the IME party. "You'll be all right," she told him, relating the specifics of his injury in terms intended to reassure him—but it simply drove home how much worse off he would have been had Bokal's aim been just a few centimeters to the left.

Turim waved someone over, and Phlox soon saw it was Director Ruehn. "That was the most foolish and suicidal move I've ever seen, Doctor, but you somehow made it work. We have the entire cell in custody. A few injuries on both sides, but no fatalities." She flushed a bit. "And our techs discovered that their cameras have an open link to the True Sons' headquarters. We've tracked it to its source and we're launching a raid on their leaders even now. Your way worked after all."

Phlox had higher priorities than saying he'd told them so. "Mettus?"

Ruehn glanced over at a subordinate and nodded. The man left the tent . . . and returned a moment later with Mettus in tow, dirty and scraped from his fall and shackled with CIB manacles, but otherwise safe and well. Phlox almost fainted from relief.

Mettus looked down at him in dull bewilderment. "I don't understand. Why did you come? Why did you"—he gestured weakly at Phlox's wound—"do *this* for someone you've hated for so long?"

Phlox's heart fell at the boy's words. "Oh, Mettus. I have never hated you. I have been furious at you. Bitter. Gravely disappointed. And deeply sad. But hate . . ." He shook his head. "Hate is a disease, Mettus. A virulent plague that infects its victims in order to propagate itself at their expense—to make them do harm to others and create more hate in return. It causes destruction to both the hater and the hated. And so it runs counter to the natural impulse of life to preserve life, to promote survival.

"That includes the natural impulse of a father to love his son," he went on, his eyes tearing up. "That is what drove my anger, my disappointment, my bitterness for all these years. But it is also what drove me to cross parsecs for you, to fight for you. That is life fighting to preserve life . . . and that is more powerful than the hollowness of hate can ever be." He lowered his head. "I only pray that someday you will understand that."

Mettus gave no sign that he did. But he offered no resistance as the rightful Antaran authorities took him away . . . for he was lost in silent thought.

October 16, 2165
Partnership planet Cotesc

At last, Reshthenar sh'Prenni stood before the representatives of the Partnership of Civilizations—their Senior Partners and their judicial council in an extraordinary joint session to hear her plea. Ambassador Jahlet stood by her side in the open, white-floored space before the curved council benches, present to demonstrate that her petition had the backing of the Federation. But the Rigelian ambassador let sh'Prenni speak, as she had wished to do for so long.

"We came to you because we believed we had a common enemy," the captain said. "We assumed you were victims of the Ware and would welcome our liberation. In our arrogance, we underestimated you. In our ignorance, we did you great harm. We should have waited. We should have listened and learned, let you tell us what you needed, so that we could come to a solution together.

"But now we see who you are, and what you have achieved. You have contended with a power that has destroyed or enslaved worlds and have tamed it, used it to build something astonishing. Something that needs to be preserved."

She stepped closer, pacing slowly before the benches to focus on the Partners one by one. "Now we truly do have a common enemy. The Klingons invade your worlds even as they begin to invade ours. And it is largely due to our own actions—mine and my crew's—that this has happened. The Klingons would probably have come for us both in time, but we set a chain of events in motion that provoked the war facing us now.

"And I speak for all my crew when I say that none of us are willing to sit idly by, to do nothing to fight that invasion.

Locking us in cells will not make amends for our mistake. Let us do what we sought to do from the beginning. Let us defend your way of life, together, as a crew."

"Your ship is wrecked," Partner var Skos said.

"And the Ware could repair it in a day," sh'Prenni replied.

"Your fellow captains have already committed their fleet to our defense," Partner Chouerd said, its tendrils swaying within the frigid atmosphere of its life pod. "What can one more ship add?"

She sharpened her voice. "What did our one ship achieve before?" It was a risk to remind them of that, but it made her point. "It is not the amount of force that makes the difference, but the precision of its use. Even in striking recklessly, we alone created ripples that affected the quadrant. What could we make happen if we directed our force more wisely?"

"Your attempts to help us have met with little success so far," pointed out Tribune Tchoneth of the judicial council. "They have led to one mistake after another."

It was her fellow Hurraait, Partner Rinheith, who countered her words. "And have we made no mistakes in this affair? In our fear of Starfleet, our own misunderstanding of who they were, we sold Ware drones to the Klingon renegades. We played our part in provoking this invasion. Let us not make another mistake out of bitterness."

Next to Tchoneth, a male Monsof named Tribune Ronled leaned over and muttered a few words in the Hurraait's ear, supplementing them with gestures and expressions. Tchoneth interpreted his question. "Do you expect that fighting in our defense will exonerate you for your crimes? Do you propose this as an alternative to implantation in the Ware?"

Sh'Prenni held Ronled's gaze firmly, for it was his question.

"Tribune, I do not expect to come back alive from this mission." The Partners murmured in shock. "I hope to, certainly. I intend, and my crew intends, to make every possible effort to achieve victory against the invaders. But it is virtually certain that not all of us will live. And it is very possible that none of us will. We all understand that." She swept her gaze across them all, her antennae cocked in determination. "So do not imagine that we ask this for ourselves."

She pivoted on her heel and returned to her seat beside Jahlet, aware of the eyes of the guards upon her every move. She had said what she needed. The rest was in the Partners' hands—as it always should have been.

October 17, 2165
U.S.S. Vol'Rala

The bridge looked as good as new, if not better, now that the Ware's repair robots had finished their work and allowed the crew to enter. Still, Giered Charas felt there was something missing as he moved to stand by the starboard tactical station. "Banerji should be here," he grumbled, tossing a glance at the science station behind him. "How can I keep sharp without someone to insult?"

"You can insult me," Zoanra zh'Vethris said idly as she sank into her seat, stroking the navigation controls with almost sensual satisfaction and trading an excited smile with Ramnaf Breg beside her at the helm. "It would be a refreshing change from being admired all the time."

"Oh, but there's so much to admire," Breg remarked.

"There. You see what I have to deal with?"

Charas frowned. "No—I can't bring myself to beat up on children."

The navigator smirked. "Now there's an insult without even trying. Good start."

"Hari's needed on the Ware project," Captain sh'Prenni reminded them. "Of all of us, he probably has the best chance of redeeming our mistake. Would any of us take that from him?"

Charas lowered his head, taking her point. "He'd better not foul it up," he insisted, and the others assented solemnly, understanding his real meaning.

Sh'Prenni looked around at Charas, zh'Vethris, and Breg; at Lieutenant th'Cheen, who stood proudly by port tactical; at Commander ch'Gesrit, who was already fiddling with his engineering console and complaining quietly about the imagined inadequacies in the Ware's repair job; at the relief science officer, Ensign sh'Thyfon, who gazed back at the captain with confidence despite her evident anxiety; and at Chirurgeon th'Lesinas, who stood with them on the bridge as he always did at the beginning of a mission. "My friends," she said, "*Vol'Rala* lives again. And she yearns to reclaim the honor of her name. Let us give all we have to aid her in that worthy enterprise."

"*Vol'Rala!*" Charas cried, echoed by the others. "*Vol'Rala!*"

Sh'Prenni lowered her strong, lanky frame into her command chair. "Are we clear to navigate?"

Ensign sh'Thyfon worked her console and reported, "The station has accepted the Partners' payment and released the mooring clamps." Charas sighed at the reminder that the Ware still blindly pursued its programming despite the Partnership's best efforts to work around it. It would be a miracle if Banerji and his colleagues could break it free of those limits. But Banerji could if anyone could, Charas knew; it was his own job now to ensure the human had that chance.

"Very good, Antocadra," said sh'Prenni. She gave Charas a tight nod, which he returned. Then she faced forward. "Ensign Breg—we have an appointment with the Klingons."

"Yes, ma'am."

Sh'Prenni took a deep breath and smiled. "Take us out."

Sausalito Harbor, San Francisco

Jonathan Archer stood numbly under the shower and let the hot water pummel him for an unknown amount of time. Normally it relaxed him, but tonight, the weight of worlds was not so easily sluiced from his shoulders.

It helped when the shower door opened and he felt a pair of soft, long-fingered hands stroke his back. The door closed behind Dani Erickson, and Archer finally let himself relax as her arms encircled him, as her warm bare body pressed against him from behind. She held on to him for some time, doing nothing more, just waiting.

"I'm not ready for what comes next," he finally said. "I've faced war before. I've stood against the annihilation of my civilization."

"More than once," Dani added.

"But I was only responsible for one ship. One crew. I didn't have to think about the fate of hundreds of ships, tens of thousands of personnel, billions of lives."

Pulling back from the embrace, Dani grabbed his shoulder and pulled him around somewhat forcefully. "Are you kidding, Jon? Most of the time, you and your crew were the ones whose actions made the difference between life and death for all those billions. In the Romulan War, the Xindi conflict— hell, even the Temporal Cold War, which was so big I can't even understand it."

He chuckled. "Join the club."

"If you ask me," she went on, "the problem is that you're not out on the front lines anymore. It's not that you feel you have too much responsibility now, but too little. You think if you were out there, facing the Klingons or the Ware or whatever comes next, you could take direct action. Say the right thing, do the right thing at the right moment to save the day."

He gave her a sidelong look at her melodramatic choice of words. Dani did like to tease him about the space-hero stuff. "But that's the thing," he replied. "I should be able to do even more from where I am now. I've tried reaching out to the Klingon High Council, tried to arrange for high-level talks to prevent this thing. But they're so divided now that no one has the authority to rein them all in."

Taking a deep breath, Archer shut off the water. "I trust my captains in the field. T'Pol and Reed, sh'Prenni, O'Neill, Shumar, Groll, La Forge . . . I know they can handle whatever the galaxy throws at them as well as I ever could. But sometimes . . . sometimes things just spiral out of anyone's control. There was nothing any of us could've done to prevent the Romulans from invading. And now it's happening all over again with the Klingons."

"We're stronger now, though. It's not just Earth—it's the Federation. And we know the Klingons. We've handled them before."

"Not like this. Don't underestimate them just because they aren't some faceless threat like the Romulans. Their weapons and ships are probably even better than what the Romulans used. And if anything, the fact that they're not afraid to face us openly might make them even more dangerous."

Archer sighed heavily. "And their fleet might be moving in

to attack Federation worlds as we speak. And I have to go in there and—"

"Hey." She took his hands. "You don't have to do anything until tomorrow. For now . . ." She moved in against him and pulled him into a deep kiss. Nothing more needed to be said.

It took a while for Archer to notice when the comm signal sounded a few minutes later. "Oh, hell . . ."

"Mmm, can't you ignore it?"

"You know I can't. Sorry."

Her eyes smoldered. "Don't be long."

Resisting the double entendre that suggested itself, he left the shower, wrapped a towel around himself, and moved out into the living room. Down by the foot of the desk, Porthos looked up from the cushion where he had been letting the gentle swaying of the houseboat lull him to sleep. But the beagle did not jump up and run over to beg for cheese as he would have in the past. It was a sobering reminder that Porthos was beyond the typical lifespan for a beagle, and that even with all of Phlox's best mad medical science, Archer would have to say good-bye to his old friend before much longer. He feared that the coming war would leave him too few opportunities to spend time with Porthos while he still had the chance.

Crouching down to scratch the little dog between the ears, Archer used his other hand to tap at the activation switch, finding it by feel. "Marcus, unless this is urgent, your timing really stinks."

"Oh, I'm confident you'll want to hear this news, Admiral."

It wasn't Marcus Williams. Still, Archer recognized the smug, nasal voice instantly, even though he'd only heard it a few times in his life. He sat up to face the gray-haired, black-suited man who'd broken into his comm channel. "Harris. What do you want?"

The Section 31 operative gave him a polite smile that Archer found less than convincing. *"This is a courtesy call, Admiral Archer. I know that recent events have placed you under a great deal of stress,"* he went on, pointedly saying nothing about just how he knew. *"So I just wanted to assure you that a solution is already in hand."*

Archer's eyes narrowed. "What the hell does that mean?"

"The less you know at this point, the better. But you'll understand soon enough. For tonight, just rest easy. You can afford to now."

Archer didn't sleep a wink that night.

October 18, 2165
Starfleet Headquarters

The explanation came as soon as Archer entered his office the next morning. The aides were in a hectic state, and Captain Williams strode through them to address the admiral upon catching sight of him. "Admiral! It's astonishing, sir. According to our intelligence reports . . . our listening posts . . ."

Had the invasion started? The captain sounded too relieved for that. "What is it, Marcus?"

"Sir, all the Klingon ships are withdrawing from our borders. The entire fleet has been reassigned. The High Council's even put out diplomatic feelers to the Federation. Sir, something's changed their minds."

Archer stared, dumbstruck. Finally he asked, "The war is over?"

"Technically, it never started. There was never a formal declaration on either . . ." Archer waved him off, and Williams nodded. "Yes, sir—I'd say it's over."

The admiral studied him. "Then why don't you look happier, Marcus?" The taller man hesitated. "Captain . . . what is it?"

"Sir . . . the Klingon fleet hasn't demobilized. It's just been redeployed."

"Where to?"

The look of concern in Williams's eyes reminded Archer that his aide's daughter was aboard *Pioneer*. "Sir . . . they're on course for Partnership space."

17

Menvoq VI, Klingon Empire

LANETH GRINNED WOLFISHLY as the command post's view-screen showed the *HemQuch* warships beginning to emerge from warp—not far from the hundred-plus Ware drones arrayed to defend the planet. "We will make short work of them," she said. "And then, to Qo'noS!"

Next to her, General Kor crossed his arms over his burly frame. "Do not fight your next battle before you have won the current one, my dear." She glared at his condescension. "Still, I admire your passion for the fight." The gray-templed general gestured in displeasure at the command center around them. "Standing here, directing dots on a screen . . . it lacks the grandeur, the intensity of the real thing."

Laneth chuckled. "It will be intense enough for the Imperials as they die."

"Yes, but why should they get all the satisfaction?"

She rolled her eyes at the nobleman's pomposity. It delayed her recognition of the anomaly on the tactical display. "Wait . . . why are there only three warships?"

The son of Kaltar stroked his beard. "A scouting party, perhaps," Kor said. "To assess our strength before the mass attack. But Ramnok and B'orel have not been so cautious in their tactics before."

"If that is so," Laneth pointed out, "we should destroy them immediately, before they can report our numbers."

"Yes, of course," Kor agreed with a sigh. "Hardly worth getting out of bed for." He gave her a courtly bow. "But you are welcome to do the honors, my lady."

Suppressing a growl of annoyance, Laneth stepped to the controls. However much she disliked Kor and his elitist attitudes, she was the representative of General K'Vagh, and she would act with the dignity that came with that posting. Besides, she relished the opportunity to direct the drones that would blow more *HemQuch* fools into atoms. They would call it dishonorable, Kor would call it mundane—but to her, it was simply progress, a more efficient and practical way of destroying one's enemies.

"Switch to visual," she ordered as two squadrons of drones moved in on the three approaching warships. She wanted to see their destruction as directly as possible. She grinned again as the drones spread into their attack formation, their command ships hanging back at a safe distance.

"Captain!" one of the sensor technicians announced. "The Imperial ships are beaming some kind of signal at the drones. Targeting the command ships most strongly, but encompassing the entire formation."

"What signal?" Laneth asked, only mildly puzzled. Surely they would not be so stupid as to think there was anyone on the command drones to talk to; by now they must know that the only life-forms aboard them were the servitors and prisoners whose brains fed their data cores.

"Unknown. It is extremely complex . . . almost like a teleportation signal, but no one is transporting aboard."

A few moments passed before another technician, this one in charge of monitoring the drones' performance, furrowed his smooth brow and reported, "Captain, there is some kind of new activity in the drones' computers. They have activated their repair programs."

Laneth frowned. "They have not yet been damaged!"

"No, Captain. I do not— Hold, Captain . . . something is happening!"

Before she could chastise him for his vague report, the visuals on the screen rendered further words unnecessary. Laneth watched the magnified views of the drones in shock as they faltered in their paths, began to dissolve from within, and finally exploded one by one.

"What has happened?" she demanded.

"I do not know!" the technician cried.

Sick of hearing that, Laneth drew her disruptor and burnt a hole in his chest. She shoved his corpse aside and began inputting her own commands.

"What are you doing?" Kor asked, moving in behind her.

"Sending the rest of the drones. We must destroy those ships before they do that again!"

But it was futile. Every wave of combat drones disintegrated before it could even reach firing range of the Imperials. The three battleships drew relentlessly closer to Menvoq VI.

They have made progress too, Laneth realized.

"Excellent!" Kor crowed, making her stare at him in bewilderment. "Let them come. At last, we can do real battle!"

"Are you mad, old man?" she demanded. "We must withdraw! Without the drones, we have too few ships to hold the planet."

"We have more than they do."

"We are two days from the homeworld! Now that these have done their job, more will surely come. Kor, if we have lost our advantage, we must conserve the ships and warriors we have. We must consolidate our forces around the territory we *can* hold!"

Clenching his teeth, he stared down at her. "Is that the will of K'Vagh?"

"It is my will. Which the general trusts me to exercise. He will agree."

For all his elitist bluster, Kor knew how to act resolutely when he needed to. "Very well. To the ships! We will withdraw to Qu'Vat and regroup for the next stage of the war."

Laneth appreciated his confidence, if only because it motivated the soldiers as they abandoned the post (readying a delayed self-destruct before they left, of course, as a trap for the incoming occupiers). But she feared that, with this strange new power the Imperials had to destroy the Ware with the wave of a hand, the war was as good as lost.

We should never have trusted that fool Lokog, Laneth thought—but then she smiled. *At least they will be coming for him too.*

U.S.S. *Endeavour*, Arvospu system

T'Pol studied the contingent of Klingon battlecruisers that had emerged from warp on the outskirts of the Arvospu system's cometary belt. The five D5-class warships would indeed present a formidable challenge to the defenders of the system. This very battle group, one of several currently invading Partnership space, had already defeated multiple drone squadrons, often several at once, by anticipating and countering their limited battle strategies. This group had lost one cruiser and sustained significant damage to several more in the process, yet had nonetheless emerged triumphant. T'Pol calculated that the addition of *Endeavour* and *sh'Lavan* to Arvospu's defense would improve the odds of success, particularly as they had been granted interface access to the command drones, able to modify their programmed responses to a certain degree. In *Endeavour*'s case, Thanien ch'Revash would direct his drone squadrons from the situation table at the rear of the bridge. Yet those odds were uncomfortably far from certainty.

Still, T'Pol had not come to fight, if it could be avoided. Negotiation with Klingons was a difficult prospect at the best of times, far more so when they were actively engaged in combat. Yet she had seen Jonathan Archer accomplish it on more than one occasion. She hoped she would be able to manage as well. "Hail the lead ship," she instructed Hoshi Sato.

The Klingon captain who appeared on the viewscreen was young but commanding in appearance, his forehead plating pronounced and edged along the temples with serrated ridges. He looked oddly familiar to T'Pol—perhaps a relative of some Klingon she had met before. *"This is General Ja'rod, commanding the Imperial invasion fleet,"* he declared. *"Stand down or be destroyed!"*

"I am Captain T'Pol of the *U.S.S. Endeavour*," she replied. "We have no wish to fight you, but we cannot permit you to occupy this system."

Ja'rod glowered at her. *"You are known to me, Vulcan. You served under Archer on his ship."*

"That is correct. And I have done business with the High Council before, most recently in the matter of Chancellor M'Rek's post mortem. I request that we parley and attempt to negotiate an honorable resolution to the current crisis."

"Your Federation's concept of honor eludes me, Vulcan. First you attempted to destroy the technology of these infernal drones, yet now you attempt to protect it."

"We seek only to protect those who depend upon the Ware for their way of life."

"They have allied themselves with enemies of the Klingon Empire. Their way of life is over."

"That was not their intent. They acted only in self-defense, but were taken advantage of by a dangerous renegade. He demanded their technology in exchange for his protection, then sold that technology to your . . . competing parties within the Empire."

"Protection from you, it seems."

"Regrettably, yes. General Ja'rod, this entire situation has arisen as a consequence of a series of misunderstandings and poor choices by a few individuals, and the willingness of a few others to exploit them for personal gain. Now it has escalated out of control, at great cost to millions. But the damage can be mitigated by a similarly few individuals, if they make the right choices here and now. You and I are in a position to become those individuals. Please, General. Do not allow us both to be swept away by the tide of circumstance that has engulfed us. Let us take control of our fates together."

Ja'rod laughed bitterly. *"Did you learn to lie so well from your Vulcan teachers, or from Archer? I said I know of you,* Captain T'Pol. *Our fates are already entangled. For I am Ja'rod—son of Duras."*

T'Pol raised a brow. That explained the familiarity of his ridge pattern.

"Yes," Ja'rod went on, noting her recognition. *"Duras, whom your human master Archer disgraced and then slew. There is blood between us, Vulcan. And even though yours is green, I know it will flow just as freely."*

"Your father's fate was the consequence of his own actions," T'Pol said for the record, knowing it would make no difference. "He left us no choice."

Again, Ja'rod laughed. *"And your Ha'DIbaH allies' fate is the consequence of their actions. So by your own logic, Vulcan . . . my choice is equally clear."*

The general signed off, and the armada returned to the viewer, looming still closer. But it was not long before Sato reported: "Captain, they're broadcasting some kind of signal. Not to us . . . toward the drones," she finished with a frown.

T'Pol addressed Thanien over her shoulder. "Commander, drone status?"

"Nominal, Captain," the seasoned Andorian officer replied. "No, wait . . . there's a power drain." He worked the tabletop controls. "The replication and repair systems are engaging. The drones are nonresponsive."

"Captain!" Lieutenant Cutler cried from the science station moments later. "The drones are breaking up!"

"Onscreen." The angle changed to a telescopic view of the nearest drone squadron. T'Pol watched intently as the blocky gray ships dissolved from within and exploded. Another familiar sight—but this time, she knew exactly what it resembled.

"Elizabeth," she said, "analysis of the signal?"

"It's our own protocol, Captain. From the botched trial at Etrafso. The signal that destroyed the Ware."

"How did they get it?" a stunned Sato asked.

"That can be determined later," T'Pol answered. "Lieutenant, has there been any progress toward a countermeasure?"

"The team's still working," Cutler said. "But they've been searching for a modification of that command set, not something to shut it down once it's been fed in. After all, it's not like they had any plans to . . . to use it."

"Uzaveh," Thanien swore. "Captain, the drones transmitted

the signal before they were destroyed! It's been relayed to other Ware within the system!"

It took only a second for T'Pol to realize the ramifications, and a second more to launch into action. "Hoshi, contact the Arvospuan authorities. Warn them to evacuate any populations dependent on Ware life support, and to sever all data and communication links with other Partnership systems immediately." While the previous shutdown signal had only been powerful enough to reach one star system at a time, this one co-opted the Ware's own mechanisms, giving it a much greater potential reach.

"If the signal's already been sent," Cutler advised, "it may be too late to save them all. And where could they go? All the technology in the system is Ware."

"Except us. Ensign," she said to Ortega at the helm, "take us back to Arvospu. Hoshi, advise Captain Sharn to follow. We shall rescue as many as we can. Advise the medical section to prepare life-support chambers."

Thanien stepped forward to her side. "Captain, the Klingons—shouldn't we try to stop them?"

"We and *sh'Lavan* could not survive a firefight, and certainly could not destroy all five battlecruisers. So long as even one survives, it retains the capacity to destroy all Ware in an entire system—or more, if we cannot successfully quarantine each system. Battle would be a futile gesture under the circumstances. Our energies will be better spent evacuating what Partners we can and working on a defense against the destructive signal."

Thanien stared. "It took over a week to get as far as creating the destruct code. Will our defense efforts be any less futile a gesture?"

She held his gaze evenly. "I do not know, Thanien. But we and the Partners must at least survive if we are to try."

U.S.S. *Pioneer*, orbiting Rastish

"The Klingon fleet is twenty minutes away," Rey Sangupta advised. "We can barely even begin to evacuate in that time. It's not just the Nierl and Xavoth and others from non-Minshara environments. There's that huge floating city in the ocean. We have a team there right now!"

"We need a way to buy time," Malcolm Reed said. He turned to the team gathered in the situation room: Tucker, Akomo, Banerji, and Vabion. "Is there any way to block the signal?"

Akomo shook her head. "There's Ware all over the system. The destruct signal only needs to reach one receiver to do its job. We made it too potent."

"Then you need to devise some kind of countersignal to negate its effect. Better yet, to immunize against it."

"We still don't know how to fix the mistakes that created the destruct code. We wouldn't know where to begin."

Vabion finally spoke. "We already have a countersignal," he said. "Think about it." His eyes fell on Travis Mayweather as he spoke.

The first officer's eyes widened. "The shutdown command!"

"The one I helped you create, yes. With our improved interface protocols, it should be easy enough to adapt into a broadcast signal. No need for Mister Banerji's probes."

"But it only works," Banerji pointed out, "with the cooperation of the sleepers. These sleepers are volunteers."

"We know the Partnership's protocols for notifying the volunteers it's time to wake up," Akomo suggested.

Mayweather shook his head. "That wouldn't be enough. When I was inside, interfaced with the other sleepers, we didn't just wake up. We actively made the Ware shut down."

"Rather, you told one another to do so," Vabion pointed

out. "A suggestion the others willingly accepted. The volunteers wish to serve the Partnership. Let us include a status advisory informing the sleepers that the system is in danger and needs to be shut down."

"What if they aren't convinced?" Akomo asked. "Most of them have missed the events of the past few weeks."

"They don't have to be convinced," Mayweather told her. "Even revived, they're half-asleep. It's visceral, instinctive. Controlling the Ware is like controlling your own body. If they feel it's in danger, they'll react by reflex."

At Reed's querying look, Tucker nodded. "It could work."

"Then get it done. *Now.*"

As the team bent to the task, Tucker addressed Vabion. "You may have just saved a whole lot of lives, you know."

The industrialist raised his chin. "I have saved a great many lives in the course of my career." He paused. "Though never, I confess, as an end in itself. Except in the belief that it provided some justification for the smaller number of lives I arranged to end." His dark eyes were drawn to the tactical screen showing the approaching Klingon armada. "Not so small a number anymore."

"Is that what you're trying to do now? Balance the ledger?"

Vabion met his eyes. "It has never been as simple as mere numbers, has it? Every life sacrificed has consequences beyond itself. Net losses that have a way of compounding." He looked away. "We can never balance them, I think, Mister Collier. We can simply try to live with them."

Oceantop City, Rastish

To Samuel Kirk, Oceantop looked like a greatly enlarged, technological equivalent of the floating sea-hornet mounds of Kaferia—a cluster of expansive, angular floating platforms with boxy protrusions extending both upward into the air and downward into the sea. Many of the lower protrusions, resembling uneven stacks of various-sized gray-white slabs, had openings and internal pools to allow the Sris'si denizens of the city to swim inside and interact with the Ware interfaces and replicators, as well as with the air-breathing inhabitants. Kirk had come here in search of a rarity: a Sris'si ex-volunteer who had somehow retained a degree of consciousness during his tenure inside a Ware data core. Captain Reed had sent him the day before in the slim hope that he could learn something new about the root-level operations of the Ware, something that could assist in bypassing the autoimmune reaction that had been the fatal flaw of the experimental control protocol.

Now that very autoimmune reaction was tearing the city in half. And Kirk was barely managing to stay ahead of it.

Val Williams and her team from *Pioneer* had found him and a dozen Oceantop residents trapped behind an unmoving hatchway as the corridors behind him flooded with water. The breakdown of the structure had flooded the subsurface bay where he'd been conversing with the Sris'si volunteer, breaking the balance of air pressure that had kept its pool from overflowing. Kirk and his interviewee had retreated in opposite directions, and Kirk hoped the Sris'si had managed to dodge the debris that sank around him. Kirk had run for the exit as quickly as he could, only to be trapped by the hatch. He had been overjoyed to see Val on the other side when she'd blasted it open. She was sweaty and bedraggled and covered in scrapes and bruises, and she was stripped to her tank top, having used her tunic as a makeshift sling for a Krutuvub evacuee ("It was torn anyway," she'd explained). She looked magnificent.

Now they ran along a clear-walled subsurface walkway that connected two segments of the city, a walkway that was bending and threatening to rupture as the segment behind them slowly sank. It gave way at the far end just as they reached the new segment, and Kirk felt the pressure increase in his ear canals. Williams shoved him through the hatch, then waited to follow until all the evacuees and the rest of her team were out, with the inrushing water already up to her knees. She hit the hatch controls, but the force of the water kept it from closing all the way. "We have to move!" she cried.

"Is anywhere in the city safe?" Sam panted as the group ran for a ramp that spiraled around the walls of a rectangular airshaft within a tower rising well above the surface.

"The team on *Pioneer* sent the shutdown signal barely ahead of the Klingons' destruct signal," Val explained as they ran upward. "Most of the Ware on the planet got shut down before the destruct code took root. The team even managed to insert a code to beam the sleepers to safety—the one part of the last experiment that worked."

"Obviously not all the Ware shut down," Kirk pointed out, looking down at the ominously rising water below.

"About a third of the data cores in Oceantop were infected by the Klingons before shutdown. They're tearing themselves apart, and every other bit of the city their transporters and robot arms can reach. The next segment should be far enough away."

"It would be if it weren't flooding!"

"There's a Tyrellian shuttle on the roof. A relief ship on its way back to Etrafso rerouted here to assist. Its freight shuttles can hold hundreds. This segment will last long enough to evacuate."

They were above the surface now, reaching a height where

the beveled corners of the airshaft became windows to the outside. Williams looked through and grimaced. "Or it would if it weren't being strafed by Klingon fighters." Gasping, Kirk ran to look out over her shoulder. Indeed, several angular, raptorlike craft were soaring by overhead, firing bolts of blinding plasma. "Come on, faster," Williams said, urging the evacuees up the ramp.

"I have . . . to give the Klingons points . . . for improvisation, at least," Kirk wheezed, trying to distract himself with banter. "As soon as the destruct code . . . gets interrupted . . . plan B!"

Williams, unfairly, was hardly winded. "Your typical Klingon warrior always has multiple backup weapons at the ready. And they're determined to destroy the Ware completely."

"The Ware, right? Not the people in it?"

"Oh, sure, they don't care how many of us get away. The evac shuttles are free and clear, as long as they aren't Warebuilt." An explosion sounded dangerously close, startling Kirk. Williams cocked a brow at him. "Then again, they don't care how *few* of us get away either."

Luckily, others cared. Through the windows, Kirk could see that shuttles from *Pioneer* and *Flabbjellah* were airlifting as many Partners as they could carry, prioritizing those unable to survive in Minshara-class conditions. Some groups were even being beamed aboard by transporter; the risk was surely minimal compared to the risk of remaining here. In the water, he could see the Sris'si inhabitants of the city carrying many of the Hurraait, Monsof, Enlesri, and others away on their backs, or towing rafts made from fragments of the disintegrating city structure. A small Balduk combat craft circled overhead, firing at the Klingon fighters. "The Balduk are helping too?" Kirk asked.

"Yeah," Williams replied, "the Klingon privateers turned tail and ran, but the Balduk stayed to honor their agreement. So much for Klingon honor."

Kirk noticed that the tower was starting to list to one side. Much of the module's "ground-level" platform below was already underwater. He could feel the slope by the time they made it onto the roof of the tower. Several open, railed skywalks connected the roof to other adjacent towers, with Partners running across them toward the large Tyrellian shuttle on this roof.

Once the Starfleet personnel reached the shuttle and helped their group of evacuees aboard, Williams turned to Kirk. "Get yourself secured."

"I'm a Starfleet officer. I can help."

"You're a historian, Sam."

"At least I can help keep people calm. Guide them aboard the ship."

"And risk getting strafed. Or falling into the water." The deck was sloping somewhat sharply now. She stroked his cheek. "I won't risk you again, Sam. You want to calm people, the ones waiting inside the shuttle will be pretty scared right now."

A loud crashing sound drew her attention. The adjacent tower downslope from them had pieces of its superstructure dissolving, evidently within range of the infected Ware transporters. Chunks of its walls had collapsed over the archway to the skywalk, pinning several people beneath them and trapping dozens more behind. And their level of the tower was sinking closer and closer to the waterline. "Just get on board, Sam. I can't afford to worry about you right now." Williams ran off, her speed and power compelling to watch.

But frightening to watch as well. As always, she was putting the lives of strangers above her own, above whatever relationship they might have. What if this was the day he lost her?

How can I lose her if I never had her? He watched how fearlessly she ran across the slanting bridge, dodging Klingon disruptor bolts, fixated solidly on her goal of rescuing innocent lives. If she could give everything for strangers, why couldn't he take a chance for her?

Love is about risk, he thought. *She risks because she cares. She cares more than anyone I've ever met.*

So how can I do any less?

By the time he finished the thought, he was already running for the bridge. A disruptor bolt hit nearby, causing him to stumble. He slid down the tilted surface of the bridge, grabbing for the railings, sustaining several painful blows to his forearms before he finally caught hold, just in time to prevent himself from flying off into the roiling, churning water below. He gasped for breath, panicking—but then he thought of Val. A moment later, he was back on his feet, jogging down to her side. He grabbed onto the heavy slab she was struggling to lift and added his strength to hers.

Once it fell clear, she threw a glare at him. "I told you to wait in the shuttle," she said, though there was admiration in her voice.

"The hell with that," he cried. "We've got a job to do. Are we going to save these people or what?"

He bent to the task, and Val grinned as she joined him. Together, they cleared away two more chunks of debris, enough to let the evacuees clamber over the rest. Two of Williams's guards had joined them, helping the injured to their feet and up the bridge that was now a steepening ramp. "Come on!" Williams cried as water began visibly flooding into the corridor behind the crumbling arch. "The bridge won't last much longer!"

Kirk checked his scanner. "Just making sure everybody's out!"

"Damn it, Sam . . ." She grabbed at his arm and pulled. "If there's anyone left in there, it's already too late. I'm sorry. This is the job." Wincing, he let her pull him away.

But the bridge was already starting to buckle and creak. "Come on!" Williams cried, grabbing his hand and practically pulling him up the slope. He ran as hard as he could to keep up, legs straining.

The upper end of the bridge gave way just before they reached it. "Jump!" Val roared, and with a final surge of adrenaline, he pushed off.

They tumbled onto the roof together, their bodies entangled. With the connection to the collapsing tower severed, their own tower started to level out a bit, at least for the moment. Kirk ended up on his back with Val's firm body resting atop him. Gazing into each other's eyes, they laughed together.

He started to pull her down into a kiss just a split second before she pulled him up into one. They met roughly in the middle, and the adrenaline rush surpassed everything he'd experienced in the past five minutes.

When it was over, Val propped herself up on her hands and glanced downward, smirking at what she felt. "Hold that thought, Sammy. For when we're back on the ship."

He flushed with embarrassment and excitement as she pulled him to his feet—and he ran a bit awkwardly beside her as she led him to the shuttle, still holding his hand. "Really? You move fast."

"Sam, I've been waiting a year for you to make a move at all. About time you started catching up."

"Good point." They paused at the shuttle entrance, and he raised her hand to his lips and gave it a courtly kiss. "I'll certainly do my best, my lady."

She grinned, enormously charmed by the gesture. "Well, you're off to a good start."

The deck groaned beneath them and the tower started to sink faster. "Uh . . . we should go," Val said.

"Good idea," said Sam.

18

"YOU NEED TO GO," Admiral Archer said.

T'Pol faced his visage on her ready-room desk monitor. "Admiral, I cannot accept simply surrendering the Partnership to the Klingons."

"I'm sorry, T'Pol. I hate it too. But this is direct from the President. We've only just managed to avoid a war with the Empire. It might start up again if you take further action in the Partnership's defense." He let out a slow breath. "Besides—most of the Klingon fleet is heading your way. Even if you had devised a countermeasure to the destruct signal, you'd still lose against that many warships. There's just nothing more you can do."

"Except rescue as many Partners as we can before their life-support systems are destroyed."

The admiral sighed. "All right—do what you can. But only until the Klingon fleet catches up with you. Then you have to withdraw. That's an order, Captain."

She narrowed her lips, her displeasure tempered by her recognition that his own was just as strong. "Understood, sir." She paused. "Have the Klingons revealed how they came into possession of the destruct protocol?"

"No," Archer said. "But I got a call from Harris just before it all started. This is Section Thirty-one's doing. Again."

"As I suspected."

He frowned. "Please tell me you don't think Trip did this."

"He has assured me that he did not."

A weighted pause. *"Do you believe him?"*

"I do. He seems certain he knows who is behind the leak, and he has expressed his intention to deal with it personally."

"I see. Even so, there will be an investigation."

"I am sure the Section will do its usual efficient job concealing the evidence."

"And in this case, we'll probably have to let them," Archer said bitterly. *"After all, they 'saved' us from a Klingon war."*

"Indeed," T'Pol said. "And all we had to do was sacrifice another civilization in our place."

U.S.S. Pioneer

Olivia Akomo met Tucker's furious gaze evenly as she let him into her quarters. "You lied to me," he told her once the door closed. "You said you'd give us a chance to find another way."

"Yes, I did," the civilian scientist replied. "Because that was what I had to do to achieve my objective. Surely you can understand that."

"Do you have any idea what you've done?" he cried. "Tens of thousands of Partners have died already. Maybe many more."

"Yes, I know. And the rest will lose their civilization. The magnificent thing they created will be lost forever."

"And they'll end up dead, or slaves of the Klingons!"

"Will they? Look at them. They can't do anything without the Ware. What good are they as slaves? Odds are, once they're no longer a threat, the Klingons will leave them alone."

"Maybe. Or maybe they'll just hunt them for sport. Even if they do get left alone, how will they sustain their population without technology? They'll go back to living like wild animals. They'll lose their knowledge, their medicine, who knows what else."

"They'll remember what they had. Maybe some will find a way to rebuild. And the Tyrellians may be willing to help them, like they have with the Pebru."

"The Tyrellians can only stretch their resources so far. Don't pretend nothing's been lost here."

"I'm not!" Akomo shouted, her rounded features contorting with fury. Tucker was struck silent. "I know exactly what I've caused, Mister Collier. I know exactly what I'll have to live with. It will be with me for the rest of my life."

"Then why did you do it?"

"Because I had to. Because saving the Federation was worth it."

"Worth hurting strangers hundreds of light-years from home."

"And hurting myself too! Do you know what your Mister Harris had to agree to in order to convince the Klingons to leave the Federation alone?" Surprised, Tucker shook his head. "We have to destroy all our data about the Ware. Everything we've learned about transporters, matter replication, computers, life support, and medicine. Knowledge that could've advanced us by centuries!" She twisted her mouth as if at a foul taste. "I had to upload the worm into our computer memory myself. It should be taking effect even now, wiping out all the scientific breakthroughs we could've made. All the good I could've done for the Federation, not to mention Abramson Industries and my own career. All thrown away."

"In the name of a greater good? Is that what you're saying?"

She shook her head. "Don't you get it, Collier? I did it for you!"

Tucker was dumbstruck. "For me?"

"You're a spy. A career liar and cheat. But somehow, despite that, you're one of the most principled men I've ever met. It's amazing that you could hold on to your principles like that, given the work you do." She smirked. "The work I now do, it looks like. I . . . I figured at least one of us should get to hold on to those principles. Somebody has to. Somebody needs to give your Section a conscience—at least for those times when a conscience isn't a liability.

"And you're much higher in the ranks than I am. You're in a better position to make a difference. So I made the hard choice, took that weight onto me, so you wouldn't have to. So you wouldn't be so badly tainted that you'd lose the ability to act as their conscience."

He stared at her for a long time, taking it all in. "Don't look at me that way," she said with a sneer. "I made a calculated, practical choice. The right tool for the right job. There was no other solution."

Tucker wanted to hit her. She was forged from iron; she could take it. He wanted to scream at her, damn her for her cool, self-righteous smugness, for the hypocrisy in her moral scorn when they had first met. He wanted to drive home the guilt of all the deaths she was responsible for, all the deaths that were still to come because of her actions.

But he saw what was behind her stony, defiant gaze. So he reached out to her. And he supported her when she fell into his arms and broke down in abject, heaving sobs.

SuD Qav

"So I have you at last, Lokog," General Ja'rod gloated from the sputtering remains of the viewscreen. Lokog crouched on his

hands and knees beside his broken command chair, bits of hot metal from the sparking wreck of the gunnery console peppering his skin and hair. Kalun and Krugt lay dead at their posts, and Ghopmoq had curled up under his console and begun crying.

"*You are truly a craven coward,*" Ja'rod went on, determined to grind his rhetorical boot into Lokog's face before finally putting him out of his misery. "*You are a pirate and a parasite, unclean and unreliable. You call yourself a warrior for your misbegotten people, but you abandon them, then flee from your own allies. You run from battle like a human.*" Lokog smirked. He had battled humans; he knew he was hardly worthy of such accidental praise. "*And now your dishonor has sealed your fate.*"

The privateer looked up at that, struck by the general's words. Lifting himself shakily to his feet, he spoke. "Yes—I'm a pirate and a renegade. I scrape by on the fringes. I made . . . one . . . mistake . . . and I got a disease! I was deformed! And because of that, I lost my ship, my crew, my standing. I had to build myself back up again however I could—but I no longer had a place in the Empire. I was pushed out! And then the *khest'n* Federation came along and pushed me out again! And then my own bedmate tried to kill me for not being ambitious," he went on, gesticulating in annoyance, "and when I killed her and tried *being* ambitious, *your* kind tried to wipe out everyone like me!"

Lokog put his hands on his hips. "So, yes. I cheat. I flee. I do what it takes to survive in a universe that seems determined to ruin me. No one else plays fairly, so why should I?"

Ja'rod gazed at him in disgust. "*It truly will be an honor to cleanse the universe of your stain.*" He ordered his gunner to open fire.

For once, now that he was out of options, Lokog faced his

death without blinking. "Your kind has no more honor than mine, Ja'rod," he said as the disruptor bolts closed in.

"You just have harder heads."

October 20, 2165
U.S.S. Vol'Rala, Cotesc system

Malcolm Reed's bearded face stared agitatedly from the bridge's forward viewer. *"Why are you still at Cotesc, Thenar? The Klingon armada will be there any minute!"*

Sh'Prenni chuckled. "Why do you ask the question if you're just going to answer it for me?"

"I'm serious, Thenar."

"So am I, Malcolm." She raised herself from the command chair, stepping forward. "The Partners on Cotesc have been working nonstop to replicate transport ships and evacuate as many people as possible before the Klingons arrive. Someone needs to run interference."

"Ware ships? What's the point? The Klingons will just hunt them down."

"Not if I delay them long enough. What I need you to do is make sure they get to Etrafso."

"Etrafso?"

"Yes." Sh'Prenni lowered her eyes, then traded looks with the others on the bridge crew. "Thanks to us, its Ware is already shut down. And thanks to you, *Kinaph*, and the Tyrellians, its people have largely managed to re-establish their subsistence needs without Ware. It's the one Partnership world that has the best chance of surviving this."

"That's a good thought, Thenar. Except you're sending a whole fleet of Ware drones Etrafso's way."

Silash ch'Gesrit stepped forward from the engineering

station. "Which is why, as soon as the last of the refugees have been unloaded, we need you to transmit the destruct signal. And dismantle the Ware that's already shut down."

"If you cleanse the planet of Ware before the Klingons arrive," Giered Charas added, "they will not see it as a target."

"And at least one small part of the Partnership will survive," Ramnaf Breg finished.

Reed thought it over. *"It's a good plan. It could work. But it'll have a better chance if you join us in carrying it out."*

Tavrithinn th'Cheen turned from his tactical displays. "The Klingon armada is nearing, Captain. All stations report ready. All particle cannons charged, torpedo tubes clear for firing."

Sh'Prenni smiled at Reed. "We are joining you, my friend. This is our part in the plan."

"Damn it, Thenar, you don't have to martyr yourselves! There are other ways to do penance."

"In principle, I agree," she said. "I'd love it if we had one. But timing, circumstances, and Klingon ruthlessness have left none of them available to us today." Her antennae took on a wistful bent. "This is what we must do. It's not about punishing ourselves. It's about protecting the innocent. It's about doing what we came here to do in the first place." She blinked away tears. "And doing it *right* this time."

Reed held her eyes for a long moment. *"It's been an honor, Captain sh'Prenni."*

"Ohh, Captain Reed." She grinned with her mouth and her antennae. "It's been a blast."

Reed's image faded before she could quantify the burst of emotion that began to sweep over his face. She could guess, though.

"Captain," Antocadra sh'Thyfon announced from the science station, "receiving a hail from the Partnership fleet."

Gathering herself, sh'Prenni nodded. "Onscreen, Cadra."

Tefcem var Skos, Rinheith Chep, and Fendob appeared on the screen, the immaculate walls of a freshly replicated Ware control room behind them. *"Captain sh'Prenni,"* Rinheith said. *"We are the last ship to depart Cotesc. All the Senior Partners are in space, along with as many Nierl, Xavoth, and Krutuvub as we could find in time. The rest on Cotesc are fleeing the cities. They will survive in the wilderness, or in the oceans for the Sris'si, and hopefully be unharrassed by the Klingons."*

"The Partners of Avathox report that they are also doing . . . as you suggested," var Skos told her. *"Many of the aerial cities' modules are being reconfigured into warp ships. They shall evacuate as much of the population as they can before . . . before the cities are destroyed . . . and then proceed to Etrafso. The Xavoth should be safe from the Klingons in the depths of their atmosphere, as long as they dismantle their Ware."*

"That is deeply gratifying to know, Partner var Skos," the captain replied. "The task force will see that they make it there safely. We shall remain here to ensure your own escape."

Var Skos fidgeted, kneading his clamplike mitts and blinking his large, round eyes. *"Captain . . . I have hated you and your crew for what you did to Etrafso. Yet now . . . it is the only thing that will save us. Your actions have made the difference—"*

She shook her head. "Don't. Please, Partner, don't try to tell us that we've made up for our crime. Your civilization would not have been endangered—uncounted sentient beings would not have died—if not for our interference. That is the fact of it, and we all must live with its consequences."

Fendob whispered a few isolated words in the ear of Rinheith, who interpreted and embellished, perhaps speaking for them both. *"Our civilization has been in danger from its neighbors for centuries. Perhaps, by attempting to tame a technology that has harmed so many others, we were always tempting fate. Sooner or later, some nation would have devised this means to destroy the Ware, or another. And we would have had no one acting in our defense when they came."*

"We are entitled to thank you, captain and crew of Vol'Rala," var Skos finished. *"To thank you, at least, for caring. And for trying."*

Deeply moved, sh'Prenni nodded in acknowledgment. "On behalf of my crew . . . I promise we will not fail you again."

"Captain," th'Cheen reported, "the Klingons are starting to emerge from warp."

"Go," she said to the Senior Partners. After a final, solemn nod from three different anatomies, they vanished from the screen.

"The last Partnership transport has gone to warp," Ramnaf Breg reported a moment later. "It's up to us now."

"Six Klingon battleships, Captain," th'Cheen announced. "Heading for Cotesc . . . now one is—three are veering this way. They've detected the fleet."

"Three isn't bad," Giered Charas said. "We can handle three, right?"

"We just have to keep them from going to warp," ch'Gesrit answered. "Barrage them with enough energy or matter to prevent a stable warp field."

"Excellent," Zoanra zh'Vethris said. "The radiation and shrapnel when we blow up should do the job nicely."

"There's that optimism I fell in love with," Breg told her.

The navigator sighed. "You were right, Vrith. I should've gone home and put my genes in the pool while I had the chance."

"Ah," Breg said, "but then we would never have been together."

"And look where that got me," zh'Vethris said with an annoyed twist to her antennae. But her hand snaked out and clasped Breg's anyway.

Over sh'Prenni's right shoulder, Commander Charas shook his head and harumphed. "I don't believe it. That damned Banerji will actually succeed in outliving the rest of us after all."

Sh'Prenni was glad at least one of them would. "I don't think he'd see it as a victory, Giered."

"No." Charas lowered his thick-antennaed head and spoke very softly. "But I do."

She smiled at him. "We know."

"One milliphase to firing range," th'Cheen announced, his confident, proud tones unwavering. Sh'Prenni smiled at him, knowing it was for the crew's benefit.

Resuming her seat, sh'Prenni hailed the medical bay. "Zhar, are you ready?"

"Don't worry, Captain," th'Lesinas replied with gravity. *"We'll keep this crew fighting as long as they're able."*

She smirked. "Not with each other, I trust."

"With this crew? We can only hope."

"You're a pillar of optimism as always, Chirurgeon. Bridge out."

Taking a breath, sh'Prenni switched to the shipwide address channel. "All hands, this is the captain. You all know what we fight for. You need no speeches, no more motivation than your own belief in our enterprise. Just look at your crewmates around you, and remember the beliefs we share. I know you will prove worthy of them."

Charas set his jaw and nodded. "For Andoria."

Breg leaned forward over her console. "For the Federation."

Th'Cheen stood fractionally straighter. "For the pride of the Guard."

Ch'Gesrit sighed and rolled his eyes. "Oh, for Uzaveh's sake."

Zh'Vethris turned in her seat and met their eyes one by one. "For the Partnership."

"For the Partnership," they all agreed in turn.

Reshthenar sh'Prenni rose from her seat and stared at the incoming Klingon fleet in defiance. "Battle stations, my friends. Let's show them all what honor really means."

19

ONCE THE TASK FORCE had done all it could in Ware space and had set course for home, the captains of *Endeavour* and *Pioneer* assembled in the latter's briefing room (for *Pioneer* was still the lead ship of the task force) for a debriefing with Admiral Archer over subspace. Joining T'Pol and Reed in the briefing were Charles Tucker, Travis Mayweather, and Hoshi Sato. *At last,* Tucker allowed himself to think. *Almost got the band back together.*

"*So Vabion is just gone?*" Archer asked over the wall screen. Through the windows behind him, the towers of the Golden Gate Bridge peeked intermittently out of the morning fog engulfing the strait for which it was named.

"We lost track of him during the resettlement on Etrafso," Travis Mayweather replied. "He may have slipped away on a Tyrellian ship, even gone with the Balduk."

"Or maybe," Tucker suggested, "he decided to stay and help rebuild, like Olivia did." At Mayweather's skeptical look, he shrugged. "So call me an optimist."

"*And you're confident the survivors of the Partnership will be safe under Balduk rule?*" Archer asked.

T'Pol fielded that one. "The Balduk are an aggressive people, but they honor their agreements, and they are highly territorial. They contracted to defend the Partnership from its enemies. Claiming Etrafso as a protectorate is a logical way to fulfill that contract in the face of the Klingon occupation."

"Except it's not just the Klingons now. This . . . Silver Armada has the Ware destruct code too."

"Evidently so, per their alliance with the Klingons. But this could be beneficial to the remaining Ware-dependent civilizations in the region. The Pegenoi are absolutely dedicated to the destruction of the Ware, but will no doubt show more consideration for the lives under its influence than the Klingons would."

"What about the conquered Partnership worlds?"

"Reports are sketchy," Sato said. "But from what Balduk intelligence could gather, the Klingons are ignoring hostile environments like the Xavoth and Sris'si homeworlds, as long as their Ware is destroyed. They appear to have occupied Cotesc, Rastish, and others, though."

"We can only hope the Klingons find the Partners too physically incapable to enslave," Reed added.

"The Klingons have now begun moving beyond Partnership space," Sato continued. "They've occupied the Pebru and set about destroying their Ware. But they're starting to get stretched thin. Reports are that other worlds with deactivated Ware are being left alone, so long as the Klingons are convinced it's being destroyed."

"Which means Vanot is safe," Mayweather said, audible relief in his voice. "They've already destroyed all the Ware that Vabion distributed there."

"I'm glad, Travis. If you'd like to swing back by Vanot on the way home . . . check in with your friend Urwen . . ."

Mayweather shook his head. "Thank you, sir. But I think it's best to leave her, and the Vanotli, with a clean break. Let them carry on without having to worry about Ware

or Klingons or anything else in space, until they're ready."
He smiled wistfully. "Besides . . . a day or two wouldn't be
enough."

"*I understand, Travis.*" After a moment, the admiral's tone
lightened. "*Speaking of which, Malcolm—I heard from Captain Williams that his daughter is now dating your ship's historian. Is that okay with you?*"

A chuckle went through the room before Reed answered.
"Assure the captain that Mister Kirk is an officer and a gentleman. As for myself, I have no objection at this point, as they
aren't in a direct chain of command. It bears watching—but if
anything, it resolves a lingering morale issue among my bridge
crew." At Archer's inquisitive look: "Let's just say a longstanding tension has been eased."

"To put it another way," Mayweather said, "we were wondering if those two would *ever* figure out what was obvious to
the rest of us."

Archer shared in the general amusement, then sobered. "*I'm
just glad something positive came out of this disaster. This has not been the
Federation's finest hour.*"

The others conveyed their agreement. "What's the mood
back home, sir?" Sato asked.

"*Somber. Confused. I think most people saw the Ware as something dangerous, destructive. The thing that destroyed worlds, that nearly provoked a
war with the Klingons. As far as anyone knows, either here or in the Empire, it was the failure of the Ardan IV attack that led to the faction behind
the invasion being discredited, their rivals put in power. That and the honor
Vol'Rala won in battle—their fearlessness that gave even the Klingons
pause, and won their respect.*"

"That much is true," Reed averred after a respectful silence.

"*Anyway, the Partnership is being seen as one more casualty of the Ware.
The complexities of their relationship with it are being lost amid the rest. I*

think it's easier for the public to cope with it that way. " Archer sighed.
*"You should see the nosedive Abramson Industries' stock has taken. Suddenly
the idea of a future full of bright, shiny robots serving our every need isn't
all that popular. Akomo was probably smart to get out while she could."*

"In more ways than one," Tucker said. "A little bird tells
me the investigation is going to show that one Philip Collier, civilian consultant for Abramson, sold classified Starfleet
intel to the Klingons, allowing them to destroy the Ware.
Collier will disappear shortly after he disembarks in Federation space."

The mood darkened. "They think of everything, don't
they?" Mayweather said.

"They certainly try." Tucker looked at Archer, at the captains, at the rest. "Are we sure this transmission is secure?"

*"I swept for listening devices and taps using the protocols you showed me,
Trip,"* Archer said.

"It's as secure as I could make it on this end," Sato added.

"Thanks, Hoshi. If you don't mind, could you and Travis
give us the room?"

The two junior officers traded a look. Both captains indicated that they were free to leave. "Sure," Mayweather said,
rising. "The less I know, the better, right?"

"If you like to sleep at night."

Mayweather nodded and headed out. Sato rose to follow,
but passed by Tucker first. "Welcome back from the dead,
Trip," she said, and leaned in to kiss him on the cheek.

Not just yet, he thought, but he merely smiled and thanked
her.

Once he was alone with T'Pol and Reed, Archer addressed
him. *"What's up, Trip?"*

"My patience, for one," Tucker said. "This is the second
time in as many years that Section Thirty-one has demanded

I sacrifice innocent lives somewhere else for the good of the Federation. First it was Sauria, and Maltuvis ended up conquering the whole planet, and who knows what he plans next. Now it's the Partnership, and a whole civilization's practically ceased to exist overnight. This is *not* what I signed on for."

"More," T'Pol added, "it was the Section's attempt to avert the creation of Klingon Augments that led to the spread of the Qu'Vat mutation, provoking the internal unrest that nearly escalated into an invasion of the Federation. Their attempts to increase the Federation's security have tended to produce the opposite result."

"I finally see," Tucker said. "The Section exists to break the rules in an emergency—to do the wrong thing for the greater good. But that doesn't work. Because the damage from doing the wrong thing doesn't just go away. It provokes more wrongs, more trouble, and sooner or later it comes back to bite you in the ass."

"But what can we do about it?" Archer asked. *"They don't legally exist. They don't answer to anyone. We could expose them, but how much could we prove? And what would it do to the Federation if people learned how much our formative actions were tainted by Section Thirty-one's involvement?"*

Reed shook his head, darkly amused. "We thought the Ware's builders had created a monster. A system meant to serve and protect, but given so much autonomy that it became impossible to contain. It seems we have a monster of our own to contend with."

"You're right, Malcolm," Tucker said. "The Section is losing its way. It's looking for excuses to break the rules to justify its own existence. It's serving itself, not the Federation.

"And I can't be a part of that anymore."

"Do you have a plan, Trip?"

"I'm workin' on it, Jon. It's a long way from ready, but I wanted to give you three the heads-up."

"Understood. Whatever you end up doing, I'll back your play."

"As will I," T'Pol said, though he hardly needed to hear it.

"Count me in, too," Reed said. "I have my own scores to settle with Mister Harris and his cronies."

Tucker smiled at them. It was a pleasure to be back among his old crew again, just as it had been a joy to return to engineering—a joy that Harris and his schemes had indelibly tainted.

Soon, he would have to give this all up once more, in order to proceed with his plans. But at least he could enjoy it in the here and now. It would give him strength for what lay ahead.

November 12, 2165
Qam-Chee, the First City, Qo'noS

Laneth stood defiantly alongside K'Vagh and Kor before the High Council. From the seat of power at its head, Chancellor Khorkal gazed down upon them for some time before speaking. Councillor Alejdar stood by his side, a place reserved for a senior advisor—an impressive height for a female to reach. But then, it was rumored that Alejdar had somehow managed to obtain the secret Federation formula that the Defense Force had used to eradicate the Ware drones. Laneth was torn between hatred toward the elegant noblewoman for her role in the rebellion's defeat and admiration at the influence she had gained despite the barriers against her sex.

Finally, the new chancellor spoke. "General K'Vagh, son of Wor'maq. General Kor, son of Kaltar. You have fought long and hard against this Council—first to attempt its conquest, then to defend your remaining territory. You have won the right to this parley." Elsewhere on the Council floor, angry grumbles came from the contingents led by Councillors B'orel and Ramnok. "There are those who denounce the dishonor of fighting with bloodless drones," Khorkal said, acknowledging the complaints. "But your warriors fought and died well in holding the Qu'Vat sector after the Ware was defeated. Some say that you have earned the right to be called true Klingons, despite your . . . disadvantage."

K'Vagh limped forward a step, leaning heavily on a thick, gnarled cane. He had been injured in the battle that had earned the parley invitation from Khorkal, and he had yet to heal completely. "I would put my warriors against any Klingon. Whatever change befell their heads, their hearts remain mighty. As they have proven time and again in battle."

"Save for those who fled like cowards and abandoned their allies." That was Councillor Ja'rod, testing out the new authority he had gained. His triumph against the Ware had earned him the seat vacated by Khorkal's ascension to the chancellorship.

"Common pirates and mercenaries," General Kor countered. "None of them were ever true warriors. We were better off without their unworthy assistance."

"Enough," Khorkal warned. "Only some say you have earned your place as Klingons. Others still insist that none with the taint of humans can stand among us. Councillor B'orel still calls for your extermination."

"Then let him come and deliver it," K'Vagh said with a smirk.

"That is just what I had in mind," Khorkal said, bringing him up short. "This dispute has gone on long enough. The leading parties are both here now. Let us resolve this in the most direct manner—with a duel. You against B'orel." He glanced at a quiet, older councillor toward the rear. "Assuming Deqan has no objection this time." A roar of laughter echoed through the hall, and Deqan made a gesture of acquiescence.

"But that is not fair!" Kor challenged. "K'Vagh is our leader, and he is injured."

"We will accept a *cha'DIch* to fight in his name."

Kor hesitated, clearing his throat as he sized up the younger, leaner B'orel. However, he appeared to be girding himself to volunteer as K'Vagh's second in the name of his family pride. Before that disaster could come about, Laneth stepped forward. "I will fight for the general!" she exclaimed.

That garnered shocked reactions throughout the hall—and an appreciative smile from Alejdar. Laneth realized she might have to start liking the noblewoman.

B'orel looked around in protest. "I will not fight a female!" he insisted.

"You may nominate a *cha'DIch* of your own," Laneth taunted, "if you are too afraid."

That did it. "I fear no common whore," B'orel snarled. "Certainly not half-human scum like you."

"Then you will die without fear. It will be the first honorable act of your life."

B'orel's eyes widened in rage and he reached for his *d'k tahg*. K'Vagh stepped forward. "Wait!" he cried. Khorkal lifted a hand, stilling B'orel. "What are the stakes?" the general asked.

"If B'orel wins, the *QuchHa'* will be expelled from the Empire, no longer to be called Klingons. Any who remain will be slain."

"And *when* I win?" Laneth asked.

Khorkal gave her a warning glare. "If K'Vagh's champion prevails, the *QuchHa'* will be allowed to remain in the Empire.

You may continue to live in your current territory. Those who have noble titles and lands may retain them without further challenge. And this Council will approve the petition of Doctor Antaak to continue researching a cure for your condition."

"We do not need a cure," K'Vagh insisted. "This is who we are now."

"Perhaps one day, your deeds will prove your equal worth," Khorkal said. "For now, you will still face much resistance. The prospect of a cure will diminish enmity toward your existence. And if you are right, and it matters not what you look like, then it will matter not if you are cured."

K'Vagh grimaced, feeling the falsehood of those words as Laneth did, but he did not dispute them now. "What about Council representation? My people will need a voice."

Khorkal gave a slight rumble in his throat, one too dignified to be called a laugh. "If your champion is victorious over B'orel, then an opportunity will present itself."

After conferring briefly with Kor, K'Vagh nodded. "Very well." He turned to Laneth, leaning in. "You are my finest warrior. My daughter in battle. Do me proud."

"No less than ever," she replied. It earned a chuckle, though she had not been joking.

Laneth swaggered forth, unfastening the top two stays of her jerkin both to convey casualness and to give B'orel a visual reminder of her femininity, so that he would underestimate her. His automatic contempt toward those unlike him was a weakness she would readily exploit.

"Good idea," B'orel said, frankly ogling her chest. "You've shown me right where to slip the knife in."

"You *would* need instruction to know where to insert anything into a female," she countered.

Once again, he proved absurdly easy to provoke. Brandishing

his knife in a reverse grip, B'orel charged her, blade poised to plunge down between her breasts. With her knife in her right hand, she slashed across his forearm as she spun aside to the left, evading the blow. He winced and grabbed his arm, but his gauntlet had minimized the damage, and the cut across his forearm did not prevent him from striking backhand at her as he went past. She crouched down below the swing, then struck at his side. He spun clear of the lunge, then kicked her in the chest, knocking her onto her back. He leapt down onto her, blade going for her heart, and she rolled away.

What followed was too frenetic for her to keep track of every move; Laneth relied on instinct. But soon she scored a second strike, then a third. With each cut, B'orel grew slower, giving her more openings. His cockiness remained, though. "You claw at me like a *grishnar* kitten," he panted. "This is the best a *QuchHa'* female can do?"

"You are not worth my best."

He roared. His lunge was sloppy, his raised arms leaving his belly wide open. She did not miss the opportunity. Dropping into a crouch, letting his own momentum doom him, she stabbed upward between the plates of his armor—and between his ribs.

A moment later, the empty shell that had once housed a vile excuse for a Klingon lay lifeless on the floor, and K'Vagh roared in triumph, jogged over to her despite his limp, and pulled her into a crushing embrace that almost achieved what B'orel had failed to do.

But soon enough, before she suffocated entirely, he released her and recovered his dignity. He then knelt over B'orel's corpse, opened his eyes, and unleashed the death scream. The Council joined in, but Laneth did not, merely taking the time to refasten her jerkin. She understood the political value in

K'Vagh's gesture, but she would not waste the energy heralding the death of a fool.

"Success is yours!" the chancellor said as K'Vagh stepped forward to stand before him, joined by Laneth and Kor. "Captain Laneth, you have proven that your people still have the honor of a warrior. No doubt the *QuchHa'* will need to prove themselves in many other battles—but you have earned General K'Vagh his place on the High Council."

Laneth bowed. "Then the honor is mine," she said.

Of course, she had known better than to rely on honor. B'orel had been dead the moment her poisoned blade had cut his skin. The rest had just been theater. These people had damned hers for an accident of mutation, one that *their* experiments had caused. Honor was defined by the victors—often as an excuse to salve their sins. Victory was what mattered, and Laneth had achieved it.

Of course, K'Vagh still held a truer form of honor highly, and it seemed to Laneth that Khorkal did as well. She respected that, but it was a relic of a simpler time. The Empire was entering an age when treachery and deceit held sway, and it was necessary to learn to wield them in the name of victory. There were those among both *HemQuch* and *QuchHa'* who shared that understanding, Laneth was sure. She would have to select her allies carefully. K'Vagh's patronage would help her secure the power she needed to survive, and to sway others to her thinking. She would need that power to defend him against all who would continue to deny and combat *QuchHa'* equality. With so many enemies, her people would need every unfair advantage they could get to hold on to their influence in the Empire.

And once the Empire had found a new balance within itself and was ready to turn its attention outward again, the

Federation and its neighbors might find themselves facing a very different variety of Klingons.

November 25, 2165
Laikan, Andoria

The monument to *Vol'Rala* and her crew was simple and taste-ful: a five-meter-high cluster of crystal spires occupying a prominent place in the capital city's central plaza, thrusting skyward at a high angle to convey a sense of boldness and optimism—the spirit of enterprise for which she had been named. Along its base, the names of *Vol'Rala*'s captain and crew had been inscribed in every one of their languages.

The only member of the crew whose name was not in-cluded on the monument stood before it now, addressing the crowd assembled for the dedication ceremony. "Some people have suggested to me that we may never know *Vol'Rala*'s true fate," Hari Banerji said in his quavering, gentle voice. "The Klingons tell us she went down in a blaze of glory taking three battlecruisers with her, but Klingons are prone to ex-aggeration, and their propaganda has little interest in escape pods. Perhaps, I am told, some of my crewmates and my friends may have found their way to the surface of Cotesc, either to live out their days there or to commandeer a Klingon ship and escape to safety. Perhaps we will learn this monu-ment was premature."

He sighed. "I would love nothing so dearly as to believe that. But I knew my shipmates too well. They would not have stopped fighting so long as a single life could be saved. They gave everything for the principles the Federation was founded on. And as I was unable to be with them on that horrible, proud day . . . all I can do now is dedicate the rest of my days to living in the same spirit. Let them be an example to us all."

"Hear, hear," Jonathan Archer muttered as the crowd applauded. He had already canceled Alexis Osman's proposal to commission a new starship bearing the name *Enterprise*. Best to leave that name in honorable retirement for a while, regardless of language, as a tribute to the fallen.

But there was more he could do in their name. He made his way over to Admiral Shran, waiting until the Andorian Guard's chief of staff finished offering his support and thanks to Commander Banerji. "It was a fine ceremony," Shran said when he joined Archer. "A fine monument. Thenar would probably have called it pretentious, but it's worthy of her, and her crew."

"That it is, Shran." He took a breath. "If you ask me, though, the best tribute we can give them will be to make sure nothing like this ever happens again."

Shran frowned in puzzlement. "What do you mean?"

"I have a proposal," Archer said, handing him a data slate. "An official Starfleet directive of non-interference." He went on as Shran warily took the slate and read it over. "We've seen what can happen when we try to get involved with other worlds' affairs, even with the best of intentions. It's just too dangerous. After this, after Sauria, it's clear that we need to change our approach."

Shran shoved the slate back into his hands. "You're mad if you expect me to support this. Just because we made a few mistakes, we abandon trying altogether? That's cowardly!"

"No, it's careful. We clearly don't have the wisdom to know when it's right to interfere and when it isn't. Maybe someday, but not yet."

"So we just wash our hands of the decision? Stand by and

do nothing while others suffer, even when we have the power to help?"

Shran began walking, and Archer hurried to keep pace. "We don't always know what *will* help. At the very least, we need to get to know other cultures first. Let them tell *us* what they need or don't need, instead of just assuming we know better than they do."

"And if they tell us they need to oppress or slaughter their people? Conquer other worlds?"

"Then that's a problem their own people are better equipped to solve."

"Their world, their problem? That's not the spirit that formed the Federation, Jon. Don't forget all the good we did in this. Dozens of worlds were liberated from the Ware. A virulent scourge has been wiped from the galaxy, never to be seen again."

Archer had to wonder about that. He remembered a similar technology that had been unearthed from an alien wreck in Earth's polar region a dozen years ago, self-repairing and exploiting living beings as disposable parts. Zefram Cochrane had claimed to have encountered it, had even said it came from the future. At times, Archer had wondered if it might have been connected to the Ware in some way. Now he knew there was no such link—which meant the Federation might someday face such a technological threat once more. He hoped that by then, they would be advanced enough and wise enough to handle it better than they had this time.

"We're always going to make mistakes, Jon," Shran went on. "Choosing not to interfere is as likely to be disastrous as the reverse. We should judge each case as it comes, not hide from the responsibility." His antennae twitched. "We've had this debate before. I'd rather not rehash it today, of all days."

"Today is when it's most important. The Federation was responsible for a terrible disaster, Shran. We have to stand up and say to the galaxy that we've learned from it, that we won't let it happen again."

Shran whirled on him. "This is *politics* to you? I thought you were better than that. What you mean is that you intend to repudiate sh'Prenni's actions. To paint her and her crew as villains."

"No, it's not about that. Shran, Thenar herself acknowledged her mistake. She and her crew gave their lives to correct it."

"And they have balanced the scales! Now you propose to drag their memories through the mud for the sake of a political statement."

Archer sighed. "I'm sorry you see it that way, Shran. Maybe this was the wrong time. Maybe later you'll understand why I think this is necessary."

"Don't count on it," his old friend said in tones that reminded him of their early enmity. "If you go forward with this non-interference directive, I will fight you. And I won't be alone."

Shran stormed away across the plaza. Archer gazed down at the slate in his hands, hoping it hadn't just cost him a friend.

November 30, 2165
Tileb Prison, Antar

"It's not so bad here," Mettus said to Phlox as they sat on opposite sides of a security barrier of transparent aluminum in the prison's visiting area. "It's nothing like I was told an Antaran prison would be. It's clean, quiet. They treat me well. The food is . . . tolerable." He chuckled. "It's actually better than I was taught Antaran *cities* would be."

Phlox chuckled even more vigorously, overjoyed to laugh with Mettus even over the smallest thing. "I hope the lack of crowding isn't difficult for you," he said.

"There are enough people around to keep me sane," Mettus replied. "But I actually enjoy the relative solitude. It gives me time to think." He furrowed his brow, so much like his mother did. "My comrades . . . back in the group . . . they never gave me much time to think. I suppose they wanted to make sure my only thoughts were theirs."

"I shudder to think what they must have done to you, my boy."

Mettus gave him a sharp look. "Don't attempt to absolve me . . . Doctor." Phlox winced. Even now, his son held on to the distance between them. "I went to them willingly. I liked what they had to say."

Phlox took that in. "And . . . now?"

The younger Denobulan sank into thought. "The Antarans still did us much harm."

"In the past. And we harmed them."

"We are very different. I still don't believe Vaneel can be happy marrying one of them."

Phlox sighed heavily. But after a moment, Mettus went on. "Still . . . spending every day surrounded by Antarans . . . I see they aren't all bad. One of the guards . . . she talks to me. Brings me books. Antaran books, badly translated . . . but some of them have interesting ideas. They admit the Antarans' mistakes. Call the war an injustice, but without blaming us. And some of them are funny. My guard is funny." He shifted, uncomfortable at what he was feeling. Phlox smiled warmly, having seen that look on the faces of so many of his children—and one or two of his eventual wives.

"I think," Mettus went on, "that I can understand now what always confused and upset me before."

"What's that?"

"How you could defend them. How you could tolerate sharing a universe with them after all their—all they did to Denobula. I thought that dishonored the memory of all we lost. Betrayed who we are." Phlox closed his eyes briefly, but he waited for his son to continue. "I think I see now . . . that it's more complicated. That the bad in a person . . . in a race . . . doesn't destroy the good. It doesn't mean . . . you can't listen to them. Can't learn from them."

Phlox leaned closer to the barrier. "There's a word for that, my boy. It's called forgiveness."

Meeting his father's eyes, Mettus blinked rapidly. "Do you think Vaneel will ever forgive me for killing Retab?"

"I know she will," Phlox said. "I know . . . that I forgive you, son." He put his hand against the clear panel. "And I hope . . . that you can finally forgive me, too."

After a long pause, Mettus's fingers pressed against the panel opposite his. "Father," he said.

Epilogue

December 29, 2165
Centauri VII, Alpha Centauri system

NOT MANY PEOPLE lived outside the colony city in the delta of Centauri VII's largest river. This was an arid world in the current epoch, still in the earliest stages of terraforming, and the vast deserts beyond the delta were deathly hot and inhabited by a variety of small but deadly arthropods, the robust survivors of the evolutionary competition to endure the planet's numerous extinction events over the past few billion years.

But every colony world had its pioneers, recluses, and rugged individualists—those who, for whatever reason, scorned the company of others and sought a degree of solitude unattainable on a civilized world. Thus it was that Charles Tucker, after an hour's travel through the desert in the fastest skimmer available for rental, found himself at the compound of Antonius Taranullus, being escorted inside by a hovering spherical drone with whining turbofans and an ominous-looking phase-weapon emitter.

The man who had until recently been Willem Abramson, and countless others before that, rose from his work etching a lithographic plate as Tucker came in, greeting him with an impressed look on his newly clean-shorn face. "Mister Collier," he said. "You are a persistent man."

"And you're a hard man to track down, sir."

"Dead men usually are," replied Abramson—or was it Taranullus? "At least, I have found so in the past. The march of technology makes it increasingly difficult to arrange my deaths convincingly. Still, I had thought my latest methods sufficient."

I certainly hope so, Tucker thought. "Believe me, Mister . . . sir . . ."

"Akharin will do."

Tucker nodded. "Akharin. You weren't at all easy to find, even knowing what to look for. This is a pretty remote place."

"As I needed it to be." The immortal sighed. "I had grown confident enough to dabble in fame and importance for a few decades, but I had forgotten how quickly fame turns to ashes in the mouth. All my ambitions for robotics breakthroughs to make a better world . . . gone now. Once again, the fiercely ethical humanity of this modern age refuses anything to do with technologies that have proven harmful. So they reject the idea of robotic servants as righteously as they rejected genetic enhancements before. As for bioneural circuitry, I doubt that research will be pursued again for generations." He shook his head. "Had the people of my original nation believed that way, humanity would have abandoned the wheel after the first chariot battle."

Tucker looked the man over, realizing that his age and origins made it conceivable that he had actually invented the wheel. "So was that the final straw?" Tucker asked. "Six thousand years living on Earth and you finally decided you were fed up with the human race?"

"As I said, anonymity grows increasingly difficult as technology matures. Particularly given the fame I gained in my last identity, despite my best efforts." Akharin raised his bushy eyebrows. "I have realized for some time that space travel created new opportunities. I suppose I should thank you for that, given your role in the perfection of the warp five engine—Mister Tucker."

That brought a wide-eyed stare, which Akharin met with a chuckle. "I am not without considerable resources of my own, sir. And I have seen so many variations on my own face that it is easy to recognize them in others."

"I guess we both know each other's secrets, then."

"Only a fraction both ways, I'm sure. But if your employers desire another service from me, let them know it is unwise to pit their resources against mine."

Tucker licked his lips. "That's what I'm counting on, sir. You see, they didn't send me. They wanted me to find you, but I gave them a false lead."

Again those eyebrows lifted. "I see. Do you expect gratitude in return?"

"No, sir."

Akharin smiled. "Then you may have it anyway." The ancient man pondered. "Come with me."

They moved through the hallways of the simple house, which Tucker noted were adorned with a variety of magnificent, oddly familiar works of art. Most prominently displayed was a series of lithographs, and Tucker recalled seeing Akharin work on another in his studio. "These are yours?" he asked.

"All of them are. But these in particular are the work of Antonius Taranullus. A series of lithographs depicting the Creation."

Tucker looked them over, but he had little understanding of modern art. "Biblical?"

Akharin shrugged. "Biblical. Greek. Mesopotamian. Hindu. Scientific. They all have common threads."

"That's interesting."

"Not unprecedented. Michelangelo's *The Creation of Adam* depicts the figures of God and His host within a shape evoking the cross-section of a human brain. The same patterns resonate through history. That is what I attempt to show here: the Creation that never ends."

Tucker studied him. "Ending with the creation of man? And woman?"

The immortal gave a faint, hopeful smile. "That is no ending."

They moved on. "So this is how you plan to make your new fortune? As an artist? Seems kinda risky."

"Perhaps. But I am not untalented in the field," Akharin replied with a slight smirk. "And I do have other sources of revenue still available to me, even without the closely watched fortune of the late Mister Abramson. My hope, eventually, is to accumulate sufficient wealth to purchase my own planet, where I can truly be alone with my work."

They reached a door, and Akharin entered a security code. "In the meantime, I make do with this."

A flight of stairs led them to an underground lab, where Tucker saw an abundance of high-tech equipment and robotics prototypes not unlike those he had seen on his initial visit to Abramson Industries. "You're still doing the work. Just in secret."

"I am."

"It'll take a hell of a lot longer working by yourself."

"I can spare the time, Mister Tucker. And I am not entirely alone. In Abramson's will, he bequeathed the fruits of his theoretical research to a Mister Arik Soong, whose acquaintance you have made. Despite his, ah, infamy, he has developed an interest in humanoid robotics and has taken quite well to the research, with some guidance from me. Eventually I will contact him—or his heirs—and guide them further."

"I wouldn't rely on Soong if I were you," Tucker advised. "He's a devious one."

"Do not worry, sir. I have other assistance." They reached the observation window of a clean room, and Akharin let him look inside. Sensing their movement, the man and woman within the clean room looked up—revealing the faces of Daskel Vabion and Olivia Akomo.

Vabion merely gave him a mildly surprised look of acknowledgment, then returned to his work. But Akomo cocked her head, gave him a rakish smile, and winked.

Tucker got the message, and spun to face Akharin. "She was working for you the whole time! I mean—"

"I know," Akharin said. "And yes. She cooperated with your employers on my instructions. Before she uploaded their worm to erase all of Starfleet's Ware research, she secured a copy for my eventual use. She also recruited Mister Vabion into my service. He is quite brilliant, and somewhat humbled by recent events . . . yet still arrogant enough to make our collaboration interesting."

"I have to hand it to you," Tucker said with a smile. "Not many people can pull one over on Section Thirty-one."

"Is that what you call it? An ugly name."

"Well, it fits."

Akharin raised a brow. "I think it is time you told me what your purpose was in coming here, Mister Tucker."

"I need help, sir. From someone who has plenty of experience at faking his death and creating foolproof new identities."

After a thoughtful pause, Akharin guided him away from the window. "I see. Such agencies rarely allow peaceful retirements. Especially for those who plan to betray them."

"Do you have a problem with that?"

"I have a problem with the way your agency had you black-mail me into their service. I have no problem with retaliating through their own man." The immortal nodded. "If you need a suitably convincing death and a new life to follow, I can arrange it." He spread his arms. "But given my current . . . more humble resources, it will take time."

"That's fine," Tucker told him. "Because before I disappear . . . I intend to bring Section Thirty-one down from the inside."

STAR TREK: ENTERPRISE ®

RISE OF THE FEDERATION

will continue

APPENDIX

Featured vessels and personnel

STARFLEET—FEDERATION SPACE

STARFLEET COMMAND

Admiral Jonathan Archer
(Human male) chief of staff, United Earth Space Probe
Agency (UESPA)

Admiral Thy'lek Shran
(Andorian *thaan*) chief of staff, Andorian Guard (AG)

Fleet Commander T'Viri
(Vulcan female) chief of staff, Vulcan Space Service

Admiral Mov chim Flar
(Tellarite male) chief of staff, Tellar Defense Force

Admiral Alexis Osman
(Human female) chief of staff, Alpha Centauri Space
Research Council

Captain Marcus Williams
(Human male) executive assistant to Admiral Archer

U.S.S. ENDEAVOUR NCC-06
(*Columbia*-class, UESPA; crew complement 132)

Captain T'Pol
(Vulcan female) commanding officer

Commander Aranthanien ch'Revash
(Andorian *chan*) executive officer

Commander Michel Romaine
(Human male) chief engineer

Lieutenant Commander Hoshi Sato
(Human female) communications and protocol officer

Lieutenant Elizabeth Cutler
(Human female) science officer

Doctor Phloxx-tunnai-oortann
(Denobulan male) chief medical officer

Ensign Pedro Ortega
(Human male) flight controller

U.S.S. ESSEX NCC-173
(*Daedalus*-class, UESPA; complement 116)

Captain Bryce Shumar
(Human male) commanding officer

Commander Caroline Paris
(Human female) executive officer

Lieutenant Commander Steven Mullen
(Human male) science officer

Lieutenant Commander Mazril
(Tiburonian female) chief medical officer

Lieutenant Morgan Kelly
(Human female) armory officer

Ensign Miguel Avila
(Human male) communications officer

U.S.S. DOCANA AGC-7-19
(*Kumari*-class, AG; complement 85)

Captain Senthofar ch'Menlich
(Andorian *chen*) commanding officer

U.S.S. ATLIRITH AGC-7-45
(*Kumari*-class, AG; complement 86)

Captain Molsetev sh'Retsu
(Andorian *shen*) commanding officer

STARFLEET—WARE TASK FORCE

U.S.S. PIONEER NCC-63
(*Intrepid*-class, UESPA; complement 46)

Captain Malcolm Reed
(Human male) commanding officer

Lieutenant Commander Travis Mayweather
(Human male) executive officer

Lieutenant Commander Therese Liao
(Human female) chief medical officer

Lieutenant Reynaldo Sangupta
(Human male) science officer

Lieutenant Valeria Williams
(Human female) armory officer

Lieutenant Samuel Kirk
(Human male) historian

Charles Tucker III (alias Philip Collier)
(Human male) acting chief engineer/Section 31
operative

Ensign Bodor chim Grev
(Tellarite male) communications officer

Ensign Regina Tallarico
(Human female) flight controller

Olivia Akomo
(Human female) mission specialist

U.S.S. VOL'RALA AGC-7-10
(*Kumari*-class, AG; complement 87)

Captain Reshthenar sh'Prenni
(Andorian *shen*) commanding officer

Commander Giered Charas
(Andorian *chan*) executive officer/security chief

Commander Silash ch'Gesrit
(Andorian *chan*) chief engineer

Lieutenant Commander Hari Banerji
(Human male) science and communications
officer

Lieutenant Tavrithinn th'Cheen
(Andorian *thaan*) tactical officer

Chirurgeon Lieutenant Zharian th'Lesinas
(Andorian *thaan*) chief medical officer

Ensign Ramnaf Breg
(Arkenite female) helm officer

Ensign Kitazoanra zh'Vethris
(Andorian *zhen*) navigator

Ensign Antocadra sh'Thyfon
(Andorian *shen*) relief science and communications
officer

U.S.S. THELASA-VEI AGC-7-48
(*Kumari*-class, AG; complement 85)

Captain Menteshay th'Zaigrel
(Andorian *thaan*) commanding officer

U.S.S. FLABBJELLAH AGC-6-16
(*Sevaijen*-class, AG; complement 38)

Captain Zheusal zh'Ethar
(Andorian *zhen*) commanding officer

Chirurgeon Veneth Roos
(Andorian *thaan*) chief medical officer (deceased)

U.S.S. KINAPH AGC-6-34
(*Sevaijen*-class, AG; complement 38)

Captain Kulef nd'Orelag
(Arkenite male) commanding officer

U.S.S. TRENKANSHENT SH'LAVAN AGC-6-49
(*Sevaijen*-class, AG; complement 40)

Captain Trenev Sharn
(Andorian *shen*) commanding officer

U.S.S. ZABATHU AGC-11-09
(*Ilthirin*-class courier, AG; complement 10)

Commander Finirath ch'Mezret
(Andorian *chan*) commanding officer

U.S.S. TASHMAJI AGC-11-15
(*Ilthirin*-class courier, AG; complement 10)

Commander Chelienal sh'Regda
(Andorian *shen*) commanding officer

Acknowledgments

LESS THAN A WEEK into the writing of this novel, Leonard Nimoy died. There are few people who deserve more acknowledgment for their contributions to the *Star Trek* universe. Everything we do, even in series where Spock never appeared, owes enormously to Mr. Nimoy's accomplishments. The sincerity and intelligence he brought to his performance helped make *Star Trek* the meaningful creation it became. For myself, I would not be the person I am today without the example set by Mr. Spock, as realized by Mr. Nimoy.

The technology I call the Ware was introduced in *Star Trek: Enterprise*: "Dead Stop," written by Mike Sussman & Phyllis Strong. Abramson, also known as Akharin and (eventually) Flint, is from *Star Trek* "Requiem for Methuselah," written by Jerome Bixby.

For my portrayal of the Andorians in this and other novels, I am indebted to sources including the novel *Andor: Paradigm* by Heather Jarman (appearing in *Worlds of Star Trek: Deep Space Nine* Volume One), the *Enterprise* episode "Proving Ground" (written by Chris Black) for the layout of the *Kumari*-class bridge, and the *Enterprise* novel *The Romulan War: Beneath the Raptor's Wing* by Michael A. Martin for information contributing to my interpretation of the Andorian calendar. (In case you're wondering, an Andorian phase is 28.14

hours long, so a centiphase is just under 17 minutes and a milliphase is 101 seconds.)

I'm especially indebted to my good friend Keith R.A. DeCandido for his contributions to the Klingon material portrayed herein. Certain events depicted in this novel, specifically the assassination of Chancellor M'Rek and its aftermath, the conflict over Ardan IV, and Captain Worik's role in that conflict, were conceived by Keith for his book *The Klingon Art of War*, and are dramatized here with his blessing. He also provided helpful advice and consultation for the Klingon portions of the book, and the character of Ja'rod, son of Duras, was his suggestion. (This is not the same Ja'rod who betrayed Worf's father in *Star Trek: The Next Generation*, but a namesake ancestor, like Duras himself.) His novel *Star Trek: The Lost Era—The Art of the Impossible* provided guidance on the Klingon Rite of Succession, while his novella "The Unhappy Ones" in *Star Trek: Seven Deadly Sins* provided information on the ancestry of the House of Mur'Eq, including the existence of Kor, father of Rynar (and grandfather of the canonical Kor played by John Colicos).

Chancellor M'Rek was established in *Star Trek: Enterprise*: "The Expanse," written by Rick Berman & Brannon Braga. Doctor Antaak (John Schuck), Fleet Admiral Krell (Wayne Grace), General K'Vagh (James Avery), and Marab (Terrell Tilford) are from *Star Trek: Enterprise*: "Affliction," teleplay by Mike Sussman, story by Manny Coto, and "Divergence," written by Judith Reeves-Stevens & Garfield Reeves-Stevens. Laneth (Kristin Bauer) is from "Divergence." Korok (Robertson Dean) is from *Star Trek: Enterprise*: "Marauders," teleplay by David Wilcox, story by Rick Berman & Brannon Braga. The

Mempa system and sector were established in *Star Trek: The Next Generation*: "Redemption, Part I" and "Redemption, Part II," written by Ronald D. Moore. Details about the specific planets in the system come from "The Unhappy Ones" and from *Excelsior: Forged in Fire* by Michael A. Martin and Andy Mangels. The latter novel provided additional information about Kor's House (therein called the House of Ngoj, but then, Klingon Houses frequently change their names), as well as details about Doctor Antaak's later career.

The class name *Tajtiq* for the fighter used by Laneth in "Divergence" is my own coinage based on a weapon name from *The Klingon Art of War*. The *Raptor* class is from *Enterprise*: "Sleeping Dogs," written by Fred Dekker. Though it was not identified therein as a Bird-of-Prey, its design was similar, and its twelve-person complement matched the description of Worik's Bird-of-Prey in *The Klingon Art of War*. The term *qa'vIn* for Klingon coffee, and its backstory as a modification of the human beverage, comes from *Star Trek: Klingon for the Galactic Traveler* by Marc Okrand. Thanks to TrekBBS poster "loghaD" for pointing this out to me.

The full name of Doctor Phlox, Phloxx-tunnai-oortann, was given in the *Enterprise* writers' bible, though it was never used onscreen. Mettus and the Antarans were established in *Enterprise*: "The Breach," teleplay by Chris Black & John Shiban, story by Daniel McCarthy. Other information about Phlox's family comes largely from *Enterprise* episodes written by Rick Berman & Brannon Braga, including "A Night in Sickbay," which elaborated on the size and structure of Phlox's family; "Stigma," which introduced Feezal (Melinda Page Hamilton) and named Vesena and Groznik as a contentious married couple; and "Zero Hour," which established that Groznik and Phlox's first wife had a child together. Though Vesena was not explicitly identified with Phlox's first wife, it seems likely to me given the dialogue in the two episodes. The suggestion that bisexuality is normative for Denobulans, including Phlox, came from John Billingsley in an article for *Dreamwatch* #123 (Titan Magazines, December 2004).

The idea of methane-based cold-planet life based on complex lipids in place of proteins (the Nierl) and that of hot-planet life based on fluorocarbons in liquid sulfur (the Xavoth) were both proposed by Isaac Asimov in his classic essay "Not As We Know It," from the September 1961 issue of *The Magazine of Fantasy and Science Fiction*. The term "azotosome" for a nitrogen-based cell membrane viable in a methane solvent was coined in the paper "Membrane alternatives in worlds without oxygen: Creation of an azotosome" by James Stevenson, Jonathan Lunine, and Paulette Clancy in *Science Advances* 27 Feb 2015: Vol. 1 no. 1 e1400067.

The destruction of Theta Cygni XII was established and explained in *Star Trek*: "Operation: Annihilate!" written by Steven W. Carabatsos. The *Marshall*-class starships first appeared in the *Star Trek Spaceflight Chronology* by Stan and Fred Goldstein, and were designed by Rick Sternbach. The *Ceres* class was proposed by the Advanced Starship Design Bureau's *Journal of Applied Treknology* site and designed by Alan E. Baker. I have interpreted the specifics of the class somewhat differently, the better to fit the continuity of the novels. The *Poseidon* class is from the video game *Star Trek: Legacy*. The Andorian starship *Atlirith* is the namesake of an Interstellar Guard ship from the alternate timeline depicted in *Star Trek: Myriad Universes*—*The Tears of Eridanus* by Steve Mollmann and Michael Schuster. The Guidon Pontificate comes from *The Tears of Eridanus* and the same authors' "Meet With Triumph and Disaster" in *Star Trek: The Next Generation*—*The Sky's the Limit*.

About the Author

CHRISTOPHER L. BENNETT is a lifelong resident of Cincinnati, Ohio, with bachelor's degrees in physics and history from the University of Cincinnati. He has written such critically acclaimed *Star Trek* novels as *Ex Machina* and *The Buried Age*; the *Star Trek: Titan* novels *Orion's Hounds* and *Over a Torrent Sea*; the *Department of Temporal Investigations* series, including the novels *Watching the Clock* and *Forgotten History* and the novellas *The Collectors* and *Time Lock*; and the *Enterprise: Rise of the Federation* series, whose previous volumes include *A Choice of Futures*, *Tower of Babel*, and *Uncertain Logic*. His shorter works include stories in the anniversary anthologies *Constellations*, *The Sky's the Limit*, *Prophecy and Change*, and *Distant Shores*. Beyond *Star Trek*, he has penned the novels *X-Men: Watchers on the Walls* and *Spider-Man: Drowned in Thunder*. His original work includes the hard science fiction superhero novel *Only Superhuman*, as well as several novelettes in *Analog* and other science fiction magazines, several of which have been compiled in the e-book collection *Hub Space: Tales from the Greater Galaxy*. More information and annotations, plus the author's blog, can be found at christopherlbennett.wordpress.com.